BETTER THAN A DREAM

Jonah sat back on his haunches and groaned, rubbed his face with his hands.

This couldn't be happening.

The woman he was only pretending was his wife was going to leave him? Taking his real baby, her pretend baby, with her? What was this? Some kind of cosmic joke?

"Aren't you going to say anything?"

From in the kitchen came an orchestra of clangs.

A week ago, his daughter had been too weak to lift her head, and now she was making such a racket it was on the tip of his tongue to tell her to pipe down.

"Jonah?" Angel leaned forward, worrying her lower lip with her top teeth. "Don't you have anything to say?"

"Nope." Back up on his knees, he easily slid her chair around so that she faced him, then cupped her face in his hands, drawing her forward for not the fanciest kiss, but one he hoped conveyed his heartfelt apology and thanks.

At first, he barely touched his lips to hers. Then instinct kicked in, and he pressed harder, and she was still there, not like in his dreams where she faded away.

No, this woman was real.

Kissing him back.

BLUE MOON

LAURA
MARIE ALTOM

LOVE SPELL NEW YORK CITY

LOVE SPELL®

May 2003

Published by

Dorchester Publishing Co., Inc.
276 Fifth Avenue
New York, NY 10001

ISBN 0-505-52538-0

The name "Love Spell" and its logo are trademarks of Dorchester Publishing Co., Inc.

Printed in the United States of America.

Visit us on the web at www.dorchesterpub.com.

For the men of Theta Tau, Upsilon chapter, who,
during the fall of 1988, provided me with my very own
toga-wearing angel. I love you, Terry!

PROLOGUE

"Look, mister," Geneva Kowalski said, trying not to be creeped out by the ever-thickening fog, the cross of smells landing somewhere between jelly beans and carnations, and, oh, yeah, as if she didn't already have enough on her plate to worry about in the fact that she was sitting on a cloud, only an hour or so earlier she'd died! "I don't know what kind of seduction thing you've got going here, but I'm not interested. I might be dead, but I'm not desperate."

The toga-wearing, patrician-looking snob cast her a look of utter disdain before scooting a good foot down the cloud. "Rest assured, my dear lady, seducing you is the furthest thing from my mind. In fact, what I'm really here to do is instruct you."

"Oh, yeah?" She flicked long strands of fuchsia and black hair over her left shoulder. It was a damn shame she'd wasted good money on a dye job just before she croaked.

1

"Instruct me in what? I'm dead. Isn't there some saying about old dogs not learning new tricks?"

The man sighed. Not an ordinary sigh, but a long, shuddering affair that thundered through the mist. "If I weren't in such desperate need of a refresher course in lost causes," he said, "believe me, I'd be casting you straight to you-know-where."

"Hell?" she teased, leaning close because she knew it bugged him. "Satanville? Land of the all-you-can-eat eternal barbecue?"

"You may joke, but believe me, if it weren't for my boss giving you this second chance at redemption, you'd be a very unhappy woman right about now."

Ha! That just showed that this guy didn't know squat about her. If he had, he'd have already been clued in on the fact that even knocking back a few wine coolers with God Himself wouldn't make her happy.

Geneva had done some very bad things in her short life.

Unforgivable things she certainly wasn't proud of. And now that she was dead, no matter what this loser said, there wasn't a whole helluva lot she could do to remedy her mistakes.

She glanced down at her nuclear green Puke & Die concert T-shirt just in time to see a seagull dive through her left boob. "Whoa!" she said, shivering in spite of the sauna-like heat. "What was that?"

The being merely smiled. "You'll get used to it. In your current state, your body consists of light beams. Actually, you have no body, but since that's a tough subject for unruly first-timers like yourself to grasp, I'll go ahead and let you keep your past form a while longer—though you might at least try doing something with your hair."

"What's wrong with my hair? At Puke and Die's concert tonight, Talon told me I looked hot."

"Oh, yes," the being said in his uptight accent that sounded more like he hailed from London than a cloud. "Master Talon. How could I forget the chap who gave you the complimentary dose of X?"

"Hey? How was I supposed to know I'd have a bad trip? I mean, up to that moment, my whole life had been a bad trip. I was just looking for some fun."

"F-U-N. Three such innocent letters that have been the downfall of so many before you, my dear Geneva McBride."

She bristled. "Don't call me that."

"Geneva?"

"No, McBride. I go by my maiden name of Kowalski." When she walked out on Jonah, she'd given up all rights to using his name.

He raised his eyebrows. "Oh? And why is that?"

She swallowed hard. Why all the questions? And why did it feel like she had a wad of tears stuck at the back of her throat? She didn't cry.

She hadn't even cried when she said good-bye to her baby, Katie, and if there had ever been an occasion to shed a few salty ones, that had been it. Her heart squeezed when she thought about her baby girl—not to mention Katie's daddy. But no matter what anyone else thought about her leaving, Geneva knew she'd done the right thing. Katie deserved better than her for a mother, and everyone in town knew Jonah deserved better for a wife.

No, no, no . . . She swallowed even harder.

I am not going to cry. Not in front of this sheet-wearing snob who looks straight off the set of a Hercules flick.

"You're not really going to cry, you know," her companion said, his voice surprisingly soothing. "You're just experiencing the memory of previous tears."

3

Geneva snapped her gaze to his. "How'd you do that?"

"What?"

"You know what. Read my mind. I don't know how you did it, but I'd appreciate it if from now on you stayed out of my private thoughts."

"As you wish," he said, pressing his hands together in a prayerlike position, then bowing his head. Beady brown gaze back on her, he said, "Well, then, now that we've exchanged pleasantries, shall we get down to business?"

Eyes narrowed, Geneva said, "What kind of con are you pulling? Is this the part where you tell me thanks, but no thanks, God doesn't want my type? 'Cause believe you me, I already know I'm going to hell and that's okay. I'll be the first to admit I deserve it."

"Why?"

She laughed. "Are you deaf? I'm going to hell because I'm bad. You know, just like in the song, 'bad to the bone.' "

He sighed, gazed at a passing flock of big gray birds that looked like they could really mess up the hood of that hot red Mustang she'd always wanted, but now would never have. Turning back to her, he said, "I'm afraid you don't understand what it is I've asked."

"Then maybe you'd better explain."

"No, that'd take too much time. I'd rather just show you a little later. You, Ms. Geneva Kowalski-McBride, have indeed done some downright foul things, but that's the upside of Heaven. My boss picks up on the intricacies of the soul, and while it's a long shot, Mr. Big believes you may be redeemable."

"Oh, yeah?" She couldn't help but lean forward. "So what's the catch?"

"Ah, yes." He smiled. "The catch. There's always a catch with creatures like you."

"Well, I know you're not about to give me this redemption of yours scot-free."

"Nope. 'Fraid not. Tell you what I am going to do, though."

"What's that?"

"Do you like games, Geneva?"

"Depends on what kind—and nothing too kinky."

"Great, then we're in luck. I don't do kink, either. What I do like, however, are games of the heart. . . ."

He made a great arc with his arm and voilà—hitching a ride on their cloud was a movie screen. "While it may seem like an hour since you drew your last mortal breath, in earth time it's been three months."

Before she could absorb that mind blower, on screen, a woman sat behind the wheel of a black Dodge Stealth. Geneva loved the vehicle's sleek lines and would know it anywhere—even as it sliced through inky darkness.

Rain fell in silvery sheets and the driver slalomed the winding road's double yellow lines. The treacherous curves looked familiar. Old Highway 74 leading out of Blue Moon?

"Whoa," Geneva mumbled. "She's looped."

"Sadly, you're right."

"So? What do you want me to do about it? Refer her to an AA sponsor? Turn her in to the cops?"

"No, thank you. What I have in mind is a tad more challenging."

From on screen came the sizzle of lightning striking close to the car, then a sickening tire squall. In slow motion, Geneva helplessly watched, her stomach churning when the vehicle swerved off the road and onto the steep shoulder, slowly, terrifyingly, smashing to a stop against the trunk of a gnarled oak.

The taillights glowed an eerie red against the black night and the horn cried a lonely wail.

Leaping to her feet, Geneva shouted, "What'd you do that for? I thought you were supposed to be some kind of angel! What if she died?"

The being tightened his lips. As he gazed at the screen, Geneva saw compassion in his eyes, and not for the first time she regretted spewing the first thing that'd come to mind. This angel dude was clearly saddened, so why hadn't he stopped the car from crashing?

The camera honed in on the woman inside the vehicle. Her delicate profile. Pale skin. Buttery hair. A nasty bruise shadowed the center of her forehead where it rested against the wheel. Something about her looked familiar, or maybe it was just a sort of kindred spirit thing in that whoever this woman was, like Geneva, she seemed to be a card-carrying member of the Bad Girl Club.

"She going to be all right?" Geneva asked.

"I don't know." He looked her way. "That depends on you."

"Me? What could I do?"

"You'd be surprised. Though at the moment it's not her body in danger, but her soul. . . ."

CHAPTER ONE

The old geezers who used to sit in the back booth of Jonah McBride's diner drinking coffee and complaining about their wives said hell hath no fury like that of a woman scorned, but as Jonah shoved the plunger in and out of the men's room john, he figured the rage simmering in him could give any woman—scorned or otherwise—a run for her money. By God, it was a damned good thing his wife, Geneva, was already dead or for what she was putting their baby and him through he would have gladly sent her to hell himself.

Nine o'clock closing time had come and gone.

Quiet surrounded him like a tomb.

The chipper scent of lemon sanitizer that commercials promised made life "sunshiny bright" did squat to mask the room's other nauseating smells. Exhaustion had long since taken hold, and more than anything,

Jonah wanted a hot shower and bed—not even nec-essarily in that order. But unlike his wife, Jonah hadn't been given a choice about what he wanted to do. This thankless job, just like so many others, had to be done.

He plunged again.

Christmas Eve, telling folks she'd taken off with a trucker . . . had to be done.

New Year's Day, driving down to Little Rock to ID her four-days'-dead overdosed body . . . had to be done.

Sitting at that damned funeral parlor pretending he missed her when the God's honest truth was that he was relieved she was gone . . . had to be done.

Plunging harder and harder, he ignored the fire burn-ing the backs of his eyes. Three months after the fact, he would not cry for her. He would not cry for her broken promises. He especially wouldn't cry for the dreams she'd been too selfish to pursue. Now, dreams of bright lights and the big city, oh, those she'd had plenty of time for.

It was his dreams she'd had problems with.

Might have been nice for her to tell him about her hatred of small towns, diners, and kids *before* they'd taken their wedding vows.

Oh, you knew, buddy. You were just too damned full of piss and vinegar to consider for even a second that you'd fail to turn her loathing into love.

Gritting his teeth, Jonah put muscle into his task and soon built up enough suction for the mess to go down. Too bad the mess Geneva had made of his life wouldn't be quite so easy to flush.

After stashing the plunger in the cabinet beneath the sink, he washed his hands, casting a passing glance at the stranger looking back at him in the mirror. Dark circles under his eyes. Dark hair in need of a cut. Dark

T-shirt in need of a wash. Yep, that pretty much summed things up—dark.

He dried his hands on a rough brown paper towel—the kind Geneva nagged about wanting him to upgrade. Right. He barely had enough cash to pay his cook, yet he was supposed to fork out dough for designer hand wipes? Pressing his lips tight, he wadded the limp paper and shot from three-point range for the trash.

He missed, and the ball ricocheted off the can's rim, rolling right up alongside the first stall john.

Why was that no big surprise?

He sighed, stooped to reach under the partition to pick up the paper, tossed it in the black trash bin, then reached for his mop bucket, intent on exchanging dirty water for clean before tackling the women's room.

In the dining area, only shadows and memories filled the seats.

Back when his father and grandfather had run the place, the town of Blue Moon had been different. Friendly. A town with a beating heart and a soul named Blue Moon Diner. Beneath the glass case holding the cash register resided decades of Blue Moon memorabilia. Calendars and mugs. Hats and matchbooks. Jonah's great-grandfather had gotten a kick out of drawing in customers through fun promotions. *Buy a burger special—get a Coke Girl pinup.* Back in the diner's not-so-distant heyday, businessmen stopped in on their way to work for biscuits and gravy. Housewives indulged in gossipy lunches over chicken salad on lettuce. Kids made out after school over burgers and fries. Families took time to really know each other—or at least pretend they did—over the meat loaf dinner special.

Most of Jonah's regulars now took their meals at the

chain places lining the so-called *improved* U.S. Highway. The impersonal 65 dissected northern Arkansas with no thought to the people it bypassed. All it cared about was speed and efficiency, kind of like the patrons who'd passed up his brand of sit-down home cooking for the flashy, drive-thru variety of food that came at value prices instead of value portions. He knew his old customers taking their business elsewhere wasn't personal, just a matter of economics, but he couldn't help but tie his failing business in with his failed marriage, and lately even in fatherhood.

The tall pie case taunted him with its flickering neon bulb. *Look at me*, it said. *I'm wearing blueberry and peach pie, apple and rhubarb, banana cream and even lemon chiffon.*

He looked away.

I'm so pretty. Just like a carnival ride, spinning round and round and round. I don't have to worry about my pretty pies being eaten because no one even comes in this musty old place anymore.

Shut up.

Your customers won't eat. Your baby won't eat. Your—

"Shut up!" He put his hands over his ears, then immediately lowered them, feeling like a fool. He was too old for this.

Too old and too tired.

Katie would be fine and so would the diner. By sheer will, he would make them fine.

Though fatigue reigned supreme, Jonah pushed through the swinging kitchen door.

Save for the forty-watt bulb over the back exit, the kitchen was dark. The hulking shapes of the stainless-steel stove and grill, and the long, streamlined counters taunted him with the fact that before the highway, at this time of night, his last customers would only just now be filing out. It'd be eleven before the kitchen was clean, and instead of Jonah doing all the work, he'd had a friend.

Chevis, a tough old bird of a black man with wiry white hair and a crooked salt-and-pepper beard so bushy he stashed his Special Edition NASCAR Marlboro cigarette lighter in the bottom fluff. Despite the fact that over twenty years earlier he'd said, "Dat's it, I'm givin' up my smokes," at any given time he might have two or three cigs poked into the bottom fluff as well. Since Jonah had had to let him go over a year earlier, Chevis now spent his time bobber fishing for bluegill off the low water bridge that crossed John Culpepper Creek at the south fork of John Peter Road.

Past the ovens, Jonah made a quick left and stepped into his office, where he'd left his desk lamp on to beat down the shadows. On the far wall, a red neon Bud sign glowed, illuminating real pine paneling and the piece-of-shit, puke-green sofa where Geneva and he had first made love. An even uglier pumpkin orange and brown afghan covered the worst of the seat cushion stains left over from the last time she'd pitched a fit.

That night, Chevis had gone home early to his granddaughter's high school graduation party, and Geneva graciously offered to help Jonah clean up.

Ha. He should have known she had something up her sleeve from the moment she asked where he kept his toilet bowl brushes. Sure enough, after she not only scrubbed both bathrooms clean but the kitchen floor as well, they'd been indulging in a late-night happy hour when she brought up the car.

Bloody Mary in hand, she'd done a sexy-slow strut across the room, looking damned fine in skimpy jean cutoffs and a black sports bra. She straddled him, pinning him to the couch with her bronzed thighs, and he smiled up at her, easing his right index finger beneath the strap of her top. "I want you," he'd said.

"You're in luck," she said. "Because I want you, too."

"Oh, yeah?" he teased, cinching her tight, pressing a kiss to her cleavage. She tasted of salty sweat and the musky perfume she'd blown sixty-five bucks on last Saturday morning at the Harrison JC Penney's. He'd been furious. He needed that money to pay the plumber for a permanent fix on the men's room john. But now all he could think about was her, and how good she smelled, and how bad he wanted into her pants—not just because he was horny but because it was long past due that they got started on that big family he'd always wanted.

His hand splayed on the back of her head, fingertips buried in jet black waves, he pulled her in for a kiss, showing her with his mouth how much he needed her.

That kiss had gone on forever, and for the first time in as long as Jonah could remember, they felt in sync. Like it was the two of them against the world.

And then she pulled away. "Um, Jonah," she said, licking her swollen lips.

"Yeah?"

"There's something I've been meaning to talk to you about."

"Anything." He kissed her throat, her collarbone, her earlobe.

"You know how I feel about being seen around town in your truck."

"Yeah . . ." Her right cheek, her left, her forehead.

"Well, on a trade, Moody Roach just fixed the transmission on Kent Holloway's Caddie."

"Yeah . . ." Her chin, her throat, that sexy-as-hell indentation at the base of her throat.

"You'll never guess what Kent traded Moody for doing all that work."

Jonah sighed. "Do we have to talk about it now? Because to be honest, I wouldn't care if what Kent gave Moody was a blow job."

"Jonah!" Pretending to go all chaste, Geneva gave him a swat. "You don't have to be crude."

"Oh, yes I do." He shifted his attention to the swell of her breasts. "Come on, Ginny, forget about Moody and Kent and spend some time with me."

"I will," she said, arching away from him to reach for the drink she'd set on the Solo box serving as a side table. When she sipped the ice chinked, giving him a whiff of the Tabasco and Worcestershire she used to spiff up her Mr. & Mrs. T mix. "But first," she said, scooping out a cube with her middle and index fingers, "I have a tiny favor to ask."

"What's that?"

She used that cube to trace the lines of her bra.

Her nipples hardened and he hardened, swallowing to catch his breath. She arched her head and moaned, running that ice across first one nipple, then the other, until all that was left were twin wet spots. "Baby," she said, "since you're always so sensitive on the subject, I hate to even bother you with this, but do we have any extra cash?"

"A—a little," he managed to choke out. "Why?"

"Oh, no big deal. It's just that Kent traded Moody for a bitchin' red 'Sixty-eight Mustang I'd look *soooo* hot in ridin' around town." Her smile widened while her gaze turned dreamy. "Can't you just see me with my black tank top on and black Daisy Dukes? And my hair all piled high—ooh, and my sunglasses. You know, the silver Oakleys you bought me in Sunglass Hut last time we went to Little Rock?"

Whoa.

As if someone had turned on the lights in Jonah's head, the reasoning behind Geneva's seduction became brutally clear. And unfortunately for him, her being on his lap had nothing to do with starting their family and everything to do with her once again wanting to blow their money.

"Jonah, baby?" Her drink still in one hand, she traced his eyebrow with the index finger of her other. "You *do* want me to have that hot car, don't you?"

"Jesus," he said, shifting out from under her. "I should have known better than to think you actually wanted to be with me."

"Then I can't have the car?"

"Hell, no."

Splash.

Double shots of tomato juice, cheap vodka, and ice matted his hair to his forehead and rained from his eyelashes. A couple of ice cubes were already melting against his denim fly. He flicked them to the carpet.

"You loser," Geneva said, hurling the glass against the far wall, where it shattered in a zillion sticky pieces. "I should have known better than to think for even a second you'd put me before this fucking, pathetic excuse for a restaurant."

"It's a diner."

"Whatever." She was standing, heading for the door.

"It's been in my family for over sixty years—and the last thing I am for fighting to keep it alive is a loser."

"Swell," she quipped, the features he'd only minutes

earlier thought beautiful looking hard. "With that and a quarter call someone who cares."

Jonah turned away from the sofa and washed his face with his hands. Katie. He'd come in here to see her, not screwed-up memories of her mother.

Across the room in her pink portable crib, she slept fitfully, wheezing on her exhales. The fuzzy yellow duck he'd bought with the last of the week's grocery money lay untouched beside her, as did a purple squirrel and a black and white polka-dotted hippo. He'd had his doubts about that hippo, but Margie down at the Tot & Shop, the only kid's store in town, told him black and white stimulated infant brain waves.

The trunk of Katie's body twisted right. She held her neck rigid. Despite her wearing what Margie assured him was the most comfortable set of baby jammies money could buy, she looked uncomfortable, and he reached into the crib to realign her, his hands big and clumsy against her painfully thin, lavender-fleece covered arms and legs.

The space heater clicked on, filling the room with its electrical hum. Jonah first worried that the heater hadn't been coming on enough, but then he pressed his fingertips to Katie's flushed forehead and decided to turn it down.

In the months since Geneva left, Katie had lost two pounds. Not much for an adult, "but for an infant," old Doc Penbrook informed him, "failure to thrive is serious business. If this little lady loses even a quarter of another pound, Jonah, I'm afraid I'll have to admit her to the hospital over in Harrison."

The thought of her trussed up to feeding tubes clenched Jonah's chest, trapping him in a man-sized vice.

Some of the women around town told him he worried too much, but where Katie was concerned, there was no such thing as too much worry. He loved her—fiercely. He'd do anything for her, and if the women around town didn't understand that, well, they could all just go straight to—

Throat thick with fear, Jonah cast his daughter one last look.

Time to get back to work. He didn't open the diner till eleven in the morning, which meant if he finished all the cleaning tonight, that'd give him extra time to spend with Katie while she was awake.

First, Jonah scrubbed the two women's room commodes, then stashed the dripping brushes in the empty sherbet bucket he kept beneath the sink.

Next, he wiped down the counter with 409.

Some lovesick teen had written *Sissy Luvs David* in race-car-red lipstick on the mirror. It took Jonah nearly five minutes to scrub the message off with Windex, and when that was done, he had to get down on all fours to pick up the paper towels someone had flung on the floor instead of in the trash.

On the way back up, the underside of the counter hit him. "Crap, that hurt," he said, rubbing the tender spot on the back of his head.

Pain and frustration had him on the verge of slinging the towels against the faded rose wallpaper when he saw a face reflected in the mirror. A woman's face. Hidden until he'd stood at that particular angle, she slept sitting up in the cramped storage alcove, hugging her knees to her chest.

Halfway expecting her to be a figment of his overtired imagination, Jonah spun around, but there she was, pale as a ghost but unmistakably human—not to mention woman, dressed head to toe in scuffed, form-fitting red leather. Bits of leaves and a twig matted her pale hair. Through the dirt smudges on her cheeks ran dry creek beds he suspected had once been rivers of tears.

Kneeling beside her, he brushed her hair back from her face and drew a swift breath. Damn. A nasty bruise marred her equally dirty forehead.

Was she sleeping? Or like *really* unconscious? And how did he tell the difference?

"Ma'am?" He put his hand on her shoulder and gently shook her. "Ma'am, are you okay?"

From behind lips so full and red they looked pursed for a kiss spilled a moan.

"That's it. Wake up." *Tell me your story.*

Her eyes opened in slow increments. "W-where am I?" she asked, treating him to a jewel-blue gaze straight off the pages of one of Geneva's *Cosmos*.

Relief turned his already aching legs rubbery. If she could talk, she could walk, which meant he was off the hook. "You're in Blue Moon, Arkansas."

"Oooh . . ." Her wobbly soft tone faded around the same time her eyes drifted closed.

Great. Just great. So, she couldn't talk. But then, judging by the sweet liquory scent of her one word, at least now there was a logical reason for her lethargy. As to how she'd gotten that nasty bruise and all that dirt, probably the same place she'd gotten soused.

He gave her another gentle shake, but she wouldn't budge. Dammit. Couldn't she see he had enough woman problems on his plate?

Despite the self-preserving voice at the back of his head telling him to set her on the front porch bench and call the town's only cab, he slid his arms beneath

17

her slight form, planning on carrying her to the piece-of-shit sofa in his office. Problem was, scooping her gracefully out of that alcove wasn't going to happen, so in the end he half-tugged, half-lifted, half broke his back trying to lug her out of there, and even through all that commotion, her eyes stayed glued shut.

Limp as she was, she made for an awkward package, but luckily, in preparation for mopping, he'd used a chair to prop open the bathroom door, so once he shimmied past that, it was no big deal to use her feet to kick through the swinging kitchen door.

Finally in the office, he settled her on the couch, then rubbed his aching arms.

After checking that Katie was still asleep, Jonah slipped into the kitchen to wet a cloth.

As best he could, he cleaned the woman's face and hands, then used his fingers to comb crumpled leaves from her hair before covering her with another butt-ugly afghan—this one red, black, yellow, and brown. God help her if she woke with a hangover and the first thing she caught sight of was that old thing. Oh, well, at least it smelled clean from Tide and the Downy Ball blue stuff he'd only just recently learned how to use.

Funny how things changed.

Back when his mom had been alive, he'd have paid good money for her to spout cleaning tips to someone other than him. Now, he'd have paid to have her here. She'd know what to do.

As for him knowing what to do . . .

He scratched his head. Eyed Katie, then the mystery woman, then the yellow smiley face clock Geneva had given him for his thirty-third birthday. He hated that clock and had been meaning to get rid of it, but at the moment that stupid clock was the least of his problems.

Hell, here it was almost ten, and instead of taking the hot shower he'd been craving, he was standing around eyeballing two snoozing blondes while he still had a bathroom floor to mop.

Sighing, he headed off to get his work done, and had just about finished when from the office came one of Katie's banshee wails.

With a small splash, he dropped the mop into the bucket and washed his hands. Time for the munchkin's bottle.

Katie's cries intensified.

"Hold on, squirt," he said, hustling for the office. Her squalling abruptly stopped.

Old Doc Penbrook's voice echoed in Jonah's head. *Failure to thrive is serious business, son. I don't mind telling you this little lady's deteriorating condition is giving me a real scare.*

Knowing he couldn't take it if something were to happen to the only thing in his life worth living for, Jonah flat out ran though the sea of dining room tables, sending a wooden chair clattering to the floor before entering the stainless steel maze of the kitchen.

Bursting through the office door, he'd imagined, then prepared, for the worst, but nothing could have prepared him for the sight truly unfolding.

The stranger he'd only a short while earlier tucked to sleep on the sofa was now seated in the big oak rocker that'd been in his family for over a hundred years—with Katie contentedly suckling her left breast.

CHAPTER TWO

"Just what the hell does she think she's doing?" Geneva hopped up from her invisible bench thingee, yanked off her black spiked heel boot, and threw it at the movie screen. "Stop it!" she hollered. "That's my baby! And my husband! I've been around the block a time or two. Don't think you can just waltz in there with your big blond hair and those baby blues of yours and—"

Angel dude clasped his hand over her right shoulder.

"What?" she said, turning away from the screen to slant him a look. "Don't interrupt me when I'm on a roll."

"Of course." His bow was so proper it could have only been sarcastic. When he straightened, sure enough, his usual serene smile looked more like a smirk. "It was merely my intention to point out a few facts that you've evidently forgotten."

"Yeah, well, save it. I'm still miffed about Blondie pulling a fast one on me. I mean, geez, I thought we had a bad girl kindred spirit thing going. I didn't have to use those powers you taught me to pull her out of her car."

"Ah, yes, and unceremoniously dump her in the weeds."

"I didn't dump her." But just in case Mr. Big might be listening, Geneva came clean. "Okay, so I'll admit her landing was a smidgen rough, but you didn't tell me how fast all this telekinesis stuff works."

He rolled his eyes. "Of course, nothing is ever your fault."

"You'd better watch that sarcasm, Hercules. At the rate you're going with that mouth of yours, you'll be making the trip to you-know-where right alongside me."

Far from looking concerned, he had the gall to yet again roll his eyes.

Geneva fumed. If she'd had a fork handy, she'd have poked his beady eyes right out of his head.

At that, the cloud turned from cottony white to stony gray, and ear-splitting lightning and thunder parted the sky.

"What'd you do that for?" Geneva asked.

"To gently remind you that you're only here by His grace. You have a lot to learn Geneva Kowalski-McBride, and it's about time you started your lessons."

"Look," she said with a deep sigh, "I did what you told me and showed Blondie the way to Jonah's diner, didn't I? I knew of anyone in that seedy town, he'd make sure she ended up at a hospital if she needed one. So, come on, cut me some slack. I'm the good girl here and she's the bad one. Doesn't she know I've only been out of the picture an hour?"

Hercules cleared his throat. "Remember how I told you about moving on to the eternal time zone? And anyway, what do you care if she makes eyes at your former husband? Weren't you the one who left him?"

"Yeah, but . . ." Geneva stilled, studied the screen and the way tiny Katie looked so at peace in Blondie's arms. And far from feeling charitable toward the woman for feeding her child, Geneva wished for a spare fork so she could poke out Blondie's eyes as well!

Jonah drew a sharp breath.

During the short time Geneva nursed their child, Katie thrived, but she'd never taken to the formula Jonah fed her like she'd taken to her mother's breast. And wasn't that how it should be? He couldn't blame his daughter for preferring nature to a plastic bottle, but how could what he was seeing be true?

He hovered in the room's shadows, fascinated by the woman's softly crooned, nonsensical lullaby. Her voice was ethereal—deep into the realm of harps and airy wind chimes. An expression of unspeakable love transformed her features, illuminating aquamarine eyes that shone wet with unshed tears.

The sight of dangerously thin Katie greedily suckling made Jonah's throat thick with not only tears of relief but gratitude. Who could this woman be? Where had she come from and how much would he have to withdraw from his meager savings to make her stay?

A long time ago, he used to go to church. Back in those days, he might have toyed with the possibility that this angel was heaven-sent, but since he no longer believed in God, he sure as hell didn't believe in angels.

She looked up and their gazes locked. The tears that had been hanging at the corners of her eyes spilled. "I'm home," she said, her voice raspy. "I'm finally home. It's been so long."

Home? So long?

Jonah stepped into the weak light pooling from the

desk lamp onto the worn beige carpet. Eyes narrowed, he moved closer to her, to his insatiable child.

"F-first there was the accident," she said. "And then I couldn't find anyone to help." With her free right hand, she pushed the hair back from her forehead, revealing a purple bruise. "I walked such a long way. . . ." With the same hand she'd used to smooth back her own hair, she now stroked Katie's golden goose-down fluff. "I missed you both so much, but . . ."

"But what?"

"But . . ." She grinned, an adorable lopsided affair that made his ever-growing urge to protect her that much stronger. "It's the funniest thing. I remember Lizzy, but I can't remember you or this place. I can't even remember my name. Favorite color or birthday. Please forgive me, sweetheart." Again, she touched the bruise. "I'm sure once I start feeling better everything will come back. The important thing is that I've found you and our baby. Now I know everything will be all right. You'll take care of me, won't you? You've always taken such good care of me."

Just as Jonah had first been grateful, now his stomach churned. When had he become so selfish? This woman thought his baby was hers because she'd obviously lost her own. Somewhere out there she had a child and a husband no doubt desperately searching for her, and here he'd stood happy as a June bug that she was feeding Katie.

"Oh, Lizzy," she said, her smile lighting not just her face but the entire room. "I missed you so much, baby. You'll never know how much."

Like out-of-tune strings on a guitar, guilt strummed through Jonah. He had to tell her that he'd never before seen her, but then what would happen to Katie?

For once she seemed at peace. What would it hurt to keep this mystery woman with her at least until morning? Because really, it was too late to try to find her rightful home now. He'd just take her to his place, see that she got a good night's rest. Then, come first light, he'd call his friend Sam—Blue Moon's police chief.

For Jonah, the ten-mile drive from the diner to his house lasted an eternity. With Katie's infant seat strapped into the passenger-side of the crotchety old Chevy pickup, that left only the center section for the stranger to sit in. With every bump, her thigh brushed his, quickening his pulse, deepening his unease. Her fancy red suit perfumed the tight space with the rich scent of leather, and whenever he lowered his hand to shift, his knuckles brushed her buttery soft knee.

Geneva would have killed for an outfit like that, and there had been a time when Jonah would have killed to give it to her. At the high point of their marriage, he'd have done anything for her, but then she changed—or had it been he who'd changed?

Expecting more than great sex.

Receiving little else.

He'd shared his woes with his pal Chevis. And Sam Lawson, high school misfit turned police chief. Both guys told Jonah to lay off the sauce—for the only explanation there could possibly be for Jonah complaining about a surplus of sex was that he'd been spending too much time with Mr. Jack Daniel's and not enough in the arms of his eternally randy wife.

Steeling his grip on the wheel, Jonah pressed his lips tight. Never having been much of a drinker, he knew better. What he hadn't told the guys was that toward the end of their marriage, Geneva had wielded sex like a manipulative weapon. Just like she'd tried sleeping her way into making him buy her that Mustang, she'd repeated the process, sometimes successfully and sometimes not, for clothes, jewelry, perfume, those pricey sunglasses. And then there were the big-ticket items she'd damn well known he could never afford but nagged about anyway. Buying a party barge, installing a backyard pool, remodeling the diner—and his favorite, altogether closing the diner and moving lock, stock, and barrel to some speck on the map where she'd said she had friends on the east coast of Mexico. With Geneva, there had always been a reason for sex—a need that went miles farther than plain old love. With Geneva, pretty much the only thing that ever mattered was what she wanted—and how she planned to get it.

He cast a glance toward the stranger, hating himself for loving the way she'd sidled up beside him. Her right hand rested on Katie's car seat and the infant reached for her index finger, cooing when she not only caught it but gripped it tight, drawing it into her puckered lips.

The woman said, "She's beautiful, isn't she? A masterpiece, even if I do say so myself." She leaned right to kiss Katie on the forehead, then straightened to kiss him on the cheek.

Jonah groaned inwardly. What was he getting himself into? The woman's simple yet fervent kiss made him feel branded. Like her searing touch implanted her essence deep within him, filling his mind with bizarre what-ifs.

What if she really was Katie's mom? His wife? How would his life be different? Without constant worry for Katie, would the added time he could have spent at the diner made a difference? Or would it still be headed for failure?

Who could say?

That was the problem with what-ifs. There was no way he'd ever know any of those answers for sure.

Even though Geneva had left him—and even though he'd emotionally left her the day she found out she was pregnant and threatened to get an abortion, the realist in Jonah gave himself a swift, hard mental kick for even wondering such things. Granted, Katie needed a mom, but he sure as hell didn't need—or even want—another wife. Another thing he didn't need was the heat building in the quarter-inch between the stranger and his thighs.

Just a little longer, he thought, consoling himself with the sensible words even as he shifted from an unwanted erection. A little longer and he'd never again have to hold his arms so tight to his chest. He wouldn't have to worry about his elbow accidentally grazing the side swell of the woman's breast. Or about the fact that she wouldn't see anything out of the ordinary about him touching any part of her. In her mind, he was her husband.

He should have called a cab for her, but where would he have told Hester, the town's only cabbie, to take her? Besides which, she was hurt. She might even need medical attention.

So why bring her home?

Why hadn't he just made the long drive to the Harrison emergency room, then said his good-byes?

Katie, giving his heartstrings a tug, answered his question with a soft coo. He'd do the right thing in the morning, but now he had to concentrate on his child, and if Katie was content, he was, too.

Hoping to uncover a clue to the woman's past, Jonah asked, "Where's your purse?"

"I don't know," she said, staring into the weak wash of headlights on the winter-hardened dirt road that was still damp from that evening's rain. The night was cloaked in black and all that could be seen on the road's shoulders were dust-covered ghosts of summer weeds, lining the way like lithesome spectators, witnessing Jonah's lies. "I guess I must've left it in the car. My accident is still so foggy." She pressed her fingertips to her forehead. "I'm sorry I can't remember more, but then . . ." She took hold of his upper right arm and squeezed, this time branding her heat through the worn flannel shirt he'd slipped on as a jacket. He wanted to jerk free but couldn't.

She'd trapped him, hypnotized him with an invisible arsenal of awareness. Before finishing her sentence, she leaned her head on his shoulder. ". . . Now that I'm back with you and Lizzy, I guess nothing else matters, does it?"

Oh, he could think of plenty that mattered.

Stuff like telling her the truth and not sinking any deeper into this charade. But then the faint expensive scent of her hair drifted to him, and its silken strands whispered miracle cures for Katie against his cheek. And then he was saying, "Nope. Nothing matters except that you're safe."

Jonah entered the house first, hugging Katie to his chest, drawing strength from her familiar baby smells of lotion and shampoo. He reminded himself while keeping busy turning on lights that everything in the house was as it should be.

The grandfather clock standing sentinel at the foot of the stairs still ticked. Yesterday's dirty black T-shirt and jeans still lay in a ball beneath the second-story landing, right where he'd thrown them, planning to later carry them to the enclosed laundry porch but never having found the time. Two half-empty coffee mugs and a Styrofoam cup still sat on one of the end tables, along with a Dorito bag and a can of Coke that'd been there so long mold sprouted out of the top. The musty smell in the air was a curious blend of all of it. Dirty clothes and dishes. Dust, mold, damp earth floating through the open kitchen window.

From in town, a late-night coal train blared a double warning to any teens planning to race it across the trestle bridge at Riverside Park.

See? He had nothing to be nervous about. Nothing had changed. Men his age brought home women for sleep-overs every night of the week.

Yeah, only those were women for them to feast on—not their babies!

With at least four more lamps shining than necessary, Jonah felt exposed. He ran a tight ship at the diner, so what had happened at home?

"I see you've missed me," his guest said with a grin he didn't want to be charmed by but couldn't help but appreciate. She stepped around a plastic tub overflowing with pureed peach–stained baby clothes to reach the coffee table littered with the paper and foil remains of take-out dinners. "Haven't been doing much cooking?"

He shrugged. "I cook all day at the diner; I figure what's the point in cooking here? It's just as easy to wrap up a burger and fries to go."

"Easy, but not healthy," she said, absentmindedly drawing a heart in the dust atop his mother's baby grand.

The instrument had been a fifteenth-anniversary gift

to his mom from his dad. Jonah remembered her sitting ramrod straight on the black leather bench, her long, slender fingers draped over the keys. She'd closed her eyes when she played, and the look on her face as she keyed Chopin and Schultz, Diabelli and Schumann, convinced him that she was the most talented, beautiful woman in the world.

Of course, Blue Moon had never been a hotbed of musical talent, so maybe that explained why when Geneva had pinged out the theme to *Ice Castles*, he'd been touched.

Every day until dying of a sudden stroke in her sixties, his mom had played this piano, filling the Queen Anne home that had been old even back then with love. She'd used her music to pour her feelings into the air. Now the piano sat fallow, a collection of dirty baby bottles riding on top, one of which had spilled a milky pond of formula into the dust.

With the sleeve of his flannel shirt, Jonah swiped the spot dry, but he was too late. The liquid had already left a mark. "Guess I've kind of let the place go to seed," he said, hating what had become of his life.

"And just think, I've only been gone a few days. What would have happened had I been gone any longer?" The woman's laughing eyes showed she was teasing, as did her quick peck to his cheek, then Katie's. Even though the moment had been fleeting, the warmth of her lips stayed with him. "Here," she said, holding out her arms. "Let me take the baby. We need to get reacquainted."

"Sure." He tried not to notice their arms brushing as he passed Katie into her waiting embrace. She'd removed her red leather jacket, revealing a sleeveless ribbed tee. White. No bra. Clinging to her curves like paint. And then there was Katie, snuggling into the woman's hold, flushed cheek resting against bare chest. Before, when Jonah had looked at his baby, he'd seen fragility and fear. Now all he saw was contentedness, her tiny body visibly limp with what in his adult mind he could only guess was relief.

The men in Jonah's family had a long-standing tradition of constructing rockers to commemorate births. The woman gravitated toward the rocker he'd made for Geneva upon Katie's birth. It sat in the room's bay window in the rosy glow of lamplight cast by a Tiffany reproduction. Geneva had hated that lamp, along with the rocker, and the rambling old house. The stranger, however, sank into the low seat with ease, then, baby held over her heart, she leaned her head back and closed her eyes. "Mmm," she said, her voice barely registering in the thick silence. "Have you ever had one of those moments when you just knew soul deep everything was going to be all right?"

"Um, no." Jonah cleared his throat. "Guess I can't say that I have."

"Well, I have. Right this minute. Lizzy feels so warm against me and her hair is soft on my chin. And she smells good—sugary-sweet, like a baby should. And you're over there, looking sturdy and handsome, hovering like a papa bear, ready to defend your two ladies should anyone question our honor."

Tell her, every fiber of Jonah's being urged. *Tell her the truth. Who you are. Who she isn't.*

He should have told her, but he didn't.

Lord help him, he couldn't stop himself from slipping ever deeper into her fantastic realm. It was late. He was bone tired. The whole scene had taken on a dreamlike quality.

He was stuck on the spokes of the vast, dreamy web she'd spun of them being a family. He was stuck on images and emotions that evoked long-buried blueprints for the way he'd planned his life to be. All he ever really wanted was to be a good husband and father, to run his diner and provide a comfortable living for those he loved—just as his father had before him.

He was a man of simple needs and even simpler dreams, yet those had always been enough.

Then Geneva left, and he thought he'd never have a shot at those dreams ever coming true, but crazy as the notion seemed, standing before this woman and his child, he knew the awareness humming through his system was far more than mere appreciation.

Maybe it was because he'd been without a woman for so long, or maybe because of the way she cradled Katie against her full breasts? Maybe it was the springtime lilt of her voice, the way her very breath seemed filled with burgeoning hope and the promise of renewed life? Whatever it was, he had the craziest urge to kneel at her feet and beg her to make everything all right.

Over the past months, loneliness and confusion had overwhelmed him. But now, here, standing before a woman with hair the shade of sweet cream butter and eyes of the purest aquamarine, he had the sensation that everything *would* be all right—at least he'd had that sensation for a few brief moments before realizing that everything had never been more wrong.

This woman wasn't his any more than she was Katie's. And first thing in the morning he had to give her back.

"Damn straight you do," Geneva muttered.
"Language, language."

31

"What? I'm supposed to be happy over this bimbo stepping into my life?"

"Your life? Aren't there a few details you seem to be forgetting?"

"Like what?"

"Like . . . you're dead."

Geneva's shoulders slumped—at least what was left of her shoulders. Geez, being dead was hard work. Dealing with Mr. Grecian Formula. Birds winging through her boobs. Riding around on a drafty cloud. When would she get to the part of afterlife where she got to lounge alongside some trippin' galaxy being served wine coolers and pizza by hunky angels, as opposed to being lectured by this snooty old know-it-all?

"In due time, my dear. In due time."

Geneva shot him a look. "Would you knock it off with the mind reading? A girl needs her privacy."

"As you wish," he said with one of his uptight bows that didn't mean diddly. She knew damned well he'd be back at it in five minutes—if he even stopped that long. He cast her a pathetically patronizing look. "Besides, you've been at this death business long enough now that you're ready to proceed with your lessons."

Geneva arched her eyebrows. "You mean learning that bimbo is taking over my family isn't enough? There's more fun ahead?"

"Watch it," Hercules said with a particularly hair singeing bolt of lightning. "You're treading on very thin ice, Geneva Kowalski-McBride. By your own admission, you gave that family away. Abandoned your very own flesh and—"

"Yeah, but—"

"Silence. I know all about your so-called reasons. How your mother left when you were a small child. And how you thought your baby would be better off without a mother *than with a mom who didn't know the first thing about being a good parent, but you know what all that is, Geneva?"*

"What?" she said, raising her chin a defiant notch.

"A cop-out. You were so into your own pain and confusion concerning the past that you didn't even try fixing the future."

She sighed. "Great. So, we established like two hours ago that I'm a fuck-up in every area of my life—or rather I was a fuck-up. Now, I don't know what I am." She slid her gaze his way. "Are fuck-ups allowed in Heaven?"

"Only if they watch their language."

CHAPTER THREE

"Well, um . . ." Jonah did the only thing he felt capable of doing, which was clearing his throat. "It's late. Why don't you let me take Katie and I'll put her to bed."

"Katie?" The beautiful stranger crinkled her nose. "Don't you mean Lizzy?"

"Yeah, sure. Sorry, I sometimes forget."

"You forget our child's name?"

"You forgot my name." Once the words were out, Jonah regretted them. He regretted the pain flashing through her eyes, but most of all he regretted not having the courage to have said, *you not only forgot names but entire lives*.

"Oops." She playfully conked herself on the head. "You got me." In an instant, her smile was back. "Okay, so let's get reacquainted. I know I love you, but I guess I need a name to go along with that love, huh?"

"My name's Jonah."

"Jonah and Lizzy. What great names for my little family."

"Yeah." Names. He'd never before thought of them in terms of carrying great weight, but obviously her baby was named Lizzy.

Her baby.

God forbid, had the infant and her father died in the car crash? As much as he'd briefly, selfishly, wanted the woman to belong to Katie and him, he'd never wish her family dead.

She furrowed her forehead. "Okay, so now I know both your names, but what's mine?"

"Angel," he said. The word came from out of nowhere to spill past his lips.

"Angel? I feel like more of a Violet or a Rose—you know, some kind of flower name. Or maybe a color?"

He shrugged, telling the truth when he said, "I only know you as Angel."

"Okay, then, if you say so." She eyed him up and down. "You look tired. Why don't you go on to bed? I slept so much back at the diner that now I'm kind of wired. I think for now I'll just stay up with the baby, then join you later."

Jonah gulped. The issue of sleeping arrangements hadn't even crossed his mind. "Um, I'll crash in the guest room. That way, you can have the whole bed to yourself."

"Don't be silly," she said with a shy, half-moon sliver of a smile. "Why wouldn't you want to share the bed with me? I've been gone for days. I missed you. Haven't you missed me?"

Oh Lord, what to do?

Tell her the truth. "Look, um, Angel, I haven't exactly been—"

Katie whimpered, then started in with one of her full-blown wails.

"Hungry again so soon?" When she talked to Katie, Angel's voice took on a cushiony-soft tone befitting her new name. "Guess we'll have to feed you, won't we?" In seconds, she bared her right breast and the hungry infant latched on.

Jonah's breath caught in his throat.

Had any man been in a more bizarre situation?

On the one hand, he was deliberately withholding the truth from this trusting woman. On the other, Katie desperately needed her. She needed not only her milk but her touch.

Sure, when Geneva had first left women from town helped him around the clock with the baby, but once he'd turned bitter, his gruff manner had gotten on their nerves. Not to mention the fact that their eternal chipperness had grated his nerves. When they started lecturing him on his lack of faith in the future, he'd given them the cold shoulder. But now he wasn't so sure he'd made the right decision. Evidently, children needed a mother's touch.

But Angel isn't Katie's mother.

Jonah slashed his fingers through his hair. Like he needed that fact pointed out yet again.

"Isn't she the prettiest thing you've ever seen?" Angel said, her lush hair cascading over her cheek and onto Katie's. She tucked pale gold strands behind her ear, then traced the baby's eyebrows with the tip of her pinkie finger. "I can't believe how much I've missed her. It feels like it's been weeks since I've seen her instead of days."

Maybe it has been weeks. "Yeah, well . . ." Jonah shifted from one foot to the other. "You know what they say about time getting away from you."

"I guess. I don't know; I'm just glad to be back." Her gaze fell again to Katie who, though still suckling, had closed her eyes. "You sound tired, Jonah. Why don't you go to bed? Really, Lizzy and I will be fine."

"How? You don't even know where her room is."

Angel rolled her eyes. "It's not that big a house, sweetheart. I lived here before and learned the routine. Don't you think I can figure it out again?"

"I guess."

"Okay, then. I'll meet you in bed."

Jonah wanted to say more on the bedroom issue but figured if he went ahead and set up camp in the guest room she'd get the hint. "Right. See you in the morning."

She blew him a soft kiss. The haunted look in her eyes told him that she expected him to return it, but he couldn't, so he headed for the stairs.

"Jonah?" she asked.

"Yeah?" He turned in time to see a single tear roll down her cheek. The urge to go to her squeezed his chest, but he stoically held his ground.

"I get the feeling something's not quite right between us."

"Oh?"

"For a man whose wife has just returned after having disappeared, I would think, or at least hope, that you'd show more emotion. I mean, I *am* Lizzy's mother. Were we . . . I mean, did we have a fight before I left?"

He sighed. How come no matter how hard he tried distancing himself from this woman, she had a knack for digging him deeper into his own lie? Still, maybe if he led her down the path she was well on her way to taking, it would at least provide a bedroom solution.

"Jonah? Please answer. Your downright gloomy expression when I asked the question tells me I'm at least partially right."

"Sorry," he said, his mind racing for a logical conclusion for why they'd fought. The first rationale coming to him were the ones Geneva used. That he was too broke and their house too run-down, and the town and their life too boring. But what right did he have to inflict those opinions on Angel when she wouldn't even be staying past morning? Now was the perfect time to tell her the truth. But why get her all upset when if he said nothing she could at least get some sleep? "You're right," he said, making a snap decision to say anything just to get through the night. "When you left, we'd been arguing."

"Over what?"

"Money."

"I don't remember that being a problem."

"How could you? You don't even remember your own name."

"Why are you being cruel?"

"I'm not. Just calling a spade a spade."

"I see."

"Do you?"

More tears. "Yes. That's why you don't want to sleep with me."

"Angel, it's just that . . ." How come this hurt as bad as if they'd been fighting for real?

"Please, Jonah. Just stop." Katie had fallen asleep at Angel's breast, and she gently shifted the baby to her shoulder before discreetly drawing down her T-shirt. "That's okay. I understand, but if you insist on us sleeping in separate beds, why don't I take the guest room?"

Why did he suddenly feel like such a jackass?

Probably because that's what I am. "I'll take the guest room," he said. "You'll be more comfortable in the master."

"Okay," she acquiesced, her gaze aimed at the floor.

He stepped toward her to take Katie, but she hugged the baby close. "No. You might feel cool toward me, but don't even think about distancing me from our child. If I no longer have you, then she's all I've got."

Those fighting words stormed Jonah's senses. Katie was all *he* had, and suddenly he wasn't all that keen on sharing. But then Katie's contented expression caught his attention and his anger dimmed. Angel meant his baby no harm. It was him she was upset with, and could he really blame her? He should try to say something to make her feel if not better, then at least comfortable. Instead he merely muttered, "Fine. I'll get you a fresh set of sheets and you tuck in, Kati—ah, I mean, Lizzy. After that, well . . . I guess we'll talk more in the morning."

In the morning . . .

Angel, pacing the lonely master bedroom, had been up most of the night pondering that line. On the most basic of levels, it meant what it implied, but she took it to mean that in the morning Jonah would give her a second chance.

Did she deserve it?

Who except Jonah knew? But obviously, whatever they'd fought about had had a lot to do with her.

Once she'd heard the sound of her husband's soft snores coming from the guest room, Angel snooped through her own belongings.

There were black leather and spike getups entirely unsuitable for the wife of a proud man who owned a small diner in a proud but simple town. There were untidy piles of vinyl platform shoes in colors that never should have even been created, let alone turned into footwear. Big purses and bigger hats.

Outside the closet, cluttering every surface, were dust-coated brass knickknacks—elephants and sailboats, twisted-wire trunk trees with dangling brass and copper leaves.

Instead of calico wallpaper that would have been charming in the high-ceiling room, the walls blared fuchsia, dotted here and there with travel posters singing the praises of Hollywood, Miami, and nighttime New York City.

Angel would have bet money she'd been to all those places and hated them, so why pollute her walls with bad memories?

In fact, she didn't find anything about the room appealing, from the bold, black-and-red-print bedspread to the dish of curried incense potpourri filling a crystal bowl on the dresser.

Stopping at the foot of the bed, she realized that judging by this decorating disaster, she didn't even like the woman she'd once been. So was it fair to blame Jonah for not liking her either?

Glancing at her T-shirt, red leather pants, and matching boots, she wondered if she was the cause of their money problems. Maybe she'd taken too much and contributed too little to not just their finances but their marriage. If that were the case, would Jonah tell her?

She closed her eyes and imagined being held in his arms. Sinewy strong. Not too pumped. Lean, with just enough of a rise to his biceps that she'd have a tough time curling her fingers even halfway around. She squeezed her eyes shut tight, trying to remember him as a lover, but when no images came, she made them up.

His naked chest. Sweat slick. Crushing her breasts as he took her against the closed bedroom door, wood grain nipping her shoulders, her fingers clutching his back, twining his hair. It'd been so long.

Faster.

Harder.

Yes. Oh, God, yes.

Eyes still closed, she cupped her hands over aching breasts. Arched her head and dreamt Jonah's hot breath on her throat. Yes. God, yes. She wanted her husband.

The question was, what was she going to do to make him want her?

"If I have any say in the matter, you're not going to do a damned thing!" Geneva yanked off her remaining boot and flung it at the screen.

Damn that bitch.

Who the hell did she think she was, trashing Geneva's choice in clothes and shoes and decor and then practically getting off with Jonah right there in their bedroom?

Fists clenched, Geneva paced, only with a measly five feet to maneuver, it was hardly effective.

"Yep," Herc said. "I'd say it's more than time to address the first of our lessons."

"Screw your lessons. Why don't you just go on ahead and send me the rest of the way to hell? Or, no, I get it, the joke's on me and I'm already there, right?" Tears caught at the back of her throat as she watched that bimbo Jonah called an angel stretch out atop the big, king-size bed, draw-

41

ing one of his downy feather pillows to her nose and dragging in a big ol' whiff. And damn if Geneva didn't smell him, too. His Prell. Girlie Caress soap she'd teased him for using. A hint of the diner's mouthwatering fried chicken.

Goosebumps spread across her forearms that weren't supposed to be real.

Herc cupped his hands around Geneva's shoulders. She tried flinching away, but he was too strong, so she went limp. What was the point in fighting this—whatever it was? She was dead. And no matter what Mr. Grecian Formula spewed, she didn't believe for a second that God was lining up screw-ups like her to hand out second chances to.

"You're wrong," Herc said. "Sit back down and I'll tell you exactly what you need to do."

Sunlight skulked past the edges of the guest room's pull-down vinyl shades, delivering Jonah a one-two punch right between the eyes. Man, was it morning already? He stretched leisurely, gave himself a good scratch, then froze.

Katie.

Her cries should have woken him hours before the sun.

Wearing only gray flannel boxers, Jonah tossed back the sheets and scrambled out of bed, bolting across the hall to her room.

Her crib was empty.

For a second, panic pounded his heart, but then from downstairs came the sound of muffled singing and the scents of fresh-brewed coffee and frying bacon. His stomach growled and, clutching the crib rail, Jonah sighed.

Angel.

Was the woman trying to give him a heart attack?

After washing his face with his hands, he noticed cloth diapers neatly stacked on the changing table as opposed to haphazardly mounded atop the nearest flat surface. Katie's pink hippo crib blankets had been prettily folded and a potted ivy had been moved from the kitchen to sit upon the newly cleared dresser. Every wood surface shone and the air smelled clean, like lemony polish.

A brief flash of resentment shot through Jonah at the way Angel, in less than twelve hours, had shown him up as a father. But then sanity returned. What was wrong with him? Angel was the best thing to happen in years. Having her in the house, caring for Katie, was like winning a human lottery.

Gravitating toward the triple bonus of his baby, a beautiful blonde, and bacon, Jonah headed for the stairs.

"Lizzy, sweetie," he overheard Angel say from the kitchen, "when your daddy tastes this, he's never gonna let me go." The tempting words drifted right along with the smells. Damn. Why was it that his cloud wasn't lined with silver but thorns?

While his grumbling stomach urged him toward the kitchen, his conscience shoved him to the nearest phone.

Police Chief Sam Lawson set his blueberry Dannon atop Mount Manila Folders and stared the plastic tub down as if it were a mass murdering druggie. Hells bells, he hated yogurt. He'd give his left nut for a doughnut and his right for a little excitement, but since Blue Moon was hardly a hotbed of crime, he turned his thoughts back to excitement of the sugary kind. A Bavarian cream-filled long John. A strawberry cake

43

doughnut with vanilla sprinkles. Shoot, he'd be tickled red, white, and purple for a plain old glazed.

Damn that cocky new mayor and the horse he'd rode in on. Old Mayor Hollingsworth never used to make him take physicals. Christ, he was still on the underbelly of forty. Jogged. Bench-pressed two-ninety on a good day. So his cholesterol was high? Big whoop. The fact that the mayor even knew Sam's cholesterol level was an invasion of privacy. An infringement upon his God-given right to avoid any food product bragging about containing live cultures!

The phone rang.

"So help me, if that's that pissant calling to nag about the Christmas decorations still being up—Chief Lawson here."

"Hey, Sam, it's Jonah. How's it going?"

Sam's shoulders sagged. "Fair to middling now that I know it's you instead of the boy mayor."

"He still harassing you?"

"Me, and everyone else in town except for that land developer from Little Rock trying to get a steel plant built out by the highway. Can you believe he turned down my new computer request yet again? I swear, Andy Griffith had a better setup than me. How'd he ever get elected anyway?"

"Andy Griffith or our boy mayor?"

"Ha, ha."

Jonah adopted a world-weary tone. "This, my friend, is what happens when it's sleeting on Election Day and the only thirty-eight people who show up to vote are the kid's girlfriend and cousins."

"Hey, I voted."

"Yeah, me, too, but two voices of reason hardly make a dent in all that inbreeding."

44

Sam eased back in his squeaky chair and grinned. "Guess you're right on that assessment. So? What can I do for you on this not-so-fine Sunday morning?"

"Other than riding the man responsible for driving half the businesses on Main Street into bankruptcy out of town, not much. Just a small favor."

"Shoot."

By the time Sam's friend finished his twisted tale, the chief had been given a new lease on life.

Hot damn. Finally a case with teeth—even better, the main suspect—or victim; her status was yet to be determined—had cooked a big greasy breakfast.

"Hang tight," Sam said, already reaching for his hat. "I'll be right over."

Angel stood outside the closed office door, hugging Lizzy. Who had Jonah called? And why had his voice been filled with such urgency? The sturdy oak door guarded the conversation's specifics, forcing her to piece together snippets like, ". . . I know, but can't you . . . Sure she's . . . I can't keep her here indefinitely . . ."

Angel sighed, nuzzling Lizzy's downy hair. Though her pulse raced, she told herself to calm down. The *she* and *her* in Jonah's conversation could have been any-one.

An employee. A stray dog.

Who are you trying to kid, Angel? He was talking about you. How he wants to get rid of you. Separate you from your baby all over again.

Angel squeezed Lizzy tighter.

No. Almost losing her once was bad enough. She couldn't go through that kind of heartache again. No matter what it took, she would make Jonah see that she'd changed. *I'm not the same old . . .*

What? Same old what?

She pressed her fingers to suddenly throbbing temples. What was wrong with her? Why did it feel as if a curtain had been drawn over her life?

Steeling her shoulders for whatever battle lay ahead, she said, "Jonah, honey? Breakfast's ready."

"Okay. Thanks. Be right there."

"Is everything all right?"

"Sure. Why wouldn't it be?"

Angel pressed her palm to the closed office door. She wanted so badly to go inside, to wrap her arms around her husband and apologize for whatever she'd done. A queasy sensation told her that she was solely responsible for what'd happened between them, but if he wouldn't open up to talk about it, what could she do to fix it? "Jonah?"

"Yeah?"

"Nothing." She sensed him on the other side of the door, imagined his radiated heat. "I-I just wanted to tell you breakfast is getting cold."

"I'm on my way."

"Okay." What she didn't say was, "Hurry, sweetheart." *Hurry.*

CHAPTER FOUR

"Come on in," Jonah said to Sam, holding open the back door. "Your timing couldn't be better. Angel's upstairs changing Katie."

"Angel, huh?"

Trailing his good friend into the house, Jonah fought the all-too-familiar knot fisting his stomach. "That's the only thing I know to call her. And no matter who she is, she has been a godsend to Katie."

Standing in the center of the sun-flooded kitchen, Sam removed his official beige hat, tucking it beneath his right arm.

Jonah watched while his friend's gaze skipped from the prettily set table with its forsythia-filled vase to platters heaped with bacon, eggs, pancakes, and biscuits.

Light oak cabinets shone from a lemon oil rub, and

even the cheap linoleum floor Geneva had forever complained about beamed beneath a fresh coat of wax.

Aside from ultratasteless silver and purple-striped foil wallpaper better suited to a disco than a country kitchen, the place hadn't looked this good since back when Jonah's mother had been alive.

As good as Geneva had been in bed, she'd been that lousy at housekeeping.

When Sam shot him a piercing stone-gray gaze, Jonah turned the other way.

"Feeling a mite guilty, are you?"

"Over what?" Jonah looked back, raising his chin.

"Defensive, too."

"Am not."

"Then why the fighting stance?"

"Maybe because I've known you all my life. Well enough to recognize one of your silent accusations. But here's the deal, Sam." Getting in his face, he said, "I haven't done a damned thing wrong. And if I'd known you'd come running over here guns blazing, I never would have called you in the first place."

"Did I say you had done anything wrong?"

"Maybe not in so many words, but I'm not stupid. Your expression says loud and clear that you think I'm using this woman."

"Are you?"

Hands tucked in his pockets, Jonah turned to the neat stack of dirty dishes in the white porcelain sink. Nudging the faucet all the way to hot, he snatched the cast iron skillet with one hand and the steel wool pad with the other, scrubbing out his frustrations on what remained of the scrambled eggs.

Still sounding far off, the morning coal train whistled. Seemed late. Or maybe he'd missed the coal train and this one carried freight.

"Jonah?"

"Look." Jonah whipped around, spotting Sam's khaki shirt with hot suds. "If you're planning on keeping up this interrogation, then—"

"Whoa—no need to get your panties in a wad." Jonah flinched when his friend gave him a few good natured pats on his back. "All I wanted to tell you is that I did a quick computer check before coming over and found exactly squat."

"Great." Jonah slung the pad into the sink.

"Wait, it gets even better. I called Doc Penbrook and he said he wants a look at your mystery woman ASAP."

"Aw, man. I don't even know how to explain your being here. How am I going to explain a doctor showing up?"

"That's easy enough," Angel said with a shimmery smile, gliding into the room with Katie tucked to her chest. "You called both the doctor and the police chief because you love me and want to make sure I'm really, truly okay." She flashed Sam a brilliant smile. "Hi, I'm Angel McBride. Forgive me if we've already met, but I seem to have misplaced the last twenty-odd years of my life—maybe even thirty." On that note, she made a face.

"As a matter of fact," Sam said, "we haven't met. I'm Sam Lawson."

They shook hands, leaving Jonah scolding himself for caring when his supposed friend held on to Angel's slim hand a little longer than necessary.

"Tell me, Sam," Angel said. "I get the feeling you and my husband know each other quite well, so how is it you and I have never met?"

Jonah said, "Sam's been out of town."

"Yeah." Sam cleared his throat. "It's, ah, good being back."

As if she wasn't quite sure she bought either of their stories, Angel flashed them both another fragile yet hopeful smile.

As for Jonah, he was stuck on the fact that even with the police chief standing less than five feet away, he'd done it again. Fallen for this woman even harder then before. Sunlight bathed her and his baby girl in gold. Gold hair, gold eyebrows, creamy-gold complexions. The pair of them in almost matching dresses looked like mother-daughter goddesses.

Katie wore a ruffled yellow smock and Angel a flowing pale yellow sundress Jonah had bought Geneva for her last birthday. Never once had she worn it. Said the garment was too dull for her sophisticated tastes. At the time, he hadn't seen her point, but now a blind man could've seen.

On Geneva, the dress had been all wrong. On Angel, it was sheer female perfection. A little long, maybe, but the whipped-egg shade of yellow transformed her already great complexion to the kind of fine porcelain he'd never been able to afford, and the dress's cut hugged her ultrafeminine curves. From somewhere, maybe his mom's old sewing basket, she'd even found a sunny scrap of ribbon to pull her long hair into a neat ponytail.

To Sam she said, "You here about my car?"

Sam nodded.

"Good," she said, heading toward the stove. "It'll be nice to at least have one mystery out of the way. But before we get down to business, let's dig in. All this food is getting cold."

Sam, ever the charmer, cast her what Jonah knew from their old swinging single days to be his best on-the-prowl grin. "That an invitation?"

"Sure," she said over her shoulder, actually flushing from his attention. "Sorry if I didn't make myself more clear."

"Not a problem, *Angel*." Sam winked before giving Jonah's supposed wife another big-toothed smile.

Eyebrows slashed, Jonah scrubbed harder.

Sam parked his hat on top of the fridge.

Leaning hard against the counter's edge, he crossed his legs at the ankles, taking it all in. Jonah's scowl. Angel's bruised forehead and easy grin. Katie's miracle. If he'd seen the pink-cheeked wonder in a carriage on the street, he wouldn't have recognized her. Had it really been less than forty-eight hours earlier that every time his office phone rang, he'd cringed? Halfway expecting it to be a heads-up from 911 dispatch that she'd had to be taken to the Harrison hospital.

Looking at her now, content on the hip of one of the most stunning blondes Sam had ever seen, even though he'd never had much of a head for math, this was one case in which he had no trouble putting two and two together. Not only had his old pal found a perfect playmate for Katie but for himself as well.

No wonder Jonah's scowl was deeper than that old fenced-off, flooded quarry they used to sneak dates to back when they were teens. Jonah knew full well no matter how much of a positive change this looker had made in his and Katie's lives, she belonged to another man—another child. A man and child who at this very moment were probably going out of their minds missing her.

"Honestly, Jonah," Angel said in a teasing scold as

she opened the cabinet beside the sink. "Next time we're expecting company for a meal, let me know. I could've already set an extra place."

"No need," Jonah said, not looking up from the sink. "Sam's not staying for breakfast."

"Sure I am." Sam lurched forward, offering to take Katie from Angel's arms.

"Thanks," she said with an easy smile. "As much as I love her, I think I must still be a little tired from the accident. My arms are sore."

"I'll bet," Sam said with a sympathetic nod, tickling his finger against Katie's still too skinny tummy.

"Jonah, honey, why don't you and Sam go ahead and take your seats?" Extra place setting and silverware on the table, she hustled to the stove to stir a bubbling pot of grits. "If you start in now, maybe at least something'll still be warm."

Sliding Katie into her high chair, Sam let out a low whistle. "This is a pretty fancy spread."

"My guy's worth it, don't you think?"

As Jonah took the seat farthest from hers at the table, she pressed a lingering kiss to his forehead. Strands of her long buttery hair swept forward, sweeping Jonah's neck. To Sam's bachelor eyes, her hair looked cashmere soft. Baby bunny soft. The kind of soft he'd only seen on fancy shampoo commercials aired during prime-time TV.

Swell. *Baby bunny soft*. Now, that was one heckuva fine piece of detective work.

Still, he thought, savoring an unbelievably tasty bite of buttermilk pancakes, who was to say great hair wasn't a clue? It could mean Jonah's angel was from the big city, where women spent more money on their hair than on mundane things like vet bills and Kool-

Aid. Or, it could just mean she had naturally nice hair.

End of story. Back to square one.

Sighing, Sam reached for a fifth strip of bacon.

Angel fought for all she was worth to keep hold of her bright smile.

Why was Jonah being so cold? He'd hardly even look at her, let alone touch her.

After filling all three of their mugs with steaming coffee, then giving the baby a teething biscuit to go along with her saucer of pureed pears, Angel joined the men at the table. Swallowing her pain, more determined than ever to ride out this rough patch in her marriage, she served herself two pancakes and a strip of bacon. "So tell me, Sam," she said, in what she hoped was a light tone, "are you married?"

"Nope." He flashed her a grin, saluting her with a forkful of scrambled eggs. "Which makes this meal all the more delicious."

"Thanks." While her words had been to Sam, Angel's gaze never left her husband. His impenetrable brown eyes. Those stern lips. Handsome, angular cheeks badly in need of a shave. God, how she loved him, hooded gaze, whiskers, and all. "I'm glad you could be here to share it with us. But since you're not married," she said, finally turning her attention to their guest, "then you can't possibly understand how devastating it was for me to have almost lost not only my child but this man." She reached one hand to Lizzy and the other to Jonah. He tried pulling free, but she wouldn't let him.

Sam looked to his plate, eyed it a good long while, then pushed it back. "You're right. I can't."

"And since you can't," she said, releasing her family to dab the corners of her lips with a white cloth napkin,

"I hope you won't mind my being blunt."

"O-okay." The big man actually gulped. "Shoot."

"Here's the deal. My husband spends his every waking moment down at that diner of his—which is fine. It means a lot to him. But that does make every second he has left to spend with me and Lizzy that much more precious. Not that I'm not always happy to meet one of Jonah's friends, but while I may have temporarily lost my memory, I haven't lost my mind. And one thing I'm sensing loud and clear is that something is going on between you and my husband that neither of you are too keen on sharing."

Jonah choked on his latest sip of coffee.

Sam toyed with his spoon. "Mind telling me what that *something* might be?"

She brushed crumbs from Lizzy's lips before admitting, "I don't have the foggiest. Just an uneasy feeling that my husband is hiding something from me."

Rolling his eyes, Jonah said, "Come on, Angel, give me a break."

"No, you give me a break, Jonah. Earlier—not that I was eavesdropping, but I heard you on the phone. At the time, I couldn't imagine who you were talking to, but now I'm guessing it was Sam here." To Sam, she said, "I mean, I know I'm a decent cook, but why else would you sit here shooting the breeze with us when I'm sure you have much more important police business to handle than my lost car? Am I right?"

"Well . . ." Sam glanced at the ceiling.

Jonah pushed back his chair and headed for the sink.

"It's okay," Angel said. "Whatever this big secret is, I'm strong enough to take it. In my accident . . . did I hurt anyone? Is the car totaled? For that matter, where is the car? And my purse? And how far did I have to walk before finding my way home?"

From the sink, Jonah said, "None of that matters."

"Not to you, maybe, but I want to know if I hurt someone. I need to know." Scooping Lizzy from her high chair to cradle her close, she added, "I mean, you two are sweet to want to shelter me from whatever is obviously bad news, but sooner or later I'm going to have to hear it. And if it's not such bad news, then please, Sam, go ahead and spill it so the three of us, Jonah, Lizzy, and me, can enjoy what little time Jonah has left before he needs to get to work."

Sam cleared his throat, casting Jonah a good, long look.

"Well?" Angel glared at the both of them, more convinced than ever that she was on the right track.

"It's like this," Sam said. "Jonah did call me this morning, but I looked you up—I mean, your, ah, accident, but found squat."

"Wait a minute," Angel said with a slight shake of her head. "You mean to tell me you didn't find a *single* mention of an accident happening anywhere in our county?"

"The county, hell—I didn't find mention of a single vehicular accident with a missing driver anywhere in the state. Lots of abandoned cars, but nothing remotely within walking range of Blue Moon."

"How about missing persons?" Jonah asked.

Angel looked sharply his way. "Why would you want to know that? I'm not missing anymore, am I?"

Jonah looked down. "Guess not."

"All right, then," Angel, still cradling Katie, said. "That settles it. Case closed. Jonah and I will return to life as usual and the insurance company will have to take my word for it that our car is gone." A shadow crossed her normally serene features. "The car was paid for, wasn't it?"

Again, Jonah and Sam exchanged glances, but it was Jonah who said, "Sure. Believe me, Angel, there's nothing for you to worry about."

Sam's gaze narrowed, but Jonah didn't care. The least he could do for Angel after all she'd done for him and Katie was put her mind at ease while she was in his home—for however long that happened to be. Sure, he could tell her the truth, but what good would that do?

It might do wonders in helping her regain her memory.

Jonah pushed the thought from his mind.

Index fingers to his throbbing temples, he closed his eyes and rubbed, but a second later, warm, slender fingers moved his aside. Angel had put down her "baby" and moved to comfort her "husband," Jonah thought ruefully, enjoying her touch entirely too much.

"Have you always had headaches?" she asked.

Jonah opened his eyes in time to catch Sam's scowl. "Nope," he answered. "Never have them. This one just popped up out of nowhere."

"Guess I'd better be on my way," Sam said. "If I hear anything, I'll give you two a holler."

"Thanks," Angel said, now massaging the back of Jonah's aching neck, shooting streaks of warmth across his collarbone and down his back. It took everything in him not to moan. Damn, this woman. Didn't she have a clue what just her sweet touch did to him? "Jonah and I both appreciate your—"

A knock sounded on the back door.

"Ugh," Jonah said, stepping free of Angel's unwittingly seductive touch to rub his face with his hands. "I'm assuming that's Doc?"

"I'll let him in," Sam said. "Good thing he showed up before I left. It'll be interesting to hear his take on all this." He opened the door. "Hey, Doc. Good to see you."

The slump-shouldered man, with most of his white hair on his soup-strainer mustache as opposed to the top of his head, opted to wave his battered black bag instead of mouthing a greeting. Not five seconds after Sam shut the back door, the man most folks just referred to as Doc zeroed in on Katie. "In all my days," he said with a sharply exhaled breath. "If I wasn't seeing this with my own eyes, I never would've believed it." He crossed to the grinning infant's high chair, scooping her into his arms. "What happened?" he asked Jonah. "She finally take a liking to formula?"

"Formula?" Angel said. "Lizzy is still breastfeeding. Isn't that what's best?"

"W-well, yes, but—" As if only just now seeing the patient he'd been summoned to examine, the old country doctor narrowed his gaze. "I'm presuming you're our mystery woman?"

Jonah cringed.

Angel laughed. "I suppose you could call me that, but I prefer to go by the title of Mrs. Jonah McBride."

Doc vaulted his bushy eyebrows high enough to serve as a toupee. After casting questioning glances to both Jonah and Sam, he said, "Well, then, guess I'd better get on with giving you a good head-to-toe look-see. Gentlemen, a little privacy."

"Oh—sure." Jonah took Katie from the doctor's arms, then ushered Sam into the living room.

Easing into a rocker too small for his frame, Sam said, "If this doesn't beat all."

"Yeah, especially the part about you coming on to her."

"Excuse me?"

"You heard me," he said, smoothing Katie's golden hair. "Lord knows I've got enough on my plate around here wondering who Angel is, who's about to show up to claim her, and what Katie's going to do once she's gone. The last thing I need is to have my best friend coming on to my imaginary wife."

Sam laughed, a great big belly snorter, but then, as if remembering there was a registered voter in the next room, he toned down his reaction considerably.

"Glad at least one of us sees the humor in all this."

"You don't?"

"Think it's funny that some gorgeous Looney Tunes thinks she's my wife and my baby's mom? Uh, no."

"Yeah, well, I sure as hell do. In fact, this reminds me of that time you and me dated those twins from Batesville. What were their names?"

Jonah sat hard on the edge of the sofa, shifting Katie to his left knee. "Carol June and June Carol."

"Right. Crazy as loons—both of 'em."

"Best I can recall, their folks were off, too."

"Remember how their grandma kept asking what size suits we wore? To this day I'm not sure if she was measuring us up for a wedding or a funeral."

Voice quiet, Jonah said, "Funny, that's kind of how I feel at the moment."

"How so?" Sam rocked forward, leaning his elbows on his knees.

"One minute it's like Angel is this saving grace. Like we've known each other forever and she really is my wife. Like we could make it official with a big church wedding and all that that implies."

"Meaning a big wedding night?"

Jonah sharply looked his way. "I didn't say that."

"No, but now that I've seen your Angel, I'd be thinking you weren't human if you hadn't had all of those thoughts and more."

"Yeah, but I shouldn't."

"Give yourself a break, man. You've been through more in these past few months than most folks have in their entire lives. So you harbored a few idyllic fantasies, a few lustful thoughts—big deal. As long as you don't act on them, you got no problems."

Yeah, right. No problems? That'd be the day.

"And the funeral part?" Sam asked.

Turning Katie to face him, Jonah held her by her hands, bouncing her on his knee. She giggled, and the sound was the sweetest he'd heard since Doc first told him Geneva had had a girl. His own melancholy grin fading to a frown, Jonah said, "The funeral part scares me. Bad. I mean, think about it. If Katie had this sudden a turnaround when Angel came into her life, it only stands to reason she'll fall just as suddenly when she leaves. And we both know it, Sam; she is leaving."

Though his buddy had the decency to give him a vague nod as opposed to a definite *yeah, you're right*, it wasn't too hard to see that Sam agreed.

Tired of his friend's accusatory stare, tired of the hall grandfather clock's tick, Jonah took Katie upstairs to change her diaper, even though it didn't really need changing. When he finished, she seemed fussy, so he tucked her belly-side-up into her crib. She kicked herself into a pint-sized fit, then settled, right before his eyes, drifting off to sleep.

Most nights he wrestled for hours just to get his eyes to shut, but she had this knack for drifting off instantaneously. Usually it worried him, but today her expression was one of profound peace. Her skin, instead of its usual grayish flush, had taken on an adorable rosy hue. Beneath paper-thin closed eyelids, her eyes moved. Her cherry red lips suckled.

"Dreaming of Angel?" he whispered, trailing his finger along the ridge of her button nose. "If you are, can't say I blame you." *Let's just hope this dream doesn't turn into a nightmare.*

"Oh, this is just great," Geneva said, glaring at the screen. "Now Blondie's taken over my baby's every waking as well as her sleeping moments?"

"You don't know that," Teach said. "What if Katie's dreaming of you?"

"Not bloody likely. And hey," she said, her gaze narrowed. "How come you don't know what she's dreaming about?"

"Do you?"

"No, but then, I'm not Mr. Expert-at-everything."

"Point of information," he said, adjusting his robe, "but even I can't see into your daughter's dreams. Not even Mr. Big Himself can do that."

"For real?"

"Have you ever known me to lie?"

"Well, no, but . . . Hey, is this some kind of trick? You know, some twisted mind game?"

He rolled his eyes. "I've already told you, I don't do kink. However, since we are on the subject of games, I'd like you to play one with me."

"Okay, but this better not involve stripping."

"As if . . ." He raised his already snooty patrician nose a good two inches higher.

"You don't have to be insulting. I'm still pretty perky for

a dead woman." She thrust out her chest, pleased to see him blanch. "In fact, the night I died, Talon—you know, the bassist for Puke and Die—took a body shot right off this tit."

Geneva was beyond pleased to see old Herc shudder. "If you're quite finished with your exhibitionist display," he said, "I'd like to get on with our game."

"Fire away."

"All right. Tell me what comes to mind when I mention the name Katie."

"Failure."

"Jonah."

"Miserable failure."

"Geneva."

"Miserable drunken failure."

He sighed. "Are you seeing the same pattern I am?"

Up from the bench, she resumed her limited pacing, careful not to catch sight of the movie screen that was still stuck on a close-up of her baby. "Look," she finally said. "It's no big secret that I was a screw-up at the game of life. Isn't that pretty much why I'm stuck with you now?"

"True, but what I'm trying to get at here is your exasperating lack of desire to change your old patterns. You're here to better yourself, yet in the time you've been under my tutelage all I've gotten from you is the same moan and groan routine. 'I'm a failure. I suck. I'm a screw-up.' Newsflash—" he said, with a twinkle of garish jazz hands right in her face. "Mr. Big doesn't make screw-ups, which means somewhere deep, deep inside of you, Ms. Geneva Kowalski-McBride, is a thoroughly decent woman dying to break free."

On screen, the picture flashed back to the living room, and to Jonah warily eyeing Blondie as that old quack doctor ushered her into the living room, then made a big deal out of helping her into a chair.

Sam pushed himself out of his cramped rocker and did his part in making the princess comfy by fluffing a pillow the doctor placed behind her back.

Geneva's only saving grace was seeing that at least Jonah still had his wits about him. Good old stoic Jonah. He wouldn't even look at Blondie.

Obviously he still held tight to the memory of his only recently departed wife.

Obviously he was a gentleman.

Sam, on the other hand, Geneva had never given two figs for. Sure, he might have a bod carved from solid stone, but ever since he turned her down that time, making her feel like a two-bit tramp, all because she was lonely and looking for a little Saturday night action while her husband slaved away at that stupid, smelly diner. And then—

"Are you quite done?" Herc asked.

"With what?"

"Lambasting the living in an attempt to glorify yourself."

"I thought you were going to knock off the mind reading."

He shrugged. "Sorry. Occupational hazard. But more to the point, what in the world were you doing coming on to Sam while you were married to Jonah?"

"Truthfully?"

"Um, let's see . . ." Finger to his lips, he said, "No, I'd much rather hear another lie."

To that smart-ass statement, she stuck out her tongue. "Truthfully, yeah, Police Chief Sam is a hunk, but I only had eyes for Jonah. Problem was, he only had eyes for that damned diner. I wanted him to notice me . . . and I guess I wanted to be noticed so bad that I didn't even care if it was for all the wrong reasons."

After she fell quiet for a moment, just staring at the events unfolding on screen, Herc asked, "Did Sam ever tell Jonah what you did?"

She swallowed hard. "Not that I know of. Guess I got lucky in that respect. They were always close. Close enough that right before Jonah married me, Sam told him not to go through with our wedding. To hold out for something—someone—better." She swiped at what felt like a tear. Funny, even when she'd had a body she'd done less blubbering than she did now as a vapor ball.

"How did that make you feel? To know your future husband's best friend not only didn't like you but didn't approve of you?"

"Duh? How do you think it made me feel? Like a piece of—" She stopped just short of admitting how she'd truly felt to instead opt for the more politically correct euphemism for her feelings. "Dog doo, all right? I felt like a big old stinky pile of dog doo. And looking back on it, after all the crap I put Jonah and now Katie through, I guess all along Sam was right. I am no good. Jonah should've steered clear of me, and—"

"And you've got that pity train of yours rolling right along the same old track. Come on, Geneva, whaddaya say just for fun we jump that track and head the train south? Miami? Rio? Pityville is starting to be such a bore."

CHAPTER FIVE

"So?" Jonah said, leaning forward from his perch on the edge of the sofa. "Let's hear it, Doc. What'd you find out?"

The doctor sighed before scratching his head. "Seeing how I've only come across one other case like this in all the years I've been practicing medicine, I'm certainly no expert, but it looks to me as if this little lady has a textbook case of posttraumatic retrograde amnesia."

Angel spilled a weak laugh. "That seems like an awfully big name for me just forgetting a few things."

"Yes, well . . ." Doc glanced her way. "This could turn out to be an awfully big problem. I don't mean to alarm you, but while you seem fine on the surface, just to be safe, I'd like Jonah to take you to Little Rock for more extensive tests."

"Why?" Angel argued. "You just said I was fine."

"You probably are, but like I always say—"

" 'An ounce of prevention is worth a pound of cure.' " Sam beamed.

The doctor and Jonah glared.

Doc cleared his throat, "As I was saying, most likely your memory will return on its own, but until then just sit tight—and don't do anything too strenuous."

"Does that mean my husband here has to wash all the dishes?" She winked.

Jonah held his breath. Was this where Doc reached his breaking point for helping to carry out what was becoming a group delusion?

"Right," Doc said. "Jonah, Sam, before I go, I need a word with you two outside."

"Sure."

Angel's expression darkened. Turning to Doc, she said, "Is there something else you're not telling me?"

"Not at all, sweetie." Jonah nearly tripped in his haste to get the doctor out of the house. "This is about official diner business, right, Doc?"

The doctor's mustache bobbed beneath what Jonah could only guess was a deep frown. He gathered his battered black leather bag, then cast his patient a feeble wave on his way out the stained-glass front door.

Outside, on the same front porch where as a boy he'd played marbles and drunk gallons of lemonade, Jonah, all grown up, found himself in the curious position of still playing games. Only this time they were deadly serious ones. He wasn't just playing with Angel's life, but possibly those of her husband and children. Sure, every bit of the deception he was carrying out was for Katie, but that didn't make any of it right, just all the more painful.

Instead of gulping lemonade, he swigged cool morning air, for ever since the mystery woman he'd christened Angel had entered his life, he never could get enough. Enough air, enough courage, enough looks into her fathomless aquamarine eyes.

Across the yard—across the whole mountain-ringed valley—a soft breeze clacked through still bare maples and oaks. The sloped pastures and lawns around the house were already greening, complete with a smattering of daffodils and dandelions bobbing their welcome to the warmth soon to come. The forsythias that'd lined the dirt drive with sunshine every spring for as long as he could remember were also deep in bloom. His mom's favorite red bud looked ready to pop, as did the dogwood he'd helped his grandfather plant when he was just a boy of nine.

Life had been so simple back then. All through his high school years, his folks urged him on to college. You'll never be happy here, they said. Become a doctor, lawyer, big-time businessman. Go out into the world and make something of yourself. Yet for as long as Jonah could remember, all he'd wanted to be was a carbon copy of his dad. Had the man died without ever realizing just how special his life had been? How idyllic in the eyes of his only child?

Swallowing hard, Jonah gazed out at the tree-lined mountains and, at their feet, the rolling hills, dazzling in the green carpet nature laid out for the myriad of color yet to come. All his life he'd woken every day to this same view. Yet today, in some indefinable way, it'd changed. Or no—maybe more to the point, he'd changed. And he wanted his old self back. The happy-go-lucky guy who saw the best in everyone. The guy who'd trusted Geneva when she told him he was every-thing she'd ever dreamed of.

Doc said, "This is some pickle you've gotten yourself into, Jonah."

"Yessir."

"When were you planning on telling this woman she's not your wife?"

Hands tucked deep in his pockets, Jonah shrugged.

Sam said, "In his defense, Doc, he's doing his best by her. But as for now, there's nothing more to be done until I figure out who she really is."

"I suppose," Doc said, "but that doesn't mean I have to like any of this. The fact that she took Katie to her breast tells me somewhere out there is a baby missing his or her mother."

"Okay," Jonah said, "message heard loud and clear. But until Sam finds that family of hers, what should I do?"

The older man took a good minute to chew his mus-tache, then, "Much as I hate to say it, after you take her to Little Rock for tests, the best thing might be nothing. As far as you comfortably and morally can, let her go on thinking she's your wife—just be darn careful about leaving her alone with Katie. Not for a minute do I think Angel would do her intentional harm, but if she has any internal bleeding, that could lead to a sudden stroke."

"Sure," Jonah said, sheepish about the euphoric relief flooding his system. For now. For maybe the rest of the day—or even week—Katie's savior could stay.

"Ha, ha! Take that, Blondie. Looks like you can't have my baby after all."

"And who exactly will this be a good thing for?"

67

Geneva slanted a sharp look Herc's way. "It'll be good for Katie, that's who. She already had one mother. The last thing she needs is another."

"Oh, really? Is that why she's thrived both mentally and physically in your absence?"

"That was different," Geneva said with a twirl of her chartreuse hair.

"How?"

"Well . . ." Hmm, looked like she'd have to think on that one, but then the answer turned out to be pretty straightforward. "Because I was dead. All kids are sad when their mom or dad dies. It's pretty natural, isn't it?"

"True, but to Katie, you didn't die, you just took off without even so much as a good-bye. Do you have any idea how stressful something like that is to a child of any age? Let alone an infant?"

"Humph. Do I know? My own mother abandoned me."

"And how did that make you feel?"

"Like if my own mother didn't love me, then how in the world would I ever find anyone who did."

"Good."

"No, that's not good—that sucked."

"Right. Of course it did, which is why I want you to remember those feelings. I want you to recall those days when you felt as if no one in the world would even notice if you disappeared tomorrow."

"But why would I want to dredge all that up? It hurts."

"Of course it does. But sometimes pain is the key to healing. This is what I keep trying to teach you, Geneva, that in order for you to right your past wrongs, you first have to face them. You have to admit that your abandoning your own child was every bit as horrific as your own mother abandoning you."

"I hate you," Geneva spat. "You're nothing more than

a pompous, toga-wearing, conceited, overbearing brute."

Lightning strobed, gnashing and slashing the air all around them.

Teach looked up, nodded, then pressed his palms together prayerlike before saying, "Of course, I completely understand."

"Understand what?" Geneva asked, darting a quick glance over her shoulder to make sure this latest—and most ferocious—lightning show was over.

"Mr. Big is displeased."

"By your lack of teaching skills?" She let loose with a snort. "Can't say I blame him. So now what? Do I get a new teacher? Someone I hope a little hunkier than you?"

Teach shook his big head. "In fact, what you have gotten, my dear girl, is your very own ticking clock."

Nose wrinkled, she said, "I don't get it."

"Precisely. You don't get much of anything I've been trying to say, which is why Mr. Big has seen fit to impose a time limit on your work. Not as a punishment per se, but as a gentle kick in the pants."

"Oh, that's great. God kicks people's asses when they screw up?" She looked to the sky only to be rewarded with three more stinging strikes. "Ouch," she squealed. "Those are getting close."

"And just think," Herc said with a tight grin, "if in six weeks' time Jonah, Angel, and Katie haven't become a family in the purest sense of the word, that's just a preview of the heat you'll soon be having to endure."

Face scrunched, she said, "So let me get this straight; just because you're a bad teacher, I'm being punished?"

"Not punished, Geneva. In difficult cases like yours, Mr. Big prefers to think of it in terms of tough love."

* * *

"Please, Jonah?"

At quarter till eleven, Jonah, Katie in his arms, had his hand on the back door. He should have been at the diner already, but after the doctor left, Angel had drilled him about what went on out on the porch. Coming up with all those creative answers took longer than he'd thought. And now this?

"Please let me watch Lizzy."

Angel's teary-eyed pleading broke Jonah's heart, but there was no way after what Doc had said, no matter how good care she seemed to give his daughter, he was leaving Katie alone with a delusional stranger. "Like I already told you," he said, hand on the doorknob, "me taking Ka—I mean, Lizzy, with me is what the doctor said is best. He said you need rest—especially after overdoing it with all that cooking this morning."

"But I feel fine."

"Angel, I—" Jonah cupped his hand round her slight shoulder, instantly regretting even this casual touch. Drawing back, he wrapped both hands safely around his child. "I know this may sound strange after the conversation we had last night, but . . ."

"Go on," she urged, tears still glistening in her blazing aquamarine eyes. Her touch feather light, she reached up to smooth his perpetually mussed hair. "I don't want anyone saying I let my husband go off to work without looking his best."

"Thanks," he said, at first annoyed by the proprietary gesture, then oddly touched. Geneva had always been asleep when he left for work, and as for her caring about his hair, she'd forever been after him to grow it long like a rock star. Like there were a lot of those roaming Blue Moon's quiet streets.

"You're welcome." Her aquamarine gaze still glistened.

He wanted to pull her into his arms and whisper that everything was going to be okay, but since he had no way of knowing whether everything would be okay, he kept his hands to himself. What he needed to do was just go. But no matter how badly he yearned to escape, he couldn't ignore his screaming need to say more. To try to make her understand that his taking Katie wasn't a personal attack—just his only way of protecting his daughter. "Look," he finally said, "I know me taking the baby doesn't make sense to you, but I'm worried about your health. That's all. Please, humor me? Just this once?"

"Under one condition." She raised her delicate chin.

"What's that?" He was almost afraid to ask.

"Kiss me good-bye?"

"Angel . . ." He raked his fingers through his hair. "In light of, well, everything . . . I really don't think kissing would be appropriate, do you?"

"If I didn't, would I have asked?" The teasing glint in her eyes was a welcome replacement to tears. "Come on, just one simple kiss."

"I already told you, I—"

"I know, I know, you don't think it's *appropriate*, but let me show you my side of the coin. Here I am, madly, crazily in love with my husband, with no memory of anything bad ever happening between us. All I want in this whole big world is to once again be your wife in every sense of the word, and yet at every turn you deny me that pleasure." She cupped her hand to Katie's head, then slid it down her back to rest on his forearm. "We took vows, Jonah. You promised to love and protect me." The tears were back, shimmering brighter

71

than ever. "I-I somehow know that I've always felt protected by you, but now, with you flinching from my slightest touch and refusing to even kiss me, I have to wonder if I've ever known your love."

Jonah pressed his lips tight. Closed his eyes. Good grief, why did she have to get all heavy on him? And why did he have to feel her pain as if it were his own?

"Look," he said, absentmindedly kissing Katie's forehead. "I can't deal with this now."

"Then when, Jonah? I can't go on like this indefinitely. We're husband and wife, yet you treat me as if I'm a stranger."

He opened the door, turned his back to her, and swallowed. "I'm sorry. Trust me when I say it's nothing personal."

"Nothing personal?" Her voice dropped to a throaty whisper. "How can I not take it personally when not only does my husband want nothing to do with me, but he obviously doesn't trust me enough to even let me spend an afternoon caring for our baby?"

Exhausted and scared and more than a little confused himself, Jonah made the mistake of turning to her. There was something about her that was so exotic, so far removed from the everyday doldrums of Blue Moon, he couldn't drag his gaze from hers. Those jewel-toned depths beckoned like deep tropical pools. Those full, trembling lips soundlessly begged for the comfort of a kiss.

She parted them, licked them slowly.

Turn away, every ounce of Jonah's body screamed. But he didn't—physically couldn't.

More wisps of her hair had sprung free of her ponytail, rioting against her flushed cheeks. He wanted to brush those wisps back. He wanted his fingertips gliding across her petal-soft skin. He wanted his mouth pressed against hers. He wanted to know her. Possess her. Be certain that when he came home from the diner that night, she'd be there. Waiting for him and Katie both. Missing them. Holding them. Yearning for them like they yearned for her.

Only the joke was on him, because he didn't even know her.

He didn't know her name, favorite food, or color. He didn't know if she liked her kisses hard or soft. If she liked her lovemaking gentle or rough.

Most of all, he didn't know if somewhere out there she had a husband who would rightfully beat the crap out of him for even thinking such things about his wife.

And so while Jonah wanted nothing more than to brighten Angel's expression by pulling her into his arms and kissing her till neither of them could breathe, he instead squeezed his eyes shut tight, banishing that image from his mind before turning his back on her and walking out the door.

The big house's silence crushed Angel, refusing to let her forget that she wasn't just alone in the present, but if Jonah had his way, she'd be alone even after he came home. All she'd wanted was a simple kiss. Why had he turned her request into such a big deal?

Even though Jonah had told her to relax that afternoon, after the humiliating way she'd just poured out her heart to her husband the last thing she felt capable of was relaxing. What she really wanted to do was crawl into a hole and die, but then she wouldn't get to see Lizzy when Jonah brought her home from the diner, so Angel instead turned her attention to tidying.

Which took a whopping twenty minutes.

Seated at the kitchen table, one elbow on the polished oak, chin in one hand and drumming the fingers of her other, she clamped down on her lower lip, trying to remember even a small morsel from her past—anything. What her favorite kind of gum had been. What her wedding dress looked like. What she'd done as a pastime during the endless hours she now knew she'd spent alone.

When nothing came to mind save for a voice of doom proclaiming that there had to be something about her accident her husband hadn't told her, Angel had had enough.

If memories wouldn't come, they wouldn't come.

No use wasting a perfectly good day moping about them.

One thing she knew soul deep was that she'd never been much of a moper. She intrinsically knew she'd been a proactive girl, and as such, she pushed herself up from the table and marched into the living room, determined to string clues from around the house into a cohesive sense of the past.

A drooping peace lily and two dead ferns told her she'd never been much for gardening.

Nose wrinkled, she hauled the two deceased ferns outside for a proper trash can burial, cleaned up the trailing mess, then watered the sole green survivor.

Great. So that took ten minutes.

Now what?

The books lining built-in shelves surrounding the fireplace were mainly classics—all blanketed in dust. At least they had been before she'd dusted them just that morning. Surely that was a sign that neither she nor Jonah were big readers.

She saw no signs of needlepoint or cross stitch. No

rug hook kits or watercolors. No jigsaw puzzles or paper crafts. A few ugly crocheted blankets graced the sofa back and easy chairs, but she didn't think crocheting would be her cup of tea.

She'd never thought to ask Jonah if, like him, she spent most of her time at the diner, but seeing how there wasn't a whole lot to show for what she did here at home, she was beginning to wonder if maybe that had been the case. And if so, could something she'd done at the diner be to blame for their marital rift?

One last scan of the room offered no additional clues. Mismatched but cozy furniture. More china and brass knickknacks. The TV and VCR. A few videos—mainly westerns and action adventure.

Hands on her hips, she wrinkled her nose. Great. Not only did she not have any hobbies, but evidently she didn't even watch TV.

From in front of the bay window she turned a slow circle, trying to absorb every detail.

Think, Angel, think.

You live here. Spend hours in this room.

There has to be something you remember.

Deciding to make a game of it, she closed her eyes and took a few dizzying turns; when she opened them, she reached to the rocker to steady herself but saw nothing of much interest aside from the piano.

She swallowed hard.

Talk about a busted mission. Fat lot of good staring at the piano was going to do—unless . . .

How could she have missed something so potentially important? The piano. Of course! She must have played the piano. Why else would such a glorious instrument hold such prominence in their home?

Anticipation made her pulse race as if she'd spent

the afternoon running a marathon. Hands pressed to her chest, Angel crept toward the massive instrument.

If this hunch didn't pan out, then what? Could she bear the pain of another dead end?

You could always have a drink to soothe your nerves.

A drink? Like a small glass of wine?

Oh, you can do better than that. Try taking a nip straight from a freshly opened bottle of J & B or Seagram's.

The gentle urging in her head was so comforting, so familiar, so absolute in the knowledge that just a few small sips of booze—any booze—would make the pounding ache go away, that she changed course.

Since the voice was inside her, it had to be right. Meaning, she had to find a drink—any drink.

She started looking in the dining room but came up with nothing but rose-patterned china and table linens. The few cabinets in the living room netted nothing but worn board games and countless photo albums.

Photo albums!

Booze search canceled.

She dropped cross-legged before the amazing array, ignoring the hardwood's chill seeping into her buns. Why hadn't she thought of this earlier? Eagerly flipping through the pages of the first album, she felt like such a fool. Finding pictures should have been her top priority.

But she felt like an even bigger fool when one album and then two and ten and fourteen netted plenty on Jonah and Lizzy—even some pretty woman with garish dark hair—but nothing, not a single image of her.

Surrounded by a sea of other people's memories, she pressed her hands to her temples and squeezed. What did this mean? How could there be photos of everything from Jonah's first steps to his first birthday, first fish, and high school graduation, but nothing of his wedding? If she hadn't known better, she'd have thought that not only had her mental memories been taken but her physical ones as well. It was as if she'd never been here or, if she had, all traces of her had long since been removed.

Could Jonah hate her to that degree? Had whatever she'd done hurt him that bad?

Who knows? Who cares? Why put yourself through all that unnecessary turmoil when you could instead be kicking back? Living the good life. Concerned with nothing but where you're going to get your next drink.

On autopilot, Angel pushed herself up from the floor and headed for the kitchen. That's where the liquor would be. That's where it had to be.

But it wasn't.

Not in any cabinets.

Not in the small walk-in pantry neatly lined with dusty canned goods and jars of homemade sauces and pickles.

Again she was pressing her temples. *Think, Angel, think. Where were you the last time you had a drink?*

Pain.

Crushing, blinding pain. Not physical, but pain of the heart—the soul. It was everywhere, surrounding her, swallowing her. Thick and black. Smoky.

Hands shaking, she took a swig from the bottle of Jack Daniel's. Just a little. Just to make the pain bearable.

She took a good, long drink, and another and another, ignoring the booze dribbling from the corners of her mouth. Giggling when it dotted her white blouse.

Air.

I have to have air.

As if clawing through hundreds of feet of inky water,

searching, reaching, Angel drank in great greedy gulps of oxygen. Looked wildly about, touching sagging pine shelves, a jar of pickles labeled "bread and butter" in handwriting that didn't look familiar. A cool bag of flour.

This is reality, she coached.

That—whatever it had been—was only an illusion.

You're here. At home. Your home. Jonah and Lizzy's home. Everything's fine. You're fine.

At least you will be once you have a drink.

Clutching the walls for support, she launched her search anew. More cabinets. The hot-water heater closet. Baskets and drawers.

Her quest finally ended at the fridge with five cans of Coors. She snatched one out, popped the top.

Her hands shook so bad, she could hardly lift the can to her lips, and when she did, the voice in her head screaming at her to take a drink stopped.

And then there was a new voice. Soft. Kind.

Not demanding, urging.

Not pushing. Holding her hand.

The baby. If you won't stop this madness for yourself, please, do it for the baby.

Her hands shook all the more, and she sniffed the open can, inhaling that yeasty smell as if it were her salvation. As if she'd worked for hours under a merciless sun and this liquid would slake her thirst.

Her tongue actually burned for the beer. And her hands shook so bad that some of the liquid spilled from the metal lip and onto the web between her thumb and forefinger.

She closed her eyes, pressed her tongue to that spill. Heaven.

Don't you mean, hell? For God's sake, look at all you've

accomplished. Do you really want to throw all of it away for a drink?

She nodded. Rolled the sweating can across her forehead and chest.

She felt sick. Really sick, like she might have to throw up. But it turned out she didn't really have to throw up, just burp, and that made her laugh and laugh and laugh. But then she started to cry, and that wasn't nearly as fun, so she took one tiny swig of beer, trying to make herself belch again, but instead of a standard belch, a little bit of breakfast came up as well in one of those deep burps that tasted like throw-up in the back of her throat.

She'd just raised the can for one more tiny swig when she caught sight of her reflection in a glass fronted cabinet. Her hair and eyes were wild. The front of her dress hung askew.

"Oh my God," she said in a tremulous whisper. "Look at me. I'm a drunk."

Maybe you are. And maybe that's why Jonah can't stand the sight of you.

"No," she said, refusing to believe she was anything other than the loving wife and mother she'd already proven herself to be.

The can she held in her shaking hand told a different story, but she told it to shut up, sending the rest of the beer fizzing down the drain before gathering the other cans, popping the tops and dumping them as well.

She gathered them to toss into the green plastic trash bin beneath the sink but then changed course.

Public trash isn't a good idea. You have to hide your evidence. Can't let them see what a closet lush you really are.

In front of the outside trash bin, beneath the accusing glare of hot midday sun, she dropped the cans clattering to hard-packed earth, lifted the bin's hinged lid, and tossed it back before kneeling to scoop up the evidence. She released the cans, but they fell with only a soft clank of aluminum against aluminum instead of falling to the bottom.

Frantic to hide the true extent of her trouble, she reached deep inside the bin, scooping up the dead ferns, crumbling the dirt and brown fronds over the cans. Only when she'd looked in the bin from every conceivable angle and knew the cans to be well and truly hidden did she close the lid, sweep her hands, and head back into the house.

Her eyes took their time adjusting to the kitchen's dim light, but once they did she marched to the sink and washed her hands with plenty of soap. It took three forever's worth of scrubbing to get the dirt out from beneath her nails, but eventually she did. And then she felt better.

And even better still when she squirreled through the fridge in the hunt for something to clean that one lonely sip poisoning her palate and found a jar brimming with dill pickles. Unscrewing the cap, she took one—*no, better make that two*—and chewed. Chewed and chewed until her pulse slowed and her breathing returned to normal.

There.

She washed her hands again.

Now I feel better.

At least she did until she smoothed her hair back from her face and strolled back into the living room. It was there she again caught sight of that mocking piano.

"I'm not afraid of you," she said, her words sounding big and brave in the empty room.

The instrument remained silent. Foreboding.

But she was strong.

Much stronger than some stupid old piano.

And to prove it, she walked right up to it and stuck out her tongue. That made her feel about three years old, but oddly better, so she grew even more bold, running her fingers along the cool black surface until reaching the cover sheltering the keys. Still standing beside the instrument rather than in front of it, she lifted the cover, pleased to see the keys in pristine condition. Dust free, all white and none yellowed or missing.

Heart thundering, she inched her way around to the front, pulled out the bench, and lowered herself onto it.

Did it feel right? Familiar?

She didn't know. Too soon to tell.

Tips of her fingers on the cool keys, she waited. For lightning to strike? For the hidden Liberace in her to burst into song?

On the verge of abandoning the whole mission, she plunked a key. F. Then another. A. And then another and another until they strung themselves together into . . . into . . . her fingers flying faster and faster across the keys, she knew the tune she played sounded familiar but couldn't quite place the name.

From that one, her fingers slowed, transitioning into one she did remember. "Georgia." And this time she even knew the words! "Georgia . . . sweet, sweet Georgia . . ."

On and on she played and sang. Gospels, rock, country, children's songs, commercial jingles, it was as if

Angel McBride were a walking encyclopedia of music.

The more she played, the more natural her movements felt. As if she'd been playing all her life—and not just piano; she had the craziest urge to check all the closets for a guitar.

But no, that would've taken too long, so she segued from Chopin into Rolling Stones, wailing, "I can't get noooo . . . satisfact—"

"Excuse me!" called out a prune-lipped, white-haired incredibly shrunken woman standing beneath the arch separating the living room from the parlor. "Does Jonah know you're in his house making all this racket?"

Once Angel recovered from the shock of a stranger waltzing into her home, she closed the lid on the keys, pushed back the bench, and stood. Pretty sad admission, but somehow she felt better knowing she was almost double the height of the glowering crone dressed in denim overalls, white T-shirt, and worn sneakers. Raising her chin, Angel said, "I should hope Jonah knows I'm in his home playing *beautiful* music—especially since I happen to be his wife."

"Oh, yeah? Since when?" The shrunken woman raised her chin. "I've lived across the road from that boy since the day he was born, and far as I know, he's only had one wife—and she's dead." Gazing heavenward, she added, "Thank you, Jesus. But that's neither here nor there. The real issue at hand is you. And the question of what am I going to do with you?"

Hands on her hips, Angel said, "I could ask the same of you. The least you could do after barging into my home and accusing me of being dead is introduce yourself."

The woman harrumphed. "Esther May Carmichael-Stevens-Plunkett. Lived in Blue Moon all my life. Buried three husbands, two fine sons, and am still burdened with a daughter who wants to shelve me in some stinkin' nursing home. I still got pretty near all my own teeth. I woke up this morning with constipation and heartburn. The cable's out. And quite frankly, being as I am on the wintry side of ninety, I don't have an awful lot of time for unnecessary chitchat. So now that all that's out of the way, why don't I just call the law and let them decide what to do with you?"

"Is this a joke?" Angel asked. "Did my husband put you up to this?"

After giving Angel a good, hard stare, Esther May Carmichael-Stevens-Plunkett ambled into the kitchen and picked up the receiver of the yellow wall phone. Angel figured she must've made a habit out of calling the police on a regular basis as she punched in the number from memory.

"Look," Angel said, hustling across the room to stop the woman in mid-dial. "I know once you listen to reason, you'll really be embarrassed about all this."

"Me? Embarrassed about stopping a prowler from having her way with my neighbor's home?" She snorted.

"But I already told you, I'm Jonah's wife. His baby's mom. If you live across the street, then surely you remember a cutie like Lizzy?"

Placing the phone slowly back on its hook, Esther took a step back. "Lady, has anyone ever told you you're one apple short of a bushel? If—like you say, you are Jonah's wife, then how come you'd be callin' his baby Lizzy? Everyone in town knows that baby's name is Katie. Just like everyone in town knows her no good momma is dead."

Geesh, what was with this woman? Angel said,

"Should I call your daughter? Do you need help?"

Esther laughed. "I'd say you're the one needin' help. Come here." She snagged Angel by the sleeve of her dress, pulling her into the living room, where she stopped her in front of a gallery of black-and-white framed prints hanging on the south wall. "See those?"

"Yes. They're wonderful." Angel put her hand to her head. "Since the accident, I'm having trouble with my memory, but I'm sure once it returns, I'll—"

"You'll what? Be able to recite them all by name? Well, guess what, sister? I can do it right now." Esther went on to do just that, stopping with her gnarled index finger poised over a shot of twenty or so laughing women dressed in full-blown flapper attire. "My eyes are closed in this one. And can you believe it? Me and that one right there—Olive Goodwilly—are the only ones still alive. Always did despise that woman. Few years back, she accused me of tryin' to steal her husband." She snorted. "Like I'd let a man named Wilber Goodwilly come within ten feet of this bod." Moving her finger to the next frame, this one of two smiling women dressed in holiday finery standing arm-in-arm beside a sad-looking pony wearing a wreathe around his neck. "That one on the left is Gloria Jean. Your husband's great-grandmother. On the right is Francie. His grandmother."

To Angel, the two women looked typical of many of the others who'd had photos taken during that era. Nothing about them stood out as special. And that hurt.

What's wrong with me? she thought, pressing her fingers to her temples.

Too bad you were so stupid about dumping those beers. Just one would've made everything so much better. And all five? Well, that would have sent you straight to the moon.

"You don't look so hot," Esther said. "Maybe I should call Doc instead of the law." Through pale blue, beady eyes, the woman stared Angel up and down. "Say, you're not one of those druggies you hear about on Jerry Springer, are you?"

"No," Angel said. *At least I don't think I am.*

"Well, that's good. Okay, on down the line here the pictures get more current. There's Jonah when he was a baby. And then on Santa's knee when he was in first grade. Got so excited he peed himself—Jonah, not Santa. And see here? That's Jonah's high school graduation. And his wedding pict—"

"I thought that woman was one of his prom dates."

"Nope. I was at the wedding. I oughtta know. Like to broke my heart he didn't marry in a church like his momma always wanted, but whatever. The bride—the now-dead bride—wanted to get hitched down at Riverside Park, but it rained that day so they did it at the house." Gesturing behind her, she added, "Marched right down those stairs."

Was it possible to feel hot and cold at the same time?

The sip of beer and pickles and pancakes and bacon churned in Angel's stomach. This Esther person had to be getting all these photos wrong. What other explanation could there be?

"And then look here," she droned on. "Here's little baby Katie day after she was born. Peed all over the doctor. Peeing at inopportune times runs in the family."

Angel summoned a weak smile.

Esther crossed her arms. "Okay, so that's everyone in the family, and not once did I see a photo of you. Have any ideas as to why that might be?" She raised her penciled-on eyebrows.

"Um, no. Maybe Jonah hasn't had a chance to get our wedding photos framed." And maybe the rest of our snapshots—the ones that should have been nestled alongside the rest of the family albums—got lost. Or haven't been developed. Or—

"Sure." Esther nodded. "Makes perfect sense." Cocking her head toward the piano, she said, "Have any idea whose piano that is you were banging away on?"

"M-mine?"

"Yours? Ha! That instrument belonged to Jonah's momma, God rest her soul. She was a dear thing. And to the best I can recall, never peed on a soul."

The pounding behind Angel's forehead hit with stereo sound. She had to sit down. Either sit down or fall down. Must've been the beer.

Bull. That one piddling sip didn't do jack. What you need is another one—or no, better yet, some of that J & B you were craving earlier.

"No," Angel said.

"No, to what? I didn't ask you anything."

"No, I mean . . ." Angel shook her head, backing to the sofa to slowly lower herself down. "I don't know what I mean. Look," she said, sending a harried glance Esther's way. "Maybe it'd be best if you leave." And be sure to take that picture of the stacked brunette you said was Jonah's wife with you.

Now along with the pounding came ringing. A tinny, far-off sound that made Angel's teeth hurt. Just to make sure they were still in her head, she pressed her two front teeth.

"You know," Esther said, aiming another beady-eyed pale blue stare Angel's way, "I think I'll call the law after all."

"No, really, I—I'll be fine. Just as soon as—" The room stops spinning.

Better get a drink, Angel. You're gonna need one when you finally get the gist of what this old crone's been trying to tell you. You're not Jonah's wife. Not Lizzy's mother. You're not anyone. Just a nameless, faceless drunk, destined to live life alone—unless, of course, you count the company of a nice, warm bottle.

No, no, no.

Angel rested her elbows on her knees, leaned forward, rocking, pressing her hands to her forehead, trying to press out the information she knew lurked inside, just beyond her reach.

Somewhere out there Esther was still talking, but none of her words made sense. The only thing that did was that mean voice in her head.

Get a drink. Get a drink. Get a drink.

She looked up, but the room was different. Spinning in a dizzying swirl of red, beige, and blue. Esther looked different.

Scary. Old.

Older than old, reminding Angel that she wasn't getting any younger. It was more than time for her to figure out what she wanted to do with the rest of her life.

But I already know. I want to get married. Stop this roller coaster I've been on and be not just a good mom to Lizzy but a phenomenal mom. I want her raised like I always wanted to be. In a small town where everyone'll know her name.

That's crap. It's all gone way too far for any of that Pollyanna shit. What you really need is a drink.

Why wouldn't everything stop spinning?

Why couldn't she catch her breath?

"Jonah?" Where was he? Angel called for him again, but her limbs turned to jelly. She was slipping, falling. She had to keep herself together. But then free will was snatched away and her world faded to black.

CHAPTER SIX

"Oh, now there's a great role model to raise my child. Are you sure about this, Herc?" Geneva looked over her shoulder to launch into their usual banter, but he was gone.

Speaking of which . . . so was her cloud. She'd been so immersed in the latest adventures of Blondie that she'd failed to notice the change in venue. Now instead of just looking at the screen she was in it—only not in it, but sort of floating just above it and to the left.

Geneva shook her head. "I've been on some wild trips in my time, but this one takes the cake."

Before her, Blondie lay sprawled out on Jonah's living room sofa, and that old biddy Esther Carmichael ran as fast as her stubby legs allowed into the kitchen to dial 911.

No—wait—she wasn't dialing 911, she was calling the diner.

"Hello, Precious?" Geneva heard Esther say. "Yes, hi,

it's me, and I don't have time for chitchat. Get me Jonah straightaway."

Geneva scrunched her nose. What was going on? And why couldn't she hear the other end of the line?

"Hey, Esther," Jonah said, sounding winded. "What's up?"

Whoa. Talk about ask and ye shall receive!

"What's up?" Esther snorted. "I hear some strange woman belting out show tunes at your piano, right? So I let myself in with the spare key, and sure enough, there's some blonde in there claiming to be your wife. Ring any bells?"

Jonah groaned. "Okay, so then what?"

"I tried setting her straight. but just about the time I got up a full head of steam she fainted on me. Fainted! Can you believe it?"

After the past twenty-four hours Jonah had had, at this point he'd have believed just about anything. Covering the mouthpiece of the phone, he said to his only waitress, a pretty teen he knew secretly had her application in at the McDonald's out by the highway, "Hey, Precious, think you can handle things around here on your own for a couple of hours?"

"If you mean can I handle giving old Earl there a refill on his twenty-sixth cup of coffee, then sure."

"Cool. I'll be back as quick as I can. And, oh hey, if things get too busy, just give me a call."

"Busy?" She rolled her eyes. "Around this snooze hole? You wish."

Ten minutes later, Jonah slammed his truck into park on the dirt drive beside the house, raced around the passenger side to spring Katie from her kid seat, then dashed up the back stairs.

Esther met him at the door. "You drove too fast."

While she reached for the baby, he pressed a kiss to her weathered cheek. "Never happy, are you, Esther?"

She shrugged before trailing after him into the house. "She's still on the couch. When she came out of it, she started asking for you, so I told her you'd be home soon. That seemed to calm her right down, so I popped one of your mom's butt-ugly afghans over her and she fell right off to sleep."

"Thanks," he said. "I think."

She pulled out a chair at the kitchen table and lowered herself to the seat. Katie facing her on her lap, she said, "Something's different with this one. She's still too skinny, but her color's better. A lot better."

"Tell me about it," Jonah said, peeking a look at the still-sleeping Angel before joining Esther and the baby—who'd been cranky the whole time they'd been at the diner but had now calmed enough to flash their guest an adorable grin.

"Oh," Esther said, a twinkle in her sharp blue eyes. "Rest assured I'm not leaving till you do."

Thirty minutes and nearly an entire pot of coffee later, Esther shook her head, "If that isn't the damnedest story I've ever heard."

"So now can you see why I'm going along with whatever she says?"

"No," she said, wagging her cup for a refill.

"I thought Doc told you to not overdue the caffeine?"

"What does he know? He's just a kid."

"Right," Jonah said, getting up to do her bidding.

"So, back to your Angel; you've got to tell her the truth, Jonah. It's the right thing."

"Even at Katie's expense? I mean, look at her." He gestured to where she sat sleeping in her wind-up swing. "She even looks healthier with her eyes closed. Even being away from Angel for a few hours this afternoon set her off. I'm sorry, but I don't have it in me to lead her back down the road she was on. I just can't risk it. She was almost put on a feeding tube, for Christ's sake."

Esther took a moment to ruminate on that before asking, "What do you think happened to this Angel's baby?"

Lips pressed tight, Jonah set Esther's mug on the table. "I wouldn't know. And to tell you the truth, sometimes I think I don't want to know—ever. I mean, look at this kitchen; it hasn't looked this good in years. Angel not only cared for Katie this morning but me. She cooked me breakfast, washed my clothes. She looked out for me in ways I haven't been looked out for since I was living with my folks."

"That what you want? Another set of parents to make everything all better?"

"No. Shoot, no," he said, raking his fingers through his hair. "That's not at all what I'm saying. Her being here just feels nice. Somehow . . . right."

"Even though you know there's a very good chance her own family is out there missing her?"

Jonah sighed. "You're missing my point. All I mean is that having her around a few more days, while it's awkward, won't exactly be a hardship. Besides, remember when Lila Stone went off her rocker and Doc told us that as long as she didn't hurt anyone we should play along?"

"Yeah."

"Well, how is this any different?"

Esther's eyes narrowed. "Cut the sales job, boy. You know full well it's different. Just promise me one thing."

"What's that?"

"That you are at least doing everything possible to find her real family."

He nodded. "Sam was over this morning. He's looking anywhere he can for leads."

"And so until he digs something up, you expect me to keep my mouth shut?"

His eyebrows lifted. "Would you?"

"I'll think about it," she said with one of her legendary snorts.

"Sure you're feeling better?" Jonah asked Angel when she finally woke around eight that night.

After sipping at the water he'd brought her, she nodded. Her expression was dazed, reminding him of how she'd looked the first time he saw her curled up in a ball on the diner's bathroom floor.

"You gave me a scare," he said, taking the glass from her to set it on a side table.

A weak laugh spilled past her lips. "I gave me a scare. One minute that neighbor of yours—Esther?"

"Yep, that would be her."

"Well, she kept needling me. Hounding me with facts about how there was no possible way I could be your wife."

"Did you believe her?" From his perch on the coffee table, he leaned closer.

"Of course not, but then she went so far as to show me this picture, that one over there—"

Jonah cringed when she pointed to the last remaining photograph of Geneva, taken right after they'd said their vows. He'd been meaning to take it down, putting it in storage for Katie along with the rest of her pictures and a good portion of her clothes and other stuff, but it must've slipped his mind. "That old thing?" he said. "That's an, ah, prom picture."

Angel's shoulders sagged. "That's what I told her, but she wouldn't let it go."

"Yeah, I love her," he said, forcing a grin, "but sometimes Esther gets her teeth into a subject and clamps hold. Speaking of teeth—did she mention she's still got most of her own?"

Nodding, Angel laughed, then winced, covering her breasts with her hands. "Lizzy's probably hungry." She shrugged off the afghan.

"Let me get her," he said, standing.

"You sure?"

He nodded, already on his way to the stairs.

"Thanks."

"You're welcome." But what he really wanted to say was, thank *you*.

"Jonah? I can't believe you didn't wake me." Monday morning, Angel rubbed sleep from her eyes and pushed herself up in the bed.

Setting a tray loaded with coffee, toast, juice, and a copy of the *Blue Moon Gazette* across her knees, her ultrathoughtful husband shrugged. "No biggee. Just thought after the rough time of it you had yesterday, this morning you might still need extra rest."

"Where's Lizzy?" she asked. "And what about the diner? Shouldn't you be there?"

"Yeah, yeah, but it's only quarter past seven. Lizzy's still snoozing and on weekday mornings—my last remaining busy time—I still employ a cook and a waitress."

"Ahh," she said with a grin, nibbling a corner of toast. "Then you're playing hooky."

"Guess you could say that."

"Well," she said, putting the toast back on the plate in favor of squeezing his hand, "whatever you call it, I like it. A girl could get used to breakfast in bed."

Glancing out the window at the sun glinting off still dewy green hills, Jonah swallowed hard.

I could get used to having Katie be this content.

Last night was the first full night's sleep he'd gotten since Geneva left, and truth be told, he brought Angel breakfast in bed probably more to alleviate his guilt over that fact than by any rampant altruistic urges.

"What're you going to do today?" Jonah asked, determined that, unlike yesterday, today's topics with his temporary houseguest would remain light.

The morning coal train wailed.

She chewed another bite of toast, swallowed. "Actually, I had a tough time falling asleep last night—I guess maybe because I slept so much yesterday afternoon. Anyway, while I was staring at the ceiling last night, I was hoping—if you have time—you'd draw me up a list of things I used to do." Fingers of her right hand pressed to her still purple forehead, she said, "I still have a hard time accepting this myself, that I can't even remember how I passed my days. I swear, you must think I'm a total nutcase."

"Only once in a while," he said, flashing her a teasing grin. "But sure. I'd, ah, be happy to make you a list. Probably be after lunch, though, until I get around to it. That okay?"

Her smile radiated through him, once again filling him with the same unfamiliar sensation he felt the very first night she'd spent in his house. The sensation that, yeah, for once, everything wasn't just okay but *very* okay.

In fact, downright great.

And for once, instead of fighting that sensation, he decided to go with it and enjoy his day.

If Sam's piece-of-crap, dinosaur of a computer had been even a smidgeon more compact, he would've hurled it at the boy mayor's picture—the one he kept stapled to the dart board on the back of his office door. Trouble was, if he had flung the damned thing, glass and plastic would fly, making one helluva mess that, since the boy mayor refused to hire even janitorial help, meant Sam would be stuck cleaning.

"Hells bells," he said, resting his elbows on the desk, then slicing his fingers through his hair. That little toad suck had made it so he couldn't even enjoy a well-earned temper tantrum.

Out of habit, he reached across his desk and into the jar of cookies his mom regularly filled. All he needed was a nice pecan sandy to soothe his nerves. Transform him from whiny kid back into Super Cop.

Then he curved his fingers around not a crisp cookie but a slimy baby carrot and a note.

Dear Sammy,
The mayor asked me to help
cut back on your cholesterol,
so please enjoy the enclosed
carrots.
Love, Mom

Sam's roar could've been heard clear to Pine Bluff.

This was too much.

He hated it when his mom called him *Sammy,* and

he especially hated the thought of his sweet, unsuspecting mother conspiring with that snake!

A boy snake, who, while the rest of the city employees sat in outdated offices too cold in the winter and too hot in the summer, sat in the lap of luxury in the brand-spanking-new municipal complex out by the highway. Funny, though, how so far, the city only had funding to finish the mayoral office portion of the building.

Boy mayor had new computers, phone, fax, and even a brass cappuccino machine, when here the town's police force of five had to make do with a duct-taped Mr. Coffee.

Here Sam was, nearly twenty-four hours into his search for Angel's true identity, and because of his outdated equipment, he'd still come up with exactly squat. Just when he was following up on a promising lead, the computer went blank.

He must've rebooted the damned thing fifteen times since six that morning.

To make matters even worse, some kid must've hacked into his fax line, and every time Sam thought he was getting a fax from one of the counties he'd queried about Angel, all that popped out were smiley faces and peace signs.

Even the regular phone lines were screwed up, filled with static and elevator music from the water department's hold lines.

Sam would've liked to blame that on the boy mayor or evil preteens, too, but seeing as he'd had a similar problem last fall and found out it was caused by mice nesting in the lines, he figured that was probably the case again.

He shook his head.

97

Back to his fax machine, this peace sign thing was exactly the kind of juvenile prank his niece, Heather, would pull, only she was too interested in the latest nail polish colors to have figured out the latest technology. Still, since Sam had told her mother he'd caught her drinking beer down by the river, he wouldn't put it past her to put one of her delinquent boyfriends up to the task.

Geneva cast her most dramatic dagger eyes at Sam.

Granted, aside from Jonah, he had the best buns in town, and okay, so his profile was way cute and those soulful brown eyes of his were enough to make any red-blooded girl all hot and bothered, but for his insinuation that a girl couldn't pull off a simple fax hack, she'd like to give him a good, hard slug.

Too bad she had no fists!

Oh, well, seeing how being dead had given her an amazing knack for dealing with all things electronic, she supposed she shouldn't dwell on that pesky matter of having no body.

Just to mess with Sam a little further, not to mention enhance the cool seventies theme she had going, she conjured up a sweet cloud of incense to perfume his musty, cop-scented air.

Watching him go nuts sniffing the room, trying to place the alluring eau de Woodstock, she grinned.

Job well done.

And equally so on her appointed task of getting Angel and Jonah together.

Ha, take that, Teach. This six-week thing was going to be a cakewalk. On an official scroll, he'd laid out her new rules. Learn six afterlife lessons and her job was done. As to what those lessons were, she hadn't a clue. Teach had told her that after accomplishing each one, she'd receive unmistakable signs. Signs he promised she'd enjoy.

Yeah, right.

They'd probably consist of little more than dorky bell ringing like in all those sappy Christmas movies Jonah always wanted her to watch.

Anyway, for the moment all she had to do was sit tight, making sure she kept Jonah and Angel together and the police chief and Angel's family apart.

Now honestly, how hard could that be?

"Crochet?" Angel said in front of the kitchen sink, wrinkling her nose at the purple, brown, and orange afghan Jonah proudly waved before her when he got home.

Katie sucked a plastic key chain, cooing in her wind-up swing.

"Yeah, you used to crochet up a storm around here. You averaged a blanket a week—even gave lots of them to charity." Jonah supposed it was mean, blaming his mom's poor taste in colors on his houseguest, but the more he got to thinking about that list Angel had requested, the less he'd been able to put on it.

What time Geneva hadn't spent complaining, she'd spent watching TV. Game shows, Ricki Lake, a few soaps.

So what if Angel turned out to be a brain surgeon? Or an astrophysicist? What if in telling her all she'd done all day was sit around watching TV transformed her from a brilliant careerwoman into a couch potato?

True, the afghan bit wasn't all that appealing a hobby—at least not to him—but it wasn't as if Angel was going to be there that much longer. And since he'd never been able to crochet, he supposed the craft did take a certain amount of finesse his bumbling hands would never possess. If she was a surgeon, she could keep up her dexterity. And if she turned out to be a mathematician . . . well, she could practice that by counting stitches.

That afternoon, Sam called the diner with the news that while because of equipment problems he hadn't followed up on any of the most positive leads, he did have a few. He promised to check them out using his home computer and phone, which meant all Jonah could do was wait . . . and, if the truth be told, hope.

Hope that like a kid who found money in a lost wallet, no one stepped up to claim it—or, in his case, *her*.

Casting him one last frown, his pretend wife turned her back on him and the butt-ugly blanket in favor of turning the chicken she had frying on the stove.

"Sure smells good," he said, stepping up behind her to inspect.

"Thanks." She headed for the sink but, not realizing he was behind her, plowed full on into him.

"Whoa." Instinctively, Jonah reached out to steady her, curving his fingers around the fleshy part of her upper arms. "Good thing Sam isn't around. He'd have to write you up for speeding."

"What was that? A real, live joke from the solemn Jonah McBride?" She grinned.

And oddly enough, he found himself grinning, too. "Hey," he said, "what can I say? Sometimes things just slip out."

"Sure. Like this." On her tiptoes, she brushed her lips across his, so soft, so fleeting, that by the time she slipped from his hold to stand in front of the sink, he was left wondering if he'd imagined the whole thing.

Running his fingers over lips still tingling way too

much for that kiss to have been imagined, he said, "Angel, I—"

"Save it," she said, turning on the tap. "I know. We're going through a rough patch in our marriage, which means I'm not allowed to touch you, right?"

"Well . . ." Had he repeated the line so often she knew his speech by rote?

"It's okay," she said. She finished washing the Mixmaster beaters she'd used earlier for whipping mashed potatoes. "In fact, thinking about the way things must've been between us reminds me of something that happened yesterday that I wanted to ask you about."

"Oh?" He took a seat at the table.

"I, um . . ." Tucking her long blond hair behind her ears, she said, "I guess I might as well go ahead and ask. Am I, or I guess it would be better to ask *was* I, an alcoholic?"

All day the question had been weighing on Angel's mind. Just getting it out lightened her heart. What didn't make her feel lighter was Jonah's gaping mouth. "I take it my question caught you off guard."

"Uh, yeah. What gave you that idea?"

She shrugged. Tried three different drawers before finding the one that was home to the beaters.

Don't tell him, said the voice in her head. *He wouldn't understand. Would never understand. You'll be labeled a no-good drunk. He'll use that to take Lizzy away, even though drinking isn't your fault.*

"Angel?"

"You know what?" she said, pasting a bright smile on her face. "Forget I even asked."

"That's a pretty loaded question to just up and forget."

"I know, but please—for me, try. I don't know what

101

even made me ask it. I guess maybe because I feel so close to you that I can't even imagine what I did that was bad enough to break us apart. So, you know . . ."

"Your imagination got the better of you and you assumed you must have been a closet boozer?" That his cold demeanor had led her to such thoughts dragged Jonah's spirits even lower than usual. Where was Sam with some news? Because faced with more pointed questions like that one, Jonah wasn't sure how much longer he could keep up this charade. It was bad enough that Angel was constantly cooking for him and cleaning for him—not to mention giving life-saving nourishment to the most important person in his life—but now she was blaming herself for the demise of their imaginary marriage. And it wasn't just ordinary blame, but hard-core stuff.

The kind of stuff he thought only a woman like Geneva would be capable of—not that she'd been an alcoholic—at least he didn't think so in the technical sense of the word, but she had liked to drink—a lot. Once or twice he'd caught her smoking pot, too, and had to wonder if she'd experimented with other drugs.

When they first met, Geneva hadn't seemed dangerous to his emotional well-being, more like an emotional kick in the pants. A wake-up call to stop taking life so seriously and start taking time out to actually live.

Problem with Geneva was, moderation wasn't part of her vocabulary. Whereas he wanted to stay the straight and narrow at least five days a week, she wanted to walk on the wild side twenty-four/seven.

Okay, so here he was with this woman who on the outside seemed so perfect he'd dubbed her Angel, yet she was asking if she'd ever had a problem with alcohol. How far off would he be in wondering if, back in her real life, at least some small part of her suspicion could be true?

After all, that first night at the diner he had smelled booze on her breath.

The phone rang, and anxious to get his mind off such serious topics, Jonah raced to answer it. "Hello . . . yes . . . uh huh . . . okay, sure. Right. Thank you, too."

"Who was that?"

"Doc Penbrook. A doctor friend of his in Little Rock is squeezing you in at ten tomorrow morning."

Sam leaned forward in his home office desk chair and punched on the computer. While waiting for it to boot up, he mused that by the time he had the toy paid off, the boy mayor would've built himself a castle complete with moat.

Sam figured on spending his evening Web surfing, looking for any news items that might pertain to Angel. If that didn't pan out, he had some buddies who were detectives with the Little Rock Police.

Now *they* had some fun toys. Angel wouldn't stand a chance of being lost around them.

"Oh, yeah?" Geneva said.

Biding her time until Sam typed in his first Web address, she worked her magic and the screen faded to black.

"What the—" Sam stood and conked the side of the monitor with his open palm. "No, no, no." No way was this happening at home, too. Taking a deep breath, he tried rebooting, but it was no use. He got the machine to turn on just fine. All self-diagnostics worked fine. He could even sign on to the Internet just fine, but when it came to surfing, forget it. Every time he tried finding something relevant to Angel, the screen went blank.

"If I didn't know better," Sam muttered, "I'd say

103

someone out there doesn't want this mystery woman found."

"Bingo," Geneva said. "Give that man a prize."

And seeing how her good buddy Sam deserved the biggest prize of all for trashing her both in life and death, she made him a festive new screen saver. One sporting both smiley faces and peace signs.

After all, he needed visuals to match all that sweet-smelling incense flooding his house!

"You sure sleep a lot," Jonah said, eyeing Angel from his seat behind the wheel. Funny how he'd been up a large portion of the night wondering what he'd talk about cooped up in the truck with her during the three-hour drive when not ten miles outside of Blue Moon she fell into a deep sleep.

"Sorry," she said, smoothing her adorably mussed hair. "Guess I should be keeping you company, huh?"

"Don't sweat it. I've kind of enjoyed the time to think."

" 'Bout what?"

A semi passed and he tightened his grip on the wheel. They were just south of Conway on I-40 and traffic was really starting to pick up. "Ka—I mean, Lizzy. The diner. Most of all . . . you."

She scrambled into a more comfortable position, tucking her jeans-clad legs beneath her on the seat. "Mind if I ask if those were good or bad thoughts when it came to me?"

"Mostly good," he said, gracing her with a wink.

"Only mostly?"

"Well, you know, I have to count off for that habit of yours of falling asleep on me."

Grinning, she gave him a playful swat. "How much longer?"

"Depending on traffic, twenty—twenty-five minutes."

"Good. Then I still have a while."

"A while for what?"

"To be normal."

He glanced her way. "I don't get it."

"You know. Be normal. If this doctor tells me my head's about to explode and I only have a few days to live, I'd rather not know. I'd rather just be oblivious and enjoy whatever time's left. You know, just go when my time's up, but knowing I had a heckuva good time getting there."

"I suppose that makes sense." Jonah pressed on the gas to pass an RV. Geneva used to call them rolling states because of how much room they took up on the road.

Lips easing into a ghostly smile, for the first time since she left Jonah realized how refreshing it was to think about one of the few good parts of their relationship. During the last couple of months, it'd been all too easy placing blame for their marriage's collapse solely on Geneva, but he'd had his faults, too. Unrealistic expectations. Always ragging her about spending too much. Guess it was high time he stopped viewing his marriage as a waste of time and started seeing it for what it really was—a learning experience. And what he'd learned was that oil and water don't mix. If he ever became involved with another woman, he'd make damn sure she was nothing like Geneva and more like Angel.

"What're you thinking about now?" she asked.

Busted.

"Marriage." Just not ours.

"What about it?"

"How it takes two to make one go bad."

For a long time he felt her staring; then, "You really mean that, don't you?"

"I wouldn't have said it if I didn't."

"So what does that mean?"

"In relation to what?"

"To us, goofy. Does this mean you're at least willing to try?"

"You mean on us? On *this* marriage?" Inside, Jonah groaned. How had he gotten himself into this mess? But maybe the even better question was, with bright spring sun streaming into the truck's cab, bathing Angel in a halo of light, why was he suddenly getting the feeling that this was one mess he wouldn't mind being happily mired in for the rest of his life?

CHAPTER SEVEN

"That's about it," the doctor said to Jonah out in the bustling hall while Angel was still in the examination room, changing from her hospital gown back into her street clothes of comfortably faded jeans and a pretty floral halter top.

Damn, she'd filled out the seat of those jeans.

Jonah kicked himself for concentrating more on what his pretend wife had worn to the hospital than on the man who was spilling the results of all those tests they'd made the trip to have performed.

"Physically," the doctor droned on, "aside from her memory loss and understandable soreness from the bruising still left from the accident, she's fine. In most cases like hers, with rest, her memory should return."

"Did you hear the good news?" Angel said, bursting through the exam room door to squeeze Jonah in an impromptu hug. "Looks like you and Lizzy are going to have me around for a long, long time."

"Cool," Jonah said, wishing for a few minutes alone with the doctor to address issues he should've broached while Angel was dressing instead of calculating the odds of her full breasts compromising the structural integrity of her thin cotton top.

"Let's get out of here," she said, an arm tucked around his waist.

He had to stall her. But how?

"If there's nothing else," the doctor said, "I should be—"

"Wait," Jonah said. "Angel? Where's your purse?" She'd put makeup and what little cash he'd given her into one of Geneva's small leather bags. Over Monday night's dinner, she'd asked him about getting her a replacement driver's license and credit cards, but he'd stalled, crossing his fingers on yet another lie when he urged her to hold off, since any day Sam would probably find her old purse still in the wrecked car.

"My purse is right here," she said, aquamarine gaze narrowed while she wagged the bag from her left shoulder.

"Did you have another question?" the doctor asked.

Rolling her eyes, Angel said, "Tell you what, sweetie, while you figure out whatever it is you wanted to ask, I'm going to go to the ladies' room."

The minute she was out of earshot, Jonah asked the man in white if Doc Penbrook had filled him in on the peculiar nature of Angel's case. When he admitted that, yes, he was aware of Angel's thinking she was Jonah's wife and Katie's mother, Jonah said, "Well, then, you must also know how badly she wants to care for my baby while I'm at work. I don't want to hurt her feelings, but I also don't want Katie being in danger."

"Of course," the doctor said. "But rest assured, I've done a thorough round of testing, and as long as Angel's not left alone with the child for extended periods of time, she should be fine."

Relieved to at least have that issue out of the way, Jonah asked, "You said in most cases like Angel's people get their memories back. What you didn't say was how long that takes."

"Honestly, she could regain full memory tomorrow, just pieces of it, or maybe none of it. The trick is to not jar her memory back, but to let it trickle in. I'm sure, Mr. McBride, that having a stranger believe she's your wife is no easy task, but you are doing a kind, altruistic thing. Memory lapses of this sort are usually brought on by trauma—and I don't necessarily mean just Angel's accident. Perhaps something even worse happened right before her accident. Or possibly was the cause of the accident. Only Angel knows for sure, and the fact that whatever happened was so painful that her mind chose to forget it rather than face it speaks volumes. If it helps, you should think of your role playing as doing her a favor."

Jonah sighed, dragging his fingers through his hair.

Checking to ensure Angel wasn't on her way back, he said, "That's just it. This connection between her and my baby. I don't know what to think of it. My Katie was on the verge of being hospitalized for malnutrition. Ever since my wife died, she just flat out wouldn't eat. Now, ever since Angel showed up, Katie's back to her old self. Even Doc Penbrook calls it a miracle."

"So? What's the problem? You and Katie and Angel

are all fulfilling mutual needs. Angel needs you. Katie needs Angel. And you need Katie to be healthy. The way I see it, for the time being anyway, the three of you make a perfect triangle." The doctor put his hand on Jonah's shoulder. "Until Angel's real family is found, you're the only family she's got, and vice versa. Instead of being bothered by that fact, Mr. McBride, embrace it. Release the guilt, embrace hope. In the end, you'll both be better off."

"Let's not go home," Angel said. "Let's celebrate."

In the tree-lined lot of St. Francis Hospital, Jonah started the truck and put it into gear. "You mean like spend the night?" This was just the kind of crazy idea Geneva would've spouted. Forget the baby and the diner, she'd made a habit of focusing solely on herself instead of her responsibilities.

"No. Good grief, I'd die spending a whole night without Lizzy, and I know you need to get back to the diner. I was just talking a fancier lunch than a take-out burger. You know," she said, jabbing him in the ribs, "maybe even a salad? Or would that be over the top?" She winked, and that combined with her easy, breathtakingly pretty smile put *him* over the top.

Lunch. All she wanted was lunch.

After all she'd done for him, how could he turn down such a simple request?

Twenty minutes later, they were seated at a quiet table in a normally hopping seafood place overlooking the Arkansas River. On weekends the place pulsed with life, but midday on a Tuesday, aside from a few other couples and one family with two toddlers and a table ringed with saltine crumbs, they had the place to themselves.

After ordering colas, salads, and a bucket of boiled shrimp, they were once again alone.

Jonah fiddled with his spoon.

Angel nibbled her lower lip. "Pardon my saying so," she finally said, "but you don't seem like you're in much of a mood to celebrate."

Glancing out the window, then back at her, he said, "Feel free to conk me upside the head. Sitting in another restaurant like this, one I know is successful, I get to feeling that much worse about mine."

The waitress brought their drinks and salads, and while Angel speared a ranch-coated cherry tomato, she said, "Why worry about the diner? Judging from the amount of time you spend there, I thought it was doing great."

"I should be so lucky," he said, unwrapping a Club cracker. He gave her the short version of the new highway project, and how it was steadily choking the life out of Blue Moon's downtown.

Eyebrows drawn, she said, "I might've only seen this on TV, but I thought renovated downtown areas—especially in quaint Southern towns, are all the rage. Put in a tearoom, antique and craft stores, a bed-and-breakfast, and a few pricey boutiques, and voilà—you've got a bona fide resort."

"Makes sense to me. Sam swears our boy mayor must be getting under-the-table cash for ramrodding all these new developments through the building committee. But so far we don't have a lick of proof other than a twenty-six-year-old mayor who drives a shiny new Jag on an official salary of eighteen grand a year."

"Sounds shady enough to me."

"Yeah, that's what we think, too, but we're the only

ones. Everyone else is thrilled—except for me and the few remaining holdouts on Main Street."

When the shrimp arrived, they spent the next few minutes in companionable silence, finishing their salads, sipping colas, and peeling hulls.

"This is nice," Angel said. "Thanks for opening up to me with at least one of your worries." She ducked her gaze before adding, "For the first time since my accident, I feel like we're starting to be a team instead of strangers sharing a house and a baby but not a bed."

"Is that bed part so important?" Jonah asked, popping a fat shrimp into his mouth.

"It shouldn't be, but I'd be lying if I didn't say it is." Lacing her sticky fingers with his, she said, "I've already lost my past with you, but I'll be damned if I lose my future."

"Maybe that's the problem," he said softly, enjoying the balmy breeze of her voice and those mesmerizing aquamarine pools.

"What?"

"You spend so much time worrying about what happened in the past, you're losing sight of the future."

"Easy enough for you to say. You obviously remember all of my faux pas. You not only remember them, but judging by your chill, you're still holding them against me. Sometimes I catch you studying me, almost as if you've never really known me at all."

"I'm sorry," Jonah said. "That was never my intention. But look, with this memory thing of yours, it is like we're strangers. I'm seeing new facets of you every day."

"Good ones, I hope." Tears in her eyes, she was once again taking his fingers in hers.

"Yeah," he said, his voice raspy with more emotion

than he would've liked. Suddenly, Angel became more than a woman with a miraculous connection to his baby. She became a woman he'd very much like to know—not for Katie's sake, but his own.

Should Angel's husband show up on his doorstep first thing in the morning, Jonah would still be better off for having truly tried to know her for even this one precious day.

What the hell. Like that doctor said, release guilt, embrace hope. Face it, one of these days, probably sooner as opposed to later, Angel's family would be found, but maybe, if her connection to him was close enough, if her true home wasn't far enough, they could at least remain friends. She could at least maintain her bond with Katie.

With that thought in mind, suddenly the prospect of Sam's hunt being successful didn't seem quite so scary.

"Listen." This time he was the one squeezing her shrimp sticky fingers. "I really am sorry about the way I've been acting."

She bowed her head, licked her lips. "Does this mean what I think it does? That you're ready to resume our marriage? Our *whole* marriage?"

He grinned. "Now you're moving a little fast for me again. Let's just take whatever it is we're feeling slow. Let's learn to be friends." Before we even think about being lovers.

Lovers.

The very word made him catch his breath. No. Angel might be gorgeous, smart, a great cook, and a temporary mother, but one thing she would never be— must never be—was his lover.

"I guess I can live with that," she said, blasting him

113

with a smile of part sadness, part hope, and all ethereal beauty.

"Toast?" he said, reaching for his cola.

Clinking her glass with her husband's, Angel tried being happy in the moment but couldn't help but feel that while his asking her to at least be his friend was progress, it wasn't near enough. Failure mired in her veins, making her mind sluggish, as if her blood had been transfused with cold syrup.

Why won't he love me? What did I do wrong?

You've done nothing wrong, baby. The voice was back. *You, are a star. He's a washed-up has-been. Let him go. Buy yourself a great outfit and five pairs of new shoes, then get thee to your nearest martini bar. No matter what he says, I say you deserve a celebration. I say you deserve a drink.*

"Damn these tears." For someone who wasn't supposed to even have eyes, let alone tears to fall out of them, lately, Geneva sure had done an awful lot of blubbering.

A chord in Jonah's speech sounded familiar, probably because he'd said roughly the same thing the night before she left.

Christmas Eve hours away, he'd taken her hands in his alongside the fragrant pine he'd cut down on the back forty and stood back up in the living room. "Listen," he said. "I know what with you just having Katie and all that lately life has been a little rough."

"A little?" She choked on her latest sip of the Bloody Mary Jonah thought was plain tomato juice. Breastfeeding, she wasn't supposed to be drinking at all, but she figured where was the harm in one small drink? After all, it was almost Christmas. "Christ, Jonah, my life's one freakin' whirl of baby feeding and baby diapers

and baby laundry. Look at me," she said, fingering lifeless dishwater blond hair. "I haven't washed my hair in
days. I've got no makeup, no decent clothes. I can't
remember the last time you looked at me."

"I'm looking at you right now, aren't I?" He flashed
her one of his disgustingly sweet grins.

"Stop that," she said. "God, I'm so sick of your eternal patience. Let's fight."

"Why?"

"Because I feel like it. And afterward let's have great
sex. Slam-me-up-against-the-wall, take-me-right-here-
in-the-living-room sex."

He sharply looked away.

"What's the matter, choir boy? Talk like that make
you uncomfortable? Forgot what it feels like to fuck?"

He turned his back on her, headed toward the
kitchen.

"Don't you turn away from me!"

"You're drunk—and you shouldn't even be drinking."

"Am not," she called out, chasing after him, not giving a damn that half her drink sloshed out on his
mother's Oriental rug. His mother. Damn, she was sick
of being held up to that dead departed saint. If he
wanted a carbon copy of his mother so bad, why hadn't
he married that old hag across the street?

In the kitchen, she said, "What's it going to take for
you to look at me like I'm a woman again—not just a
mommy?"

"Is being a mommy so bad?" he said, locking the back
door and flicking off the lights. Raking his fingers
through his hair, he said, "Geez, Ginny, you're the
mother of my child. Do you have any idea how much
that means? You're worth so much more to me than a

115

quick fuck on the living room floor. You're worth roses and a soft bed covered in satin sheets."

She shook her head. "That stuff's for movies and books."

"So? Once you've healed from Katie's delivery, who said we can't copy 'em?"

"Life, that's who. We can't change who we are. It's ingrained. Imprinted on our souls."

"That from a movie?"

She shrugged, downed another gulp of her drink.

"If it is, I've got another line for you." Removing the glass from her hand, he set it on the counter behind her, then settled his big hands around her waist. "I always thought life was what we make it."

"What movie's that from?"

Lowering his lips to that sexy indentation at the base of her throat, he said, "Beats me."

"Mmm," she said. "Does this mean now we get to fuck?"

He froze. Took a step back. Eyes narrowed, he said, "You don't get it, do you?"

"Get what?"

"That as my wife, as the mother of my child, I want to make love to you. I want to put all this crap we've been fighting over for the past few months behind us and start over."

She rolled her eyes. "You're such a sap. What? Just because it's almost Christmas are we supposed to take our magic Santa wands and wipe the past away?"

"We could at least try."

Lips pressed together, she snorted. "Yeah, and while we're at it, let's call Jimmy Stewart over for beer and pizza."

Jonah quietly left the room.

"Hey!" she called after him. "He's past his prime, but after we eat wanna have a threesome?"

Geneva swiped the backs of her hands over her eyes. That night Jonah reached out to her, offered to treat her like a lady, and what had she done? Thrown that offer in his face.

She'd been a horrible person. Crass. Mean.

For the first time in her life, or maybe that would be death, she was sorry. Truly, deeply sorry—not that that would do her much good now.

Far and away, Jonah and baby Katie were the best things to ever happen to her, yet she'd been too wrapped up in her own self-pity to see it. What had she been depressed about? Had it really been so bad not driving the hottest car or living in a creaky old farmhouse instead of a high-rise condo? At least she'd been loved. And that was a helluva lot more than she could say right—

Her bubble grew into a room filled with light. The sparkly kind that comes from giant disco balls at the very best night-clubs.

A black-velvet-curtained stage appeared at the end of the room, and through those curtains swaggered young Elvis. Sexy lip curl, tight black leather pants and jacket, slicked-back hair, and all. "Evenin', Geneva. How's it goin'?"

She rubbed her eyes.

No way.

She'd seen a lot of strange things since she'd been in Heaven, but this one took the cake. "Are you really Elvis?"

"Either that," *he said with a rogue's wink,* "or a darned good impersonator."

"Does this mean for once I did something right?"

"Beats me. I show up wherever the Colonel says I have a gig." *He reached for a guitar perched on a nearby stand, slung it over his shoulder, and began strumming the tune to*

"Love Me Tender." Soon he began to sing, and the velvety depth of his voice combined with the unfamiliar emotions in her heart brought on more tears, but instead of cursing them away she embraced them, and herself, swaying in time with his words.

"Care to dance?" Teach stood beside her, and instead of his usual toga he wore faded jeans, black biker boots, and a white T-shirt.

"This is too much," she said, stepping into his arms.

"No, Ms. Geneva Kowalski-McBride, you're too much. Congratulations. Though you went about it in an unconventional manner, you've finally managed to learn something. One lesson down, five to go."

By the time Jonah pulled the truck into the drive, what had been a brilliant sunset made room for a purple velvet blanket tucking in the mountain-ringed valley. By this time of night, usually the yard's night watcher came on, diluting the view, but the light was burned out, and he hadn't had the energy to call the power company to fix it.

Angel was asleep again, but this time with her head on his shoulder. They'd spent the afternoon talking, laughing, walking in a riverside park, oohing and ahhing over simple things like a family of turtles sunning on a log and a barge passing through the lock and dam.

As if they'd been strangers on a blind date, they told each other their favorite things—or, in Angel's case, she took wild stabs at her favorite things, looking to Jonah for answers on the rest. He denied her request, putting the blame on her doctors for his not being able to instantly shed light on her past. At first helping her discover herself had been awkward, but then, the more they became friends, the more fun he had helping her write a new life script.

After buying six ice cream cones from a street vender, they decided her favorite was strawberry cheesecake. For choosing her favorite movie, he gave her butchered outlines of popular films, many of which she had enough memory of to decide she liked *ET* best. From the sea of human and animal traffic cruising the park, she decided she loved small dogs and hated big ones.

Jonah confessed he'd never had time for either.

When he pressed her for her favorite color, she looked to the cloudless sky and announced blue. But then she looked to the spongy moss carpeting the rock they'd perched on to finish their ice cream and changed her answer to green. Later, when a red tugboat passed through the lock, she changed her mind again to red.

She'd asked so many questions. How old Katie was, her birthday, their anniversary. Her own age and birthday. Katie's vitals had been easy enough to furnish. As for their anniversary, he'd taken the easy way out by providing his and Geneva's October 31 date. He'd been more for the Valentine's Day romance theme, but Geneva being Geneva had wanted devilish fun. As for Angel's birthday, he flaked, telling her the doctor had forbidden him to tell her any personal information since it would be healthier for her to remember that sort of thing on her own.

She'd pouted for a good fifteen minutes over his lack of cooperation but eventually got over it, immersing herself in picking a new favorite song.

Jonah turned off the truck's ignition, closing his eyes to invite the image of her clad in buttery soft red leather. Did she have any idea how hot she'd looked

119

that first night? If she was married, what kind of husband would let her out of his sight for even a second dressed in such a racy number?

Hell, for such a careless move, he deserved to have her snatched up by another man.

Whoa.

Jonah's old friend guilt slugged him in the gut. Nobody was talking about snatching anyone. He and Angel were friends. Period. He owed her at least that much. And as for what she looked like in red leather, one of Geneva's old sundresses, or even a halter top and faded jeans—didn't matter. Not because he didn't care but because he *couldn't*. For his own well-being, he wouldn't let her get that close.

"We home?" Angel asked, voice scratchy from sleep. He expected her to rise up and scoot to her end of the bench seat. Instead, she pressed her hand to his chest, snuggling deeper into his loose hold.

"Uh, yeah," he said, doing his damnedest to ignore the tightening in his groin. Hoping to ease the pressure, he shifted positions, but that only worsened his condition by releasing the floral scent of her shampoo. Geneva's shampoo that on her had never come close to smelling this good. "We ought to get inside," he said. "I'll bet Esther is running out of steam."

"Sure. But before we go, I have something to say."

Hand already on the door handle, he said, "Shoot."

Using his chest for leverage, evidently not noticing— or not caring—about his thundering heart, she pushed herself to his eye level. Never had he wished more for the obnoxious white glare of the night watcher. But then, what did he need light for when his senses told him everything and more that he needed to know?

Her lightest touch burned through his cotton shirt.

Her breath smelled minty sweet, like the peppermints the waitress left on the tray with their bill. Jonah, never a big fan of peppermint, had planned on leaving them, but Angel scooped them up, telling him they'd be good later. On her, he had to agree.

Even in the dark, he felt her stare. Felt her moving closer, closer. He told himself to move, get out of the truck. But that invisible stare acted like some superhuman seat belt, rendering him powerless to move.

"Thank you," she said, her mouth close enough to his that her minty breath brushed his lips. "It's been a really nice day."

He tightened his jaw.

What happened to him today? How come where he once felt strong in his resolve to steer clear of this woman, he now felt marshmallow weak? She froze, close enough for butterfly wisps of her hair to tickle his cheeks.

Go away, his conscience screamed. She was the temptation in his own private Eden.

But then the bulge beneath his fly tightened to a new degree, wearying him of this nonsensical game. Plain and simple, no matter what the end result, he wanted her. Bad.

Stop playing games and kiss me, dammit. Because if you kiss me, then it's not my fault. I can't be held responsible.

But it turned out he needn't have worried as she resolved the whole issue by sliding to her side of the seat and opening her door, leaving him cold, starving, irrationally mad, and a whole lot thankful for the dark so she couldn't see either his flushed face or his woody.

"How's Lizzy been?" Angel asked Esther, pulse still hammering from her last-minute decision not to kiss her husband.

121

"Fussy as the devil at St. Peter's dinner party." Esther passed Lizzy like a deflated football into Angel's outstretched arms. Not only was the baby wide awake but red-faced, as if she'd spent hours crying. "I don't know what kind of hold you've got on that babe, but I can tell you this—it isn't natural for a child to be this attached to a woman who isn't even her—"

"Thanks, Esther," Jonah said from the door. "How much do we owe you?"

The old woman waved him off, gathering her purse and a tattered copy of GQ. "I don't want your money. As miserable as that child's been all day, I still like looking after her. 'Night all."

"Here, let me at least walk you home," Jonah said, hustling to open the front door.

"Lordy, no. I need peace and lots of it. Lived here all my life; I think I can find my way across the road and up my own drive."

With Esther gone, Lizzy in her arms, Angel gravitated toward her favorite rocker, her breasts aching. "I wonder what could've happened?" she said raising her halter and unfastening her nursing bra. Lizzy didn't need an engraved invitation to latch on. The poor thing was starving. "She seems fine now. Just a little flushed and tired." Lizzy grunted and sighed, closed her eyes. "Was this how she was when I was gone?"

"Yep."

She looked up to find her husband leaning against the still-open front door. In her haste to feed Lizzy, she hadn't turned on any lights beyond the dim lamp Esther had been reading by. Jonah had flicked on the porch light, but in his current position had it blocked. It backlit him, making it impossible for Angel to read his expression.

"Would you mind either scooting or switching on a light?" she asked, stroking Lizzy's flushed forehead.

"Sure." He flipped the overhead switch.

The instantaneous brightness startled Lizzy and she started to cry.

"Here," he said, "let me take her."

"She's not done."

"I don't care."

"Well, I do. She's already had a rough day. Why would you want to make it any rougher?"

Glowering, he perched on the end of the sofa.

"Jonah? What's wrong?"

"Nothing." He pressed his lips tighter.

"Come on, don't ruin what has been a perfect day."

With a sharp laugh he turned away, slashing his fingers through his hair. "You don't get it, do you?"

"Get what?" She wished she could go to him, put her arms around him to tell him everything was going to be okay. Not only was there the logistical problem of Lizzy being in her arms, but at this point in their lives she had no way of knowing whether everything would be okay.

Was their marriage back on the right course? Or were they headed down the road to divorce? One thing Angel did know was that if they were headed for a final split, Lizzy was staying with her.

But that was worst-case scenario.

She and Jonah were nowhere near that point. Right?

"Please, Jonah," she urged yet again. "Talk to me. What am I supposed to get?"

He stood, paced to the fireplace and back. "Okay, it's like this. For as long as I can remember, Esther has been like a mom or grandmother to every kid in town. Babies love her. Dogs and cats love her. Everyone loves her—everyone, that is, except my daughter. She only loves you."

"What's wrong with that? Lizzy's going through a clingy stage. Most babies do."

"To this degree?"

She shook her head, trying to clear the confusion. What happened to the easygoing, carefree spirit she'd spent the day laughing and sharing ice cream cones with? "You're talking crazy. So Lizzy loves me. She loves you, too, Jonah."

"Does she? Let's just see."

Before Angel could stop him, he took Lizzy, who'd fallen asleep at her breast.

Startled awake, the baby wailed.

Angel sighed, tugged the flap to her nursing bra up and her halter down. "That doesn't prove anything other than that you gave her a fright."

Jonah handed the baby back and her crying stopped. After a few more sniffles, Lizzy rooted at Angel's breasts.

"Still hungry, sweetie?" In seconds, Angel was back to nursing her child.

Jonah slowly backed away, planting himself against the far wall.

"I know," Angel said to her precious daughter, smoothing the backs of her fingers against the infant's velvety cheek. "Daddy's in a grumpity mood. He'll be better in a little while."

"The hell I will," Jonah hissed. Face in shadows, he said, "What have you done to her? Purposely turned her against me?"

"No," Angel fought back, swallowing tears. "She adores you. Why would I ever do anything to hurt that bond?"

He laughed. "Damn good question. Once you're done answering that, tell me why she refused to eat the whole time you were gone."

"That was only a few days. She's fine now."

"Right. She's fine now, but what happens when you leave again? Who's left to pick up the pieces?" He poked his index finger at his chest. "Me. Only that's the problem, Geneva, Katie doesn't want to be picked up by me, rocked by me, fed by me. She wants you."

Angel drew Lizzy closer. "Jonah, stop. You're scaring me."

"Good. I want you scared. I want you to know how I've felt every day since you first walked out that door."

"Y-you called me Geneva. You called Lizzy Katie."

As if forcing himself to wake from a nightmare, her husband shook his head. "I did?"

She swallowed hard. Nodded. She'd long since ceased to rock.

Hollow-eyed, he stared at her, but not really at her, more like right through her. And then he crossed the room, fell to his knees, and dropped his head in her lap.

She'd never heard him cry, but cry he did now, with ugly racking sobs that tore through her with more power than if they'd been her own.

"Don't leave us again."

Smoothing his hair, crying right along with him, she said, "I won't, sweetie. I promise." And just like that, Angel McBride was once again whole.

CHAPTER EIGHT

"Oh, man," Jonah said a few minutes later, raising his head from Angel's lap. "I'm sorry. I don't know what brought that on." *Can't freakin' imagine what brought that on.* He stood, rubbed his hand over his stubbled jaw. He needed a shave. A shower. And while he was at it, how about a brand-new, squeaky-clean life?

"Why are you sorry?"

"Why do you think? For being a blubbering idiot. Geez, I haven't bawled like that since I was ten and fell out of my tree house."

"Maybe that's part of the problem."

A sharp laugh escaped his lips. "It's a problem, all right. A sure-as-hell sign I'm teetering on the edge of a breakdown."

Gazing at the baby, *his* baby, with the sweetest smile any woman had ever given a child, she said, "Funny. I see what just happened as more of a breakthrough." She lifted that jewel-toned gaze of hers, seducing him with nothing more than the voodoo of her aquamarine stare. "You opened up to me, Jonah. Thank you for telling me I left. That was something I needed to know. I mean, no wonder you've been cool with me. I don't blame you for being mad."

"I'm not mad," he said. "Just frustrated." With a dead woman. "Look, can we drop this? I've had all the touchy-feely stuff I care to participate in for the next fifty or so years."

"Great. Then let's go to bed." Katie had long since fallen back asleep in her arms. "Here, you take the baby."

He did, instantly contrite upon holding the reason for all of this in his arms. Gazing into his daughter's sleeping features, he'd never wished more that she could talk. Tell him what was behind her mysterious link to Angel, and why his love wasn't enough.

Her head resting on his shoulder, he made his nightly rounds, locking doors, turning off lights.

He heard Angel mount the creaky stairs and wished he could find words. Words to express how sorry he was. Sorry for his flash of injustice, sorry for freaking out on her like that, and, most of all, sorry for not being man enough to put his own petty jealousies aside in order to spend every remaining second Angel lived in his house thanking her.

Even though in her mind she was doing nothing more than honoring vows she believed she'd made long ago in some quaint country church, he knew better.

He knew better, and by God, if it killed him, he was going to start behaving better. Treating Angel with the kindness and respect she deserved.

She'd never asked to be put in this situation, yet how many times had he wished for a miracle cure for Katie that he'd feared might never come?

Leaving on one small lamp on the table at the base of the stairs, he climbed them, every muscle in his body creaking from even this minor exertion.

At the top, he found the bathroom door shut.

From inside came the sounds of Angel brushing her teeth. She turned the water off, just like him. Geneva always left the water running. He'd asked her countless times to turn it off. Every dime they saved would help. Toward the end, he figured she left it on just to spite him.

Katie still cradled to his chest, he stood there, taking it all in.

The faucet going on for a final tooth rinsing.

The chink of Angel placing the new toothbrush he'd rummaged up for her in the hot pink porcelain holder Geneva bought at a flea market for five bucks. She'd paid too much. Which in turn made him pay by having to work even harder, worry even harder, to make up for the money she frittered away.

The bathroom door opened, giving him a start.

"Jonah," Angel said, hand to her chest. "You scared me."

"Me, too. I mean, you scared me." Listen to him. The comely wench attracted him to the point that he couldn't even speak. Did she have any idea how pretty she looked with her hair all piled high, wavy tendrils damp from where he guessed she'd held a washcloth to her face? She'd changed into an ivory satin nightgown that provided a shimmering showcase for her every curve, straining against hard nipples he wouldn't have been a man if he hadn't noticed.

She tried getting past him without touching, but the old house had a narrow upstairs hall. Arm to full breasts. It couldn't be helped. Neither could the shift beneath Jonah's fly.

"Excuse me," she said. "Want me to put the baby to bed?"

"Nope. I can handle it."

She smelled good. Like the expensive lotion Geneva bought at the Harrison JC Penney to match that pricey perfume. He'd been mad as hell over that, but catching a whiff now only made him appreciative, and sad that he'd felt he had to yell at Geneva for spending all that money on what he'd considered useless when, in actuality, perfumed lotion was providing him with an awful lot of pleasure.

"Okay, then. Good night." On her tiptoes, she pressed a kiss to his cheek. "Thanks again for today. I really did have a great time."

"You're welcome." Only after she'd closed herself into what used to be his bedroom did he lift his palm to his still warm cheek.

"Dammit." Wednesday morning, Sam slammed his palm to his desk. "Thelma! When you get a sec, could you please come in here?"

The station secretary, big as a rambling farmhouse and just as cozy, had been with him ever since he won his first election over seven years earlier. Though he'd never asked, he guessed her age to be somewhere in her early forties. After work she went home to raise three rambunctious boys all on her own—thanks in large part to her cross-eyed, wife-beating husband, who was now in the state pen for counterfeiting hundred-dollar bills on State Farm Insurance's color copy machine.

Thelma stood at his office door, in the hand where she usually had hold of a doughnut was a celery stalk.

Sam groaned. "Don't tell me the boy mayor's on your case, too?"

She nodded. "Said if I don't lose fifty pounds by Christmas, he's gonna see what he can do about canceling my health insurance."

"He can't do that."

"Who says?"

"I say."

She laughed. "You only wish you had that kind of power. Face it, Sam, in these parts that boy's akin to God."

Sadly, as he glanced at the paperwork stacking up ever since his computer went down, Sam had to agree.

"Anyway, what's up?"

"Can you believe it? Now I can't even get a dial tone on this damned phone."

Chomping a bite of celery, panty hose swishing between her thighs, she sashayed around to the far side of his desk. "Don't suppose this could be your problem?" she asked, her tone sassy as she wagged the unplugged phone cord in his face.

"Oh, hells bells," he said, rubbing his jaw. "I'm sorry. I forgot about tripping over it last night when I was in such an all-fire hurry to get down to that fire at Cecil's."

Thelma plugged in the phone. "True what folks are saying about him torching it for the insurance?"

Sam shrugged. "After the trouble he's had trying to unload it, and now with his mom having cancer, couldn't say I'd blame him if he'd tried." For over forty years Cecil Stump had run Stump's Hardware on Main

Street, located just two blocks south of Jonah's diner, right in front of the prettiest stretch of Riverside Park.

Six months earlier, right about the time the new super-discount store went up alongside the highway, Cecil's business fell so sharply he'd had to shut the doors. The building had been up for sale for quite a while, but so far, Bev Harding at Rusty Pine Reality hadn't had a single nibble except for some guy from Little Rock wanting to put in a strip club and bar. Even though it probably would have been bursting at the seams every night of the week, that idea had gone over about as well with the mostly Baptist planning commission as the time Stacy Clements tried turning the old drive-in into an outdoor disco with rock videos being projected onto the screen.

"Oh—" Thelma said. "Before I forget, it might make you feel better knowing I got a juicy fax this morning from Dallas on Jonah's missing woman."

"No kidding?" Hot damn. At least one part of his day was looking up.

"I'll get it."

When she was gone over five minutes, Sam pushed back his chair and ambled into the front office. "Everything all right?"

On her knees in front of the fax machine, she'd removed the upper lid and paper tray. On the worn brown carpet, smiley face and peace sign faxes ringed her. "What's wrong with this thing?" she asked with a deep sigh. "I swear, not twenty minutes ago you had a fax from a Dallas detective. It had a photo of a real pretty blonde and a handwritten note asking, *This your girl?* Now it's gone."

Geneva beamed. Damn, I'm good.

* * *

131

"You sure you two ladies are gonna be all right?" At ten past six Thursday morning, Jonah was surprised both of them were already up. Katie sat in her high chair, glopping a teething biscuit in Cream of Wheat, while Angel sat at the table beside her, nursing a cup of decaf tea. The welcoming aroma of coffee she'd brewed specially for him still lingered, as did the feeling of warmth stealing through him at the thought that even after his blow-up Tuesday night, she wasn't holding a grudge.

"Of course we'll be all right," she said, taking another sip. "Give me some credit, Jonah, for having at least gotten this far in life."

Frowning, he said, "You know what I mean. Now, I left the truck keys in the bowl by the back door. Be extra careful until I can get Sam to get you a new license."

Hand over her heart, she said, "I hereby promise not to go over forty and to obey all road signs and safety laws." Her toothy grin, not to mention the sparkle in those tropical pools she called eyes, nearly steered him straight down the road to ruin. Damn, how did the woman manage to look so hot in a robe?

Focusing on Katie, he said, "You remember how to lock Lizzy into her seat?"

"Yes, Mr. Worrywart."

He had the craziest urge to seal his instructions with a kiss, but thankfully, a chugging truck engine and honked horn salvaged what little was left of his sanity. "That'll be Leon," he said, thumbing the back door.

Angel just grinned.

"Anyway," he said, kicking himself for grinning right along with her, "I left the diner number next to the phone. Call if you need anything. Oh—and I left a twenty by the truck keys. I know it's not much, but I'm running short—"

"I know," she said, rising in one graceful motion from the table to meet him by the door. Her robe parted, dazzling him with a view of her long, lean legs that led straight to Heaven. Black-pantied Heaven. "Don't worry. Stretched right, twenty bucks'll go a long way."

Dear Lord, I'd like to stretch you right over my—

Leon honked again.

Mouth dry, he looked to the back door. "Guess I'd better go."

"Yeah," she said, licking her lips.

Was it just wishful thinking on his part, or had that deceptively innocent robe of hers slipped open at her throat?

"I'll miss you," she said, reaching up to smooth his hair. "Gotta have my guy looking good for work."

"Thanks," he said, catching her hand to give her fingers a quick squeeze. He looked out the door toward his cook, then back to her. "I'll miss you, too."

"Do you mean that?"

He winked. "Wouldn't have said it if I didn't." Standing there in a pink flannel robe—gift he'd given Geneva—her hair all morning mussed, she looked the very embodiment of her name. *Angel*. Impossibly pretty. Impossible to hold. A fleeting spirit to look at but never touch.

"Good."

That same crazy urge to kiss her welled in his throat again, but as he did with all his urges these days, he swallowed it, choosing instead to walk out the door. But then he was back. "Oops," he said, rushing inside. "Almost forgot." Jogging across the kitchen, he kissed Katie on her forehead, rubbed her tummy, and tweaked

133

her button nose. "Bye-bye, sweetie. You be good for Mommy."

Mommy. How easy the word came. Just as easy as the lie.

Leon honked again, this time twice—each blast with extra urgency.

"Okay," Jonah said. "All that other stuff was just a drill; this time I'm really leaving."

Where's my kiss? Angel longed to call out as Jonah ducked out the back door, leaving her with nothing more than a grin and a jaunty wave.

Flattening her palm against the cool windowpane, she squeezed her eyes shut tight.

Patience.

Time. All she needed—all *they* needed—was time.

Though she knew little more about what had driven her and Jonah apart than that she'd left both him and the baby, it was more than enough to tell her Jonah was justified in his distrust.

What she needed was to inch by inch bring him back to the magical place she knew they used to share.

"Oh, Lizzy," she said, joining her daughter back at the table. "Help me, babe. Help make not only me remember, but your daddy, too, how good things used to be."

"Damn, boy," Leon said when Jonah bounded into the old Ford truck. "Took you long 'nuff. If I din't know better, I'd've thought you had a woman locked up in there."

Leon was Chevis's brother-in-law.

When the diner started nosediving to the point Jonah knew he'd have to start letting people go, Chevis volunteered to leave first, seeing how when he wasn't out fishing, he made extra money doing yard work. In confidence, he told Jonah that seeing how Leon's wife, Delilah, spent nearly every dime he brought home on fancy church hats and shoes—not to mention the fact that Leon's son and three kids had moved back in— he needed the steady income more.

"A woman, huh?"

"Stands to reason," Leon said, grinding his truck into gear. "After all, why else would you be needin' a ride to work when your truck's sittin' there lookin' perfectly healthy to me?"

Jonah shot him a sideways glance. "Out with it. What's Del heard?"

"Thought you'd never ask."

By the time Leon lurched his truck into its usual spot behind the diner, Jonah had told him the gist of Angel's story—leaving out the parts about his downright shameful attraction.

"Like her, don't ya?"

"S'cuse me?" Jonah choked while climbing out of the truck.

"You heard me. Del says her cousin Kendra saw you two drivin' in from Little Rock last night. Said that woman of yours was sittin' *real* close."

"Give me a break," Jonah said, sliding his key into the diner's back door. "She fell asleep on me, that's all." Stepping inside and flicking on the lights, he said, "For all I know, she's got a husband and kids out there, which makes her strictly off limits."

"Um hmm." Leon trailed after him. "You jest keep right on talkin'. Maybe sooner or later you'll even start believin' yourself."

As usual, the diner smelled of decades' worth of bacon, coffee, and cheeseburgers. Jonah drew strength from the familiar scents, as he did from the muted rush of the river winding its way through Blue Moon's downtown.

"Mornin', Jonah. Leon." Pauline, his morning shift waitress and Precious's mother, paraded through the back door with a pat of her helmet hairdo and a bold wink. Her daily uniform consisted of the pale blue dress Jonah provided topped off with a sparkly silver apron to which she pinned photo buttons of her daughter's many shining moments. There was the ninth-grade baton twirl-off she won down in Searcy. Her annual cheerleader uniform shot, going back all the way to peewee football. Two prom pics, and even a shot of Precious doing a perfect split at last year's Fourth of July picnic. Pauline's passion was pageants, so her every move was calculated to win a judge's eye—not for herself, but for her daughter. Seeing how you never knew when the judge of a local pageant might wander in, all those pictures of her pride and joy ensured she never missed a chance to sing her baby's praises. Hanging her silver-sequined purse on the hook beside the back door, she said to Jonah, "Heard you've got a houseguest."

"Oh?" Hoping if he ignored her she'd go away, Jonah headed for the front room to turn on the lights.

No such luck. Pinning on her beaded name tag, Pauline followed him. "Esther told my momma that she's a real looker—has talent, too. Said if she so much as put on a little eyeliner and a touch of mascara she'd be a shoo-in for at least Miss White River—that is, if she weren't already married with a baby."

"Yeah!" Leon shouted from behind his grill. "Jonah's baby!"

"All right, that's enough," Jonah said, midway between the two. "Just to set the story straight, sometime

Saturday night she must've wandered into the ladies' room,'cause that's where I found her after closing. Next thing I knew, she had Katie in her arms and the little traitor was eating like there was no tomorrow. Somewhere in her travels the lady lost her memory, so I volunteered to keep her with me till Sam gets a handle on where she's supposed to be. There. End of story. Satisfied?"

Pauline turned to Leon. "My sister, Melvine, said her best friend, Nancy, saw Jonah and this mystery woman cozied up in his truck last night when they came into town from Little Rock."

"You don't say," Leon said, separating sausage patties and slapping them onto the grill. "My wife's cousin Kendra saw the same thing. We think the boss here's got a thing for that mystery woman."

Pauline cast him an understanding nod. "Only be natural, what with her saving his baby."

"That's what we thought," Leon said.

Jonah pressed his lips tight. "Would you two listen to yourselves? Hell, here I don't even know the woman's real name and you've got me married off. I'm giving the lady a place to stay until Sam finds her rightful home. That's it."

"You know, Jonah," Pauline said, hand on his shoulder, green eyes brimming with concern, "I'm here if you ever want to talk to me—you know, about your understandable attraction. Melvine said Nancy—you know, her friend who owns the Kut and Kurl—well, she said even from behind she could tell this woman of yours had really great hair—maybe she's even a natural blonde. Nancy couldn't tell with it almost being dark and all if she had any roots."

"Really?" Jonah asked, raising his eyebrows. "I'm surprised with that X-ray vision of hers, Nancy didn't catch me slipping my hand up Angel's dress."

"Naw," Leon said with extra conviction. "That couldn't have happened even if you tried."

"And how do you know that?" Jonah turned his fury from Pauline to him.

" 'Cause Esther told Frieda Wilcox your woman wore jeans and one of Geneva's old hippy shirts to the Little Rock doctor."

From there, Jonah's day wouldn't have needed much to go straight into the toilet, and luckily fate was standing close by, ready, willing, and able to give him a shove.

By noon the coffee machine gave up the ghost. Some crazy woman must've called eight times, dialing the diner as a wrong number. The last stall in the men's room john overflowed. And to top all that off, they'd had only a whopping six customers all day.

Few enough that he sent Pauline home early to watch her soaps and sew beads on one of Precious's pageant gowns. Fortunately, Pauline's husband was an engineer at the town's only factory—a BB gun plant— so she really didn't need the money she earned at the diner; she just liked to have a little of her own cash to subsidize her penchant for sparkle. So far, Precious had only won the title of Grape Queen way over in Tontitown, but Pauline had set her sights on one day having her daughter be crowned no less than Miss Arkansas herself. Although judging by Pauline's tenacity, Jonah wouldn't be surprised to one day see Precious crowned Miss Universe—or, at the very least, Miss Ed's Tire, Brake & Transmission.

* * *

138

Worrying her lower lip with her front teeth, Angel snuggled Lizzy closer, grasping her basket with the same hand she had tucked beneath Lizzy's ruffled rump, and rapped on Esther's front door.

A quick peek past parted curtains netted the discovery of no lights; and beyond the sound of the next closest neighbor's chugging tractor, all else was quiet.

For early March, the day was sheer perfection. Not a breath of wind, a downright balmy temperature, and the whole valley fairly glowed with the promise of spring. On the far porch rail, a pair of wrens squabbled. Lizzy grinned at their antics.

"Well, sweetie," Angel said to the baby, "looks like our mission failed. Miss Esther isn't home."

After one more peek through the window, Angel turned away from the door to head for the stairs, secretly relieved to have been temporarily reprieved from making nice. It wasn't that she didn't want to be friendly with their neighbor—she very much did. The truth of the matter was that with all Jonah had told her about how well-loved Esther was in their small town, Angel was more than a little intimidated. While Angel might not have known much about herself, one thing she knew for sure was that she had a deep need to be accepted. To truly belong.

"Thought I heard company." Esther, dressed in overalls, a red T-shirt, and a big straw hat, ambled up the stairs and onto the porch.

"Hi," Angel said. Heart in her throat, she hated feeling as if she *had* to have this woman's approval. Still, she was here now, so she might as well follow through with what she'd come to do. She held out the basket she'd found in the pantry. "I made these for you."

"Oh?" Esther took the basket. Lifted the green gingham dishtowel covering two dozen oatmeal cookies. Angel had wanted to add raisins, but they'd been fresh out, and she sure didn't want to pad the grocery bill with extras.

You mean extras on top of the beer you had to buy Jonah to replace the ones you dumped?

"I hope you like oatmeal," Angel said, shifting Lizzy to her other arm. "I feel bad about the other day, and then when Lizzy set up such a fuss. Well . . ." She flopped her free hand. "Jonah said you wouldn't accept money for spending so much time with her, but I thought . . ."

"You thought right," Esther said, giving her hand a firm squeeze. "I've been out in the garden and could use a snack. With this warm weather, I'm plantin' early. Worked up a powerful hunger and thirst. Care to share a few of these cookies and a glass of lemonade? It's just from mix, but still wet."

"Thanks," Angel said. "That'd be nice." But what was even nicer was the almost giddy feeling of acceptance Esther's casual invitation brought on.

Trailing after the older woman into her shadowy house, it wasn't the faint scent of menthol rub that caught Angel's attention or the tinny country song playing on AM radio in the kitchen. It was the wall behind the silent TV that screamed loudest for attention. The whole thing—top to bottom—was covered with love. Blue-backed pictures of grinning elementary school kids missing their front teeth. Hundreds of crayon drawings of sunshine and horses and rainbows. Even a couple of pinup posters of hunky, half-naked men.

"Pretty neat, huh?" Esther caught Angel staring.

"Amazing."

"I've only been keepin' 'em for the last couple years. Whenever I get to feelin' lonely, I look over at my happy wall and everything just seems better." Esther looked her way. "Aw, now, what's the matter?"

"Nothing." Angel swiped at a few tears before blasting her new friend with what she hoped was her brightest smile. "Absolutely nothing is wrong with me. Just looking forward to that lemonade." *And to the day when I'll have earned as much respect and love from my friends and family as you.*

Ha! said the voice in her head. *You? Earning respect and love? That'll be the day.*

Angel pressed her temple, warding off the accompanying flash of pain.

Esther eyed her but didn't say a word other than, "Here, take a glug of liquid refreshment, then follow me. There's more work to do."

Ten minutes later, Angel had been taught the fine art of deadheading marigolds. Esther had all sizes, shapes, and colors, ranging from deep orange to sunshine yellow. While Lizzy lounged on a blanket beneath the cool shade of a red bud, Angel laughed and laughed over Ester's recollections of Jonah as a little boy. Picturing him as an eight-year-old dressed in his best cowboy duds selling gold-painted rocks he claimed were nuggets straight from his mine only made her love him more.

"Tell me what you remember about me," Angel asked once they'd finished with the marigolds and weeded the rest of the bed.

Esther wiped her forehead with a hanky she'd tucked into one of her overalls' many pockets. "Downright unnatural heat for this time of year."

"Esther? Please?" Angel urged from her seat on the

porch steps. "Anything you could tell me I'd be grateful for. Jonah, he—" she looked down, wringing her hands on her lap. "Well, he says the doctor told him it'd be best for me to remember everything on my own, but . . ."

"But it'd be easier if I just told you everything I know now?"

Grinning, Angel nodded.

Esther patted her knee. "Sorry, child. Much as I'd like to help, I promised Jonah I wouldn't interfere." She snorted. "Not that he has a clue what he's doin', but I pride myself in always stickin' by a promise."

"Appreciate it, Leon." Eight that night—due to the lack of customers he'd closed early—Jonah climbed out of the truck. Hand on the still open door, he said, "See you same time tomorrow?"

"Wouldn't miss hearing your next soap installment." He winked.

Still shaking his head when he walked in the back door, Jonah had to look twice to make sure he'd entered the right house.

Sure enough.

There was Angel seated at the table, dressed in a lacy ivory dress, her hair up with a few spiraling tendrils kissing her cheeks. "Hi," she said, her smile unusually shy. "Lizzy's already tucked in for the night, so I thought we'd have a party."

From the oven came the tantalizing aroma of a cheesy Mexican casserole he hadn't had to make. *Olé*. Let the festivities begin.

Seeing his pretend wife all dolled up, smelling a great dinner, both of those things he'd halfway expected, since she'd called him about six, asking him not to eat at the diner. The kitchen, on the other hand, blew him away.

"Hope you don't mind," she said. "I know it was probably me who picked out that horrible silver wallpaper in the first place, but I was rummaging through the attic and came across this. Much better, don't you think?"

The new-and-improved paper boasted a clean white background with a field of intertwining daisies. Just weeks before Jonah's mom died, while he'd been living in an apartment down by the railroad tracks, she custom-ordered it from Day Glow Interiors. He hadn't had the heart to take it back, so he stashed it in the attic, paste and all. Years later, he came across it while putting up Christmas decorations. He asked Geneva if she wanted him to replace the faded calico. Oh, she'd replaced it all right. With her very own kitchen night club! Now, smelling the paper's newness, sensing how happy his finicky mother would be to see Geneva's disco stripes forever gone . . . well, damn if he wasn't tearing up.

"Jonah? I'm sorry. I didn't mean to make waves. If you liked the other paper better, it pulled off easy. Maybe I can salvage some of it from the trash and redo your office?"

"No," he said, pulling her out of her chair and into a spontaneous hug. "Hell, no. I like this much better." Releasing her, he told her about his mom spending a month picking it out, and how she never got to see it hung. And how some small part of him felt better now that the job was finally done. Laughing, he said, "What is it about you that keeps making me spill my guts?"

"Beats me," she said with a flirty batting of her lashes. "Guess it's my irresistible McBride charm."

143

As rotten as his day had been, his night was that good.

Her spicy chicken and cheese casserole hit his burger-weary taste buds like ambrosia. But as great as her cooking was, her conversation tasted even better.

After giving him a glowing report on his daughter, Angel mentioned listening to a radio talk show while she'd papered and he mentioned having heard the same show. After a good-natured political debate, she asked him what he planned to do with the garden plot out back, and if he'd mind if she redeemed her murder of all the houseplants by trying her hand at growing a food crop.

Over dessert—a pineapple upside-down cake brought over by Esther—Angel asked, "You probably would've already told me if you'd heard, but did Sam ever find out what happened to our car?"

Wham. Just like that, she unwittingly jolted Jonah from his fantasy that this kind of domestic bliss was to be his every night for the rest of his life. "Nope. He's still trying, though."

"What about insurance and replacing my license? I know you're busy. Want me to call?"

"Um, no. I'll handle it."

"Really, I don't mind. It'd be no big deal for me to make a couple of calls."

"I said I'll handle it." He slammed his fork to his plate harder than he'd planned.

Her aquamarine gaze grew haunted.

"Sorry," he said, cupping his hand over hers. "It's just, well, the insurance agency is right down the street from the diner. No trouble at all."

"O-okay," she said. With her cloth napkin, she

dabbed at the corners of her lips. "I guess that's settled, then."

"Right."

After a few minutes of awkward silence, she asked, "Did you get enough to eat?"

"If I ate anymore, I'd pop."

"Good." She reddened. "I mean, not that you'd pop, but—"

"I know."

Had he done this?

Just like their day in Little Rock, he'd taken what had been perfectly cozy conversation and reduced it to stilted chitchat.

"I'll clear the table," she said.

"No. Let me."

"No way, Jonah. You've worked hard all day."

"So have you," he said, gesturing to the walls. "Come on, please. It's the least I can do."

"Okay. Thanks." While he began clearing, she fidgeted with her hands. "Guess I should check on Lizzy."

"No. Stay. Tell me more about your day." Jonah couldn't fathom what made him voice such a request, but seeing the glow those simple words restored to her amazing eyes filled him with the certain knowledge that if that was the kind of touchy-feely type thing it took to make her smile, he'd just have to start doing it more often.

Angel had just turned off her bedroom lights when a rap sounded on the door.

Heart pounding, she licked her lips before saying, "Come in."

Was this the night her husband reclaimed his side of their bed?

"Hey," Jonah said, peeking his head through the cracked door. "I didn't wake you, did I?"

"No."

"Good. Well, I won't keep you, just thought with this heat and all you might need this." He came the rest of the way in, and the hundred watts spilling from the hall silhouetted a box fan. "Mind if I turn on the lights?"

"Go ahead," she said, sitting up in bed. She wore the only tasteful item in her nightie drawer, an ivory spaghetti strap satin slip she'd been sleeping in to try to counter the heat.

Her eyes took their time adjusting to the sudden glare, but when they did, she saw Jonah hadn't budged from the door.

"Thought you might need this," he said, wagging the fan's cord.

"You already said that."

"Sorry." He looked away, setting the fan on the dresser facing the bed before tugging the piece of furniture out from the wall. "In this old house," he said, "you never can find an outlet where you need one."

"I'll be all right without the fan."

"No, I'm sure there's an outlet back here somewhere." He went down on one knee, giving her a mouthwatering view of his jeans-clad derrière and broad shoulders. He wore no shirt, and the farmer's tan around his neck and biceps didn't detract from the hard muscles rippling across his back. She knew full well he didn't have time to work out, which meant these muscles were earned the hard way. Lifting boxes of canned goods. Carrying loaded trays.

She closed her eyes, and for a split second her mind's eye flashed on that image she'd had of him her first night back in their house. The one of him taking her standing, back pressed against the bedroom door, her legs hooked about his waist. They both glistened with sweat, the room's heat almost as unbearable as the pent-up heat throbbing between her legs.

She raised her hands above her head, grasping for purchase where there was none, but then he was there, pinning her hands at the wrists. Her full, aching breasts thrust against his bare chest. Milk leaked, seeping through her satin gown, lubricating his already sweat-slick chest.

In and out he thrust, and when she gasped, he covered her mouth with his, probing with his tongue, dizzying her with—

A sudden breeze pressed the bodice of her satin nightie to her breasts, fingered the short hem.

Jonah stood. "That's better."

No, no, that wasn't better. Nothing will be better till you take me into your arms.

Tucking her hair behind her ears, she licked her lips. "Seeing how it's actually pleasant in here, why don't you stay?"

Hands in his pockets, he gave her a long, hard appraisal. Had she only imagined it, or had his breath caught when his gaze settled on the vee between her legs? *Had I known you were coming, love, I would've skipped the panties.*

He withdrew his right hand, raked it through his hair before backing toward the door, gesturing with his thumb. "I, ah, really ought to get to bed. Long day ahead of me tomorrow."

We could start sharing long nights. Might make your days go a little easier. "Okay, sure. I understand."

"Well, then. Good night."

"Good night."

CHAPTER NINE

"Isn't that special." Geneva sat down hard on her cosmic bench, crossed her arms, and scowled.

Never once—not even when they dated—had Jonah looked at her like he was looking at Blondie, let alone spent hours talking like he had over dinner.

'Course, to be honest, every time he'd tried talking to Geneva about one of his high-brow subjects, she'd been bored to tears, suggesting they change the topic to something exciting like handcuffs or vibrators—not that good old, disgustingly wholesome Jonah had ever been too keen on either of those good time items. But, hey, Geneva considered it her duty on behalf of bad girls everywhere to at least get him to give them a try!

At first, living a leisurely life of watching TV talk shows all day, then having sex all night hadn't seemed like a bad gig. But then she got bored. She'd tried looking for a job, but Blue Moon wasn't exactly a hotbed of career choices for an enterprising young woman such as herself.

The only dye jobs the Kut & Kurl specialized in were platinum blond, jet black, and little old lady blue. She'd always thought she'd have made a damned good tattoo artist, but there wasn't a tattoo parlor within a hundred miles of that one-horse town. She'd tried a brief stint as a cake decorator for the local IGA, but that lasted less than a week once she found out she had to be in by six to help make doughnuts.

Anyway, with the lovebirds finally asleep, Geneva pushed the off button on her cosmic viewing screen.

Now what? It was too early to try getting to sleep herself—not that she felt comfortable yet with rolling around on a cloud.

Good grief, Heaven was a snooze.

And where were all the rest of her songs? Angel and Jonah did little more than fawn all over each other—at least that was how they spent their time when they weren't trashing her taste in decorating!

Maybe she was working so fast that Mr. Big didn't know what to make of her. In fact, maybe she was doing such an awesome job that Mr. Big was having to create a whole new division of Heaven. Maybe he'd call it the Bad Girl Zone? And maybe instead of those boring old white clouds to float around on, they could have something nice and flashy—something to replace all that pretty wallpaper Blondie so callously tore down?

Eyes closed, Geneva drifted off to sleep, dreaming of a sparkly, silver-clouded Heaven where no other women were allowed—just her and lots and lots of hunky bad boys wearing nothing but silvery-sparkle Speedos.

Hmm, silvery-sparkle clad buns.

Now that was her idea of heaven!

* * *

Saturday morning, Angel had just sent Jonah off to the diner with a determinedly chipper wave instead of the lingering kiss she'd have preferred when a knock sounded at the front door.

She opened it to find Esther dressed in her usual overalls, but instead of a T-shirt and sneakers, she'd opted for a frilly floral blouse and pink heels. "Yard sale day," she said.

"Excuse me?"

"What? Are ya deaf? I said it's yard sale day. Grab your purse and the babe and let me show you how it's done."

"Well, I don't have much money—and what little there is should go to groceries. Besides, I—I really should see about working in the garden. I thought it might be nice to plant a few tomatoes. You know, to help save on money."

Esther waved her hand. "You and me can put in a garden Monday. No yard sales on Monday."

Angel glanced over her shoulder at the flotsam of baby paraphernalia that had a way of gathering on every flat surface of the house. "If I'm not gardening, I should be tidying. The place is a mess."

"Tidy-schmidy. No one'll be over 'cept for me, and I'd rather have company to my sales. The lack-of-money thing could be a problem, but with a little bargaining, I guarantee you a whole new wardrobe for under ten bucks."

"No kidding?"

"Honey, I thought we'd already established the fact that at my age I got no time left to kid." Patting her crown of tight white curls, she said, "Come on. I see Jonah left you the truck. You can drive."

Ten minutes later, Lizzy tucked in her baby seat, gnawing on plastic keys, and Esther just to the right of the gear shift, Angel got the truck off to a rollicking start, managing to hit every one of the driveway's dozen or more potholes before finally careening onto the dirt road.

"Maybe next time I should drive," Esther mumbled, clinging her arthritic hands to the dash.

"Sounds good to me," Angel said. "That way I could sit back and do nothing but side-seat drive."

Patting Angel's right knee, Esther let loose with a full-on belly laugh. "I like you," she said. "Yup, you and me, we're gonna get along just fine."

By noon Esther had purchased over a dozen picture puzzles—her favorite of which was of a Chippendale's dancer that, when you pressed your fingers to his tight leather pants, body heat made them vanish. In addition to puzzles she'd picked up a scary black wig for her favorite great-great-granddaughter to play dress up in, a set of rusty golf clubs for her least favorite grandson-in-law's fiftieth birthday, and a box of stubby crayons to melt into candles for her Sunday School class. Esther later admitted she wasn't sure if this would even work, but for a quarter, she figured it was worth a try.

As for Angel, she had indeed found an awful lot of pretty dresses for her ten dollars—not that a single one of them fit, but since Jonah promised she wielded a mean set of crochet needles, she figured she might as well try her hand at sewing. A few of the dresses were large enough that there'd be fabric left over to make a dress for Lizzy.

The best part of all about the morning, though, wasn't the items she bought but the friends she made.

Esther knew everyone. Every yard sale hostess. Both

mailmen making their rounds. Every curious dog. Every kid on a bike or selling Kool-Aid and cookies.

Agreeing to be Esther's escort for the day had bought Angel a kind of instant acceptance. And while every person she met gave her odd glances upon her announcement that she was Jonah's wife, by the time Esther finished with her ever bigger, bolder, flashier version of her accident and resulting memory loss, no one batted a further eye. If Esther said she was one of them, she was one of them. And that suited Angel just fine.

"There's one up on that corner," Angel said, pointing to a leaning hot pink garage sale sign. "Look," Angel said, aiming the truck in that direction. "It says they have lots of toys. Maybe that means puzzles."

Esther made a face. "I know that address. Belongs to Callie Cook. Those kids of hers are walking disasters. Can't hardly keep their wits about 'em, let alone puzzle pieces. Nah, I'm pooped. Take me home."

"If you say so," Angel said, pulling into a convenience store lot to turn the truck around.

During the twenty-minute drive home, sun shone brightly into the truck's cab, warming the interior. For a while the two of them shared chitchat, but that soon fell into companionable silence, and not too long after that Angel spied Esther nodding off.

Just before settling into a full-fledged nap, she yawned, then said, "I like you, Angel Whoever-you-are."

Patting her newfound friend's gnarled hand, Angel said, "I like you, too, Esther—even if you can't remember my name."

* * *

Saturday afternoon the diner was so dead that Jonah sent Precious home to help her mom sew on evening gown beads for the Miss Pine Lodge pageant.

On weekends Jonah rarely had need for Leon, so he was all by his lonesome behind the counter when Angel walked in, Lizzy held in the crook of one arm, a paper sack in the other.

"You two sure are a welcome sight," he said, truly happy to see them. What a difference a week made. Last Saturday at this time not only had he been faced with his business going under, but Katie had almost been hospitalized. Now, to look at her, you'd never even know she'd been sick.

His diner was another matter. Too bad Angel couldn't do something about that, as well.

"I ran into Leon's wife at a yard sale. She gave me these free of charge. Said to bring them down here. That you might be craving company." Angel withdrew a plastic freezer bag from the sack, then bustled behind the counter for a plate, arranging Delilah's legendary lemon poppy seed muffins in a pretty spiral.

"Yard sale, huh? Don't tell me Esther connived you into chauffeuring her around all morning."

"Actually, it was fun. Besides, she said next time she'll drive."

"Oh, she did, did she? Did she also tell you she had her driver's license revoked back when I was in sixth grade?"

Angel nodded. "So that's why she raised such a fuss over gas being over a dollar a gallon."

"Shoot," Jonah said with a laugh, "last time she bought gas it was probably a quarter a gallon. Anyway, I appreciate you stopping by. Delilah always did make

153

the best muffins." He unwrapped the paper before popping half the treat into his mouth.

His pretend wife grinned. To Katie she said, "It's a good thing we came down, Lizzy-babe. Who'd have thought the owner of a diner would be sitting here starving?"

Jonah's chuckle echoed off the dozens of empty seats.

Cinching Katie tighter, Angel said, "Where is everyone?"

Jonah shrugged. "Probably Mickey D's. Dairy Queen's pretty popular, too. The new Braums is going to put the last nail in my coffin."

"Things are that serious?"

"Look around," he said, gesturing to the ghosts of customers past. "Most days this is all I see from six-thirty to eight. I used to stay open till ten, then nine, now eight. Some mornings we still get a crowd when they get tired of McMuffins, but then they go back in the afternoon for those famous fries. Braums'll be even worse. Hell, even I go by Braums' every chance I get over to Springdale. Ice cream. Good, hearty breakfasts— even better greasy burgers and fries for lunch. Even if they are fast food, they get it—really get the concept of serving fast food with a country flair."

"Sounds like maybe you should apply for one of their managerial positions. I'll bet they even have health and dental benefits."

He held his arms across the counter for Lizzy and Angel passed her to him. Over the past week the three of them had fallen into such a comfortable routine, she knew what he wanted without him even asking. With his grinning baby snug in his arms, he walked out from behind the counter, trailing his fingers along the cool, gold-speckled laminate top.

"I celebrated my kindergarten graduation in here," he said. "Riding my bike without training wheels. My first kiss. So did my dad. You can't imagine how many memories these walls hold. Sure, I can and probably should run to those advance hiring people sitting in that trailer down by Braums. But as long as I've got even a penny in savings, I feel like I owe it to this squirt here to at least try keeping the doors of her legacy open."

Beaming a sarcastic smile she hadn't even known herself capable of his way, Angel saluted his speech with a nice, slow round of applause.

"What's that supposed to mean?"

She lowered herself onto one of the counter stools and spun around. "It means that while I fully sympathize with you on how hard it must be watching this place die, I also think it's high time you got your head out of Nostalgia Land and faced facts. What kind of legacy is Lizzy going to have with her daddy in bankruptcy court? How were you planning on paying for college? Oh—that's right, with any luck, she'll have this diner to toil in for the rest of her life."

"That's enough," Jonah said, his words a low growl. Who did this woman think she was? She was a stranger, dammit. What gave her the right to stroll in here preaching about what was best for *his* baby?

"No, it's not anywhere near enough," she said, hopping off the stool to cup her hand to his cheek. He flinched away, but she followed him back, trailing those perfumed fingers down his neck and then atop Katie's head, cupping her downy hair. "I always thought as a parent I would want more than what I have for my child. I don't want Lizzy to have to do her own dishes and cook at home unless she wants to, let alone spend fourteen-hour days doing it for strangers."

"The people who come in here are hardly strangers. They've known me and her all our lives."

"Is that supposed to make the work better? Easier?"

"What I do is a noble profession. Okay, so I might not wear a fancy suit to work every day, and I might not drive a Lexus, but when I fall off to sleep at night I've got a good tired. A hard-earned tired. And nobody, sure as hell not you, is going to tell me that's bad."

"I never said that was bad, sweetie." Her voice softened when she was once again cupping his cheek. "All I said was that for Lizzy, I want choices. You and me, we chose this life. It's a hard one, but a good one. This is the only life you've ever known, and you love it. You're able to cope with the stress of not knowing from one day to the next whether your livelihood'll be snatched away by some corporate giant, but Jonah, even you've got to admit there are days you'd like to just chuck it and start over from scratch. Maybe learn some nice, boring trade like accounting that you know people are always going to need."

Jonah turned his back on her. On her sensible words. Right now, he didn't want sensible.

In just this one afternoon he'd had enough harsh reality to last the rest of his life. If he were a smart man, he'd be down at that Braums' trailer begging for a job—any job. But evidently he wasn't smart, because no matter what kind of logic his pretend wife spouted, he wasn't buying it. At least not till his banker forced him to post a FOR SALE sign in the front door.

Gazing about the lofty space, Angel said, "How many presidential elections has this place seen?"

"Don't know. Never counted."

"These old brick walls ooze history. Did you ever

think about changing the diner's format? You know, spiffing it up, then trying to appeal to a more sophisticated crowd?"

"You mean like yuppie types?"

"Yeah. This place has the kind of historic, feel-good vibe they'd eat right up."

He flashed her a weak smile. "Thanks, but no thanks." Not six months after Geneva and he tied the knot, she'd gotten it into her head that the diner would make a great tearoom—only not just any ordinary tearoom; she wanted a head banger tearoom. That idea had been lame, and so was Angel's.

Face it, he was a meat-and-potatoes, no-frills guy, running a meat-and-potatoes, no-frills establishment.

"Anyone ever told you you're stubborn?"

He grinned. "Mom used to say I was more bullheaded than a bull."

"Yeah, well, your mother was right. And whether you like it or not, as your wife, I'm going to tell you what I think."

Jonah groaned, rolling his eyes.

Big mistake. That really got her going.

"You think this is funny? Maybe me not speaking up for what I believe in is partly to blame for us now being miles apart. Maybe if instead of you being so mule-headed you'd just for a second really listen to what I'm suggesting, you might find something in my idea that's workable, both for your income and your pride."

Hugging Katie tighter, nuzzling the crown of her downy head, Jonah turned away from Angel's beady stare. His real wife had never even talked to him like this. Where did this stranger get off? "I think you'd better leave."

"Is that how things work in this family? I say one

little thing that gets your goat and I'm dismissed?"

"No. I just think it'd be better for all of us if—"

Katie started to cry.

Angel was instantly there, reaching out for her. "She's probably hungry."

Reluctantly, Jonah handed Katie over. Her cries instantly stopped, which only added fuel to his fire.

"You've got a bell over the door, don't you?"

"Yeah."

"Good, then let's take this conversation to the office, where we can all be more comfortable."

In the office, seated in her favorite rocker with Lizzy feasting away, Angel felt more capable of keeping their conversation constructive as opposed to letting it grow into a full-out war.

Jonah, however, must have felt differently, as he had yet to even enter the room. He stood glowering in the open doorway. Not looking at her. Not looking at Lizzy. Just glowering, with his dark stare aimed somewhere between the neon Bud and Coors Light signs.

"Ever considered applying for a liquor license?"

He snorted.

"What?"

"My parents would roll over in their graves."

"So? Let them. If it means the difference between keeping their dream—your dream—alive, what would it hurt?"

"Dammit, Angel, I said no. Would you please give this whole topic of restructuring the diner a rest? It isn't going to happen."

"Fine. What time do you want me to pick you up tonight?"

"Don't bother. I'll find my own ride home."

* * *

For once, though it pained her to admit it, Geneva had to agree with Blondie. Though she'd never said it in so many words, maybe she should've. Jonah was a flat-out fool for not at least trying to take the diner in a new direction.

Granted, maybe her idea of a head banger tearoom wasn't all that hot, but she could see Blondie's idea of turning it into one of those yuppie places working out.

However, since saving Jonah's diner wasn't in her job description, Geneva remained focused on what was. And at the moment that meant keeping Sam from getting to his appointment with that nosy Little Rock detective.

"Oops," she said, popping one of his patrol car's tires while he slowed to round a curve.

"Dammit," Sam said, dragging the wheel right to compensate for the blowout.

What was up with this? How come fate was messing with what had so far been a pretty good day?

He'd found a new flavor of yogurt that, if he pinched his nose when he ate it, actually tasted like key lime pie, his phone had worked long enough for him to confirm his three o' clock meeting with his detective buddy, Luke, and he'd even managed more than two words to Stacy Clements—the hottest blonde in town. Change that. She *had* been the hottest blonde until Angel showed up. But seeing how Angel had been taken off the market—twice—she didn't count on any of his local hottie compilations.

He pulled the cruiser to the tooth-jarring dirt shoulder and climbed out of the car just in time to see the other rear tire pop.

"*That's for me not being at the top of all of your lists!*" Geneva said with an otherworldly flick of her black and fuchsia hair. "*After all, I may have been taken, but back when I was alive I put every other woman on the planet to shame."*

"Damn." Being a Saturday, Sam wore jeans, a red Razorback T-shirt, and a Blue Moon Bulls ball cap, which he removed to swipe beading sweat from his forehead. There was a downright unnatural heat for this time of year—especially for where he was—smack dab in the middle of nowhere. Hardwood forest and snaking vines arched over the equally snaky road, but what little sun did manage to filter through was merciless.

"Oh, and now you're bitching about the weather, too?" On her weather meter, Geneva had gone straight to hot. Not that she was allowed much tweaking beyond seasonal norms, but even a little bit of tinkering had been a hoot.

To show him what kind of girl he was messing with, Geneva kicked over a dead tree to the right of Sam's cruiser.

Sam leapt clear of a falling oak.

"Hells bells!" Gazing at the sky as if trying to guess where the next hazard might fall, he clutched his hand over his chest.

A jay called out.

The sharp cry came in big contrast to the sudden racket raised by a couple of spring peepers, making him jump all over again.

"This place gives me the heebies," he said, pausing at the driver's side door, darting glances to his right, left, behind his back, all in an effort to shake the feeling someone was watching him.

"Damn straight I'm watching you. For the way you treated me, all high and mighty-like when I was still alive, you deserve a whole lot more of a scare than this, but seeing how I'm on probation, guess I'll be good and at least allow you to radio for a tow. After that . . . anything's fair game."

And to prove it she popped both front tires, too.

* * *

Just past six—seeing how he hadn't had a customer since three—Jonah decided to close up early, then go home and hit the sack. In the process he hoped he'd avoid all contact with his opinionated pretend wife. Because, hey, if there was anything worse than being saddled with an opinionated real wife, it was being stuck with a fake one!

As eager as he'd been inside to climb into bed, standing on the diner's front sidewalk Jonah was that glad Leon took his time coming to get him.

Seeing how Geneva and now Angel both tried ramming their opinions on saving his diner down his throat, he figured that, also like Geneva, Angel would be waiting for him at the kitchen table, ready to pounce.

Once she'd had hold of a particularly controversial topic, Geneva loved duking it out to the death—which usually meant he'd end up caving to restore peace.

Sighing to see his buddy pull up alongside the curb, Jonah prepared himself to face Angel. He assumed he was in for one toad sucker of a night. Thankfully, Leon was too preoccupied, rambling on about Delilah's penchant for pricey shoes, hats, and purses, to drill Jonah as to why Angel wasn't picking him up.

After muttering a quick, sympathetic apology for Leon's troubles and a curse for women in general, Jonah thanked him for the ride and slid out of the truck.

The walk up the drive through the balmy night air felt akin to a death march. Crickets chirped warnings to turn back. In town, a train whistled. Was it traveling too fast for him to hitch a ride when it passed the mill pond?

Hand on the back door, he took a deep breath, hardening his jaw. "Dammit," he muttered, "this is my house. Angel gets too ornery, I'll boot her out."

Yeah, right. Who're you trying to kid? Even with Geneva at her worst, to the bitter end you tried to salvage what was left of your marriage.

Now, for Katie's sake, he was trapped in that same old quicksand, trying his damnedest to play nice with a woman his child had chosen to love.

Dragging in one more deep breath of the unusually steamy night, he turned the back doorknob and headed inside.

"Jonah!" Angel cried out. "You're home early. And look at me—everything's a mess." Dressed in jeans, his old football jersey, and one of his mother's lacy white aprons, her hair caught up in a high ponytail, more tendrils escaping than contained, smudges of flour across her nose and left cheek, the mere sight of her took his breath away. And then there was Katie, grinning up at him from the rag rug in front of the sink, clanging a stainless steel lid against its matching saucepan.

"Looks fine to me," he finally said. Better than fine—assuming all this domestic bliss was real.

He dropped his keys in a wooden bowl on the counter. Withdrew his wallet and set that in there, too.

Okay, he told himself, steeling his shoulders for the grief yet to come. This had to be a trap. Like Geneva, Angel was a clever girl. Obviously all of this was nothing more than her misguided attempt at wooing him over to her way of thinking. Since she knew he wouldn't fall for sex, she must've been working on his stomach. Good thing he finished off a chocolate cream pie just before leaving the diner.

"Yeah," she said, "but I feel really bad for badgering

you this afternoon. To make up for it, I wanted tonight to be extra special."

"Okay . . ."

She ushered him into a chair, then said, "What am I thinking—I'm sorry. You probably want to wash up first." Grasping him by the upper arm, she pulled him back from the table. "You go ahead."

Eyeing her, he crossed to the sink, kneeling to ruffle Katie's downy hair before notching on the tap. Immersing his hands in the water's warm flow, he closed his eyes and leaned his head back, working his shoulders.

"Let me help," Angel said, stepping up behind him and starting to rub.

Heaven. There was no other word to describe the feel of her strong fingers easing the day's tension.

"A big part of these knots was probably caused by me," she said, continuing to rub. "Knowing how much the diner means to you, I should never have butted in the way I did."

Jonah turned off the faucet, then wiped his hands on a damp orange dish towel lying on the counter beside a bowl of fresh-snapped green beans. He swallowed hard. Enough was enough. He was more than ready for her to declare her true intentions. Hardening his jaw along with every other muscle in his body, he slowly turned to face her. "What do you want?"

"Excuse me?"

"You heard me. What do you want? Money? A new car? Because whatever it is, I can't afford it. Hell, forking out the dough for all those fancy medical tests of yours nearly wiped me out. I'm already working twelve-to fourteen-hour days."

Her aquamarine gaze welled with tears.

Oh, she was good. "I'm not saying the magic you work with Ka—Lizzy is anything less than a miracle, but—"

"Stop." Palms pressed to his chest, she made a little choking sound, then pushed herself away. Crossing her arms over her chest, she turned her back to him, angling toward the stove. "Just stop." She halfheartedly stirred gravy simmering on one of the back burners.

The old part of him—the tenderhearted man Geneva hadn't destroyed—ached to cinch his hands about her slim waist, nuzzle her hair, but what would that accomplish other than showing Angel that her tactics worked?

Katie, blessedly numb to the goings on around her, clanged ever harder on her pot.

"You know," Angel said, removing the wooden spoon from the saucepan, tapping it a couple times on the edge before slapping it to the counter, "I'm getting sick and tired of this cold shoulder of yours, Jonah. I'm sorry for whatever I did to you. More sorry than you'll ever know, but that woman, whoever she was, isn't the same woman I am today." With the backs of her hands, she slashed away tears. "I desperately want to make this marriage work, but not enough to condemn myself and my child to a life with some . . . some coldhearted prick who doesn't know the—"

"Prick? Did you just call me a prick?"

She notched up her chin. "Yes. Yes, I did call you a prick."

He laughed. Laughed so hard tears sprang from his eyes. Katie stopped clanging to stare.

"What's so funny?" Angel asked, her hands on her hips.

"You. Calling me a prick. Something about the image of you standing there all Suzie Homemaker with flour on your nose, hurling out that rank an expression."

She stood her ground. "Yeah, well, there's plenty more where that came from."

"Give me one."

"Well . . . dickhead."

"Great. Love it. Give me another."

"Jack-off."

"Another."

"Slimeball."

"Ugh." He made a face. "That was weak. Come on, surely you can do better than that?"

"Sure, um . . ." She fumbled with her fingers to her mouth, looking at him, the floor, the baby. Her aquamarine pools welled again, and then she broke into sobs. Really ugly, hacking sobs that ripped open a hole to Jonah's soul.

What had he done?

She really was sorry.

She really had meant her dinner to be nothing more than a goodwill gesture, and here he'd gone and blown it by accusing her of being no less a conniving bitch than Geneva.

He looked to Katie, who was back to playing with her pans, then chased after his wife.

He found her curled up in the rocker by the big bay window, crying and crying and crying.

"Go away," she spat. "I never want to see you again."

"I don't blame you," he said, kneeling beside her. "Hell, most days I never want to see me again, but what can I say? I'm here, and you're here, we might as well make the best of it."

"How can I with you constantly talking in riddles? I

165

feel like I'm on trial for crimes I didn't commit."

"I know. And I'm sorry."

"That's not good enough," she said with a vehement shake of her head. "I want more. I deserve more and I demand more. Either you're going to be married to me—and I mean in every sense of the word—or I'm leaving, and this time I'm taking Lizzy with me."

Jonah sat back on his haunches and groaned, rubbed his face with his hands.

This couldn't be happening.

The woman he was only pretending was his wife was going to leave him? Taking his real baby, her pretend baby, with her? What was this? Some kind of cosmic joke?

"Aren't you going to say anything?"

From the kitchen came an orchestra of clangs.

A week ago Katie had been too weak to lift her head, and now she was making such a racket it was on the tip of his tongue to tell her to pipe down.

"Jonah?" Angel leaned forward, worrying her lower lip with her top teeth. "Don't you have anything to say?"

"Nope." Back up on his knees, he easily slid her chair around so that she faced him, then cupped her face in his hands, drawing her forward for not the fanciest kiss but one he hoped conveyed his heartfelt apology and thanks.

At first he barely touched his lips to hers. It'd been a while since he'd done anything like this, and he wasn't quite sure where to start. But then instinct kicked in, and she was so very alive beneath him, and so he pressed harder, and she was still there, not like in his dreams where she faded away.

No, this woman was real.

Kissing him back.

Shuddering beneath him, increasing the pressure. Though his head reminded him this was to be merely a friendly kiss, he took it one level higher, parting her lips with his tongue, meeting up with hers for one, two, three wildly forbidden strokes.

Okay, so he'd really gone too far now, but try telling that to his pounding heart, or the aching fly of his jeans.

"Make love to me," she moaned, her mouth tasting of tears. Tears he'd made her cry.

"Yeah," he managed to croak. "Oh, yeah." Anything to make her never cry again.

From the kitchen came Katie's cries.

"No," Jonah moaned. "Oh, hell, no."

Looking dazed, lips swollen and eyes looming even bigger and bluer than usual, Angel said, "I'll get her."

"No, let me."

"Okay. But come right back."

"I will." More than a little dazed himself, he kissed her again.

In the kitchen he found Katie half in, half out of the cabinet that held all his mom's old baking stuff. Aluminum cupcake pans and tin pie plates and the flour sifter. Right after Katie was born, Jonah had gone through the house baby-proofing. Back then, he'd still had that rush that comes from being a new dad.

And now, thanks wholly to Angel, that wondrous feeling was back.

Scooping up this new and improved Katie who'd somehow landed on her back and was wiggling her arms and legs like an upside-down turtle, he brought her to his chest, loving the feel of her actually snuggling into him for comfort. Angel had dressed her in

167

fuzzy pink footie pajamas and she smelled like pink baby lotion and that yellow baby shampoo.

A rush of happiness surged through him, taking him completely by surprise at the notion that all in one night he'd had to worry about his kid making too much noise, then getting herself into trouble. This amazing kid of his who just a week earlier wouldn't even eat was now turning into a hellion. And he loved it— her—so much that he laughed. Right there in the middle of his kitchen, out loud for the world to hear.

Yes. For the first time in he couldn't remember when, Jonah McBride was happy.

CHAPTER TEN

"You're kidding, right?" Saturday night, finally back at his office, seated behind his desk with the phone tucked into the crook of his neck and right ear, Sam closed his eyes, ran his hand over his jaw.

No way.

No freaking way that after coming up without a single lead for a week was he now going to be faced with this. And here Jonah was, thinking this Angel was his savior when, if Detective Neil P. Mercoup of Boudreaux Parish, Louisiana, was right, Angel might be his worst nightmare—hell, all their worst nightmares.

"No, sah. If your gal's same as ours, she's a bona fide she-devil."

"Can you fax me a picture?"

"Not tonight." Static crackled through the line. "We got us a storm raging down here. Everything's out 'cept for the phone and emergency lights. Shoot, t'only reason I'm here is 'cause my muthah-in-law's down from Shreveport."

Hells bells, Sam hated doing this. What if he was wrong, and Jonah's Angel wasn't this crazy Mary Peters?

Yeah, but what if she is? You really want your friend and his baby hanging out with a psycho even one more hour?

Expression grim, Sam said a quick thanks, made his good-byes, then grabbed his hat. Good thing Ed's Tire had been so fast fixing his car.

"What's so funny?" Angel asked, leaning her shoulder against the kitchen door.

"Nothing. Everything." Jonah spun to face her, her ethereal just-kissed smile. Her luminous aquamarine eyes. He felt about like a kid making puppy eyes at his first girl and his first dog, asking his parents if he could keep her. "I can't get over what a difference a week makes."

She hugged him with Katie stuck in between them, fisting his T-shirt. "Dinner's probably all dried up," she said, her voice muffled by the baby and his chest. Her words felt all breathy and warm against him and he couldn't tell where Katie left off and Angel began.

For all he knew, maybe they were one.

Maybe all this was a crazy dream.

Maybe he should quit worrying and go with it—her.

"I don't care," he said, hugging both.

"You will when you're chewing pot roast that has the consistency of week-old bubble gum."

"Mmm, that does sound tasty. You're right. You'd better cook. Need any help?"

"Nope." On her tiptoes, she kissed him, then the baby. "You tuck in Lizzy. It's already thirty minutes past her bedtime, isn't it, my little cutie patootie?" She tickled her on her belly and Katie grinned.

Grinned!

Jonah snatched Katie's tiny hand in his and waved. "Good night, Miss Angel."

"Miss Angel?" She scrunched her nose. "Mommy will do just fine."

And seeing how in the week she'd been there she was already more of a mother to Katie than Geneva had ever been, Jonah would've wholeheartedly agreed. Trouble was, the same old problem kicked him in the ass every time he got the slightest bit comfortable around Angel. That niggling issue of her most likely belonging to another man. Another baby.

And that hurt. Hurt like someone stabbing him with—with shards of glass, blunt-tipped screwdrivers, pitchforks, and hoes.

"I thought you were going to tuck Lizzy in."

He looked up with a start. "Right. Be right back."

Angel sighed, watching her husband mount the stairs two at a time. It was on the tip of her tongue to tell him to slow down with the baby, but seeing how he hadn't taken too kindly to her advice over the diner that afternoon, she doubted he'd appreciate her counsel on the fine art of walking as opposed to running.

Dare she hope that he was in such a hurry to get back to her?

Fingertips to her lips, she closed her eyes, savoring the memory of that kiss. Just thinking of him made her breasts ache and much lower parts hum. Would tonight be the night Jonah once again became her husband in every sense of the word?

Unable to bear the thought that she was getting her hopes up for nothing, she reasoned that even if Jonah didn't make love to her tonight, at the very least that kiss had been something to celebrate. There had been nothing chaste or even remotely innocent about that kiss. It'd plain and simple been the kiss of a man wanting a woman.

A happy woman.

She allowed herself a jubilant squeal and quick hug, then focused on dinner.

If food was the way to a man's heart, then by the end of the night she'd have her course to Jonah mapped out. Pot roast. Mashed potatoes and gravy. Steamed green beans, and for dessert blueberry pie—still warm from the oven.

"Sure smells good in here," Jonah said.

She jumped. "You scared me."

"Sorry. Truth be told," he said, standing beside her at the stove, "back there in the living room, you—that kiss, scared me. I shouldn't have—"

She pressed her fingers to his lips. "It was wonderful. Let's leave it at that."

"Yeah, but—"

"But nothing. Help me get these green beans on the stove, then as soon as they're done we'll eat."

Not five minutes after they sat down to dinner, a knock sounded at the back door.

Jonah shot the door and the shadow lurking behind the calico curtain a dirty look. "Wanna pretend we don't hear whoever it is?"

The shadow knocked again.

Angel sighed and pulled her cloth napkin from her

lap to set it on the table. "Great idea, but looks like whoever it is, is persistent."

She started to get up, but Jonah beat her to it. "Let me," he said. "Hopefully it's just a neighbor wanting to borrow milk or sugar. I'll load 'em up, then send 'em on his way." He winked before opening the door.

"Do I have a knack for showing up at the right time, or what?" Sam said. "Mmm mmm, I could smell that pot roast all the way out at the car." He removed his hat on his way through the back door, parked it in its usual spot atop the fridge, then shook Jonah's hand. Looking over to the prettily set table brimming with home cooked food, Sam cast Angel his biggest smile. "Don't suppose I could charm you into setting an extra place for a friend?"

"No," Jonah said, slamming the back door.

"Jonah?"

Sam watched as Angel gave him one of those shame-on-you looks only a wife could pull. Interesting.

To Sam, she said, "Of course, I'll get you a plate."

"Let me," Jonah said, hand on her shoulder when she started to stand.

"I promise to eat fast," Sam said when Jonah plunked a plate, knife, and fork on the table. He drew out the chair beside his hostess and across from his glowering host.

"No need to hurry," Angel said, forking a bite of green beans. "Maybe later we could even play cards."

"I'm pretty beat," Jonah said. "No way I could stay up for cards."

Sam caught Angel passing her *husband* another look. Either she was awfully polite or Sam figured he'd interrupted way more than dinner.

Aw, man, his old pal Jonah wasn't stupid enough to

have actually fallen for her, was he? Sure, she was gorgeous, seemed sweet—she was even a damned good cook—but there was also a very good chance she was already taken. After that phone call with Detective Mercoup maybe even worse—the implications of what that meant Sam didn't even want to consider. But he had to concede that the more time that passed without him digging up anything on her only added to his already bulging list of suspicions.

Housewives didn't just up and vanish. Which meant if Angel wasn't someone's long lost wife and mother, for Jonah's sake, Sam had to at least explore the possibility she could be Louisiana's homicidal Mary Peters—not wanting to be found.

Jonah cleared his throat. "Been a long day, Sam. Mind getting to the heart of your visit?"

"Got a few questions," Sam said.

"About my car?" Angel set her fork on her plate. "I thought we'd been all over this. Jonah, you told me you called the insurance company."

"He did," Sam said, jumping to his friend's defense. "Trouble is, nobody—not me or the insurance company—can find hide nor hair of your vehicle. And that's not all. Every time I try digging up info on this case, either my computer goes dead, the tires blow out on my car, or my fax machine prints out all kinds of crazy shi—stuff."

"And this is our business how?" Jonah asked. " 'Cause seems to me all this equipment trouble should be taken straight to the boy mayor."

"Already done."

"So? What'd he say?"

"The usual. Send my deputies out to catch more speeders and the department would have more money."

"Sounds like him."

"Okay, so wait," Angel said, fingers to her temples. "What does any of this have to do with my car? Shouldn't it be on the side of the road somewhere, clogging some ditch?"

"That's what I thought," Sam said, helping himself to a generous serving of pot roast, then burying it in gravy. "Trouble is, it isn't."

"So what do you want me to do about it?"

"I suppose nothing." He toyed with a roll. "On the other hand . . ."

"What?"

"Maybe you know more about the car than you let on. Maybe—"

"That's enough," Jonah said, jumping to Angel's defense faster than Sam would've liked. "Can't you see she's upset?"

Sam shrugged. "In my line of business that's something that can't always be helped."

"Sure it can," Jonah said, leaning forward in his seat. "All you have to do is shut up and tell my wife how good her pot roast tastes."

"Your wife?"

"Yeah. My wife."

"Jonah, look, man, you know I love you like a brother, but—"

"But what?" Angel shrieked. "Just say it! What horrible thing is it you think I've done?"

Jonah placed his hand over hers, "Angel . . ."

"No, I want to know, Jonah. He barges in here uninvited, and even though we've offered to share our meal—not to mention our friendship—I can't help but feel he's not my friend." Pushing her chair back from the table, she added, "And for that matter, maybe he never was yours."

Working his jaw, Jonah looked from his best friend to the woman to whom he owed his baby's life. One allegiance was strong, but the other . . . They were talking Katie's life. He couldn't let Sam ride all over Angel this way. He couldn't. He wouldn't. Still, there had to be some way to settle this peacefully. "Angel, honey," he finally said, "please, sit back down. I've known Sam all my life and I'm sure he didn't mean—"

"Yes, Jonah, I did." Sam pushed his chair back, too.

"You can't be serious."

"H-have I committed some kind of crime?" From her reflection in the kitchen's bay window, Jonah could see Angel's complexion had turned waxen. "Because if I have, I have rights. You can't just—"

Sam sprang from his seat, stepping deep into Angel's personal space. "Barge in here and haul you down to the station for questioning? As a matter of fact, yes, I can."

"Jonah? Do something."

He was already on his feet, hands fisted, ready to blow. "That's it, Sam. Get out."

"Not until I—"

From upstairs came the sound of Katie's cries.

"I'll get her," Angel mumbled, already halfway across the room.

Jonah let her go, glad for the time alone with his one-time good friend. "Mind telling me what the hell this is about?"

Sam sighed, raked his fingers through his hair. "There's no good way to say this, Jonah, so I'm just gonna spill it. Angel—she, well, I just heard some news from a detective down in Louisiana who says she just might be the devil herself. If your Angel's the woman he thinks she is, she's wanted for armed robbery. Kidnapping. Grand theft auto. The list goes on and on."

"This is bullshit and you know it."

"No, bud, I don't. Which is why I'm here. If she is this Mary Peters, do you really want her spending one more second alone with your kid?"

"She's not."

"How do you know?"

"I know, okay? I'd feel it. Some kind of wild kingdom instinct thing would kick in. I'm Katie's father, for Christ's sake."

"Yeah, you really got a lot of mileage out of that when she refused to eat, didn't you?"

"Take that back."

They stood toe to toe.

Eye to eye.

Nostrils flared.

Hands fisted.

Whoa, whoa, time out. Geneva squeezed between the two bruisers, flattening what was left of her vaporous palms against their chests. Each man's pain shot through her in waves.

"Sam really is only looking out for your best interests," *she told Jonah.*

"She's okay," *she told Sam.* "Angel's not that crazy woman."

"And how would you know?" *Teach barged in on her big rescue.*

"Geez!" *Now Geneva was clutching her own chest.* "Couldn't you have at least knocked before popping into my space?"

He shrugged. "Too late now. Anyway, what have you found out about Jonah and Katie's Angel?"

177

"She's a good cook, has rotten taste in wallpaper, and seems to have a genuine fondness for my husband and baby."

"That's it?"

"What do you mean, that's it? Keeping an eye out on old Sam there is taking every ounce of my time and then some. He never sleeps. Did you know that? He's even started going to pay phones to try to get outside information on this woman. Do you have any idea how much energy it takes to zap a pay phone? And then there was his attempted trip to Little Rock. I popped more tires today than a kid with a stinkin' case of bubble gum."

Teach rolled his eyes. "If you must use an analogy, please at least try to ensure it makes sense."

"Geesh, are you dense? Popped tires? Popped bubbles? What don't you get?" More than annoyed, she blew him off, turning her attention back to Jonah and Sam.

"Get out," Jonah said.

"Not without taking her with me."

"Are you insane? She's probably up there breastfeeding my child. What kind of gun-toting redneck whores you know take time out of their busy schedules to breastfeed a helpless baby?"

Sam worked his jaw. "All I'm saying is—"

"Get out. You get hard evidence, maybe—*maybe*—we'll talk. Until then, you stay the hell off my property."

"You don't mean that."

"The hell I don't."

"So it's come to this? After all the years we've known each other, you're gonna let a woman—a strange woman—come between us?"

Jonah stared his friend hard in the eyes. "Guess so."

Sam shook his head, eyed his friend one last time,

then snatched his hat off the top of the fridge and exited out the back door.

Watching him leave, Geneva released a wall of breath she hadn't realized she'd been holding. Heck, for that matter she hadn't even realized she needed air.

"I must say, that could've gone better."

"And I must say . . . mind your own damned business. I'm doing the best I can."

"Which isn't anywhere near good enough."

"So what do you want me to do? If I let Sam get the goods on Angel, then she's gone. If I don't, then she's gone anyway,'cause the first second I'm concentrating on Jonah and her becoming a family, Sam's off on some wild-ass tangent with guys like Buford T. Justice."

"Who?"

"The sheriff from the Smokey and the Bandit movies. Classics. Burt Reynolds and Sally Fields? They used to date, but—"

He held up his hand. "Enough." Then put that same hand to his forehead. "Never, in over a thousand years of teaching, have I run across a pupil as difficult as you."

She preened. "That just proves you need to get out more."

"Sorry about all that," Jonah said from the open nursery door.

Angel looked up. Lizzy had fallen asleep at her breast and she tugged her bra and his jersey back in place, feeling a sudden urge for modesty. "It's okay."

"No," he said, crossing to her, "it's not. This is our home. And in our home I demand my wife be treated with respect."

It might have sounded old-fashioned, but at that moment with Jonah's protective words ringing through her

179

head, Angel could've swooned. She swallowed hard, tracing her finger along Lizzy's silken brow. "You really mean that?"

"I wouldn't have said it if I didn't." He knelt beside her, cupping her face with his big, strong hands. His warmth, his strength, seeped into her, through her, until the two of them merged into one.

"I love you," she said, meaning it with every fiber of her being. Sure, they still had a lot of issues to work through, but for the most part they were right back on track.

Jonah didn't return her words, but he didn't have to. His love for her blazed from the depths of his dreamy brown eyes.

He said, "Let me take Lizzy from you. Tuck her back into bed." His hold on the baby could've hardly been called fluid. It was awkward and clunky, as if he wasn't handling his child but a priceless piece of china.

Angel had never in all her days seen a more beautiful sight. Beaming up at him, she said, "She won't break, you know."

"That's where you're wrong," he said, lowering the infant into her crib. "Before you came along, I almost did break her." He pressed his fingers to Lizzy's bow-shaped lips. Her button nose. "She just stopped eating. Hardly ever slept. It was like she was willing herself to die. I didn't know what to do."

"She's fine now."

He looked up. "Because of you."

"Okay, then," she said, pushing herself up from the chair. "We're even, because the only reason I'm alive is because of you."

Jonah groaned before taking her into his arms, pressing a hard kiss to the top of her head.

"What does that mean?"

"That I'm tired and going to bed."

She looked to the floor. "Want company?"

Hands in his pockets, he thought, *Yes. Lord, yes.* He said, "Thanks for the offer, but not tonight."

Monday morning, coated in sweat and layered with dust, Angel wiped her brow, sitting back on her haunches to tip her face toward a sky of dizzying blue. For planting her garden she'd worn faded jeans and borrowed one of Jonah's T-shirts. Forest green that soaked in the day's heat. When Esther wasn't looking, she closed her eyes and breathed in his scent, still lingering in the fabric's soft folds, pretending the heat warming her back and arms was from him instead of the sun.

"We've gotten a good piece of work done," Esther said, surveying the neatly tilled rows of the ten-by-eight plot. Who'd have guessed Esther wielded a mean Rototiller? "Rate we're goin', should be ready to set plants this afternoon."

"Thanks again for helping me with this, Esther. I wouldn't have had a clue where to start."

She waved off the gratitude. "Does my heart good seeing this old plot back in use. Back when Jonah's momma was still here, she used to work nearly half an acre. Should have seen her out here on her tractor. That woman was a dynamo. Marcus, her husband, Jonah's daddy, used to use a good bit of what she grew down at the diner. Made the best eggplant parmigiana you ever did taste."

Angel glanced Lizzy's way. She sat up in her playpen, gumming her favorite wooden block. Esther had helped rig a tarp between the tool shed and clothes line so the baby would have a patch of shade.

"What about me?" she asked.

"What do you mean? Can't recall ever tastin' your parmigiana."

"No," Angel said with a half-grin. "I mean, did I ever help Jonah's mom with the garden?"

Esther started to answer, then clamped her lips, wagging one of her leather-gloved fingers at Angel. "Shame on you, tryin' to sneak information out of me. And it almost worked."

"Then why not just go ahead and tell me?" Angel asked.

"Because a promise is a promise."

What about the promise Jonah made me? The one to be my husband our whole lives long? Angel swallowed hard.

Esther snorted. "Quit that poutin' and get your gloves back on. We've got work to do."

For Jonah the next week passed in a blur. A blur of nagging doubts, but most of all, hope.

More and more, he and Angel and Katie were starting to feel like a real family. Angel, smoothing his hair back on Friday before he left for work, tactfully urged him to get it cut. He returned home to a rave barbershop review. Tuesday, he'd hinted how much he'd enjoy it if she and Katie dropped by for lunch. That afternoon they'd spent nearly an hour in a back booth sipping iced tea and musing about what Katie's future boyfriends might be like.

Even better, the more time Jonah and Angel spent together, the more Sam stayed away, spending his time dealing with the variety of problems cropping up from the freak heat wave—least of which were two more

Main Street fires, this time blamed on spontaneous combustion.

These parts were famous for hot summers, but March was generally pretty mild—sometimes downright cold. Not this one, though. With still a week until April, every day had been a scorcher—well above ninety.

Jonah assumed that where Sam was concerned no news was good news, but after that last bombshell his supposed friend had thrown, Jonah thought he could be biding his time, waiting for just the right piece of evidence to blow Jonah's newfound happiness to smithereens.

"What're you thinking about?" Angel asked on a Thursday night over after-dinner coffee and tea. She'd prepared baked chicken and creamed spinach and a sweet potato casserole so tasty he could've wept.

"How good that meal was." He reached for her hand, lacing his fingers with hers. Katie had been snoozing for over an hour and the kitchen's only sound was the slow drip from the sink faucet he'd been meaning to fix.

The room was hot.

Too hot for coffee, really, but as with most things having to do with Angel, when she offered, he couldn't refuse. In a perfect world he would've switched on the central air, but that was just the first in a long line of luxuries they'd have to do without.

"Thanks."

"You're welcome." Her hand felt good in his. Like they'd always been together. Like they always would be together. "What'd you do today?" he asked after a few minutes of companionable silence.

"Esther's been looking for an X-rated mug to match

her Chippendale's puzzle, so she conned me into taking her to a couple of flea markets."

"Fabulous. What did I buy?"

"If you drop the sarcasm," she said with a sassy wink, "I'll give you a hint."

"Sorry. It's just that with savings at an all-time low, it doesn't leave much room for frills."

"Which is why I didn't spend much." She hopped up from her seat, planted a not-nearly-as-long-as-he-would've-liked kiss on his lips, then dashed off to the living room.

He'd barely had time to sip at his lukewarm coffee when she was back, holding something small and wrapped in brown paper behind her back. "I wanted to wrap it properly, but in the spirit of saving every dime we can, I even made gift wrap. Ta da!" Beaming, she placed the package on the table in front of him.

"What you bought is for me?"

"Yes, it's for you."

"Wow. Thanks." Never once, in all the years of their marriage, had Geneva bought him a gift. Oh sure, he'd been given loads of naughty nighties to take off her, perfume he was allowed to smell on her, and even chocolate syrup and whipped cream he was supposed to drizzle on and then lick off her, but never once had she bought something just for him.

Angel had decorated the brown-paper-bag wrapping with red hearts and stars. "I hope you like it," she said. "I know I was excited when I found it, but I hope it doesn't make you sad."

"Sad?" he asked, slipping his finger beneath the tape.

"Not really sad—more nostalgic in a traumatic way."

He frowned. Gave the package a mock hard scowl. "Hmm, maybe I don't want it."

184

"Go ahead," she said, her smile lighting every dark corner of the room.

And so he did. And the crushing pleasure/pain of what he found inside was almost more than he could bear.

Standing behind him, Angel circled his shoulders in a hug. "Mr. Neimowitz—he owns the flea market—he gave it to me for free. Said he'd come across it at an estate sale in Batesville and thought you might want to have it. He's been meaning to give it to you but hasn't had a chance. What's wrong?" she asked when he couldn't stop staring. "Last time I was at the diner I noticed your collection of memorabilia. Do you already have this one? Or don't you like it?"

"Like it? I—I love it." In the box rested a ladies' paper fan. On it was the quintessential proper Forties woman seated at the diner's counter with tidy blond hair, a form-fitting baby blue suit, big red lips pursed into an *o*, perfectly plucked eyebrows raised, blue eyes gazing in wonder at the forkful of mystery meat in her left hand, and the flag in her right. The caption beneath her read, *I eat at Blue Moon Diner where the food is always tasty and leaves me with enough dough to buy War Bonds! Happy Fourth of July 1943!*

Jonah had seen one of these fans once when he was a little kid—maybe six or seven. But that one hadn't been in this awesome condition. His great-grandfather handed them out that Independence Day as promotional souvenirs. Over the years he'd gone on to do calendars and matchbooks, but nothing in the glass case beneath the register topped this.

"Really? You really like it?"

"Do you even have to ask?" Setting the fan gingerly

back in its box, he pulled her onto his lap. "This is the best present—ever."

And to show his appreciation, he kissed her square on the lips. And this was no trial kiss but a full-on frontal blitz he hoped demonstrated the depth of his gratitude.

Angling to get a better hold, he slipped his right hand under the fall of her silken hair, pressing her mouth closer. With his tongue, he parted her lips, drinking her in, stroking her tongue. He drew back for air, sweeping the pad of his thumb over her arched brow, drowning in her amazing aquamarine gaze. "You're beautiful," he said on a ragged breath.

"So are you," she whispered back.

He laughed. "I've been called a lot of things, but never beautiful."

"Then every other woman you've been with was blind."

He refused to think of her being with another man.

Sliding his hand up and under her shirt, he molded his hand around the fullness of one of her breasts. Though the front of her bra was damp with milk, at that moment—or maybe it'd been days before and he'd been too entranced to acknowledge it—he stopped thinking of her as wet nurse to his daughter and started thinking of her wholly as a woman.

His woman.

He kissed her lips and cheeks and the tip of her nose. He nibbled her ear lobe, drawing it into his mouth for the lightest of nips, loving it when this elicited a scrunched-neck squeal. He moved on to her neck, winding his way to that sexy-as-hell indentation at the base of her throat. She wore a no-frills short-sleeved minty-green oxford that, while it granted him easy enough access to his heart's desire, didn't begin to do her lush figure justice.

She should've been draped in a gossamer gown. He wanted that throat of hers encircled in priceless pearls.

For the first time in his life, he regretted his chosen profession—not because he was ashamed of it, but because it wouldn't buy her the luxuries she deserved. He wanted to make love to her on a bed of not roses but tropical birds of paradise that matched the Bahamian blue of her eyes. Change that—those plants could be spiky. How about making love on silk sheets surrounded by vases brimming with birds of paradise? And after that he'd buy her diamonds and furs and a new Mixmaster and blender.

Nothing was too good for her. Nothing too extravagant or unique.

One by one, he slipped open the buttons of her shirt, finding her skin dewy with sweat. Earlier, he'd wished for money to turn on central air, but now he had doubts. He kind of liked her sweaty, tasting faintly of salt and the baked-in goodness of the roasting hen she'd prepared especially for him.

With her shirt all the way off, he pressed hot, openmouthed kisses to the top of her cleavage.

Her fingertips pressing the back of his head, urging him still closer, she said, "Make love to me."

"Yes. I mean, no."

"Why?"

Because you're not mine. But soon, babe. So soon.

Screw Sam. If it took every last dime he had in savings, Jonah would hire his own private detective to find out who Angel really was. He'd find out, and then, once he was sure she wasn't married, he'd marry her himself.

"Jonah?" She drew back, her eyes pooling.

He shook his head. "It's not that I don't want to—I—"

She hurled her hand back and slapped him, then immediately drew that hand to her mouth, then to his reddening cheek. "My God, I'm sorry. So sorry." She kissed him. Raining a hundred—no, a thousand—tiny kisses all up and down his cheek. "I'm sorry. So sorry."

"No, I'm sorry. I have no right to toy with you this way." Fumbling for her shirt, which he'd tossed to the table, he drew it over her shoulders.

"Jonah, I'm your wife. You have a right to not only kiss me but so much more. I want you to kiss me. I want you to take me straight to bed and not let me up for a week."

"I want that, too, but—"

She stormed to her feet. "You know what? Maybe I'm glad I slapped you. Maybe I should do it again."

"Maybe you should," he said, hardening his still aching jaw. Maybe that'd knock some sense into him.

"What do I have to do, Jonah, for you to forgive me? What will it take?"

"Nothing. This has nothing to do with you and everything to do with me, okay?"

"No." Tears streamed down her cheeks. "No, that's not okay. Dammit, Jonah, I love you. I've apologized for whatever I did in the past, but I'm done. I don't know what more I can do. Time after time I pour my heart out to you, but it's never enough."

He sighed, raked his fingers through his hair. "One of these days you'll understand."

"Understand what? Is there another woman?"

"No. Hell, no."

"Are you gay?"

He laughed. "You felt the havoc you caused beneath my belt. You tell me."

"This isn't funny," she said, swiping at more tears.

"No, it isn't. And believe me, this forced celibacy is every bit as hard on me as it is you."

"Then why do it?"

"Because I—we—have to."

"That's stupid."

"I agree, but, the um, doctor—the one in Little Rock—he said until your memory returns, we should abstain from any marital relations."

"That's crazy."

"That's what I told him, but he insisted. Said it could really mess you up emotionally."

"More than this constant rejection?"

He stood, pulled her into his arms. "Baby, baby, no." Now he was wiping away her tears. "God, no, don't think of this as me rejecting you. Think of this as me protecting you. I'm so proud to claim you as my wife in so many ways. God, where to start? You're beautiful, great with Lizzy. You're a fabulous cook. You work wonders inside the house and outside—your garden is growing like gangbusters. And all that, as amazing as it is, doesn't scratch the surface of how much I admire in you."

Jonah stood there hugging the woman he'd rather be making love to. His lies sounded good in theory—even to him. But that fact gave little solace in light of the fact that he was facing yet another endless night alone.

What if she's already married?

What then? Could you and Katie bear knowing you had your whole lives to live alone?

Frowning, Jonah figured he'd think about those questions in the morning. He was only capable of handling one crisis at a time, and at the moment a cold shower superceded all other needs.

CHAPTER ELEVEN

"That's so sweet," Geneva said, literally blubbering up a storm. She'd gotten to know Mother Nature's son, Thor, quite well during her off hours, and all the heat she'd been conducting reacted with the humidity of her tears.

Lightning struck the hill behind Jonah's house, and Geneva jumped from the resulting clap of thunder.

"You find it sweet that your ex is dying little deaths every time he merely thinks Angel's name?"

Almost used to Teach's nasty habit of popping in uninvited, Geneva didn't bother replying to his question. After all, he read minds; if he wanted the info bad enough, he could retrieve it himself!

What she thought was sweet—disgustingly so—was the way Jonah was really starting to care for this woman.

At the rate Jonah and Angel's relationship was so nicely progressing, Geneva figured she'd be sporting those wings in record time. Even baby Katie seemed deliriously happy. Who cared that Geneva couldn't remember the last time she'd heard Elvis. In her heart of hearts she knew she was on the right track with her assigned lovebirds, and that was good enough for her.

Teach released a decidedly unangelic snort. "Yes, well, if all of you mortals got to decide your own fates, the world would be in an even sorrier state than it already is. Sorry to burst your bubble there, sugar, but you're doing a simply abominable job on your assigned tasks."

Hands on her hips, Geneva said, "How's that? I'm keeping Sam hopping with all sorts of lame missions. He doesn't have a clue who Angel is and at the moment is so busy clearing the road of overheated cars, escaped cows, and burned-out musty old buildings, he doesn't even have time to look. And geesh!" She pointed to her view screen, splitting it in two to show the wide-eyed, tossing-and-turning horn dogs Jonah and Angel had become. "Those two are so hot for each other they can't even close their eyes. Wait—I spoke too soon." Angel was closing her eyes, all right, closing her eyes and cupping her great big boobs! "I rest my case. She wants him bad, and look at him. Think there's supposed to be a tent stake beneath those sheets?"

With a flamboyant wave, Teach erased the screens.

"Hey, what'd you do that for? This was just getting good."

He sighed. "We are not peeping Toms, my dear Geneva. We are angels-in-training."

"I thought I was the only angel-in-training and you were already the real deal."

"I was speaking metaphorically. Now, if you will kindly cease interrupting me, I'll get to the point of my visit. In case you've forgotten, Mr. Big imposed a time limit on your mission, and as of right now you have only twenty-three days remaining to see Jonah, Angel, and Katie live happily ever after."

"They already are."

"You call that *happy*?"

The screen flashed back to an appropriately blurred view of Jonah cringing from the sting of a biting cold shower.

Geneva winced. "I get your point. So what am I supposed to do?"

"Finding out the truth about Angel's background might be a good start."

Angel kicked off her sheets.

Outside, rain hammered the earth, doing little to cool the steamy heat inside the house. At least tomorrow she wouldn't have to water the garden.

The box fan Jonah gifted her with in what seemed like another lifetime did more harm than good, fingering the satin gown she wanted her husband's strong hands gliding up.

"This is madness," she said, sitting up in the bed.

Lightning strobed, reflecting off the brass knick-knacks Angel hadn't yet gotten around to getting rid of. Instead of shopping other people's yard sales, she needed to host her own. Maybe that was the problem. Maybe because of all of her clutter, Jonah didn't feel comfortable in his own room.

Rolling thunder shook the walls and the dangling leaves on the brass tree gracing the top of Jonah's highboy dresser. The one that now stood empty since he'd moved his clothes to the guest room.

Too antsy to remain lying down, she bounced out of bed, planning to pace, but another flash of lightning showed rain pooling on the windowsill, so she changed course. Creaking open her door, she padded into the hall, intent on grabbing a towel from the bathroom to sop up the mess.

The hall was spooky dark.

Had the storm knocked out the power?

Days earlier, Jonah had had a crew out from the power company to fix the yard light. Since then, even in the thick of night there'd been a daylight glare through the window at the top of the stairs.

Lightning momentarily illuminated her path, shining through not only the hall window but an open door at the end of the hall.

Jonah's door.

Usually he kept it closed.

Sometimes she'd even heard him lock it. But tonight there it was, drawing her beyond the bathroom, beyond all good judgment and into the heart of the true storm. The floor beneath her shook from thunder. Or was that her hammering pulse?

No, just driving rain, battering the old house with the fury of a thousand hammers.

I only want to see him, she told the warning bells pealing in her heart. *I won't touch him; I won't even enter his room.*

Just one look.

One look was all she needed.

Yeah, right, just like that one drink you've been craving?

The voice had been blessedly quiet for the past few days, but now it was back with a caustic vengeance, forcing Angel to stop, pressing fingers to her temples to make it go away.

You don't need him. You don't need anybody. You're a freakin' star. All you need is a bottle and a stage and you're good to go.

"No," she whispered, not hearing her voice above

the rain. "I don't need anything except my Lizzy and my husband. They're my life."

Great, only Lizzy's dead.

Lightning struck close.

Thunder boomed, and the old house shuddered.

"No. No, that isn't true. She's in her crib, sound asleep." And to prove it, Angel dashed down the hall, throwing open the door to Lizzy's room.

Running to the crib, she bent over it, scooping her baby into her arms. Her warm baby. Her very much *alive* baby.

"There," she said to the voice. "There, see? Just like I told you, she's fine."

The voice only laughed. *Sure, you go right on believing everything's fine. Meanwhile, your real life, your real you, is out there just beyond your reach, falling apart.*

The pain was too much, so Angel gave Lizzy a final hug, then set her back in her crib, freeing both hands to clutch at her forehead.

More lightning.

More thunder.

More rain, pounding in time to the blinding ache in her temples and heart.

Jonah. I need Jonah.

She went to him, navigating the hall by rote. Lightning showed her the way, thunderous rain applauding her each and every step. Not much farther now. Not much farther and she'd crawl into bed beside him, melting against his strength.

His love. That's all she'd ever wanted.

Standing in his open doorway, to the accompanying strobes of the storm, she drew her satin gown over her head, pooling it on the floor. She bent to remove her

195

panties, slipping one foot out, then the other, dropping the lacy scrap atop her gown.

Jonah lay spread-eagled with the sheet twisted around his legs, pulled only waist high. His chest gleamed bare, damp with sweat.

The four casement windows were open to the storm, gauzy curtains writhing in the wind. Rain pooled in lightning-reflecting droplets on the sills and wood floor, but she didn't care. She was beyond caring about anything but the crazy need that had been building within her for days.

She needed Jonah's touch like she needed air, and this time, unlike the others, she refused to let him turn her away.

Now seeing with the acuity of a nimble cat, she crept toward the bed. Once there, she ever so slowly drew back the covers. Had she been dreaming, she couldn't have woven a more spellbinding sight.

For only an instant lightning kissed her husband's rock-hard form. Thighs of steel. Chest sculpted from marble. Arms of the most glorious flesh-toned granite. He'd thrown his head to the side, and in profile she saw both his beauty and his pain.

Like her, he wasn't all whole.

But tonight—right now—she would fix that.

She would complete him.

And come morning, when all this rain was wiped clear by dawn, he would thank her. And the two of them would once again be one.

Jonah groaned.

Damn, that felt good.

In his dream a woman—no, an angel—*his* Angel—leaned over him, sweeping his chest with her long silken hair, pressing soft, hot kisses to his abs.

Instantly hard, he shifted, hoping she'd get the hint that he wanted all of her on top of him, saddling up for a nice, long ride. Too bad this dream Angel was a tease, for the moment only into kissing.

But hey, that was okay.

He wasn't opposed to taking things slow. What he was opposed to was taking them nowhere, like he had with Angel for the past couple of weeks.

Outside, or maybe in his head—didn't really matter which—the storms that'd been stoked all afternoon under the tender ministrations of tropical heat were only just now reaching their climax.

As for him . . . he had quite a ways to go.

Grabbing his dream Angel by her upper arms, he dragged her up the length of him, loving the softness of her silken curves against his solid steel.

Steel? Come on, Jonah, my man. Layin' it on a bit thick there, aren't ya, bud?

Burying his fingers in this temptress's hair, he told the voice in his head to shut up. This was his dream, and by God, he'd be made of steel if he damn well pleased!

Her mouth fell even with his, and he kissed her hard, making up for all the times he'd wanted to kiss her but couldn't. Needed to kiss her but knew he shouldn't.

In the real world odds were she belonged to someone else. But in this world she was his for the taking, giving, loving, and before the night was out he intended to do all three.

Her lips pressed pliant and warm against his, and when she groaned her pleasure he sent one hand sliding into a deeper exploration of her wild hair, the other on a trek down her back. Cool velvet was the only way to describe the sensuous slope of her spine, rising up into the sweetest mound of backside God ever created.

He intensified their kiss, memorizing the feel of her tongue stroking his, the forbidden honey-sweet smell and taste of her breath. This moment, this memory, might be all of her he ever had, and with that in mind he intended to milk it for all it was worth.

With a grunt of pure, masculine pleasure, he turned the tables, spinning her over to land himself on top.

Time for more than kisses.

Time for breasts and belly and inner thighs and all the delectable places in between.

"I love you," he said, because in this dream world he could.

And with her left nipple swelling in the palm of his hand, she replied in a fevered, raspy voice that she loved him, too. And that was all he needed to drive him over the edge.

All at once he was kissing her again, telling himself over and over that if he wished it hard enough, if he willed it so, he could somehow make it possible for her to stay. To keep being a mother to Katie, a wife to him in every single way—most especially the one they were currently engaged in!

She was kissing him back, squirming and bucking beneath him, running her fingers through his hair.

The two of them flowed like a windswept song, frantically exploring in rising and slowing pitches.

He drew first one of her life-sustaining breasts into his mouth and suckled and, when milk came, though she pushed him away, he returned to her other for more.

He moved on to her belly, feasting there in greedy nips and laves. And then he was moving lower, pressing his hand between her thighs, finding it damp there with sweat and desire.

Shifting to a sitting position between her legs, drawing those endless golden limbs around his waist, he granted himself full access to her womanly core.

She squirmed against him, claiming he shouldn't, but he was right there reminding her that this was his dream, and ever since he'd first laid eyes on her all those days ago at his diner he'd wanted to pleasure her in ways she hadn't dreamed possible. And so she acquiesced, tossing her head to and fro with each thrust of his tongue.

By the end of this night he hoped to ruin her for all other men. He hoped to brand her with lovemaking so intense, so carnal, so elemental and raw and exquisitely right that even if she was married, she'd have no choice but to leave that other man—that nobody man—for him.

In this dream land, far from his real life, Jonah chose his destiny, and that destiny began with making Angel his wife.

He brought her to climax twice.

Once with his fingers, again with his tongue, and while the storm battered the house around them, he sought shelter deep within her velvety folds.

She was hot, slick, and ready, drinking him in like a potion or spell.

And he rode.

Rode and rode like a madman through the storm.

He was once again pulling her up, setting her astride him so he could feast on both her magnificent breasts and her kiss-swollen lips. He could lose his fingers in her thick hair, bury his face in the sweet curve of her neck.

Outside lightning slashed, thunder roared.

Inside he roared, for in her, he'd become king. Master of his ship and destiny. In Angel, he could do anything, be anything. If only for this one moment, this one night. All fear was gone, replaced by joy and hope, building within him like the brightest, most brilliant rays of the sun.

And then he was coming, coming, and she was reaching out for him, meeting him along the way. Hugging, laughing, kissing, they rode together, beating back the storm, becoming one with it, reveling in cooling rivulets of rain.

Cupping her face in his hands, he said, "I love you. I adore you. No matter what, you must promise to always be mine."

Lightning illuminated her aquamarine eyes, and they shone huge, and he couldn't tell whether tears fell from them or rain, but it wouldn't have mattered either way, for the smile lighting her face shone a thousand times brighter than any mere flash from a storm. Her light came from within, filling him with her magic and her awe.

And while the rain raged around them, he ever so gently lifted her from him, easing her back to the bed, where he nestled a downy pillow beneath her head.

True, all of it had only been a dream, but even dream angels needed their sleep.

And with that thought in mind he lay down beside her, spooning her, the gentle curve of her belly warming his palm.

Geneva switched off her view screen and fell back on her newly installed supple cloud couch.

Wow. Wow, oh wow, oh wow.

NAME: _____

ADDRESS: _____

_____

_____

TELEPHONE: _____

E-MAIL: _____

_____ I want to pay by credit card.

__ Visa   __ MasterCard   __ Discover

Account Number: _____

Expiration date: _____

SIGNATURE: _____

Send this form, along with $2.00 shipping
and handling for your FREE books, to:

Love Spell Romance Book Club
20 Academy Street
Norwalk, CT 06850-4032

Or fax (must include credit card
information!) to: 610.995.9274.
You can also sign up on the Web
_at_ www.dorchesterpub.com.

Offer open to residents of the U.S. and
Canada only. Canadian residents, please
call 1.800.481.9191 for pricing information.

What was the one thing missing from Heaven?

Cigarettes.

No, she hadn't stayed around to watch all of Blondie and Jonah's big show, but what little she had seen left her horny as hell and needing a smoke.

Geesh, she'd spent her entire mortal life looking for a little excitement, a little grace, when all along it'd been right there under her nose in the form of her husband.

Make no mistake, she and Jonah had shared some pretty hot nights, but nothing like this. For the few minutes she watched, she hadn't just seen the love flowing between those two but felt it.

Felt it in a way she'd never experienced love herself.

What she'd missed out on was genuine depth. Substance. And that made her sad. Not just for herself, but even for her daughter, because if she hadn't been such a coward when it came to opening herself up to true emotions, she could have so easily loved her child.

Now it was too late for her, but at least in hooking up Angel with Jonah, she'd given both he and Katie a second chance—at least she would if she could decipher Angel's mystery before Sam did.

The question was, how to go about informing herself without tipping him off? After all, if the news did turn out to be bad where Angel's past was concerned, it was Geneva's duty to provide instant damage control.

But how?

Rubbing what she thought was her forehead, Geneva jumped to hear footsteps coming up from behind her.

There was Elvis, swaggering her way with his guitar slung across his shoulder and his handsome mug sporting a lethally sexy grin.

"Geesh," she said, "what is it with you people, always sneaking around?"

201

"And here I thought I'd be playing to a friendly crowd. Want me to come back some other time?"

"No. In fact, maybe you can help."

She explained the basics of her problem, after which, the King snapped himself a chair, took a seat, and played her a charming acoustic rendition of "Stranger in the Crowd."

"Mind keeping it down?" Sam glared out his bedroom window at the rain pelting his window.

As if flipping him a cosmic bird, lightning struck uncomfortably close. The resulting thunder shook the house like some rotten teenager out to avenge his latest speeding ticket by lobbing a live grenade down Sam's chimney.

"Thanks," he said to the heavens. "Yeah, that was real nice."

He gave his cheap, poly-fil pillow a couple of punches, swearing that if he ever got a raise he'd blow it all on comfortable bedding.

He rolled over for a glance at the glowing red numbers on his alarm clock, but the power must've gone out, because the rectangular box was black.

Finding some solace in the fact that at least he wasn't out on patrol working a wreck, he rolled back over and promptly fell into a shallow sleep. A sleep filled with freaky psychedelic imagery like floating tie-dyed peace signs and mushrooms and hippies reclining on big pillows smoking joints.

He should've arrested the lot of them, but a couple of the chicks were hot, wearing hip-hugging jeans cutoffs and leather halters with lots of beads and fringe. And boy, oh boy, look at the cleavage. Mounds of it. Enough to keep him happy for many nights to come.

Even better, they had boxes and boxes of greasy pizza!

And then this one particularly hot chick glided through the pot-smoke haze, dancing all Mata Hari–like to slow Led Zeppelin.

Sam just stood there, staring like a junior high kid freaking over his first public boner, as she danced his way, gyrating saucy hips and bouncing her red hots around in that macramé halter.

He'd freakin' explode if he couldn't at least kiss her, but when he tried she skittered away, laughing, teasing, shaking her sweet derrière in time to the music.

"You know what you need to do," she said.

"Take you right here on the floor?"

She grinned. "Sounds like fun, but that's not it."

"What, then? Hells bells, just give me a hint." She'd sassed her hips within grabbing distance, and he slipped his hand behind her back, cinching her close.

"Naughty, naughty," she said, pushing herself free, wagging her finger at him like she was scolding a bad little boy. "Mustn't touch—at least not until you tell me what I need to know."

"What? For you, I'm an open book."

"All right then . . ." She was back, standing on her tiptoes, slipping her arms around his neck to draw his ear to her delectable mouth. ". . . Tell me everything you know about searching for missing persons."

He frowned. What kind of crappy dream was this?

"Oh," she moaned into his right ear, filling the cavity with her moist, hot breath. "I promise, Chief Lawson, if you tell me everything I need to know, I'll fulfill your wildest fantasies."

"Promise?"

Presumably to show him she meant business, she

kissed him, writhing her way into his senses with her nimble tongue, doing things he'd never even read about in *Penthouse*!

"Do we have a deal?" she asked, stepping back.

"Lady, for you, my mind is an open book."

CHAPTER TWELVE

Crashing thunder jolted Jonah awake.

It was light outside, which meant he was already late for work. And tired. Tired didn't begin to describe the bone-deep weary he felt coming on.

Damn this crazy weather. The booming kept him up half the night. And those dreams.

Talk about X-rated.

Grinning about his dreamland prowess, he reached low for his usual morning scratch, only instead of meeting up with cotton boxers he found nothing but skin. No cause for alarm, though; he vaguely remembered stepping from his second cold shower straight back to bed.

He sat up.

What he needed was a quick peek at his baby girl, then a steaming shower—all while carefully avoiding

Angel. His dreams of her were still too fresh. Too real. Real to the point that it looked like his morning shower would have to be cold, too.

He'd just pushed himself to his feet when he spotted an inconsistency in standard Jonah McBride bedtime procedure.

Every night since he'd turned eighteen and his mom quit giving him flack about too many pillows being bad for his back, he'd slept with two. Both neatly stacked. Even when he'd shared his bed with Geneva, every night he slept the same way. So how come last night should have been any different?

Different enough that one of his pillows was off the stack, nestled sweetly right up alongside it? And how come in the center of that pillow was a very long, very blond hair?

Jonah wasn't sure whether to clutch his head or gut. Either way, suddenly he didn't feel so hot.

The crazy night had been *just* a dream, right?

Hand on the cast-iron footboard, he turned the corner only to face still more condemning evidence. An ivory silk nightgown and matching lacy panties were pooled beside the head of his bed.

No. He shook his head for further emphasis. No way was this happening. The night's fun—hell, the night's magic—had been a dream. Nothing more. All this other stuff could be easily explained away.

From down the hall came the sweet sounds of Angel singing a lullaby to Katie.

Leaping into action, he pulled on boxers, then jeans. Not bothering with a shirt, he stormed down the hall. "Angel?" he called out.

"In here."

He found her in the nursery's rocker, pink flannel

robe slipped over her left shoulder as she nursed his daughter. Katie balled her chubby hands into fists, kneading the breasts that, with cheeks flaming, Jonah recalled quite vividly having tasted himself.

"Good morning, sleepyhead," Angel said, looking up with a sunnier than usual smile. "I hope you don't mind. We, um, didn't get much sleep last night, so I called Leon and asked him to cover for you."

Mind? Jonah put his hand to his forehead. Expelled a deep breath. "Mind telling me why we didn't get much sleep?"

"In front of the baby?" She grinned. "Shame on you. A father shouldn't discuss such things in front of his daughter."

He looked to his bare feet. "Angel, I'm serious. Nothing happened between us, right?"

Those big eyes of hers got all teary. "You don't remember?"

Oh, I remember all right. Only this was one time I was hoping all of it was just a dream.

Katie had fallen asleep. Angel slid up the shoulder of her robe before saying, "I made breakfast. Just a second and I'll fix you a plate."

She made efficient work of laying Katie in her crib, pulling a light flannel cover over her bare legs before brushing past him.

He caught her by the shoulders, turned her to face him.

"What?" she said, her voice raspy and more than a little hurt.

To put it in her terminology, he felt like a prick. "I'm sorry."

She shrugged. "Doesn't matter."

"Of course it matters." He released her to raise his

207

hands, only to drop them against his thighs. "Honestly, I thought the whole thing was a dream. Angel, you know what we did—it never should have happened. It wasn't right."

"How can you say that?" she asked, tears streaming down her cheeks. "After the things we did—said. How can you possibly say that?"

"I said I'm sorry."

"I don't want an apology, Jonah. I want you to stand by those things you said. I want you to stop this stupid protector thing you've got going toward me and just be my husband. I want you to be the man you were last night. The man who held nothing back, either in words or actions."

"That it?" He flashed her a hopeful grin.

"This isn't funny," she said, pummeling his chest.

He caught her wrists. Used them to pull her close. "Let's get one thing straight."

"W-what?"

"Every damned word I said—I meant."

"Oh."

"Yeah, *oh*, Angel. There's a lot going on here you can't possibly understand."

"Then tell me. Let me at least try."

He shook his head.

"Wait. Let me guess. Doctor's orders?"

"Yes, as a matter of fact."

She struggled to get away, but he held firm.

"Let me go," she said between clenched teeth.

"Not until you cut me some slack."

"For what? Giving me the best night of my life, then claiming it was all just a dream?"

"I never said that."

"No, but you wanted to."

Releasing her right wrist, he curved his open palm to her cheek. "God, you're beautiful," he said, leaning forward, grazing her lips.

"Tell me something I don't already know." A smile tugged at the corners of her lips.

"Oh, so now you're getting feisty on me?"

She shrugged. "Maybe."

"So what if I do this?" He released her left hand as well, slipping both of his hands around her wisp of a waist, tugging her close, close enough that even if he didn't remember details of their night, his body did. Arousal struck hard and fast, and to give himself some glimmer of release, he pressed her even closer. "Now do you believe me?" he said on a groan into her ear, the heat of his breath catching in the fragrant web of her hair.

Her back to the door, he covered her lips with his, parting them with an irrepressible shuddering hunger. In a mere three weeks' time she'd bewitched him. Completely and utterly made him her all too willing slave. Nothing like Geneva, Angel was everything he'd ever wanted in a woman and so much more. "Woman, what have you done?"

After sidling free of his hold, she blew him a kiss. "Hopefully made you see that this nonsense the doctor said about you having to protect me is just that—nonsense. Now hurry up downstairs. Your breakfast is getting cold."

"Hot damn," Geneva said, eyes wide at just how well her osmosis computer lesson worked. She'd tried only a few of the tricks Sam taught her—computer tricks—none of the juicier stuff. She was an angel-in-training. Wouldn't want to mess up her rep now, just when things were going good.

Anyway, the information on Jonah's Angel was flowing. And compared to her, Geneva felt like a bona fide saint!

Whew, talk about your dirty laundry.

From the day she first set eyes on her, Geneva thought she looked familiar, and now she knew why. Blondie had a naughty past that read like a racy summer novel—not that Geneva was put off by any of the information. If anything, she had a newfound respect for her. Knowing she'd made her share of mistakes and lived to tell about them meant they had things in common beyond their love for Jonah and Katie.

Sure, she might be the image of the model wife now, but wow . . . Jonah was going to blow a gasket when he found out—if he found out.

The way Geneva saw it, Blondie's past wouldn't change anything about the person she'd become except in Jonah's eyes. If he treated his new woman anything like he had her, he'd expect her to be a perfect paragon of motherhood and sainthood and TV sitcom mom and wife that no real woman could ever live up to.

So here was a brand-new problem: how to erase Blondie's past without Jonah finding out about it.

Geneva plunked down hard on her cosmic couch.

Looked like she had her work cut out for her. A man to erase. A child. A whole other—

"Knock, knock."

She jumped. "Dammit, Teach. When are you ever gonna—"

"I did knock. Is it my fault you weren't listening?"

She flashed him her fiercest frown. "What do you want? I'm busy."

"I hear that. You're thinking loudly enough to have interrupted my beauty sleep."

She laughed.

"I'm here to do you a favor, Geneva."

"Oh, goody."

He glanced over his shoulder. "You'll be thinking goody after I give you this heads-up."

"What now?"

"You can't magically erase Angel's past."

"Why?"

"Because part of her personal journey is learning to deal with past mistakes."

"Yeah, but she's made some doozies and I'm down to what? like twenty-two days to get those two together?"

He glanced at his gold Rolex. "Try twenty-one."

"Great. That's just dandy. I know Jonah, and when he hears about this, he's gonna freak. He might be hot for her now, but believe me, once Sam reads him Blondie's rap sheet, that'll be the end of this cozy setup."

Teach frowned. "Even in light of all she's done for his baby?"

"Especially because of that. Shoot, I'm Katie's mother and even I wasn't good enough for her. You think for a second this new fallen angel will be?"

"Trying to fatten me up?" Jonah asked twenty minutes later, slipping a cloth napkin onto his lap. As usual, the kitchen table was set with his mother's best china, silver, and a vase brimming with flowers—this time pink and white tulips and red bud branches. Spread before him was a feast of scrambled eggs, bacon, French toast, syrup, juice, and coffee.

"A man needs plenty of good food to build stamina, don't you think?" Slipping a strip of bacon onto his plate from her still sizzling pan, she winked.

"What I think is that you're trouble with a capital T."

She set the pan back on the stove before joining him.

They'd been eating a few minutes in companionable silence when she said, "I've been thinking lately about ways we can save more money."

Bacon to his lips, he said, "Let's hear it."

"Well, I know how sensitive you are on the subject of the diner, but—"

"Aw, man." He dropped the bacon on his plate. "I knew all this was too good to be true. What do you want?"

"What is it with you and always thinking I want something?"

A little something I learned from my first wife.

"Why won't you for once consider maybe I'm wanting to give?"

"Give what?"

"My time. I sit around here all day, just me and Lizzy. Yes, I've made some improvements in the house, but that's not enough. I want to get out and do something. Be productive."

"You saying you want a job?"

"Not just any job. I want to work with you. At the diner."

"No. Absolutely not. Out of the question."

"Why?"

"B-because . . ." Because he'd tried it once with Geneva, and for that one week she'd made his life a living hell. Always acting like she knew best. Suggesting he cut costs by cutting portions. Being rude to his best customers. Refusing to wait on people because she thought it was beneath her. To her way of thinking, she was strictly management material.

Yeah, but that was Geneva. This is Angel. What if she's

as night-and-day different from Geneva at the diner as she is at home?

"Please, Jonah." She covered her hand with his, filling him with inexplicable warmth. "Just for today, let me and Lizzy come with you. I'll wait tables, do dishes—whatever. I just want to feel like I'm making a contribution."

"You are. The difference you've made in Lizzy means the world to me. But the diner—it's not fun. Most days, it's boring as hell. Going through the motions for nothing. Cooking lunch and dinner specials nobody eats. Baking pies that rot on the shelf."

"Fine. I'm prepared for all that and more. I . . ." She swallowed hard. Looked to her plate, then to him. "Especially after last night, I want to share everything with you. Good and bad."

"You know the pay's lousy," he offered as a final argument.

She grinned. "I work for kisses."

Leaning across the table, he did just that, kissed her sweetly yet urgently. Nothing this amazing, this right, could last. Sam was good. One of these days he would unravel Angel's mystery, but until then Jonah was determined to take each minute as it came.

Living, laughing, loving.

Oh, sure, he knew better than anyone he was doing all that in a fantasy world, but how did a man force himself to wake from the dream he'd waited his whole life to live?

"What's she doing here?" Sam asked, seated at the diner's counter.

"She's my wife. What do you think she's doing here?"

His friend's response gave Sam instant indigestion.

The one lead he thought he'd had on her vanished, right down to the detective's name, number, and precinct. If he didn't know better, Sam would've sworn the same teens messing with his computer and phone lines were messing with his head. Leaning across the counter, he all but hissed, "Don't you mean your *pretend* wife?"

"Don't start," Jonah warned, swiping a wet rag across the counter.

"What's the matter?" Sam asked, slanting a look Angel's way. "Long day?"

Jonah laughed. "Even longer night. Damn storms. If I got ten minutes' worth of sleep I'd be surprised."

"Yeah. Me, too." He finished his coffee. "Had some of the kinkiest damned dreams of my life."

Jonah blanched. "Thanks for sharing."

"You bet."

Across the room, Angel sat in a window booth, singing "Itsy Bitsy Spider" to a grinning Katie.

"She's got a helluva voice, doesn't she?" Jonah stopped his cleaning to simply stare. His expression turned all warm and fuzzy. Beat anything Sam had ever seen. It was like he'd fallen victim to a spell. Sighing, Sam waved his hand in front of Jonah's glazed eyes. "Earth to Jonah."

"What?" His tone was sharp as a bratty ten-year-old's whose mom called him away from cartoons to take out the trash.

"Not that you probably even care, but Cecil's place—looks like it was arson. Even worse, Cecil has a solid alibi."

Jonah cleared the remains of Sam's meat loaf special, a white plate, a water glass, and a crumpled paper napkin. "So?"

"So? He was my number-one suspect. I thought for sure he did it for the insurance. But now . . ."

"Jonah, sweetie?" Angel called out from across the room. "Come here; Lizzy just did the cutest thing." Forehead against the baby's, she cooed, "Didn't you do the cutest thing, sweet cheeks?"

Sam groaned when Jonah abandoned him to watch his kid blow a spit bubble.

Rubbing his jaw, Sam supposed he should be happy for Jonah. A few weeks earlier Katie had been in a bad way. Now, judging by the empty tables around him, it was just the diner in a bad way, but Jonah had his head so far up his ass making goo-goo eyes at Angel, it was like he wasn't even living on the same planet.

Sam would've been happy for Jonah if what he shared with Angel was the real deal, but as far as he could tell, she was nothing more than a Band-Aid covering the worst of Jonah's wounds. Take her out of the equation and his life would be as rotten as ever.

And therein lay the rub. Maybe not today, or even tomorrow, but she *would* be taken out.

For as long as he could remember, Sam's only passion in life had been solving mysteries. He'd helped out old Police Chief Stutts back in high school—even played a big part in solving the town's only murder.

Now, in less than a month, their normally quiet town had a strange woman making moves on one of its most respected citizens and an arsonist flaming half the historic downtown. Oh, sure, initial findings proved those second two fires were caused by oil-soaked rags and heat, but Sam wasn't buying it. They were too close to Stump's Hardware to have been coincidental. And the worst part of all this was, as long as Sam was saddled with the crappy equipment down at the station, he couldn't do a damn thing about any of it.

Oh, make no mistake, if he found a phone that worked, Sam knew damn well he could work miracles with at least Angel's case. But with the way things had been going, he might as well be working blindfolded, both hands tied behind his back.

Snatching his hat from the counter and plunking it on his head, he pressed his lips tight, eyeing the happy threesome laughing it up in the corner.

This couldn't help but end bad.

"Come on, Earl," Angel said, setting the elderly man's sausage and pancakes on the table. On only her second day waitressing, she already loved her job. And who said the pay was lousy? She'd already raked in a bundle in tips, and getting paid her hourly wages in Jonah's kisses made her feel rich as a millionaire. "You don't really want me to sing that old song again."

"Yes, yes, I do," he said with a clack of his dentures. "You sing purdy as a bluebird buildin' its nest."

"That's quite a compliment," she said, her hands on her hips. "For that, maybe I will have to sing it again." She launched into the song Judy Garland made famous, "Somewhere Over the Rainbow," oblivious to the other diners looking on. Doing her performance solely for the pleasure of this dear old man who'd said his now deceased wife used to sing this song to their babies. Babies who were now well into their fifties!

In the kitchen Leon said to Jonah, "If that don't beat all."

Jonah looked up from the pie crust he was rolling. "What?"

"The way that woman's singin'. Looks like she's been doin' it all her life."

Jonah shrugged. "Sings all the time around the house. Lizzy loves it. You should see her green eyes sparkle every time her momma launches into a song." Feeling his friend's stare, Jonah glanced up. "What?"

"Don't you mean Katie?"

Jonah sighed, fitting the flattened dough into a pie plate. "Most days I don't know what I mean. Guess she's growing on me."

"From the looks of it," Leon said, gesturing to the almost full counter crowd, "she's growing on everyone else, too. Word's spread fast."

"You think I'm wrong?"

"For what?"

"Not telling her the truth about how she came to be here?"

"Hard to say. Guess you could tell her the truth, but then most times she looks so happy, I'd kinda hate burstin' her bubble."

"You said *most times*." Jonah glopped the apple pie filling he'd already prepared into the shell. It smelled richly of cinnamon and butter and apples. "When have you seen her not looking happy?"

"Mostly 'round you. When you're in one of your strong moods where you think you're doin' her some big favor by not lettin' her get too carried away playing the part of your wife."

Jonah slapped the top crust on the pie, pinching the sides.

"Then there's times when you forget all about her bein' a stranger. Those times I catch you lookin' at her tendin' to little Katie. And she'll look at you and you look at her, and damn, boy, if it don't make my heart nearly burst just lookin' at you two."

"So what do you think I should do?" Jonah asked, sliding the pie into the oven.

"If it was me, I'd do nothin'. Lord knows there's precious few good times in this life, might as well enjoy the ones you get."

From the dining room came thunderous applause along with plenty of wolf whistles. Through the kitchen pass-through, Jonah watched, equally as dazzled as any one of those old geezers seated at the counter as his pretend wife took one last bow before freshening all of their coffees.

The day before had been the first day in over a year the diner turned a profit. Coincidence it also happened to be the same day the woman who single-handedly saved his baby now seemed to have turned her special magic onto his dying business as well?

The queasy churning in his stomach told him no.

Far from coincidence, Angel was meant to be in his life. Question was, for how much longer?

"You know, your fans are going to be royally ticked you're taking today off?" Hand-in-hand on Easter Sunday, Jonah and Angel walked the verbena-strewn field behind the house. The weather was balmy perfection. Not a cloud in the sky. Not a breath of wind. Over by the pond, a bullfrog croaked, and already there were plenty of insects about, buzzing and humming and chirping about the earth's good fortune.

Many March Easters Jonah remembered cold drizzle that devastated little girls and even big ones having to wear coats over their pretty new dresses, but on this sublime day gals would've been happy in bikinis. Come to think of it, that would've made the guys around these parts happy, too!

With Katie napping upstairs in her crib after spending a busy morning gumming plastic eggs and a big chocolate bunny, he and Angel were finally snatching a moment for themselves. Jonah carried the baby's new monitor in his free hand.

"Let them be ticked," Angel said. "Spending today together—as a family—is more important. Although Esther had her heart set on us going to church."

"I think she just has the hots for Reverend Matthews. Wants to suck up to him by padding the church roll."

Angel laughed. "I think you're right. Last Saturday we ran into him at a yard sale, and she said he had unusually tight buns for a man of the cloth."

"That sounds about like Esther. What about you?" he said, loving the way her buttery hair flowed with her every step.

"What about me?"

"What do you think of his buns?"

"There is only one set of buns around here that turn me on—yours." She brazenly pinched him on the right pocket of his faded jeans.

"Ouch. You've got mean fingers."

"That's not all I've got." She stopped walking to face him, press her palms to his chest. "Make love to me, Jonah."

"Here? Now?"

She nodded.

Sweeping stray locks of hair from her cheeks, he stared deep into her fathomless aquamarine eyes. "You know I want to."

"Then what's stopping you?"

"You know that, too."

She stood on her tiptoes to kiss him. It was a branding kiss, one that said he was hers with bold, brazen strokes of her tongue. When she pulled back, she said, "There. Did that seem like the kiss of a woman who's confused about anything? Least of all the man she loves?"

"Angel, I—"

Fingertips pressing the back of his head, she ground him to her, changing gears from need to desperation. "Please, Jonah," she said, pausing to catch her breath.

Pushing her lightly away, yet still keeping his hands curved atop her shoulders so she knew he wasn't pushing *her* away, just their actions, he said, "Not here. Not like this."

"But why?" Tears glistened in her jeweled eyes.

Sliding his hands to her cheeks, with the pads of his thumbs he brushed away her tears. "Because I—it's crazy. Truth? Because I love you too damned much."

"Y-you love me?"

Unable to catch her stare, not because of insincerity or shyness, but because he knew soul deep what he was doing was wrong. Because she wasn't his to love. He swallowed hard. Finally able to meet her searching gaze, he said, "When this is over, I'm going to marry you all over again."

"When what's over?"

He pressed a kiss to her forehead. "This thing with your memory."

"What if it never comes back?"

Good question. Then what would he do? Claim her like a stray cat or dog? Live years believing everything was fine, his and Katie's lives were perfect, only to one day have their rug jerked out from under them?

Just a week ago he might've said no, he wasn't willing to put either himself or Katie through that kind of possible hurt, but now . . . now his bond with Angel had reached the point where he had to consider her feelings. She was far too precious to put through a single second's hurt.

"Jonah?" She searched his expression.

"We'll know."

"How?" She wrinkled her forehead. "I mean, will you set a deadline? Like, say, if my memory doesn't return in a month, then will you agree to blow off everything the doctor said?"

"A month, huh?" Hands in his pockets, he turned his back on her to take in the lush fields and hills he'd spent his whole life viewing but not truly seeing. Being with Angel changed everything for the better. Whether it be washing dishes, changing diapers, or sharing something as simple as the springtime view, she made life worth living.

She transformed mountains into verdant ridges of green so vivid they registered deep purple and lavender and a hundred shades in between. Today, with the air crystalline clear, he felt as if with her hand in his he could see clear to forever. Some days these mountains were cloaked in fog or snow or raging thunderheads, but always he knew they were there, just like he knew no matter how hard he tried getting Angel out of his system, there was no way she'd go.

Like Blue Moon itself, she'd become a part of him.

No matter if her rightful husband along with a half-dozen babies claimed her tomorrow, he'd still love her.

Just like these mountains couldn't be moved, neither could his country boy's heart.

Jonah pulled Angel in for another hug. How long was a man legally, but most of all morally, supposed to wait to declare himself heir-apparent to another man's wife? "Yeah," he said, his voice unexpectedly coarse with emotion. "I guess a month sounds about right."

When she pulled back her eyes shimmered again, but this time he hoped with happiness. Her kiss-swollen lips parted in a wide grin, making her expression way brighter than the sun. "You're sure? I can start planning for our second wedding?"

If for no other reason than that financially he wasn't capable of supporting Angel the way she should be, he should have stalled, but after all she'd been through—after all *they'd* been through—he couldn't bear to ever again lose sight of her smile.

"Yeah," he said, brushing her sweet, salty lips with his. "A month and a few days—but don't go tellin' everyone just yet."

"Why not?"

Because I want to do some investigating of my own. At the moment I might not care for Sam, but he's always been a damn good cop. Conscientious to a fault, always getting his man, whether it be a shoplifter or the town's only murderer. If after both of them tried digging up Angel's past and failed, then maybe she was heaven-sent.

And maybe, seeing how she'd already cured Katie and was well on her way to giving the diner its first successful week in over a year, she'd been meant to fix that, too.

"I'm waiting," she said, standing on her tiptoes to kiss him again. "And don't you know it's rude to keep both your past and future bride waiting?"

"I know," he said. "Color me bad."

"Jonah McBride," she said, cupping his latest erection, "even without a memory, I know full well you've never been bad at anything."

CHAPTER THIRTEEN

Wednesday morning Jonah glanced through the diner's kitchen pass-through, falling more in love with his beautiful wife every minute—so much so that he kept forgetting the part about her being his pretend wife.

She crooned a song about love and yearning to Randy, the UPS guy, and damned if he didn't look like he was about to ruin his soup with drool.

Jonah's eyes welled with pride.

She's mine. This one-of-a-kind miracle woman is all mine.

Well . . . almost.

Angel chose June 15 as their wedding day. She'd wanted it earlier but ultimately decided that was the perfect day to become a June bride.

Just thinking about the hole he was daily digging

deeper had Jonah alternating between beyond belief happy and downright ill.

What had he done? Without knowing the truth about Angel, he couldn't marry her. How would they even get a license?

He had a home computer to research her on, but over a year earlier he'd canceled his Internet connection to save money. Knowing online would be the first logical place to start, he took Tuesday afternoon off under the guise of making a supply run to Harrison. Leaving Leon on his own to work with Angel and Pauline felt strange, but he'd done it not by choice but necessity.

Dammit, he'd made Angel a promise he full well intended to keep. If she wanted to be a June bride, then by God, she would.

Unfortunately, a two-hour search using the Harrison Public Library's computer netted him diddly other than adding one more question to the dozens already floating through his head. How much did a guy have to shell out for a forged wedding license?

Wednesday night Esther led the crowd of seniors she'd invited for dinner at the diner in a boisterous round of applause.

Angel had just serenaded them with the prettiest a cappella rendition of Pasty Cline's "Crazy" that Esther had ever heard—outside of hearing it sung by the great Ms. Cline herself on a long-ago visit to the Grand Ol' Opry.

Wearing one of the dresses she'd bought for a quarter at a yard sale and transformed into a full-fledged, form-fitting evening gown, Angel looked, sounded, and performed like a real live star.

Gerald Jorgenson actually had tears in his eyes. "You weren't kiddin', Esther. She's good."

Esther snorted. " 'Course she's good. Think I'd be springin' for all of y'all's dinners if she wasn't? Help me get the word out that Jonah's place might cost a little more than the senior citizen center, but the entertainment's much better than all those same old wacky hits of the fifties Emily keeps playin' over and over. Shoot, if I wanted to hear Martians beep beeping, all I'd have to do is double up on laxative." Emily was the senior center's head honcho. Nice girl, but she had no taste when it came to good tunes.

Just as his wife launched into a new number he didn't know the name of, Jonah pushed through the kitchen door, jockeying his way through the golden-age crowd to give Esther a quick hug. "Thanks," he whispered in her good ear.

"Thank *you*," she whispered back. "This one's a real keeper. Guess you knew that from the start, though, didn't you?"

He shrugged, not missing the sparkle in her pale blue eyes and hoping like hell she couldn't see the wet shine he knew must be in his own.

Times like this, with Katie cooing on one of her adopted great-grandmothers' laps, Angel singing up a storm, the diner filled to near capacity with both strangers and friends, he couldn't help but feel like the luckiest man in the world. He hadn't just dodged one bullet with Katie's health but another in the diner. And the more time went on, the more he was suspecting—hoping—he'd dodged another with his soon-to-be-real wife.

And what if not only were things looking up for the diner but the rest of the town? What if Bev Harding

225

rented the empty building beside his, and that business attracted even more? And what if all that business suddenly did exactly what Sam and a lot of other one-time business owners had dreamt about for years? Which was transforming Blue Moon from a forgotten place in time into a vibrant tourist destination. The kind of place with bed-and-breakfasts and antique stores and a real, live old-time restaurant called the Blue Moon Diner?

Yep, life just kept getting better, and Angel—*his* Angel—shone at the heart of everything good.

"You've got to be kidding." Covering the mouthpiece of the phone, Sam rolled over, stealing a glance at his bedside clock. Just past three in the morning. He rubbed the sleep from his eyes before saying, "No, Frank, you did the right thing. I'll be right down."

Fifteen minutes later Sam stood on Main Street beside Frank Churchill, Blue Moon's fire chief. What a year earlier used to be Sweet Treat Bakery—seven doors down from Jonah's diner—had burned to the ground. While the main structure was brick, the supporting interior was constructed of well over hundred-year-old dry oak timbers that'd lit up like tissue paper. The surrounding wing walls crumbled, leaving a jagged pile of still smoldering brick.

Sam's nostrils flared at the acrid sweet smell. "What do you make of this?"

Hands on his hips, watching his crew douse the charred remains, Frank shook his head. "No way to tell till we get all this cooled off. By the time we were called in, it was already too late to save the structure."

"Who made the call?"

"Callie Cook. Says the only way to get that new baby of hers to sleep is drivin' it around. She got us on her cell. Calm night. If there'd been even a breath of wind, we'd be lucky if we didn't lose the whole damn block."

Never having been prone to pussyfooting around, Sam asked straight out, "Arson?"

Frank sighed. "Off the record. This being number four in just under as many weeks, that'd be my guess. But who knows?"

"Yeah." Lately that phrase summed up a lot in his life. Who knew who was systematically burning his way through Blue Moon's historic downtown? Who knew what was going on with his computer, phone, and fax? Who knew if Angel was friend or foe?

Back to the fires, Sam had his short list of suspects. A few disgruntled teens, Cecil, or, for that matter, maybe they'd all been accidentally caused by itinerant bums. Hells bells, at this point everyone in town was suspect, from the boy mayor to Angel. Hardening his jaw, Sam said, "Yep, who knows?"

"If this don't beat all," Leon said, standing on the sidewalk in front of the diner, surveying the too-close-for-comfort damage. "And just last night the wife told me Bev Harding rented the place to Mary Alice King. Said she was gonna open a flower shop."

"Would've been nice," Jonah said, incapable of even imagining the heat that must've been generated to take out such a sturdy brick building.

An early morning thunderstorm might've cooled any leftover hot coals, but the steamy air only intensified the charred-sweet smell. Even inside the diner the stench was inescapable.

"How awful," Angel said, stepping out of the diner's door. "It's even worse than it seemed driving in the truck."

"You get Lizzy changed?" Jonah asked.

"Yeah, she's in her playpen. Pauline is with her, assembling silverware and napkin rolls."

Jonah nodded, slipping his arm about Angel's shoulders.

Why? Just when everything for once seemed to be looking up, did something like this happen? Had it only been the night before that not only his future but the town's looked bright?

"You okay?" Angel asked.

"Truthfully? I don't know."

Leon said, "Let's get on inside. Folks be linin' up soon to hear their angel sing 'em through breakfast."

"You go on," Angel said. "We'll be right in."

With Leon out of earshot in the kitchen, Angel said, "Tell me what's going on in that handsome head of yours."

He squeezed her hand. "I've lived in this town all my life."

"Yeah, so?"

"So, I find it a little odd that all in the same month four buildings that've been here since—since, hell, even before Esther was born, should just go up in smoke."

"I thought they proved the first one was arson."

"They did."

"And the others were what? Spontaneous combustion?"

"Supposedly."

"So you're thinking this one wasn't accidental?"

Shrugging, he said, "I don't know what I'm thinking. Just seems odd. I mean, if it *is* arson, why would anyone even bother taking these old buildings out?"

* * *

228

"After you," Jonah said, late that night, unlocking the house's back door, then pushing it open, gesturing for Angel to step through.

"Such a gentleman," she said, sleeping Katie tucked against her chest.

"I try."

She blew him a kiss.

Once inside he flicked on a few lights. The house's peace came as a welcome break after the frenzied pace of the diner.

He was out of practice.

He'd been sure the fire would keep people away, but in supposing that he'd underestimated his Angel. The place had been packed. Maybe folks were there to hear his wife; others, to pay their respects to a dying downtown. Whatever the reason, he'd run out of both chocolate cream pie and meat loaf.

Money in his pockets, a healthy baby and a beautiful woman in his arms—hot damn, did life get any better?

Yeah, the day he slipped his ring on Angel, making all this bliss a permanent thing.

"Come here, you two," he said to Angel and Katie, pulling them both close. He kissed the baby on her sweet-smelling forehead, then his soon-to-be-wife full on her lips. She tasted of the lemon meringue pie they'd shared on the way home. "Have I told you lately how much I love you?"

"Actually, no," she said, that smile he so loved playing about her full lips. "Tell me again. It's something I can never hear enough."

Lifting her by the waist, spinning her and Katie round and round, he said, "I love you, I love you, I love you."

"Jonah!" she shrieked. "Put us down. You'll hurt yourself and the baby."

"Nah, I'm too happy to be hurt."

"Me, too."

Both breathless, they kissed some more, swaying beneath the kitchen light's hundred watt glare to the silent music playing in their hearts.

For once Geneva didn't bother swiping at the tears that weren't supposed to be falling. The sight of Jonah and Katie and Angel laughing and loving struck a chord deep in her long frozen soul.

Maybe until just now she'd never even truly believed in love, but watching those two, seeing the positive physical manifestations their love had brought about, how could she not believe?

Love makes the world go 'round, and for once she felt as if she was on the receiving end. For once she understood that old saying, "It's better to give than to receive." Because, essentially, she'd given Blondie to Jonah and Katie.

Oh, sure, at first she'd been a little shaky on the idea, but now that all her plans were finally coming to fruition, their wedding in sight, she was soon to be on the express train to heaven. Even Teach himself couldn't stop that!

"I like your style," Elvis said, creeping up behind her dressed in white leather sprinkled with a rainbow of rhinestones. "Those two look great together."

"Thanks." Geneva preened. "Speaking of looking great . . . wow. Super outfit."

"Thank you," he said. "Thank you very much."

After they laughed a little more, flirted a little more, and Geneva pinched what was left of herself over the realization that she was starting to have a thing for the King, he said, "You ready for another song?"

"Thought you'd never ask."

He snapped his thumb and forefinger and bam—she sank into a scandalously rich lounge chair upholstered in purple faux fur.

A low stage appeared beneath Elvis's feet, and omnipresent lights made the rhinestones on his suit glitter so brightly she wished she had shades. But then the light softened, and a ghostly drummer appeared, tapping out a catchy beat on a high-hat. And then Elvis was crooning the sweetest tune yet, "A Pocket Full of Rainbows," making Geneva feel as if she had a destiny full of rainbows.

Yep, this song was proof she was finally heaven bound. And after all Teach's preaching, look how easy it'd been.

Easy breezy. Easy as pie.

As Elvis launched into a beautiful chorus, she laughed for the pure joy of being alive . . . er, rather, dead. Regardless of the cosmic state she was in, she was happy.

"Jonah," she whispered, "I have to agree with you. Though we've gone our separate ways, life and death are for once looking good."

Thursday night, Angel nursed Lizzy, then tucked her in for the night. Jonah was downstairs nuking the burgers they'd brought home and tackling breakfast dishes they hadn't had time to wash earlier.

Angel loved the positive changes the diner's increased traffic made in Jonah's mood. She loved performing for his customers, and especially spending so much time with him during the day, but for all of that pleasure, she could already tell it was going to be tough keeping up the pace.

Jonah knocked on Lizzy's door. "This a private party?"

"Sure is," Angel said, gazing up at him with more

love in her heart than she'd ever thought imaginable. "Good thing I put you on the exclusive guest list."

A sharp pain nipped Angel's temple.

"Look, lady, I know you're a big-time star and all, but for the last time, you're not on the list. Get a clue. The club's owner doesn't want you here. Says you're trouble."

Swigging off the pint of cheap vodka she'd had her limo driver pick up on the ride over, she waved the bouncer away. "Now, I can see where he used to think that. But that's all changed. See?" She flashed him her sexiest smile. "I'm all better."

The six-foot bruiser snorted. "Yeah, lady, you've changed all right—for the worse. Beat it."

"Angel?"

She looked up to see Jonah eyeing her oddly.

"Where'd you go?"

She shook her head. "I don't know."

Yes, you do. Hey, baby, I'm back.

"Okay, well, I just came up here to run an idea by you."

"Sure, shoot." She managed to hide her face and, hoped, her pounding pulse by tidying the lower shelf of the changing table. "No matter how many times I straighten these diapers, they always tip over."

"Leave that," he said, drawing her up and into his arms. "Come on, let's head downstairs and talk. I want to run something by you."

Seated at the kitchen table, their burgers and fries transferred from foil wrap to paper plates, Jonah finished his latest bite, then said, "You know how much folks seem to love your singing?"

"Yeah." And she loved performing, which was why she didn't understand why that scary voice was back.

Why now? Why just when everything was going so great?

"Well, I was thinking, you can't keep up this pace forever." He cupped his hand to her cheek. "I can already tell it's taking a toll."

"I feel fine."

"I know, but you've got to be tired."

"Really, I'm not that bad—especially since you hired Chevis back, and Precious has been coming in after school."

He beamed. "Interesting you should mention Precious. Has Pauline told you yet about her beauty queen aspirations?"

Angel snatched a fry. "I remember hearing something about the Miss Ed's Tire and Transmission competition. She wanted to know if you'd sponsor her." She looked down. "Seeing how we've had all this new business, I kind of told her that, in exchange for really good seats at the pageant, we'd cover her entry fee."

"How much is it?"

"A hundred bucks—but that includes a cool trophy—win or lose. And free lifetime tire balancing. She's young—that could end up being worth a bundle."

Jonah grinned. "I'm happy to be part of such a grand mission—and this'll be good, because my idea is that, seeing how folks around here are loving this serenading bit, how about asking Precious to cut back on her waitressing duties and start singing?"

"That's a great idea." She bounded from her seat to wrap him in a hug.

"Really? You think it'll fly?"

"Absolutely. This'll be great exposure for her. I remember starting out small, then—"

"Whoa." He brushed fallen sweeps of hair back from

her eyes. "What do you mean, you remember?"

She released a half-hearted giggle. "I guess I did say that, didn't I?"

"So? What do you remember? Have you sung like this before?"

"I don't know," she said, pressing her hands to her temples as she slid off his lap. "You tell me."

He shook his head. "Oh, no, doesn't work that way. The doctor said you have to remember on your own or it doesn't count."

"The doctor says!" she all but shrieked, grabbing a coffee cup from the counter and pitching it into the porcelain sink, where it shattered in a dozen pieces. "I'm getting goddamned sick of always hearing what the doctor says. I'm fine, dammit. Goddamn fine. Why won't anyone believe me?" Surveying the damage, she froze, her hand flying to her mouth, then scurried into action, picking up the broken shards.

By the time Jonah reached her, her hands were crisscrossed with tiny cuts and she'd dripped blood onto the counter and her pale yellow sundress and the floor and her face and hair.

"I'm so sorry," she said. "I don't know what came over me. One minute I was fine, the next . . ."

"It's okay," he said, grabbing two clean dish towels from the drawer beside the refrigerator, then wrapping her hands with them. When she had one green mitt with cows and a blue one with geese, he tucked her hands against his chest and enveloped her in a hug. "You scared me."

"I'm sorry."

"Don't be. We all have our moments. Come on." He took her by the goose hand, led her out of the kitchen, and turned out the lights, then led her up the stairs and into the hall bathroom. Still holding her, he sat on the edge of the claw-foot tub, turning on the taps, then adjusting the temperature so that it wasn't too cold or too hot, but just right.

He kissed her.

Nothing heavy. Nothing sexual.

Just a simple kiss. A hi-I'm-here-for-you-if-you-need-me kiss.

Next he unfastened the white daisy-shaped buttons on her dress, and when he'd opened all of them to her waist, he slipped the dress off her shoulders, grazing it past her hips, letting it whisper to the floor. She wore her nursing bra, and he reached behind her to unfasten it, too. He fumbled, and she tried reaching around to help him, but her mitts got in the way, and so he shooed her away and she just stared at him, great aquamarine eyes shimmering with unshed tears.

Her breasts were beautiful heavy orbs, nipples large and dark, pomegranate red. He hooked his thumbs into her panties, sliding them down, down, easing her left leg up and out, then her right.

She stood before him naked, unashamed, arms at her side.

"Get in," he said, his voice husky with words he didn't begin to know how to say.

He helped her into the tub, and when she was in and the water was steaming, and rising, rising, he stripped, too. Jerked his T-shirt over his head, kicked off his shoes, unbuttoned his fly, and dragged down his jeans and boxers, tamping them into an untidy pile.

When she eyed him with those aquamarine pools, he said, "Scoot."

And she did.

He got in behind her, easing her buttocks between

his legs, easing her back against his chest, the back of her head into the arch of his throat. With his right big toe, he turned the faucets off, then smoothed his hand over her forehead, the crown of her head and back, over and over, until he felt her breathing slow and she fell limp and warm in his arms.

Only with his Angel asleep did Jonah succumb to sleep himself, deliberately blocking out her remembrances right along with the violence those remembrances had bred.

There'd be time enough in the morning for analyzing.

Right now all he wanted was sleep. Wonderful sleep.

"You mean it?" Precious said Friday afternoon after school. "I can practice my pageant songs right here in the diner?"

"Yep." Jonah got a kick out of for once seeing the teen jazzed.

"And you'll pay me and everything?"

"Yep."

"Jinkies, Scooby Doo, this is so cool. I can't wait to tell Mom."

"She already knows. I ran this by her first."

"Oh, well, sure. Then just wait till I tell Heather." Heather was Sam's niece and Precious's best friend from the Blue Moon High School pom squad. "Can I call now?"

Seeing how the diner was in the lull between the lunch and supper crowds, Jonah waved her back to the office, where Angel was nursing Katie.

The bell over the diner's front door jangled when Sam walked in.

Tension still ran pretty thick between them, so Jonah was surprised to see his friend. Surprised, and instantly nauseous. Was he here with news about Angel's past?

"Jonah," Sam said, tipping his hat.

"Sam."

He mounted a counter stool. Took his hat off and parked it on the stool beside him. "Heard you've been doin' bang-up business around here."

"It's been okay." Jonah swiped at the counter with a wet rag.

"I hear more than okay. I hear you've had so much business you even had to rehire Chevis."

"True."

"I'm happy for you," Sam said. "No one deserves a piece of good luck more than you."

Jonah froze, eyed the man he'd done everything with, from fishing for bass to chasing after pretty women. "You serious?"

"You know me better than to think I go off spouting things I didn't mean."

"Yeah, I know. Thanks."

"You're welcome."

Jonah leaned closer. "Now that the pleasantries are out of the way, why are you here? Ready to blow me out of the water?"

"Whoa." Hands in the air, Sam leaned back. "Put your gun back in its holster there, Tex. I still don't know any more about Angel than I did the first day you called."

"How is that possible?"

"You think that's not a question I haven't asked myself twenty times a day since she got here?"

"Sorry."

"You should be." Sam leaned closer. "I'm on your side, pal."

"What about you thinking she's some psychotic, kidnapping ax murderer?"

Sam shrugged. "It's the cop in me. Hells bells, maybe she is, but at least if you go down, you'll go down happy."

"Ha ha. Can I get you anything?"

"Double cheeseburger, onion rings, and a chocolate malt—heavy on the malt."

Jonah tucked his order pencil behind his ear and whistled. "Boy mayor know you're on a bender?"

Sam laughed. "Funny you should mention the little pissant. He's the real reason I stopped by."

"Mmm." Angel leaned her head back and closed her eyes. "This was a great idea your mom had about setting up a picnic table back here." *Back here* being the grassy area behind the diner.

From there, the White River was just a stone's throw beyond the parking area. Beyond that, the railroad track that brought in coal to power stations on the other side of the state. This time in the afternoon the tracks were silent, as was the rest of the world, aside from chatty birds and the soft rustle of new leaves in maples and red buds and century-old oaks. The normally moody river had settled into a glassy flow, with sunbeams spotlighting dust motes dancing above the water.

Angel stretched, luxuriating in this oasis in her busy day.

Precious winced. "Actually, Mom isn't the one who did most of the talking. That would've been—" The teen fell silent.

"Who?" Angel asked, shading her eyes from the sun before checking on Lizzy, still content on a blanket beneath the shade of a dogwood, making buzzing noises while checking out her toes.

"No one. I forgot what I was going to say."

"You were talking about your mom, and her working as a tag team with someone else to convince Jonah to—"

"I'm going back inside to try Heather again. I'll bet she's offline by now."

"Precious, wait. I—" Too late; the teen was already through the screen door.

Angel frowned. Just one more incident to file away in her ever growing Twilight Zone drawer.

The door creaked open, and Angel glanced that way to see Jonah strolling into the sun. Just looking at him stole her breath away. His thick muss of dark hair and the dreamy dark eyes that she lost herself in and that made her feel not just safe but adored. "Hey, handsome," she called out, too lazy to get up from her seat, where she leaned against the picnic table's top.

"Hey, gorgeous."

"How're you feeling?"

"Fine. Why?"

He shrugged, taking the seat beside her. "Things have been so hectic, we never have had a chance to go over what happened last night."

She glanced at her bandaged hands. "Do we need to?"

"I don't know," he said, glancing her way. "Just thought you might. Seems like I read in a *Cosmo* one time that women like to talk."

"We do, but not all the time."

"Gotcha. Next time I'll keep that in mind." They

stayed quiet for a long while, staring at the river, at the lacy leaf shadows cast by golden afternoon sun. Jonah broke the silence with, "You'll never guess who was just in."

"Santa?"

"Little early."

"Easter Bunny?"

"Too late. And his gut and ears aren't quite as big."

"Ooooh," she said, casting him a grin. "Must be Sam."

Jonah winced. "I'm sure he'd be thrilled to know how easily recognizable he is."

"What'd he want?"

"To apologize."

"That's long overdue."

"And to run a theory by me."

She groaned, arched her face to catch more sun. "It's such a gorgeous day. Do you really want to ruin it?"

Trailing his index finger along her throat, then her collar bone, Jonah said, "How do you even know whether this theory is good or bad?"

She shot him a look. "If it originated from Super Cop—it's bad."

"Okay, so it's bad. You know all these fires?"

"Kind of hard to forget when a stiff breeze still blows ashes this way."

"He's wondering if the mayor could be behind them."

"What?" She sat up straight. "I know you guys aren't fond of him, but—"

"I know. Out there, isn't it?"

"And then some. Did you tell him he's just as wrong about that as he was about me being a closet criminal?"

CHAPTER FOURTEEN

"Go, go!" Geneva cried in the back seat of Sam's police cruiser, bobbing in her bubble as he chased down the bad guy. "Get him, Sam, get him!"

The guy driving a beat-up primer gray Lincoln pulled off old Highway 74 and onto John Peter Road. This particular stretch was dirt, and she'd have given anything to be able to slap Sam a high five for taking the curves good as any NASCAR driver.

She popped into the front seat, loving the fierce look of concentration in the police chief's stony gray gaze as he pressed even harder on the gas. To coin a phrase she'd learned from her new friend Elvis, geez, what a hunk o' burnin' love.

Back when she'd been alive, Geneva's friend Mindy used to live out on this road. About a quarter mile up there was a wide spot school buses used for turning around. Sam used *that now to pass the bad guy, effectively cutting him off by vrooming across the low water bridge, then slamming on his brakes, using his car as a barrier to stop the Lincoln from getting across.*

Sam jumped out, running around to the opposite side of the car to the concrete pilings placed to stop debris from taking out the bridge when the water was high. Today, though, the water was low. Maybe a couple of feet deep—five or six in the fishing/swimming hole old folks and kids used for weekend entertainment.

The road narrowed with steep embankments on either side, leaving no opportunity for the Lincoln's driver to turn. Either he had to back all the way to the school bus turnaround or surrender. Or Sam supposed there was always Option C, go for the "Dukes of Hazard" maneuver and try blowin' straight through his car.

Aw, hells bells . . .

From across the river came a series of guttural vrooms.

Sam darted out from behind his concrete wall just long enough to see a flash of light behind the Lincoln's tinted windows, then all hell broke loose when the kid gunned it, rear tires sending dirt, dust, and gravel flying halfway cross the county.

Frozen by what he could only guess was morbid fascination, Sam watched the whole thing unravel. The Lincoln hitting the bridge at what had to be fifty, a barefoot woman wearing hip-hugging, belly-baring jean cutoffs and a leather-fringed halter leaning against the driver's side door of his squad car, then moseying across the bridge.

"Nooooo!" Sam shouted, springing into action in what he prayed would be enough time to shove her out of harm's way, but before he even reached the bridge the driver must've caught sight of her and instinctively veered, for the Lincoln careened off the low water bridge and dove nose-first into the deepest portion of the fishing hole, the grill of the car stabbing into the clay bottom with such force that it now stuck straight up, rear-end ten feet above the water's lazy current. The driver must've landed face first into the horn; it hadn't stopped blaring since impact.

"No way . . ." Sam muttered, looking first for the girl, then back to the driver. But the girl was gone, and that horn was grating on his very last nerve, so after he waded chest deep to the Lincoln to check on the status of the driver, he made the sloshing, cold-as-hell trek back to his car to call Thelma.

Looked like they'd need a tow truck and an ambulance and the fire station's hazmat crew. No need for the EMT guys to hurry.

The driver was already dead.

"That was some trick you pulled," Teach said, strolling across the bridge, right through a tow truck and a burly guy named Ed who had hair the color of a dusty potato. "I don't know who taught you that, but Mr. Big asked me to inform you that physical manifestations are strictly prohibited for a student at your level."

Geneva cradled her forehead in her hands. "You've got to be kidding. What else was I supposed to do?"

"Let fate take its course."

"Sam could've been killed."

"What's it matter to you? You've stated on more than one occasion that you can hardly stomach the man."

"Yeah, but . . ." Geneva let her words trail off in favor of watching the man she was starting to love to hate.

* * *

"Dammit, Frank," Sam said, shaking his head. "There had to have been something I could've done. It didn't have to end this way."

Frank looked to the wall of green beside the creek before emitting a sharp laugh. "After what we found in the trunk of that boy's car. And after I think about how long all that gas is gonna be clogging up this creek—a creek me and my dad and my granddad and now me and my boys fish in, that kid can go straight to Hades."

Sam looked up, shaking his head. "You don't mean that."

"The hell I don't. You have any idea how much damage that punk has done in our town?"

"You pretty sure he's the one?"

"You tell me, Sam. What else would a kid his age be doin' joy ridin' with twenty milk jugs of gas stored in his trunk? You're damned lucky nothin' set it off. And if he was so innocent, why was he runnin' from you in the first place?"

Sam washed his face with his hands. "I don't know. It was a slow day and the boy mayor had just rode my ass like Zorro about my department needing to bring in more ticket revenue, so I saw this kid speeding with a busted brake light and decided to take my frustrations out on him. Shocked the hell out of me when he ran. And now this gas thing. How do we know he wasn't just working for some lawn company and made a run to fill up their tanks?"

Frank slanted him an incredulous look. "How long you been police chief?"

Sam sighed. "Long enough to know better. Much as I'm having a hard time believing it, I guess I just killed our arsonist."

"Correction, old friend," Frank slapped him on his back. "Our arsonist killed himself."

Round about eight-thirty, when Jonah glanced through the kitchen pass-through to see Sam stroll through the diner's door, wet, dirty, and reeking of gasoline, he hustled through the swinging door, leading the room in a round of applause.

Sam flashed the dozen customers a wave. "Y'all stop," he said. "What happened this afternoon isn't something I'm proud of."

"But just think," Randy, the UPS guy, said, "of how much more of our downtown you must've saved."

Sam mounted a counter stool. "You don't know that. We've got a long way to go until it's proven he's our man."

George said, "Frank told me there's not a doubt in his mind this is our guy."

Sam shook his head. "I'm glad Frank's conscience is so clear. Mine, on the other hand, could use about a pound of hamburger and an extra-large side of onion rings."

"You already had that for an after-school snack," Jonah thoughtfully pointed out.

Sam flipped him a halfhearted bird.

"Okay, then, looks like you'll be having it again for supper."

When Jonah returned to the kitchen to get started on Sam's order, he heard the bell over the door ringing but didn't pay much attention—that is, until he was back at the grill, back at his view of the pass-through, watching the boy mayor saunter up to the counter to shake Sam's hand.

"Who's that?" Angel asked, stepping up behind him.

She'd been in the office nursing Katie and missed Sam's big entrance.

"That is the infamous boy mayor."

She wrinkled her nose. "I've seen him."

"Sure. He's always lurking around town, trying to convince voters he cares."

She shook her head. "That's not it." Still pondering where she might've seen the man, she pushed through the swinging door and pasted a bright smile on her face in preparation for approaching Blue Moon's Man of the Hour. She still couldn't say that, after all of Sam's asinine accusations, he was one of her favorite people, but tonight, in ridding the town of that arsonist thug, he'd done them all a big favor.

Who knew? Maybe the diner would have been next?

After she gave Sam an awkward thank you, which he awkwardly accepted, the town's "boy mayor" offered his hand for Angel to shake. "And you might be?" he asked.

She fought to hide a grin. Sam and Jonah's name for the slight man fit. The fact that the mayor had baby cheeks that looked as if they only needed shaving once every other week didn't help in aging his button nose, comb over hairstyle, or the khaki pants and white button-down complete with tie and suspenders that looked more like a school uniform than mayoral garb.

Sam said, "This is the woman I've told you about, Mayor. Jonah's wife."

"Oh—oooh, of course. How could I forget?" Angel surrendered her hand to him, and in that instant blinding pain seized her left temple.

Even for one of her concerts, the backstage crush had reached almost unbearable proportions. Booze and cocaine were just the appetizers to what she soon feared would be-

come an all-out orgy. Once upon a time she'd thought she'd
be into that sort of thing. She'd thought good, old-fashioned
rock and roll was her ticket out of the lame hometown where
she'd ripened into womanhood only to feel like she was
withering on the vine.

After a month in LA, she signed with a legendary manager, and the rest had been history. She hadn't known just
how rare her easy success or her talent were until it was
too late to salvage either.

Tonight she longed to run and hide. Drown her sorrows
in a liter of vodka or rum. But now, she thought, rubbing
her rounded tummy, she couldn't even do that. The tabloids
accused her of getting fat, but only her manager and a
precious few others knew the truth.

Would the baby change things?

She hoped so, but gazing across the smoky, noisy room
at Talon, her baby's father, she doubted that where he was
concerned anything would ever change. A brunette with
practically neon fuchsia stripes in her hair had laid herself
out in front of him, begging him to do body shots off her.

She'd been watching for a good ten minutes when he
nestled his shot glass between the woman's ample breasts
and wrapped his lips around the glass, jerking the shot back
only to spit the glass out before sucking fresh-squeezed
lemon juice off yet another bare-chested woman's nipples.
He sucked salt off still another woman.

Sickened by what her life had become, how far it had
strayed from the one and only thing she'd ever wanted,
which was to belong, to be loved, she looked sharply away,
right into the face of a clean-cut kid, eyeing her black leather
stage get-up that, with its Empire waist, managed to hide
her tummy while thrusting her breasts high enough to be the
answer to his every wicked prayer.

"How much?" he asked above the music's throbbing beat.

247

"Excuse me?"

He waved a twenty in her face. "What'll this buy me?"

She shook her head. "I don't know what you're talking about."

"Sure you do," he said, tucking a stray piece of her hair behind her ear. When her only answer was a blank stare, he said, "Oh, I get it, this is all part of the game. You play hard to get, then I cough up more dough." Fishing in his back pocket, he pulled out his wallet and this time presented her with a hundred. "Don't want it said that I'm cheap."

"Oh, no," she said, slapping him hard enough that her fingers left an imprint on his boyishly pink cheek. "Lots of sins are forgettable, but being cheap isn't one of them."

"You okay?" the boy mayor asked, tightening his hold on Angel's hand.

She blanched. "I—I haven't been feeling all that good. I must need some air." Not knowing what else to do, she pushed through the kitchen door and ran out back, dragging in gulps of rich, river-musky air. Out here, a symphony of tree frogs and crickets did the only singing, and she was glad, for all of a sudden, far from bringing her joy, her musical talent scared her—bad.

The diner's screen door creaked open only to slam shut. "Angel?" Jonah strode across the small patch of lawn.

"Over here," she called from the river's edge.

"What's the matter? Sam said you turned white as a sheet, then ran outside."

She flashed him a smile. "It was nothing. Just too much excitement, what with the arsonist being caught, and meeting the infamous mayor, and the kitchen's heat. You know . . . too much."

Cupping her cheek, searching her face in the sliver of yellow light escaping the diner and the pale wash of moonlight filtering through the canopy of leaves, he said, "You scared me. I didn't know what was wrong."

She threw her arms around him for a tight hug. "Nothing." *As long as I have you, nothing could ever be wrong.*

In the morning, seeing how Katie was still sleeping at six, Jonah let Angel sleep, too, calling Leon to stop by and give him a ride, just in case his-soon-to-be-official wife wanted to drive herself down later.

The breakfast crowd was nuts.

All the old-timers had a thing for Angel, and when they found out she wasn't around to croon Patsy Cline's greatest hits over their biscuits and gravy there was grumbling all around.

At eight the phone rang. It was Angel, wanting to know why he hadn't woken her up. A fierce rush of affection streaked through him just hearing her voice. Unlike Geneva, who'd slept till noon every day without ever giving it a thought, Angel not only had an amazing work ethic but a conscience. She was amazing. And he loved her. And come hell or high water, on June 15 she'd be his.

They talked for a few more minutes, but he could tell she was still groggy, so he urged her back to bed, wishing like hell he was there to share it with her.

Hands trembling, Angel hung up Jonah's office phone extension.

She'd woken from a nightmare, run downstairs in search of Jonah, needing his strong arms, only to find him gone. Just like in her ugly dream—she was alone.

In her nightmare, like the other visions, she wasn't an amateur performer but a star.

Traveling from town to town, always visiting, never

belonging. A drifter without family or home. She thought her fans would love her. Take care of her. But they only wanted a piece of her. To touch her hair. Kiss her. Try taking her to bed. They didn't care about the hurt deep inside. The gnawing emptiness that no matter how hard she partied or drank never really went away.

Which was ridiculous, she thought, drawing her body to sit cross-legged in Jonah's big leather chair. Like the house, the chair was old and creaky and had a personality all its own, but it also provided a certain comfort. She liked knowing that, just like Jonah and herself and everything in this house, the chair had a history.

From outside came the faint whistle of the coal train passing through town. Just hearing its lonely wail reminded her how alone she felt without Jonah.

From down the hall came fitful cries, and Angel grappled out of the chair to care for her child.

The nightmare was stupid.

She was stupid for having given it a second thought. After all, it wasn't as if she had any real singing talent, and as for her being alone, she had more friends than she knew what to do with. Everyone knew her name and her life story, and in less than a month everyone she knew and loved most would share her joy when she married the man she loved most.

Scooping Lizzy into her arms, she said, "Momma's gonna make you the prettiest dress. You'll be the best-looking flower girl at any wedding ever."

Lizzy grinned, and the sight of it warmed Angel soul deep, washing away the previous night's ugliness and replacing it with sunbeams and rainbows.

Her, some kind of leather-wearing rock star?

The very idea was ridiculous.

She was a mother and a wife, and to prove it, she fed, bathed, and dressed Lizzy in record time. After all, she had some singing to do for her husband's lunch crowd.

"Ed Jackson, you know better than to leave that car sittin' there." Sam rubbed his eyes. Only ten on a Saturday morning and already his head felt ready to bust. Hells bells, Ed's Tire was one of the town's still bustling businesses. Didn't Ed have anything better to do than hassle him?

"I think people got a right to see it."

Sam groaned. "Come on, Ed, that car is evidence."

"It's also—"

Jonah stepped outside the diner, Angel right behind him, Katie in her arms. "What's up?" he said to Sam.

"See that?" Sam said, pointing to the mud-encrusted, busted-up Lincoln the arsonist had been driving. "Ed thinks it oughtta stay right here on Main Street for a while. You know, kind of like a warning to anyone else who gets a sudden hankering to torch one of our buildings."

Ed crossed his arms, pressed his lips tight.

Jonah whistled. "That thing's in pretty sorry shape."

"That's why I think it needs to be out here," Ed said. "People gotta know that here in Blue Moon, we don't take kindly to folks messin' with what's ours."

While the men went round and round on the issue of whether or not the car needed to be positioned for public viewing, Angel cradled Lizzy close, nuzzling her downy hair, gently rocking, staring, mesmerized by the crystal hanging from the dead arsonist's rearview mirror.

It caught a glint of sun, sparking for just an instant,

251

like a child's Fourth of July sparkler prematurely burned out. And then the pain was back, sharper than ever, like a hundred pushpins jabbing her eyes.

Desperate for air, she ran from the backstage party. The throbbing bass. The booze. The laughing. The cloying smoke from Marlboros and pot.

At the end of the dimly lit, dingy hall was an emergency exit. And she laughed, figuring if there ever had been an emergency in her life, this was it. Reaching the door, she pressed her palms flat against the cold steel panic bar, dragging in gulps of the frosty late December air.

It was four days before New Year's.

New Year's Eve she had a show in Vegas. A world away from this Little Rock gig that she'd only agreed to as a favor to her manager, who had ties and debts to the town.

Outside, she found herself in a service alley somewhere behind the arena she'd just played. The way her luck had been running, the door would lock behind her and she'd have to hoof it back around to the waiting limo. She tried it, and sure enough, it'd automatically locked.

Oh, well, she thought, already heading somewhere, anywhere, she hoped led to warmth. You wanted air and now you got it—all fifteen degrees!

She rounded a corner to face three stoners garbed in leather and sprawled across a brown expanse of grass.

"Dude," a wiry guy with hair longer than hers called out.

"Dude," she answered back, stepping over his legs to continue on her impromptu journey. She was rounding the arena's south corner, hoping it would be the last before she found her ride, when a glint caught her eye.

On the street beside the service alley sat a primer gray Lincoln, headlights on, exhaust cloud rising gray against the black night.

An object hanging from the rearview—a crystal, maybe,

caught a far-off streetlight's glow, sparking for just an instant, then falling to black.

The driver leaned out his head and waved another man over. The other man didn't fit. A pretty boy amid what had only an hour earlier been a sea of black leather and denim. The same pretty boy who'd offered her a hundred to take him to Heaven.

"Got my cash?"

Pretty Boy shushed the driver, casting darting glances over his shoulders before jogging to the passenger side and climbing in.

Continuing around the edge of the building, her lips curved into a half-smile. First-timers were always nervous about drug deals. Since alcohol had always done the job for her, she'd never tried harder candy, but she had plenty of friends who had, and Talon—Talon popped treats for any and all occasions.

She cast one last look at the transaction, then rounded the arena's corner. Three limos waited alongside the equipment trucks.

"Hey, Rose!" one of the guys called out, his breath white in the thin night air. "Talon was just lookin' for you."

He was? She quickened her pace, rubbing her hands along her bare shoulders, suddenly ready for the lights, the party, the heat. Talon's heat.

Back on Main Street, full sun raining heat on her suddenly chilled arms, Angel squeezed Lizzy tighter.

"I ain't movin' it," Ed said. "Me and the boys all agree that—"

Sam said, "Move it or I'm ticketing your truck. And then I'm hauling you in for tampering with a suspected crime scene."

"Aw, now, Sam, you wouldn't go and do a dumb thing like—"

"You callin' me dumb?" Sam snatched his cuffs off his utility belt only to slap them onto Ed's left wrist, then his right.

Jonah stepped in between the two of them. "Come on, Sam, I'm sure Ed didn't mean—"

"The hell I didn't."

"Did!"

"Didn't!"

Lizzy wailed.

"Would all of you stop!" Angel cried. "Look what you've done. You've scared poor Lizzy half to death."

"Lizzy?" Ed wrinkled his forehead. "I thought Jonah's kid's name was Katie."

Sam elbowed him in the ribs.

Thirty minutes later Angel pressed her hands to her forehead, willing away the swirling noise and color.

She was lying on the sofa in Jonah's diner office.

Lizzy gummed blocks on the rag rug.

A knock sounded on the door, then Jonah stepped in. "Sam and Ed are gone—as is the arsonist's car."

"Good," she said without opening her eyes. "That thing gave me the creeps."

"Yeah, the ladies from the First Baptist Church Bible Study Group came down to complain, too. Even the mayor stopped back by to make sure it was gone."

At the end of the couch, he wrapped his big, warm hands around her ankles, lifting her legs, sliding in under them, to massage her bare feet. "Lizzy seems okay."

"Are we?"

He stopped rubbing. "I don't get the question."

"Are we okay? You and me? Our relationship?"

Raising her left foot to his lips, he kissed all five toes. "These are cold. Better warm them up." Foot still to his mouth, he fogged her tootsies with warm breath, then blanketed them with his hands. He did the same for her other foot before admitting, "I've never loved you more."

"Forever?"

"What's up, Angel?"

She dropped her gaze. "I'm afraid."

"Of what? For once, everything looks great. Lizzy's healthy and happy. The diner's making a profit."

"Let's get married tonight."

"Why? We already are married." And, in Jonah's heart of hearts, his last statement wasn't a lie. He loved this woman more than he'd ever thought it possible to love. "Besides," he said, hoping to lighten the mood by tickling the toes he'd just kissed, "what about your fans? They've come to expect your singing meat loaf."

The headache, the voices, were back.

"What about your fans, Rose? You can't let them down. You have to go onstage."

"What about me, Grant? I'm tired. I'm seven months pregnant. I can't keep this up."

Her manager's expression hardened. "You signed contracts, Rose. This concert isn't something you can call off on a whim. We're talking at least fifteen thousand rabid fans out there."

"It's not a whim. I'm exhausted. We've been touring for months. Night after night putting up with Talon's BS. Squeezing my D-cup boobs into this stupid C-cup leather joke. The drinking, the drugs, the sex. I can't do it anymore. I won't."

His answer was a cold laugh. "That's where you're wrong, babe. You will, because I say you will."

"No," Angel said, jerking her feet from Jonah's lap,

clinging to her end of the long couch. "I'm not singing. Not tonight. Not ever."

Jonah's stomach sank. "But the diner. Your singing is what's bringing people back. You don't think they're in here for my cooking, do you? They're all hoping for a glimpse of you."

She stood, hands on her hips, and said, "What don't you get about the word *no*? I thought you were different, Jonah. Better. But you're not. You're just the same. Only after me for one damned thing. I thought you loved me. I thought—"

He was instantly on his feet, gripping her by her shoulders. "Let's get one thing straight. Yes, I love what your singing has done for this old place, but more than that, I love what it's done for me—what you've done for me. When I wake in the mornings and you're crooning lullabies to my daughter . . ." He cupped her face in his hands, drawing her to him for a lingering kiss. "That's what matters to me. That's what's important. Not the diner. Not whether old Earl's gonna get his panties in a wad if he doesn't hear you singing Patsy Cline while he's slurping his grits. You, baby. You're the only thing that matters."

Tears streamed down Angel's cheeks, and damn if Jonah didn't feel close to shedding a few of his own.

What was up with her?

She wasn't herself, but then the joke was on him, because he'd never known her true self. The woman she was today was due in large part to his molding. What if this latest outburst was her way of rallying against that molding?

Was he using her to keep the diner open, just like he'd used her to feed Katie?

Kissing Angel, stroking her hair, the curve of her

hips, he told himself over and over no—he wasn't using her. Would never use her. But if that were true, then how come his old friend guilt was back? How come he felt as if everything he'd spent these past weeks working toward was nothing more than a house of cards on the verge of collapse?

"Marry me, Jonah." She clung to him.

"Angel?" Still gripping her shoulders but searching her eyes, he said, "What's going on with you? You're shaking."

She was once again crying. "I'm afraid."

"Of what?"

"Losing you."

Funny, since he was the one afraid of losing her. "Baby, that's one thing you never have to be afraid of. Trust me," he said, wiping away her tears. "I'm yours for as long as you'll have me."

"Promise?" she asked, gazing up at him with eyes impossibly blue, impossibly racked with unnecessary confusion and pain. "No matter what?"

"No matter what."

CHAPTER FIFTEEN

Geneva scowled. "Oh, Jonah, I hope that's a promise you're prepared to stand by."

"And you, Geneva?" Teach said, popping himself onto her cloud. "What promises are you prepared to stand by?"

"I thought all I had to do was get them together. Don't they have to sort out the rest?"

He sighed. "Have you learned nothing?"

"What do you mean, 'have I learned nothing?' " she said, mocking his haughty tone. "I've worked my a—butt off trying to get those two together, keeping ol' eagle-eyed Sam off Angel's case. I've learned a lot about not only those two but myself. Haven't you heard all my serenades?"

"Certainly. But what I've also heard is your fascination with Blue Moon's dapper police chief getting the best of you. Do you have any idea how short you're running on time?"

"What? I've got two whole weeks. Jonah's already proposed. As long as he never finds out who Angel really is, I think it's a done deal."

"You think? All your life, Geneva, you have only considered what you think. Now you are being tutored in the fine art of considering what others think. For instance, how would your former husband feel if he learned the woman he thinks he's in love with is in reality you—only a thousand times worse?"

"Hey!" she said, leaping up from the couch, hands on her hips. "Take that back! I was never even half as bad as her—at least not until the night . . . well, you know."

"Yes, how well I know." He rolled his eyes. "Which is precisely why I'm now wondering if maybe Jonah and Angel aren't meant for each other at all. In fact, what if you made a mistake and Angel isn't the true soul mate he's supposed to be with?"

"I made a mistake? I've only got fourteen days to find out if I get to rush that big sorority in the sky and now you're telling me I might have to start over?"

He shrugged.

"Answer me! Don't just sit there like an overfilled jelly doughnut."

"The answers are for you to find, my dear."

"I've had it with the hoity-toity euphemisms," she said, snatching him by the lapels of his fancy-schmancy black suit. Either you tell me if Angel's the real woman for Jonah or else!"

Angel stared at the TV sitcom but didn't really watch. Jonah was in the kitchen cleaning up the dinner dishes. After her outburst at the diner he'd packed up Lizzy, called in still more newly hired reinforcements—two friends of Precious's who sang in her high school and church choirs—then ushered Angel to the truck, strapping in the baby before driving them both home, where he pampered them like crazy. Fixing Angel her favorite orange spice tea. Letting Lizzy play extra long in the tub. Preparing Angel an extra-special dinner of fresh trout that one of their customers brought in as a gift.

Working side-by-side to make a salad, they'd shared heated glances and touches and soft, nibbling kisses and giggles and sighs. He once again told her he loved her, but if that were true, why wouldn't he take that love all the way? Why wouldn't he renew their vows immediately? Why, when she merely mentioned the idea of them sleeping together, did he practically leap away?

And what was with these visions she kept having?

Were they dreams? Nightmares? Snatches of her former self? And if that were the case, how did she reconcile the woman she was today with the woman in those sometimes shocking images? That wasn't the kind of woman she'd ever wanted to be. Was that why she and Jonah had grown apart?

Hand to her forehead, she slid her fingers into her hair and pulled. Physical pain was preferable to this constant confusion.

Jonah came into the living room, bearing still more tea. "Thought you might be thirsty," he said, setting his mother's best silver tray on the coffee table.

Gazing up at his dear, handsome face, at those dreamy dark eyes and that angular jaw always in need of a shave, she grinned, her mood lifting a hundred times over just to see him. "You wanting to float me away?"

"Never," he said, pressing a kiss to her forehead before sitting beside her on the sofa. "Because then I'd just have to swim after you—and I've never been all that keen on swimming."

Tucking her legs beneath her, she angled to face him. "You know how, don't you?"

"Of course I know how. Just had a bad skinny-dipping incident as a teen."

"Mmm, got caught, did you?"

"Oh, yeah—and by Sam's predecessor."

"Oooh, a case of *I fought the law and the law won?*"

"You know it." He dragged her giggling onto his lap.

"Know what I think?" she said, lying with her legs hooked over the sofa arm and her head in Jonah's lap.

"Oh, boy, I'm afraid you're going to tell me."

She jabbed him in the gut, but his reflexes were faster and he hardened up, reminding her—as if she needed reminding—of his amazing abs. "What I think," she said, breathless from more laughing, "is that you just haven't been skinny-dipping with the right girl. I never get caught."

"And you know this how?"

"Come on, Darren, just jump. We won't get caught."

She already stood on the impeccibly manicured lawn of Sulphur's richest citizens—the Philmoores. La dee da. Like they'd even notice if she and Darren took a quick dip in their pool.

He jumped the fence but still didn't look all that happy about their mission.

"Come on," she said, dragging him by the hand toward the glowing blue water. Dew had already settled on the grass, soaking through the thin canvas of her sneakers. They were new. A welcome-to-our-home gift from her latest foster family. They were nice—the shoes, and she guessed the family was okay. But their kids wore the hottest leather Reeboks, and there she was, stuck with plain old white canvas—and they weren't even Keds, but some cheap, knock-

off brand. The rubber rim around the soles wasn't even the same height all the way around.

"Rose, damned if you aren't going to get us in trouble again."

"I thought you had fun that night."

"I did, but"—he glanced over his shoulder—"you sure these people don't have guard dogs?"

She rolled her eyes, dragging him deeper into the yard, deeper into their illegal escapade. Finally they were there, poolside, so she pulled the one stunt that always reeled Darren all the way in.

She stripped.

The pool was quite a distance from the house.

Closer than the tennis court but farther than the putting green, so she took her time, tugging her T-shirt up nice and slow, loving the kiss of summer night air against her belly and breasts. She wore no bra—didn't have to, much to the happiness of her last foster dad, who had a penchant for copping feels.

His motto had been, more than a mouthful's a waste. She swallowed the bile rising with her all too fresh memory of the time he'd tried putting that motto to the test.

Centering herself in the here and now, Rose forgot about him. He was gone. Darren was the only one who mattered now. Pleasing him. Making him love her like she loved him.

With a pop of her hip, she carried on with her own motto: no matter what, the show must go on.

"Oh, baby," Darren said, settling onto a lounge chair. "Now that's what I like."

She swayed to a slow Prince song playing in her head.

The music.

It was always about the music with her. Music was her security blanket. Music would one day be her ticket out.

Unhooking the button on her frayed jean cutoffs, she slid

those down, too, taking her worn white cotton panties along for the ride, wishing they were a silky scrap of lace so she could use them as a prop to work Darren into a genuine lather. Not that it would've mattered; he was already right where she wanted him, his attention off the remote chance of them getting caught and solely, completely, on her.

"I j-just know."

"Angel? Baby, you okay?"

"Don't call me *baby*."

He flinched, searching her face. "Sure. Whatever you want. Sweetie, okay?"

She curved her lips into a half-smile, hoping, praying, he couldn't see the real her—whoever that was. "That'll be fine." One of his big hands rested on her left thigh, the other played in her hair. She slid his lower hand up the length of her until he was covering her breast. Just as her nipple hardened, so did he; she felt him swelling against the back of her head.

Yes. I'm back in control.

Now, if I just had a damned drink, I'd be—

Jonah slid his hand back to her thigh, giving her a gentle squeeze. His erection lost its sharp edge. "No," he said softly, still twirling a lock of her hair.

She swallowed hard.

I'm losing him. Just like Darren. Just like Talon. Just like every other man I've loved, I'm losing him.

Grabbing a throw pillow from the opposite end of the couch, he bunched it beneath her head before sliding out from under her.

"Where're you going?" she asked when he abandoned her on the sofa.

His gaze met hers and they stared at each other for a good, long time. She felt him searching her face and desperately wanted to know what it was he was searching for.

Signs that I'm not your wife, but the same lost little girl I've always been? Struggling most of my life to claim some space in this world. No one has ever loved me for me. They loved what I could give them. What housing me and feeding me would do for their fine, upstanding reputations. When I was a kid I was a master at stealing candy for my gang of hoodlum friends. As a teen I mastered sex. As an adult, still more sex until stupidly falling for Talon. But then I immersed myself in song. And for a while that had been good. Almost enough. But then things changed. And somewhere along the line I got lost. Lost in too few true friends. Too much booze.

Spending every night in a different town. Never belonging. Never fitting in. Never—

Go away! Angel screamed at the voices zinging through her head. *I'm not lost! I'm Jonah's wife. Lizzy's mother! I have friends! Lots and lots of friends!*

Angel squeezed her eyes shut tight, pressing her fingers to her temples, trying to ease the ever-increasing pain.

Somewhere in another part of the house she heard footsteps, and the kitchen tap being turned on and off. From town came the lonely call of the night train. More footsteps, and then Jonah was back, settling beside her, pressing a cool cloth to her fevered head.

"Want some aspirin?" he asked.

"No, thanks." *All I want is you.*

"Something to eat? Drink?"

"No!" The word came out too sharp. "I'm sorry," she said. "It's just these headaches."

He got up again.

"Where are you going?" *Why won't you stay with me?*

264

"I'm calling Doc. Something's wrong with you, Angel. You've been acting strange."

"No, really, I'm fine. It's just sinuses. Esther told me how this time of year, they're always bad, but the heat is making everyone worse."

"Then I should still call the doctor. Maybe he can prescribe something to help. You shouldn't have to put up with this kind of pain."

Why not? Pain is the only thing I've ever had that's been a hundred percent mine.

"Okay." She nodded. Swallowed hard. "I'll take some aspirin."

"Good."

While he left to get it, she sat up, darting wild glances about the room.

Think, Angel, think.

She pressed her fingers to her temples.

What you have now is real. Who knows where all this crap in your head is coming from?

Maybe a movie or book? Maybe one of those sappy TV movies of the week? What you have with Jonah is the real deal. You share a child. No doubt countless happy memories that one day soon will all come floating back. Right along with the photo albums and dried corsages and other mementos of your life that, per doctors' orders, your husband tucked away from your view.

"Here," Jonah said, handing her two white tablets and a glass of water. "Hope these help."

"Me, too," she said, willing the tremor in her hands to still. After she swallowed the pills and set her half-empty water glass on the coffee table, Jonah gathered her into his arms. "Where are we going?"

"We're going upstairs, then *you're* going to bed."

"Alone?"

He sighed. "I'll stay with you until you fall asleep, but after that"—he kissed her nose—"you're on your own."

Jonah kissed his sleeping Angel on her bare shoulder, drew up the sheets to cover the spot he'd kissed, then slipped off the bed, sneaking out of the room to ease the door shut behind him.

Her headache must've been a doozy; she fell asleep within five minutes of her head hitting the pillow. Within five minutes of that, Jonah was on the phone with Doc Penbrook.

He relayed Angel's symptoms. The headaches. Sudden mood swings.

When he finished, the doctor said, "Think she's regaining her memory? Some specifics she may remember from the accident could be frightening."

"She hasn't said anything about the accident or remembering anything." *Thank God*, Jonah added with a pounding heart. Was this it? Was this how he'd lose her? One more headache and bam—she'd be back with her former husband, baby, and life?

"Hmm." Doc stayed quiet for a moment, then, "I'm sorry, Jonah, but without examining her, for all I know she could just be having sinus trouble. Lord knows, what with this weather we've been having, I'm hearing enough complaints. Fierce sinus headache'll turn anyone into a bear."

"I know," Jonah said.

"Want me to have my nurse call you in the morning to set up an appointment?"

Yes, said the man who loved Angel and was genuinely concerned about her health and well-being.

No, said the selfish bastard who didn't give a damn

about anything other than his own happiness. With Angel in his house, in his arms, his life—Katie's life— worked. He never wanted her to get her memory back. And truth be told, every night he prayed Sam's fax and computer stayed permanently busted.

"Jonah? What about that appointment?"

He cleared his throat. "Um, thanks, Doc. But she seems fine now. I'll call you in a couple of days."

Clenching his jaw, Jonah stared at the phone.

Score one more for the selfish bastard.

Tuesday morning, during the lull between breakfast and lunch crowds, Jonah left Angel and Katie with Leon, Pauline, and Chevis to run down to the IGA for vanilla. When he'd been making pies, there'd been nearly a full bottle that had had an *accident*.

New bottle in his back pocket, he doubled back through the alley to the police station.

Already the temperature hovered in the high eighties. The forecast for their part of the state said temps could hit record-breaking mid-nineties by the end of the day.

His navy T-shirt soaked up the sun, and his back had already started to sweat. But then, that probably had more to do with the crow he was about to eat than anything to do with the weather.

"Hey, stranger," Thelma said when he walked in the door. She put her half-eaten Snickers beneath an open procedure manual. So much for the mayor's new health plan. "Haven't seen you in a while."

He flashed her a weak grin. "Been busy."

She winked. "I'll say. That Angel of yours is a real looker. The whole town's smitten."

"Thelma!" Sam called from his office.

"What?!!"

"Quit harassing our customer!"

"It's only Jonah."

Sam strolled out of his office, leaned against the doorjamb, and crossed his arms. "You showing up on my turf mean I'm forgiven?"

"That depends."

Sam straightened, ushering Jonah into his office. "Let the negotiations begin."

Jonah relayed the specifics of Angel's odd behavior, then leaned forward on a rickety wooden chair, resting his elbows on his knees. "Look, Sam, I know I've been pretty much a jackass over the past few weeks."

"Yeah." He cracked a grin.

Jonah flipped him the bird. "I'm serious here. I need your help. Christ," he said, slashing his fingers through his hair. "I don't know how or when or even why, but I've fallen for her, man—hard. And now . . ." He straightened, flopping his hands on his lap.

"Now, you don't know what to do."

"Right. That's it exactly."

"Tell me something I don't already know—hells bells, Jonah, the whole town knows you've fallen for her."

"So what do I do? What if these mood swings are connected to her memory? What if she wakes up tomorrow remembering her real husband and real kid?"

"I don't mean to be cruel, but you knew the risks going into this thing." He rifled through the short stack of dead-end leads on his desk. "This is all I've found on her. It's like she's ghost."

"What does that mean? In general, is it good or bad when a person's untraceable?"

Sam shook his head. "Jonah, I—"

"Tell me."

His old friend dropped his stony gaze.

"Great. That's all I needed to know."

Upon his return to the diner, armed with no more information than he'd left with, Jonah wasn't in the best mood, but then he caught sight of Angel, seated in the rocker in his office with Katie at her breast, and he felt nothing but a surge of protective love.

God help him, he knew loving this woman was wrong, but he couldn't help himself.

Even worse, he didn't want help.

Oh, sure, he'd gone to Sam looking for answers, but the sad truth was, far from being put off by Sam's negative take on there being no info on Angel, Jonah chose to take the no-news-is-good-news route.

"Hi, handsome." She looked up, drowning him in her aquamarine pools.

"Hi, yourself, gorgeous." He sauntered her way, kissing Katie on her cheek, then her new momma on her lips. To hell with Sam. Jonah figured what he and Angel shared felt too good to be wrong.

"We were starting to worry about you. Have to run to Little Rock for that vanilla?"

He took the small brown bottle from his back pocket. Gave it a shake. "Just took me a while to find it—and this." From his other pocket he withdrew a small sack of those peppermints she'd liked so much on their way home from Little Rock.

Her face lit up at the simple gift. "Thank you. Is it my birthday?"

"Nope." He unwrapped one and popped it into her mouth, letting his fingers linger on her soft, moist lips. Instantly hard, he took a swift breath and backed away.

269

"Admirable attempt, though, of trying to weasel information."

"Can't blame a girl for trying." Smoothing Katie's hair, she said, "You were gone an awfully long time."

"Uh huh."

"Go anywhere else?"

"Sam's."

"What for?"

He sat on the sofa. "I know you and Sam aren't exactly best friends, but—"

"Friends? The man all but accused me of being an ax murderer."

Making a face, he said, "I wouldn't go that far. He was—"

"He was what, Jonah? Protecting you? From what?" Katie had fallen asleep at her breast, so she fastened her bra and tugged down her scoop-necked white tee. "Your wife?" Standing, cradling Katie close, she said, "Yep, I'll bet folks for miles around have been locking up their kids, warning them away from that dangerous Angel McBride."

"Cut the drama. Nobody thinks that."

"The funny thing is, Jonah, I wouldn't care if anyone did think that—anyone but you."

"And I've already told you I don't. So can you and Sam call a truce?"

"Is that what he wants?"

Cupping her cheek, he said, "That's what I want."

"Okay, then. That's all you had to say."

"Just like that?" *No negotiations? No, if I buy you perfume, you promise to play nice?*

Eyes tearing, she nodded.

He pulled her into a tight hug, his emotions swelling. What had he done to deserve her? She was everything

270

he'd ever dreamed of finding in a woman and more. And even though he couldn't yet legally make her his, he could publicly stake his claim. And as luck would have it, she'd unwittingly already given him the perfect tool with which to do it.

CHAPTER SIXTEEN

Saturday night, Jonah stood beside the diner's cash register, surveying a crowd of about forty of Angel's new-found friends. "Okay, now," he said, "when she walks in, is everyone clear on what you're supposed to do?" Instead of the nods of agreement he'd hoped for, he got about forty blank stares.

He arched his head back and groaned.

No way were they going to pull this off. Something was bound to go wrong.

Esther probably already blabbed the surprise. Earl would dig out the center of the cake before Angel even got to see it. Angel was going to call from home and say she was too tired to come. Or Katie was too cranky to come. Or Katie was already sleeping.

I have to get hold of myself, Jonah thought, taking an

extra deep breath. *This night's gonna be perfect because by sheer will I'll make it perfect.*

That fact established, he posed his question again. "Are we clear? 'Cause if not, we can go over it one more time."

Precious, face hidden behind her Aunt Melvine's Camcorder, cracked her gum. "Like, we know, Jonah. It's not too tough, you know, just yelling 'surprise.' "

He made a face for the camera. "Cut me some slack. Is there a law against wanting this night to be special?"

"What's the occasion again?" Esther asked from her end seat at the diner's counter.

See? This was just the kind of thing that had him most worried. Referring to the twenty-foot banner strung between the back wall's row of booths, he read, " 'Happy Birthday, Angel.' Everybody got that?"

Esther scratched her head. "But how do you know it's her birthday?"

"I don't," Jonah said. "It's kind of her birthday."

"This the anniversary of the first night she came to town?" Pauline asked.

"Yes. Yes, in a way it is."

"Whaddayou mean? In a way?" Ed asked. "Is it or isn't it?"

"It is," Jonah said. "Yes. This is what? Week five she's been here?"

"I can't remember her not being here," Esther said. "She's a lovely girl."

"Here, here," Earl said, raising his third beer.

His third beer? Jonah hustled across the room to cut him off, on his way giving Esther a quick hug.

"Drink this," Jonah said, replacing Earl's Michelob with a tall glass of iced tea.

273

"Thought this was a party," Earl grumped. "I don't want no stinkin' iced—"

The bell over the door jingled. Angel walked in, Katie in her arms. "Hey, everybody," she said. "What's going on?"

"Surprise!" half the crowd yelled. The other half was still watching the drama unfold with Earl.

"Sing!" Jonah shouted. "Sing!"

As the crowd launched into a heartfelt rendition of "Happy Birthday," Angel put her free hand to her mouth. Before settling on him, her aquamarine pools filled with tears.

In that instant all the confusion, all the fear, was gone, distilling the true heart of the matter—their love—into one enchanted island in time that no matter what, the two of them would always share. "I love you," he mouthed.

"I love you, too," she mouthed back, cuddling Katie.

Gazing upon his girls made Jonah teary, too.

Yes.

His plan to prove his love to Angel—shoot, the whole town's love—had worked. Now all that was left to do was party—and wait for Angel's final surprise.

After the crowd finished singing, Frank, as previously instructed, fired up a newly installed jukebox. The only way Angel was going to be providing entertainment at her own party was if she chose to, if it benefitted her to do so, he thought with a small smile—not because she felt pressured in any way by a need to help him.

The whole time they'd been together, he'd fought that damn voice in his head accusing him of using her, but no more. Starting tonight—here, now—they were forging a partnership.

True, he might not be able to legally marry her, but

in his heart—and if she could talk, he assumed in Katie's—in every sense of the word, Angel had become his wife and his baby's mother. For all he knew, maybe tonight was her birthday. Or maybe her real birthday had been the night he found her huddled on the bathroom floor.

Precious filmed like crazy, trailing Angel through the human sea of laughter, well-wishes, and warm smiles. Across the room, Jonah waited patiently for Angel to hug her way to him. It took longer than he'd hoped, but that was okay. They had all the time in the world and she was certainly worth the wait.

"Hi, handsome," she said, finally in his arms.

"Hi, gorgeous." Enough talk. Time for kissing. Claiming.

As the party roared around them, to the accompaniment of some crazy alternative rock only Precious and her friends would've picked out, Jonah cinched Angel close, pressing his lips to the curve of her neck, loving it when she scrunched her head and giggled.

"That tickles," she said.

"You've never much minded before."

"You've never done it in front of so many people."

"Mmm," he said, doing it again. "An audience only makes it that much more interesting. Happy birthday, Angel."

Leaning into him, loving him, Angel could've melted with happiness.

In a million years her husband couldn't have found a more perfect way to make her feel loved. All her crazy visions, all her confusion and fear, all of it *had* just been bad dreams.

This was real.

These people were real.

This wonderful man kissing her and hugging her and laughing with her was real. And tonight was her birthday. Her birthday!

The only possible way Jonah—or any of her friends—would know this was the day she was born was to have been there—or at least known when and where that event had occurred.

Gazing up at Jonah's fresh-scrubbed, fresh-shaven, sexy-as-sin face, she said, "How old am I?"

He shook his head. "You know better than to ask me something like that. Remember what the doctor said? You have to remember everything on your own."

"Then how come you're throwing this party?"

"Because I love you."

She thought about pouting the information out of him but decided the act would take more energy than it was worth. Besides, why waste one minute even pretending to be sad when the night still held so much fun? "Come on," she said, taking her husband by the hand and leading him to the center of the room, where tables had been cleared for a dance floor. "I like this song. Let's boogie."

Hours later, bathed in a happy birthday glow, Angel snuck another piece of her yummy chocolate cake. Good thing she had connections with the chef. With any luck, she could con him into making her another one even when it wasn't her birthday.

"Having fun?" Esther asked from high atop the same stool she'd been on all night.

Angel nodded.

Esther grasped her hand and squeezed. "I'm glad. You've been very good to me," she said above the pulsing music. "Accompanying me to all my sales, saying my rubbery old pineapple upside-down cake tastes good. I'm so happy for you. You're just gonna love the gift me and Pauline helped Jonah cook up."

Angel gave the dear woman a hug. "Thank you, Esther, but you've already given me the best gift of all in your friendship."

The old woman snorted. "That sounds like a goddamned Hallmark commercial—but I'll take it just the same."

Finally used to Esther's unique way of stating things, Angel didn't even blink.

"See that guy?" Esther asked, pointing across the room to a heavyset man dressed in a black suit that looked far too hot and formal for the weather and the occasion. He sat alone in one of the back booths, nodding his head to the beat, taking it all in.

"Who is he? Do I know him?"

Esther shook her head. "I don't know him either, but anyway, he's your present."

Angel frowned. "What do you mean, he's my present?"

Esther winked.

"You mean like he's a male stripper? And if that *is* the case, wouldn't he be more suited to you, Miss Chippendale?"

Esther swatted Angel's forearm. "Don't be fresh. What I meant is that he's here for you—to listen to you."

"Listen to me what?"

"Sing, stupid. One of Pauline's pageant people knows him. He's a part-time celebrity-type reporter, part-time talent scout for some hotty-totty LA agency."

"But, Esther, I—"

Putting her thumb and forefinger to her lips, Esther whistled loud enough to get everyone's attention. She made a mysterious hand signal to Jonah, then he flicked on the lights and off the music. The added light brought attention to an area of the room Angel hadn't even noticed that used to house a booth big enough for eight. The booth had been removed and in its place was a small stage, complete with lights, upright piano, and red velvet curtains.

"What's this?" Angel asked Esther, still confused.

"The stage is Jonah's gift, the piano's mine, plus he helped me and Pauline track this talent fellow down. Had to call him in three different states. Cost more than a new washer and dryer to fly him out here from California."

Suddenly Jonah was at Angel's side, leading her toward the stage. "Jonah, I—"

"Shhh," he said in her ear. "Relax. This is for you. All for you."

"But—"

"All I ask is that you give this your best shot. I don't want you to ever feel you're here in Blue Moon out of any obligation to either me or Lizzy. I want you here because you want to be."

"Jonah," she said, searching his dear face for signs as to what could've brought this about. "I am here for you. Why would I ever want to go anywhere else?"

He shrugged. "The other day, when you accused me of using you—your talent—to keep this old place alive—I thought long and hard about that. And the conclusion I came to I didn't like. Maybe you're right. Maybe—"

She pressed her fingers to his lips. Shook her head with tears in her eyes.

"You've got to be sure," he said. "I want you to see

where this singing of yours can go. In short, I want you to see if you can fly."

Was this finally it? The root of why their marriage had almost been torn apart? Had she dreamt of pursuing some crazy dream of Hollywood while he wanted her here? Was that what all the visions meant? Had that been her subconscious trying to tell her what a mistake chasing that kind of life could be?

"Don't you know anything?" she said. "All I want is you. All I've ever wanted is you."

"Hey," the man in the suit said, eyeing her unnervingly closely. "I don't mean to interrupt, but I've got to head back to Little Rock ASAP. Tomorrow I've got an early flight home."

"Sorry," Angel said. "But I'm afraid my husband's dragged you all this way for nothing."

The man raised his eyebrows, looked to Jonah, then again to Angel, staring extra hard, almost as if he was trying to place her.

"You'll have to forgive my wife," Jonah said. "She's had way too much punch." He gave her a light shove, and suddenly she was onstage.

The overhead lights were out again and she was immersed in the wonderland of a whirling disco ball, scattering the stage's blue lights on all four walls of the room.

Someone set a mike stand in front of her.

She tapped it and found it hot.

Surprised, she jumped back with a nervous giggle, which made everyone else in the room laugh, too.

"Sing, already!" Earl hollered. "We've been waitin' all night."

"Yeah!" someone else cried out in the dark.

"Um, okay," she said shyly into the mike. "Does anyone have any requests?"

The suit was back to eyeing her funny. He made her nervous, so she concentrated on pretending he wasn't even in the room. After all, it wasn't as if he was likely to declare her the next singing sensation and whisk her off to LA.

"How 'bout Patsy Cline?" shouted Esther's friend, George.

"I like her Judy Garland better!"

"Linda Rondstadt!"

"Karen Carpenter!"

Precious ducked out from behind the Camcorder to shout, "Gwen Stefani!"

"Wow," Angel said. "That's a lot of requests. Don't know if I can handle that many."

The suit stepped forward. "How about Rebel Blue?"

"Excuse me?" She wrinkled her nose. "I'm not familiar with any of her songs."

" 'Fallen.' 'High Tide.' 'You.' Any of those ring a bell?" He was looking at her again. Staring. Staring so hard he made her itch.

Was this stage fright? Was she about to break into hives?

Her only response was another nervous giggle. "Let's leave songs like those to rock and roll professionals. I'll stick with the sentimental old stand-bys." Before he could tell her anything different, she launched into Miss Patsy Cline's "Crazy," and the crowd went wild.

Everyone, that is, except for the suit. He stood, arms crossed, right hand holding a microcassette recorder he'd pulled out midway through her song.

Ignoring him and his toy, she sat at the piano, quickening her pace with Whitney Houston's "I Wanna

Dance With Somebody." That especially got the younger crowd going and, surprisingly enough, her, too. It'd been a while since she'd sung anything fast—what was she saying—like she'd *ever* sung anything fast!

On and on she sang, pounding on the piano's keys until her voice grew hoarse and her fingers ached.

By that time the suit had vanished just as mysteriously as he'd appeared, and her spirits soared. Performing like this, in front of Jonah and all of her friends. Perfect. The night had been absolutely perfect.

Laughing, eyes pooling from the amazing outpouring of love, Angel finally said, "Really, you guys, I've got to stop."

"Aw, come on," Randy, the UPS guy, hollered. "Just one more!"

"Really," Angel said, hand on her throat. "I'm flattered you asked, but I can't—not tonight, anyway." She winked, blew the still cheering crowd a big kiss.

"You did it, babe!" Grant shouted above the still roaring crowd. "Not only did you fill your first arena, but you blew them away! This crowd loves you!"

Caught up in the excitement, she stepped into his outstretched arms, loving it when he hugged her tight, lifting her off the stage to spin her 'round and 'round.

"After tonight," he said, "You'll never want for anything. You're set, baby! You're a star."

"Really?" she asked once he set her back on the stage floor. *"You really think so?"*

He laughed. "Look at them." He nodded to the still cheering crowd. "Do you even have to ask?"

She did as he'd suggested. Really looked at them. At the teens screaming their love for her in the front row. At the hundreds of flash bulbs, blinding even after nearly three hours of show. The banners, offering anything from free joints and coke hits after the show to marriage. All her life, this was it, this was that mysterious, elusive something she'd always been missing. Love. Finally, finally, she had a family. Ten thousand moms and dads and brothers and sisters.

"Come on, Rebel! Surely you can do at least one more?" The male request came from the back of the room, and Angel put her hand to her forehead, shielding her eyes from the lights. She needn't have looked too hard, though, as the man in the suit made his way to the stage.

"Sorry," she said. "But it's been a long night, and . . ." What was it about the man's accusing stare that made her feel as if her stomach had been turned inside out?

"And you're afraid if you keep this up too long, someone might guess your dirty little secret?"

"E-excuse me?"

Jonah stepped to one side of the man, Sam to the other.

Jonah said, "I think you'd better leave."

The man held up his hands, slowly reaching into the chest pocket of his suit to pull out a press ID. "Hey," he said with a sharp laugh, "last thing I want is any trouble. But seriously, you all can't be buying this woman's scam? She's no innocent country princess, singing for her supper. This is Rebel Blue, Queen Bitch of Rock and Roll. No one sings harder or parties harder than her." He laughed again. "Hell, Rebel, even I can't imagine why you'd be hanging out in this hick town."

"My name's Angel," she said, her voice holding less conviction than she would have liked. "I don't know what you're talking about. I don't even know *who* you're talking about."

He grinned. "You just go right on believing that, babe. I know the truth." He searched the faces surrounding him. The angry faces. "Come on," he said. "Can't you all see she's just here killing time? Duping you until the roar of her latest scandal dies down?"

Sam picked up where Jonah left off. "For a man claiming not to want any trouble, you sure have a funny way of going about avoiding it. Mind telling us what that last statement was supposed to mean?"

Angel felt sick. This stranger meant more than trouble; he meant her outright harm. She couldn't fathom how or why. The knowing was nothing more than an uneasy roar behind her eyes. Nothing less than the feeling that she was standing at the edge of a cliff with nowhere to go but down. "I've got to go," she said, not realizing her mumbled words had been spoken directly into the mike.

"No," Jonah said, stepping up onto the stage beside her, putting his arm about her shoulders. "The only one leaving is this guy."

"Look," the stranger said, "if you'd just drop the loyal protector act and let me talk, I promise I can—"

"That's it," Jonah said, hardening his jaw, stepping off the stage and back to the floor. "Sam, help me get this creep out of here."

Sam sighed before releasing the man.

Under his breath, Jonah said to his long-time friend, "What the hell are you doing? Can't you see how badly this guy's upsetting my wife?"

Sam's gray eyes turned to stone.

"Come on," Jonah pleaded. "Help me. Help me get him out of here."

Sam looked to his friend, to Angel. "I'm sorry—to both of you—but Jonah, this has to end. You knew eventually it would."

Tears streaming down her cheeks, Angel shook her

head, pressed her fingers to throbbing temples. "Please, Jonah. Please, make both of them leave."

Jonah was back at her side, wrapping his arm about her shoulders, leading her down from the low platform and across the crowded room. "Sorry, folks," he called over his shoulder, "but the show and party are over. My wife needs rest."

"You all go on," Esther said, patting Angel's arm as they passed. "We'll clean up and look after Lizzy."

"Stop it, Esther," Sam called out. "Her name is Katie. And she isn't Angel's daughter but Geneva's. Just like Jonah isn't her husband."

Free hand clenched, Jonah said to Esther, "We appreciate your offer of help, but me and my *wife*, will be taking *our* baby home."

Angel glanced at the cluster of her gaping friends. Why were they all just standing there instead of helping her husband defend her against Sam and that horrible man in the suit?

The teens formed their own animated circle, eyeing her with a combination of awe laced with fear. As if she were someone to look up to, but also someone to be wary of. "Precious," she softly said. "Why are you looking at me that way?"

The teen, who had long since put down her camera, sharply turned to her mother.

One swift elbow to the ribs was all it took for Heather to entice Precious back. Brunette heads touching at the crowns, they whispered all the more.

They know, Angel's voice said. *Give it up, honey. Before this night is out, everyone's gonna know all your dirty secrets.*

Angel shook her head, hiding her face against Jonah's very solid, very real chest.

This is my reality, she fought, railing against the demon in her head. *This man, this baby, all my friends. Why would any of them host a birthday party in my honor if they didn't even know my real name? The whole idea's nuts!*

"Hells bells, Jonah." Stepping in front of him, Sam shook his head. "What's it gonna take to get it through that thick skull of yours? The game is over. I don't know who this guy is," he said, thumbing toward the suit. "But whoever he is, he obviously knows a helluva lot more about our mystery woman than we do."

"Jonah," Angel said, tucking her face against his chest. "Please take me home."

"Step aside," Jonah said to Sam, his teeth clenched.

In Esther's arms, Lizzy began to cry.

Angel reached for her child, cuddling her close. "It's past your bedtime, isn't it, sweetie?" Why wouldn't the man leave? Why was he insisting on ruining her party?

The suit narrowed his eyes. "Christ, Rebel . . . what kind of drug are you on?"

"That's it!" Jonah said, releasing Angel to rear back his fist.

Sam stepped between him and the man hurling insults at his wife, clamping a hold on both Jonah's wrists. "You don't want this."

"The hell I don't," Jonah said, thrashing to get away.

"Screw you people," the suit said, shaking his head on his way out the diner's front door. Shuffling the last few feet backward, he said, "You think you've got trouble now, Rebel Blue—what with losing your baby and finding out your kid's father was shacking up with about a dozen other women. Not showing up at that rehab center? You just wait till I leak this to my tabloid buddies. They're gonna have a field day. They're gonna—"

"Stop!" Angel cried, ducking her face against her baby. "Please, Jonah, make him stop!"

Her request was all it took to give Jonah extra strength. Wrenching free of Sam, he lurched across the room to let that bastard have it, punching him clean in the jaw.

The guy stumbled back. Rubbed his already bruising face. "You'll hear from my attorney."

"Good," Jonah said. "I'll tell him how you slandered my wife."

Hand on the door, the suit shook his head. "You pathetic country hick. Get a life."

Jonah's friends released what sounded an awful lot like a collective growl.

Probably to ensure the guy didn't get lynched on his way out of town, Sam followed the suit outside.

Jonah, mouthing good riddance to both, ushered Angel and Katie toward the office, again shouting along the way, "Party and show's over, folks. Time to call it a night."

Everyone began talking at once. Speaking in low rumbles, as if nothing they'd just heard dared be spoken aloud.

Jonah rubbed his forehead, his mind reeling from the implications. What if the suit was at least partially right?

Leon clapped his grizzled hand around Jonah's shoulder. "You go on back to the office. Me and Pauline and Chevis gonna clear everyone out. Everything's gonna be all right. Jest you wait and see."

On autopilot, Jonah said, "There's going to be a few needing rides. Earl in particular."

Leon nodded. "Don't you worry 'bout a thing. I'll take care of it."

"Thanks, Leon," Jonah said, searching his long-time friend's expression for any sign as to what he'd thought of the suit's outburst, but Leon's face was a mask. A mask of sympathy and kindness, but a mask just the same.

Jonah wasn't sure how, but before Angel quit sobbing on the office sofa they had the place to themselves.

"Why did he do that?" she finally asked. "What could he gain by digging at me that way?"

Hugging her with Katie in between, Jonah said into the fragrant fall of her hair, "I don't know, baby. I don't know."

She pushed back, staring up at him with a haunted, tearstained stare of the purest shimmering aquamarine. "And all that stuff about poor Lizzy—and you. All of it was downright mean."

Was it? that old nag in Jonah's head asked. *Or could he have been telling the truth? You've known from day one that Angel has secrets. How could any of what that stranger said be more bizarre than the days you've already shared?*

And what if even a fraction of that stuff was true? What if your so-called Angel could've given Geneva lessons on the true meaning of bad to the bone? And if that is the case, how does it feel knowing for the second time in your sorry life that you and your inane longing to play house have led you down not the road to bliss but humiliation? Because face it, bud, in your heart of hearts you already know the woman you thought you loved is gone—that is, if she was ever even there.

"Jonah? You're scaring me."

"Sorry," he said, fingering her hair.

"Then take me home—no—farther. Away from the diner. From Blue Moon. I never want to see any of those people again."

"Why? I've known them all my life. They're all I've got."

"What about me?"

A muscle ticked in his jaw. "Where do I begin?"

"How about by saying you love me? That you know full well every word out of that man's mouth was garbage."

Jonah swallowed hard.

I can't give her up, one side of him warred. *If I do, what happens to the diner? To Katie? Me? How can I— we—live without her?*

One day at a time.

One second at a time. Just like he'd done before.

"Jonah, please," she said, her vast aquamarine gaze scanning his face. What was she looking for? A sign that he really wasn't the bastard he was in having done the very thing she'd accused him of all these many weeks—using her. Squeezing Katie tighter than ever, she said, "I can't live with their stares. They all looked at me like I was a freak."

Maybe you are.

No. He had to believe at least some of what they shared was real.

He looked away. Enough.

His heart couldn't take any more.

Sure, he could probably play this out indefinitely— at least until Angel's memory returned fully, but what would that prove? Here. Tonight.

He had to tell at least a portion of what he knew to be the truth.

One part of him longed to take her hand in his, but the part already letting her go stoically held his hands in his lap.

Searching. He felt her gaze searching. "Oh, my God,"

she said on a choked gasp. "Don't tell me you believe that man's lies?" Wild-eyed, she shook her head. "How could you? I'm your wife. I've been right here in Blue Moon—with you. All our lives. How could any of that be true?"

"Think about it," he said, pushing himself up from the sofa to pace.

"I have thought about it. Every day for the past five weeks. I've thought of little else aside from what could have gone so terribly wrong between us. Is this it? Is this what you think I did? Ran off to become a rock star?"

"Stop it," he said, wishing he could shake her memory back into her. "God, would you listen to yourself? You're not even making sense. Look, I don't know if any of what that guy said is true. What I do know to be truth is that you're not my wife, Angel. I made it all up—no, no, that's not true. *You* made it up. Right here in this office, you spun this fairy-tale image of me, you, and Katie living happily ever after, and I wanted to believe, but . . ."

"Stop it," she said, cupping Katie's head. "Do you think I could nurse another woman's baby? Now who's the one being stupid, Jonah? Not to mention cruel?"

CHAPTER SEVENTEEN

Jonah forced a deep breath. "At least that part's true, Angel. I know you don't want to believe it, but—"

"No," she raged. "It's not that I don't want to believe it—I won't. I refuse. I've already lost one baby, never again will I lose another." Her hand flew to her mouth, and she broke into rasping sobs, clutching Katie tighter than ever. "Lizzy. Oh, God . . . Lizzy."

Jonah might have been a jerk for lying to her, but he wasn't a monster. He crossed the room, pulling her into his arms, smoothing her hair. "I'm sorry. So sorry."

"Then it's true?" she said after finally catching her breath. "All of what that horrible man said is true? I'm not your wife but some rock-and-roll freak from LA?"

Jonah looked to his feet. "Judging by the red leather getup I found you in, I'm guessing so."

Angel pressed a kiss to Lizzy's forehead. This was all

too much to comprehend, let alone absorb. But if Jonah wasn't her husband, who was he, and why was he keeping her here?

Pain shot through her forehead. White and at the same time red hot. Nausea roared, chugging up then crashing down in a derailment of fragmented thoughts and memories. Just like that, the life she'd have rather forgotten bullied her back into a little girl.

The lonely years after her parents died, being passed from one foster home to another. *You gotta watch out for this one. She's a pistol.* The gamble she'd taken to escape Sulphur, Texas. Hitchhiking to LA to follow her dream of becoming a star, and how that dream ultimately become a nightmare. All of what the suit and that voice in her head had said was true. The alcoholism. Talon's cheating. And the baby.

Oh—dear, God, the baby.

Angel/Rebel Blue/Rose—she didn't even know her own name—fell to her knees, clutching Lizzy unbearably close, terrified that if she gave in to the grief it might consume her. "No," she cried. "No, no, no, please, don't let me have lost my baby." But even as she cried the words, she knew they were true. Her baby, her precious Lizzy, was dead.

The child she held in her arms, as much as she loved her, was a stranger after all.

"Oh, God, Jonah," she sobbed, still on her knees with him easing onto the floor beside her. "I remember. All of it. It was so cold the day of her funeral. It was raining and fans and my record company sent all these flowers, but I didn't want them. None of them meant anything without her. She—Lizzy—was born too soon. Her tiny body was just too weak to survive. A nurse had me pump breast milk to feed her through a tube.

The doctors said the milk contained special nutrients that would make my baby strong. But it didn't. And one by heart-wrenching one, Lizzy's systems failed. And I had to sit there helpless, knowing there was nothing I could do but watch my precious baby die." Rose took a deep shuddering breath before continuing. "A-all of that happened right after New Year's. I was in Vegas doing a New Year's Eve show. The doctors said I'd been pushing myself too hard. I knew, Jonah. I knew—and yet I let them. Talon, my manager, all of them; I let them do this to me, to my baby." She swiped her hand beneath her nose. "No, no, I did this. I could've refused, but I didn't. I wanted their love, so I did it anyway. But they didn't love me. They never really loved me. No one ever has. They just used me to make themselves feel better."

She looked up, only just now realizing what she was saying. No one had ever loved her—not even her precious Jonah.

He shook his head. "I—I don't know what to say."

Squeezing her eyes shut tight, she prayed when she opened them that he'd have gone away. But he hadn't. And so she carried on with what she knew she had to do. Once again, say good-bye.

Palm pressed to his dear cheek, she said, "I love you."

Watching a war rage within him, Rose realized the part of him who'd fallen for Angel probably did love her. But hey, like the suit so eloquently pointed out, she was no angel, but Rebel Blue. Rock and roll's queen bitch.

Swallowing hard, she pressed one last kiss to his baby's forehead, then released her to her rightful parent. "I love her, too," she said, standing and turning for the door.

"I know you do," Jonah said. "She loves you."

"That's why I have to go."

"What do you mean, go? It's the middle of the night."

"Knowing Sam, he's still at his office. He'll be only too happy to give me a ride out of town. Surprise, surprise," she said with a hiccuped laugh that caught on the tears looming at the back of her throat. "I'm a millionaire. I can buy anything in the world—anything but a little joy."

Jonah grappled to his feet, put Katie in her playpen before following her through the office door. "Please, stay," he said. "Just the night. We can talk. Then, in the morning, I'll take you anywhere you want to go."

Her heart felt trapped in a vice. This was classic Jonah, a gentleman to a fault. Saying all the right things, the kind things, but the one thing he wasn't saying was that he loved her in return. And now that he knew the kind of woman he was really dealing with, words of love from him were something she'd never be likely to hear. But then, what was she saying? Why would she even want love from a man like him?

Just like all the rest, he'd used her.

Used her as a wet nurse.

A housekeeper and cook.

A cheap entertainer to keep his two-bit diner alive.

He was worse than Talon or her manager. At least neither of them had ever claimed to be anything other than what they were—both out to scam on either her talent or her body. What they'd taken from her—her pride—she hoped she could one day get back. But Jonah had taken her very soul, and she didn't know if she'd ever recover.

Giving him one last stare, she raised her chin, determined not to cry. Never to cry. "Good-bye, Jonah," she said, her voice a brittle shell. "When Lizz—I mean, Katie gets old enough, please tell her how special she was to me."

"Don't," he said, a muscle twitching in his jaw.

"I have to," she said, trying desperately to hold back tears. "I have to regroup. Mourn. Most of all, try to forget."

"At least let me walk you to Sam's. You know, make sure he's there. I don't like the thought of you being out at night alone."

"Oh, Jonah," she said, sadly shaking her head. "My whole life I've been alone. Day or night, doesn't much matter."

Gazing at him one last time, the man she alternately loved and hated, she squeezed her eyes shut, then spun on her heel and walked out the door.

And just as she'd known he would, Jonah let her.

For he was a Boy Scout. Dependable to a fault, but when it came to knowing how to handle a bad girl like her, he was helpless as a babe in the woods.

Geneva sat on her cloud, staring out at the moon, wondering how in the world she could've gotten this so wrong.

Teach popped in. Figures he'd show up just in time to gloat. "That couldn't have gone worse," he said, sounding chipper, as if all she'd lost was a two-dollar bet on a long-shot horse.

"Bite me," Geneva said, hardly in the mood for small talk.

He rolled his eyes. "Why so snippy? You do still have a week to go before your deadline."

"Great. Angel/Rebel/Whatever-her-name-is can't stand Jonah, and he's scared to death by the prospect of even

talking to her." She pointed to the screen. "Look at him just standing there. If he had even an ounce of brain in that empty cranial cavity of his, he'd be running down the street after her."

Teach cleared his throat. "In his defense, he is watching out to make sure she meets up safely with Sam."

"Big consolation. I thought I knew him better than this. How can he just stand there, letting the best thing that ever happened to him or Katie walk away?"

Pulling Geneva into his arms, Teach made a sympathetic clucking sound. The lights went down and the music went up. And doing more hugging than dancing, Geneva cried to the accompaniment of Elvis's "Only the Strong Survive."

A tune she found ironic in light of the fact that after tonight's events, she was headed straight to hell.

Jonah, Katie asleep in his arms, pushed open the back door and stepped into a dark house.

No—it was more than dark.

Without Angel, it was lifeless—soulless.

Taking one step farther, he closed the door behind him, somehow managing to get to the table and pull out a chair. He closed his eyes and heard laughter. His, Katie's, Angel's. He smelled her pot roast and blueberry pie. Tasted her kisses. Felt the full, warm curves of her breasts.

What had he done?

How could he have just let her go?

He should have run after her. Physically stopped her from getting anywhere near Sam. He couldn't think without her. Couldn't breathe. And what about Katie? What was she going to do? Sure, Angel had gradually introduced her to solid foods, but would a few teething biscuits and pureed pears be enough?

A snoozing Katie tucked against him with one arm, Jonah cradled his forehead in the other, feeling pretty much the fool. All along, folks told him his attraction to Angel would turn out bad, but there he'd been, falling for her, not giving a damn what anyone said—least of all that nagging voice in his own head warning him to steer clear.

Oh, no, what had he done with Sam's warnings? Esther and Doc's? Laughed, then gone on to plan a wedding. A wedding! To a bride with no name.

Swallowing back still more bitter tears, he laughed. Oh, yeah, that would've been the social event of Blue Moon's non-existent season.

I, Jonah McBride, do solemnly swear to keep my head up my ass for however long it takes to get my fill.

He might've claimed his love for Angel had been strictly about Katie, but the real truth was that Jonah loved her for himself. Yes, he loved the changes she'd brought about in his daughter, but most of all he loved the changes she'd made in him. She made him happy. Made him forget his troubles at home and at the diner, allowing him for the first time in he couldn't remember how long to laugh, smile, deeply breathe and look forward to his next day—his next minute—of life.

"Angel," he whispered, finally giving in to tears. "Oh, God, what have I done? Where are you? How could I let you go?"

Simple, the realist in him pointed out.

He let her go because the woman he fell in love with didn't exist. He'd created her. The real Angel was a rock star. A freakin' rock star! And he thought Geneva had been a bad-news party girl. She'd been tame compared to the stories he vaguely remembered reading in newspapers and magazines about Rebel Blue.

Without her Goth makeup and vampish leather costumes, without her hair teased and her breasts thrust out, she'd looked nothing like the star "Entertainment Tonight" once dubbed a female Ozzy Osborne.

Turning to Katie, he kissed the top of her head. "We're better off without her, squirt. The last thing we need around here is another wild child like your mom."

Right. And just who exactly is it you're trying to convince, Jonah? Your sleeping four-month-old or yourself?

"Thank you, Sam," Angel said at the Little Rock airport the next afternoon. "And please forgive me for all those times I snapped at you for doubting me." A sad, strangled laugh passed her lips. "Turns out you were right. I am bad news." Instead of clutching Lizzy to her chest, she clutched a bulging manila file. Late into the night, she and the police chief had surfed the Web for information about Rebel Blue. Her drinking, her partying. Her rock-and-roll way of life. The old Rose would've blamed all of it on someone else. Foster parents, her manager, Talon. But the new Rose accepted her faults for what they were—her own.

The night of her accident, she'd been headed to an Ozark Mountain rehab center. Not only was it secluded and discreet, but judging by the pictures in the brochure, she thought it might be a good place to heal, seeing how the trees and hills reminded her in small ways of the town where she'd grown up in Texas—the one she'd always wanted to belong to but never had.

"Who are you going to hassle now that I'll be out of town?"

Sam shrugged. "Guess there's always the boy mayor."

Rose conked herself on the head. "Speaking of him, I guess I should've told you earlier, but you've kind of been the last person I've wanted to talk to."

Sam dropped his gaze, shrugged. "Sorry I was so rough on you. What can I say? I love my boy Jonah and his baby girl."

Me, too, she thought, swallowing hard.

Taking a deep breath, she said, "The other day, when I met the mayor at the diner, I remembered meeting him before."

"Outside of Blue Moon?"

She nodded. "At one of my concerts, of all places. It was in Little Rock. He crashed the backstage after party. Offered me a hundred bucks to sleep with him."

"No way," Sam said, scrunching his nose. "The boy mayor is a legendary saint. Strictly into Christian rock and rumored to be the oldest living virgin. And anyway, what would it matter—other than the fact that if it was him, he's an even bigger sleazeball than I figured. Although a sleazeball with great taste in women and music."

"Yes, way." Rose swatted Sam's arm. "Think about it. He doesn't exactly have a face anyone's liable to forget. And it matters because I got the feeling he wasn't just there to listen to me."

Sam feigned a gasp.

"This is serious," Rose said. Surprised to find herself still able to grin, she gave him a bonus swat. "Now, listen up. The day Ed had the arsonist's car parked in front of the diner, I remembered seeing the car at my concert, too—or, more specifically, the crystal flashing from the rearview mirror. I wouldn't have given it a second's thought, but the night I saw the mayor, I'd ventured outside the arena for fresh air and locked myself out. I was hoofing it around the corner of the building and saw your favorite guy approach the Lincoln.

At the time I thought he was buying drugs. He looked all nervous and edgy—you know, with a lot of glancing over his shoulder. But who knows? Seeing how you and Frank suspect the guy driving the Lincoln to be the arsonist, there might be a connection."

"Did our fair mayor get in the car?"

"Yes. Passenger side. I saw him in there just before catching up with my own ride."

"Wow," Sam said, scratching his head. "This is definitely something to think about. I mean, I've always suspected the creep was up to something, but what if he really was?"

Hand on his arm, she said, "Maybe the better question would be, what if he still is?"

"Boggles the mind, doesn't it?" Still shaking his head, Sam said, "Thanks again. Don't know whether this'll lead anywhere or not. Could be our mayor was just buying drugs. Who's to say a guy who'll commit arson isn't also into selling dime bags for pin money?"

"Yeah. Anyway . . ." After an awkward silence, Rose shrugged. "Now that that's out, guess I'm not sure what else to say."

She offered her hand for him to shake, but her one-time nemesis pulled her into a fierce hug. "There's nothing else to say, Rose, other than maybe thank you."

"What do you mean?" she asked, swallowing hard. "All I've done is cause Jonah more pain—and as for him using me like he did . . . well, that's just unforgivable."

Hand on her chin, Sam tipped her head back, forcing her to meet his gaze. "Don't you think you did an awful lot of using each other?"

She didn't answer.

"And no matter what Jonah said to you, I've known him all my life—well enough to know what amazing changes you made in a guy who'd become about as exciting as a brick. He loves you, Rose. So does Katie."

Tears flowing freely now, she shook her head. "The woman he loves doesn't exist, Sam. As much as I'd like to be her, I can't."

Rose's manager, Grant, both wired her the money for her return trip to LA and met her at the airport. The whole drive to her Malibu beach house, a description of which could be summed up in five words—soaring white panes of glass—he gushed about how big he planned to make her comeback. Looking healthy and more beautiful than ever, she'd become every manager's wet dream. And just think—she was all his.

Rose fired him on the front steps of her house. Right after he'd handed over her Ferrari and Mercedes keys, along with the key to her house.

She told him to never contact her again, and she meant it.

And now, on a Monday morning, reclining on a sleek lounge chair, drinking in the full-on ocean view beneath the baking Malibu sun, she figured she might as well be adrift on the ocean for all the comfort it didn't bring. Sure, the house, with its plush white carpet and custom white leather chairs and sofas and chrome and glass tables, was beautiful, but it wasn't her. None of this was her, but what was? And how did she go about finding out?

She closed her eyes, soaking up the sun, the roaring waves.

Somewhere down the beach seagulls cried and the air smelled crisp with the barest hint of brine.

How was it that she'd outright owned this house for five years, yet it felt less familiar than the one she'd shared with Jonah for five weeks?

There, she'd loved the feel of the morning sun soaking through the back of whichever one of Jonah's T-shirts she'd worn to tend her new garden. The rustle of breezy spring secrets tittering through leaves. Calls of mockingbirds and robins and jays. Coal trains' lonely wails. The old house with its creaks and cozy smells of morning coffee and bacon and Katie's baby lotion and shampoo. Recalling Jonah's unique scent would bring unspeakable pain, so she forced open her eyes. Forced herself to face reality. This was her life now. Jonah and Katie were gone.

Eyes open, heart pounding with a raw ache, she brought her hands to her breasts, for they ached, too.

What she missed most from Blue Moon weren't sounds and smells—but people. Her family. Her adopted baby. Sure, in her head she knew Katie had only been a beautiful dream, but her body still hadn't adjusted to the fact that she no longer had reason to produce milk. Since she'd been on a regular schedule of pumping milk for Lizzy ever since her New Year's Eve birth, when Rose ended up with Katie in her arms just three days after Lizzy's death, her body had been all too cooperative in keeping up the masquerade that her baby was still alive.

Lizzy.

Sweet, sweet Lizzy.

Rose swallowed hard. The day she found out she was pregnant, joy didn't begin to describe her elation. She'd been so certain hearing the news that he was about to be a father would be all it took to settle Talon into a loving husband and father. She couldn't have been more wrong.

"Don't you turn away from me!" she'd said to him backstage in Memphis. In the cloying smoke clouding their dressing room, Rose snagged the man thousands of women called Talon by the hard black leather of his vest, spinning him around. His dark hair hung long and loose about his shoulders and his dark eyes loomed bloodshot and wild. Unlike all those masses who night after night chanted his name, Rose knew the real man behind the name. "Greg, don't you get what I've been trying to say? I'm having a baby. *Your* baby."

He laughed, and the sharp note pierced her heart.

"You think it's funny?"

He shook his head. "I think it's pathetic. Look, kid, you're beautiful, and everyone on God's green earth knows you've got lungs, but you've also got some stupid notion of settling down to your white picket fence and face it—" He curled his lips into a sneer. "That just ain't me."

"You could change, Greg. You're going to be a father."

He gripped her hard by her shoulders, giving her a rough shake. "What's it going to take to make you listen? The man you call Greg is dead. In his place arose Talon. That's who I am, baby. All I ever wanted to be."

Holding back a wall of tears, she shook her head. "You don't mean that."

"The hell I don't." He reached into his back pocket for his wallet. Opened it and plucked out a couple of hundreds, flinging them at her. "Here. Abortions are cheap. Take care of it."

"It? You're calling our child—the child we conceived from love—an it?"

"Whoa. Nobody ever said love around here but you. I was only going along for the luscious ride. If you'd ever listened to a word I'd said, you'd know I'm hardly a happily-ever-after kind of guy."

She slapped him.

"Mmm," he said, cinching her close. "Now we're talkin'. You know I've always liked it rough."

Geneva hung her head in shame.

To think she'd left Jonah in pursuit of a man more like Talon. What a joke. What a damned shame that she'd ever given Jonah up. And now here Rose had made the same stupid mistake with an equally tragic outcome. Sure, Jonah had his faults, and technically, yes, he had been using her, but not in the same sense that Talon and Grant used her. Those two yo-yos used her purely for their own financial gain. Jonah used her to help heal his child and his heart.

So how come if even an insensitive angel reject like herself saw that difference, Rose couldn't?

Was this it, her big cue from the sky to pack it in?

"Not just yet." *Young Elvis approached. Wearing faded jeans, a white T-shirt, and scuffed black boots that matched his jet black hair, the mere sight of him left her for once without words and gaping.* "Mr. Big said you need a song."

"But I'm failing. How am I ever going to get those two back together with Jonah stuck in Blue Moon and Malibu Barbie there back in her natural habitat?"

Shaking his head, Elvis clucked his tongue. "Shame on you, Geneva. If there's one thing I've learned since being up here, it's that you gotta have faith."

"Right. I've got about as much faith in this all working out as—"

303

He cut her off in mid-whine with a downright depressing rendition of "Heartbreak Hotel."

Just as Elvis strummed the final few notes, Teach popped in, giving the King a round of applause. "You just keep getting better," he said with a shake of his head. "Ever think of giving life another go as a member of one of those hot boy bands?"

"Nah." Elvis waved him off. "I've got things good up here. Why would I want to go back?"

Teach nodded. "Excellent point. Well, then"—with a sharp sigh and a click of his heels, he turned to Geneva—"looks as if I'm back to dealing with you."

"Forget it," Geneva said. "I'm a lost cause."

"Giving up so easily?"

"Easily? Ha! You were the one who told me Rose probably isn't even Jonah's true soul mate, so where does that leave me? With like billions of other women to sift through looking for just the right one?"

"Good point," Teach said with a solemn nod. "I hadn't thought of it in quite those terms. Yes, I suppose you're right. At this point, with only five days until your official deadline, there's not a thing left for you to do but wait."

She slanted him a dark look. "Even you're giving up on me?"

He shrugged. "Everyone else has—including yourself. Besides, Sammy Davis Junior and Mozart are giving a concert in fifteen minutes. Don't want to be late." With a jaunty wave, he was off.

Under ordinary circumstances, Geneva would've flipped him the bird, but she was too depressed.

Even her own teacher had turned against her. What kind of screwed-up Heaven was this?

She'd worked her vaporous buns off getting Jonah and Angel together. And if it hadn't been for that stupid talent

*scout/reporter guy, she would've already been tooling
around in her flashy new wings! So there, none of this mess
was her fault. And what about the fact that before that guy
showed up, Jonah, Angel, and Katie were so happy? That
had to count for something! Didn't that prove they were all
meant to be together? And if that was the case, didn't that
mean Geneva still had a chance at busting through those
pearly gates?*

"Damn straight," she said with a calculating smile.

*She'd come way too far to waste a single second being
sad. Now was the time for Geneva Kowalski-McBride to
get mad.*

"Would you all give it a rest?" Jonah said Monday afternoon before flipping a burger. "For the last time, Angel's gone—and she's not coming back."

He looked up just in time to catch Pauline roll her
eyes. Chevis and Leon shared a look. The size of
Chevis's grin made the NASCAR lighter and two cigs
hitching a ride in his beard bobble.

"What?" Jonah said, slapping a piece of cheese onto
the patty. "You think I'm kidding? She's bad news. I
say . . . good riddance." Muttering that last part while
holding himself together took superhuman effort. He
didn't want to, but Jonah missed Angel/Rebel Blue/
Rose/Whatever with a powerful force. He missed hearing her crooning lullabies to Katie and he missed her
delicious cooking and her laugh and her aquamarine
eyes and even goofy little things that used to annoy
him like the way she'd smooth his hair every morning
before he walked out the back door for work.

"You know you don't mean that," Pauline said, edg-
ing around the side of the stove to wrap him in a sideways hug.

He sloughed her away to slide the burger off the grill and onto a toasted bun. "Leon? Those fries ready?"

"Gott'um right here," he said, waving the fry basket in front of the fryer. "Only I don't s'pect I'll be giving them to you till you admit you had a thing for her."

Jonah gritted his teeth. "Fine. Then I guess I'll get them myself." He did just that, wrenching the basket from his friend's hand, then dumping the contents beneath the warming light and shaking on salt. He scooped a couple dozen onto the burger plate, then held it out for Pauline. "Can you handle delivering this, or is my waitress on strike as well?"

Spying tears in her eyes made him feel like the jerk he was. "I'll take it," she said, lifting her chin. "What I won't take is any more of your attitude."

"I'm sorry," he said, plate in hand, heading for the dining room. "Last thing I intended was to take any of this out on you. But facts are facts, and the fact is, my Angel was no angel."

Pauline started to speak, but he managed to escape the kitchen before hearing her.

Jonah set the burger and fries on the counter in front of Randy, the UPS guy.

"Mmm, mmm," Randy said. "Forgot how good your burgers are. Twice as thick as the fast-food places."

"Thanks," Jonah said. "Glad you like it." At least someone was happy with him this afternoon.

Glancing across the crowded room, a prickle of guilty pride swept through him. The place was packed, just like in the diner's heyday. Just like in his dreams. Dreams that now felt curiously empty without sharing them with the woman who'd helped bring all those dreams to life.

"Jonah!" Pauline's sister Melvine called from her

booth across the room. "Could I trouble you for more tea?" She wagged her empty glass, tinkling the ice.

Had he really wished for increased traffic in the diner? Maybe he liked it empty. Gave him more time to sit in the office, licking his wounds.

"While you're here," Melvine said, patting Jonah's hand when he served her the drink, "I want you to have this." She reached beside her onto the orange vinyl seat, pulling a videotape from her purse. "It's the tape Precious took of your Angel's birthday party."

"She's not *my* Angel," Jonah said, taking the tape from her only to set it on the table beside her sweating glass of tea. "Never was."

"Oh, well." Reddening, she fussed with the sugar dispenser for a moment before pushing the tape back his way. "Just in case, I thought you might like to have it."

"In case of what?"

She sighed. "In case you come to your senses, all right? No matter who she *used* to be, the woman we all came to know and love is sweet as cherry pie. Now take the tape, or I'm walking out of here without paying on the grounds that your just plain mean disposition ruined my lunch."

Rose frowned. The state-of-the-art microwave might as well have been from outer space. All she wanted to do was nuke a bag of popcorn. Did she really need all these buttons?

And it was cold in here, too. Ever since leaving Blue Moon, she'd felt chilled. Just as soon as she figured out how to make her snack, she'd get back to finding a manual on how to shut off the AC. She'd tried earlier, but the computerized heating and cooling system was equally as complex as the microwave.

Just one more thing to thank Grant for. To him, image wasn't just about the character she portrayed onstage. It was a full-time gig. If he'd had his way, Rebel Blue would have resided in a dark gothic mansion deep in the heart of old town Beverly Hills as opposed to the beach.

"If you insist on living in a sand castle," he'd argued when she'd bid on a simple yet cozy thousand-square-foot cottage, "at least make it a true castle."

And that was how she ended up in not a castle but a palace. Fifteen-thousand square feet of blinding white elegance that used to have a full-time cook and two housekeepers—but right after Lizzy's death Rose let them all go. It wasn't as if she'd used even half the place. She was rarely even home to eat. She did still have two gardeners in her employ. Two very surprised gardeners this morning, when she helped them deadhead a bed of yellow marigolds. Esther would get a kick out of seeing Rose's elaborate gardens—not that she could take credit for growing them, but they were pretty just the same.

An elegant series of chimes sounded.

Figuring it was Armande with a question about the tomatoes and zucchini she'd asked him to plant beside the roses, she abandoned the microwave to answer the door.

"Hey." Talon leaned against the glass block entry wall. Mirrored sunglasses cloaked his dark eyes. Black leather pants hugged his long, lean legs. On his feet were black biker boots. On his chest—nothing. His pecs and abs were perfectly tan and perfectly ripped— both feats achieved through hours spent with his tanning bed and personal trainer. After giving her what she could only guess from her reflection in his glasses was a head-to-toe appraisal, he said, "You're looking good."

"Thanks." Having left Blue Moon with nothing—the same way she'd entered the small town—Rose had trouble accommodating her new, simpler tastes in clothes from her former outrageous wardrobe. At the bottom of a dresser drawer she'd managed to find a white T-shirt and jean cutoffs. She wore her hair in twin braids. No makeup. And standing before this man she'd once thought she loved more than life itself, it took everything in her not to hurl from a sudden case of nerves.

He pulled her into a hug. "Long time no see."

Not until after he pulled back did she notice the scent of stale cigarette smoke clinging to his skin and hair. "Yeah. I thought we'd pretty much said all we had to the day of Lizzy's funeral."

"I didn't go," he said, shifting his weight from one foot to the other.

"That's my point."

"So what? You're holding a grudge?"

"You think I shouldn't?"

He glanced over his shoulder. A photographer dove behind a bougainvillea. "Look, can we take this inside?"

She stepped back, hugging the door's edge to allow him to pass. "I'd forgotten about paparazzi."

He shrugged, sliding his sunglasses atop his head. "Another day, another tabloid story. No biggee. Remember the first time they said we were an item?" Nudging the front door closed with the tip of his boot, he said, "You used to love that shit. Remember how we'd lounge by my pool naked, reading the *National Enquirer*, drinking pitchers of margaritas?" While he talked, he'd slid his hands about her waist.

She pushed him away. "I won't deny we had a few good times, Greg, but that's over."

"Call me Talon."

"Forgive me," she said, rolling her eyes. "I forgot. The stage lights never go out for you, do they?"

"That's a low blow, Rose."

"Is it?" Crossing the mechanically cooled white tile foyer, her bare feet felt frozen. Seated on the massive, C-shaped white leather sectional, staring out at the foaming surf, she reached for a white faux fur pillow to slip over her toes. Closing her eyes, she wished Jonah were there to warm them the way he had that day in his office when he told her he loved her.

Talon sat beside her. "I don't blame you for being mad. I've flaked on a lot of things." He looked to the view, then back to her. "Grant told me you've been shacking up with another guy."

"Shacking up?" she spluttered. "I had amnesia. I thought I was his wife. His baby's mother."

"Deep." He paused for a moment as though letting her words sink in. "Where does that leave us?"

"I thought you said there never was an us."

He groaned, slid across the sofa to pull her into his arms. He smoothed the hair back from her forehead, meeting her gaze. "Damn, you've got gorgeous eyes. Guys in the band say your ass is your best feature, but I always said it's your eyes."

"I'm touched," she said, her pulse racing.

He curved his lips into the smile that had seduced women all over the world—including her. "God, I've missed you," he said, his voice husky and his breath smelling faintly of beer and cigs and the lifestyle she thought she'd abandoned but, in light of the pain she was going through over losing Jonah and Katie, suddenly didn't look all that bad. "We used to be so good together." He came in close for a kiss, and the part of her that'd for years loved him heart and soul, that would've at one time given her very soul to have heard him mutter those very same words melted. "We could be good again, you know."

"What are you saying?" she asked, drawing back to search his inky dark eyes.

"Want me to spell it out?"

She licked her lips. Nodded.

"I was thinking we could do like you've always wanted. You know, have a big wedding. Invite all our friends."

"And then what? Would you still want to spend all our time partying and touring and making more albums? Or are you ready to settle down?"

He nodded and shrugged. "Oh, hell, yeah. Grant says I should let you pop out that baby you've been wanting; then we can get back out on the road."

Her blood chilled. "Grant says?"

"Well, yeah. He told me I should come talk to you. Said some nonsense about you firing him." He pulled her close, pressing openmouthed kisses to her neck and throat.

His actions, his words, his acrid smell all repulsed her, and she shoved him away. "Get out."

"What do you mean, get out? I just got here. Don't we need to call a wedding planner?"

Silent tears streamed down her cheeks. "There isn't going to be a wedding, Talon. There could've been, but you messed that up the night you told me to abort your daughter."

"You should've. Would have saved us all a lot of grief."

Though her palm itched from wanting to slap him, she held it in her lap. "Get out."

He stood. Graced her with a simple bow, then walked out the door.

CHAPTER EIGHTEEN

Jonah, with a sniffling, cranky mess of a Katie in his arms, paced the length of the living room, trying his best to jiggle her and sing as he walked. Overall, she'd been better than he'd expected since Angel left. And since Angel had introduced her to solid foods, she was at least eating a little, though she still refused to drink from a bottle.

He hadn't opened the diner Sunday, and Monday Pauline had moved Katie's playpen into the dining room so folks could visit with her while they ate. This worked out fine during the day, but here he was Wednesday night and his best girl wasn't at all happy.

"I know you miss her," he said on his way past the piano, shooting the instrument a dirty look. "I miss her, too. But you have to trust me, squirt. Her leaving is for the best."

Katie launched into a whole new fit of wails.

"I'm sensing you don't agree with Daddy's decision?"

Her answer was a particularly cutting *waaaaah*.

He jiggled her faster, but when that didn't help, he tried jiggling her slow. Rocking. Humming. Nothing helped.

He headed into the kitchen to get her a teething biscuit when he spotted the corner of the video Melvine had given him on Monday poking out from beneath a stack of unopened mail. Since today was Wednesday, that showed where viewing that tape landed on his list of priorities. Still, what if watching Angel on TV helped calm Katie?

Yeah, but what was it going to do to him?

The very thought of seeing her again, hearing her ethereal voice—it was too much. Just thinking about it made his heart race and his palms sweat.

Then Katie launched into a fresh round of wailing and his throbbing head demanded he at least give the tape a try.

Holding his squirming baby with one hand, he fit the tape into the VCR with the other. Turned on the TV and hit play.

A picture of himself scowling filled the screen.

Precious, voice tinny, said, "Like, we know, Jonah. It's not too tough, you know, just yelling 'surprise.' "

He made a face for the camera. "Cut me some slack. Is there a law against wanting this night to be special?"

From an end stool at the counter, Esther asked, "What's the occasion again?"

Precious panned the camera back to him as he pointed at the banner he'd had made at the copy shop. "Happy Birthday, Angel," he said. "Everybody got that?"

314

Jonah sighed.

That night felt like a million years away. Hard to believe it'd only been what? Four days?

The commotion with Earl broke out, and then the bell over the diner's door jingled. In walked Angel, Katie in her arms, still flushed from her walk from the car.

"Surprise!"

The crowd burst into, "Happy Birthday," but instead of panning, Precious kept the camera tight on Angel. On her amazing smile and blazing aquamarine eyes. She looked across the room, and Precious followed her gaze, settling on him. Jonah blinked, caught off guard at the sight of himself, eyes welled with tears, heart in plain sight for the world to see.

"I loved her," he said, hand to his mouth. "I really, truly loved her."

"What? You thought this whole exercise was just a game?" Geneva slanted him a dirty look. *"Of course, you loved her. And you still would if you hadn't been such a hard-nosed Goody Two-shoes about women being purer than driven snow."*

Jonah looked to Katie. He'd been so wrapped up in watching the tape, he'd forgotten all about having turned it on in hopes of calming her. But calm her it had. She seemed fascinated by the action unfolding on TV. Precious had turned off the camera for a while, and now he was presenting Angel with her surprise.

Ha. The surprise was on him. What a nightmare that talent scout turned out to be.

Angel sang Patsy Cline's "Crazy," and while he fell for his pretend wife all over again, Katie was all smiles, bouncing up and down and giggling and pointing at the screen.

"Mmm-ah," she said over and over. "Mmm-ah."

"What the—?" He turned his baby girl to face him. Damned if it didn't sound like she was trying to say momma. But how? She wasn't yet five months old.

She wriggled back around and pointed at the screen. Angel was singing some pop tune requested by Precious that he didn't recognize. "Mmm-ah! Mmm-ah!"

He shook his head and groaned. No way. No way in hell this was happening.

"Oh, but it is, Jonah. Listen to what our baby's trying to tell you."

Watching that tape, Jonah wished more than anything things could've turned out differently with him and Angel. At first, when the reality of her true identity sank in, he'd been relieved. At least she wasn't married, though he was deeply saddened by the news that her baby was dead. Still, sorry as he felt for her, that didn't mean she was any better mother material than Geneva.

Geneva laughed. "My God, Jonah, would you listen to yourself? When did you become such an expert on great mothers? Look at our daughter, damn you. Look at her all but trying to hug the TV, then think back to what a terrific job of parenting Angel did. That girl was running on pure instinct. Skills like that can't be taught. She was loving our baby the way she'd want to be loved."

Jonah scratched his forehead. He'd become a swirl of conflicting emotions. On the one hand, he wanted desperately to give Angel a second chance—to beg her to give him a second chance. But on the other, he was scared. Geneva was his proof that no matter how hard he wished it, people don't change. True, aside from her few questions about drinking, Angel had never shown him signs that she was anything other than the amazing

316

image she presented, but then again, how did he know that was the real her?

"*Ever heard of a little thing called faith?*" Never had Geneva more desperately yearned to pound some sense into a man. "*Please, Jonah. Just this once, let loose of that almighty control. You don't have to master every situation. All you have to do is have faith. Please, Jonah. For all our sakes.*"

Sam's boots made no sound as he walked across the cushy Oriental carpets lining the hardwood floors of the boy mayor's outer office.

Gretta Sturgis, the pinched-nose secretary guarding his door, said, "He's taking a call, Sam. You'll have to wait."

Sam waved her off. "Got good news, Gretta."

She bustled out from behind her desk, trying to cut him off at the pass, but Sam's legs were longer and faster. "He's not going to like being interrupted."

"Oh, I promise," he said with a dashing wink, "he's gonna love hearing this." Gently shoving her out of his way, Sam opened the mayor's mahogany door, stepped inside the posh antique-furnished digs, then shut the door behind him.

This was going to be fun.

Hot damn if Angel—he still had trouble thinking of her as Rose—hadn't been right about this snake. Sam had no way of proving beyond her statement that the mayor was ever in Little Rock, but he did have a couple of hair samples he'd found in the arsonist's car. He'd sent them off for testing and had just gotten word back on a positive match with one in particular.

Gretta had been right. The boy mayor didn't look pleased to see Sam barging into his pleasure palace. He mouthed something unintelligible into the phone, then hung up. Adjusting his tie, he said, "This might be a small town, Chief Lawson, but that doesn't mean we don't adhere to protocol."

Sam removed his hat, parked it on one burgundy leather guest chair and himself on the other. "Protocol, huh? Interesting you should mention that as I'm here on just such a matter."

"Oh?" The mayor raised his neatly trimmed eyebrows.

"Seems not too far back—'round about Christmas to be exact—you took a trip to Little Rock."

"Christmas shopping," he said, straightening an already straight pile of manila folders. "Mother and I go every year. It's a tradition."

"Sure," Sam said with an understanding nod. "The trip I want to know about, though, is the one you took after Christmas. To a concert?"

The mayor fisted a pink receipt lying atop the folders.

"I'll take that as a yes? You did attend a concert?"

He pushed a button on his phone. "Ms. Sturgis?"

"Um hmm?"

"Hold all my calls."

Early Friday night, the sky behind her ablaze in deep oranges and reds, Rose climbed out of her black Mercedes sedan—license plate REBEL—and onto the scenic lookout of an endless Texas highway she'd forgotten the name of. The arid air she thought she needed to smell dried her nose and made the back of her throat itch. The view she thought would cure her of life's woes struck her as beautiful in a sparse, tragic way, but nothing so spectacular as to have felt her very life was in peril if she didn't get a second look.

A lone cricket chirped. A far-off coyote yipped.

For as far as she could see, rolling hills barely supported scraggly cactus and weeds and scrub oaks washed in the setting sun. Yes, the scene was peaceful. Gorgeous, if you were a fan of Clint Eastwood westerns, but this was what she'd driven all this way for? This was supposed to answer the dozens of questions roaming free range through her head?

Rose eased her lips into a ghostly smile.

The town of Sulphur was still a good twenty miles down the road, but she could already see the few twinkling lights, and from the look of it, nothing much had changed.

Still one main business strip, with side streets feeding off that. On a Friday night all the proper citizens would be seated around their dinner tables, sharing their days—or at the very least sharing bowls of popcorn over their first of the night's rented movies. As for the rest of them, they'd be making out down by the abandoned feed mill or nursing beers and playing pool in one of the town's two bars.

A long time ago, back before her parents died, Rose belonged to Group A. What some folks called the Churchies. She'd lived a normal life. Been bored, afflicted with what she now supposed were normal growing pains, but essentially, she'd been happy—until her rug got jerked out from under her.

Closing her eyes, she took an extra deep breath, remembering. Helping her daddy round up their few cattle for feeding, helping her momma in the kitchen and garden. Learning to sew. Play the piano and her daddy's guitar. Going to church. Always going to church.

When her parents died in a car wreck she was ten. Hovering on the verge of becoming a woman, utterly thrown into a tailspin by the changes in her body and her life. Then came a succession of foster families where she felt like the proverbial square peg trying to fit into a round hole.

Her church family took turns doling her out. She never stayed more than six months in any one house. Meaning, since the death of her parents, she'd never felt like she belonged again—at least not until ending up in Blue Moon. It was there that her most basic small town roots and a loving, hardworking man proved to be her salvation. It was there she realized her singing career meant nothing without loved ones to share her songs with.

Wednesday she'd spent at the cemetery, tending Lizzy's grave. She'd planted pink roses and had a good, long talk with the daughter she'd always wanted but, sadly, would never have the pleasure of knowing. She'd dreamt of mornings spent playing Barbies and brushing hair. And, later, of giggling about boys and trying on different shades of lipstick and eye shadow.

Throughout that day as Rose thought of all she'd wanted to experience in the future with Lizzy, she found her mind wandering to Katie. Wondering how she was doing and if she missed Rose half as much as she missed her.

After Rose's meeting with Talon, one thing had become abundantly clear—the fact that she wanted nothing to do with LA. The lifestyle or the people. Did that mean she never wanted to sing professionally again? She couldn't say. All she knew was that she needed roots, and singing her heart out in a different city every night was no way to ground herself.

Thursday morning, when she'd embarked on this journey, she thought those roots might be found in Texas, but now she realized she'd been wrong. Yes, she felt affection for a few of her foster families, and especially for her parents, but she didn't love those ghosts enough to want them revisited beyond sending Christmas cards to the living and leaving flowers and prayers at the graves of the dead.

Now the roots she'd set in Blue Moon—those were an entirely different story. Even if they were shallow roots, the life she'd briefly led in Blue Moon had for those few shining weeks lifted her higher than a sold-out arena's applause. She hadn't been Rebel Blue, stage presence, but Angel McBride, beloved wife and mother.

Oh, right? Like Angel wasn't a character you were playing? How was she any more real than Rebel?

Sliding her fingers into her hair and pressing her scalp, Rose wished she could blame all that confusion on the nagging voice that'd lived inside her during her bout of amnesia, but trouble was, now that she knew the voice was all hers, she'd just have to add it to her ever-growing list of things to deal with. Her continuous urge to find solace in a bottle. Her love for Katie. What she thought was her love for Jonah.

Staring out at the arid rolling hills she'd driven over a thousand miles to see, it was then Rose realized it wasn't this landscape that was important, or seeking out any of her few former friends. What was important wasn't the past but the here and now.

Yes, she'd lost one child, but there was another child very much alive who didn't give a damn what her name was, only that she held her tight.

As for Jonah, Rose didn't have a clue what she'd say

to him were she to see him again; all she knew was
that she had to give what she felt for him—with him—
one more try.

*"Yes!" Geneva did an impromptu happy dance right there
on the side of the road. It was about time Blondie came to
her senses. Lord knew, with that Texas road trip Geneva
had been trying to steer her in the right direction, but an
angel in training could only do so much. Now, when she
got her real wings—watch out!*

*And the way Geneva's mission was suddenly looking up,
surely getting Jonah and Angel permanently hitched by Saturday night would be no big deal. After all, if Rose drove
all night, she could be in Blue Moon by morning, which
meant Geneva could have her wings by Saturday afternoon.*

"Mmm-ah! Mmm-ah!"

Bright and early Saturday morning, Jonah turned his
attention from a pan of scrambled eggs to Katie to
check whether all that wriggling she was doing
might've loosened the belt on her high chair, but from
the looks of it she was still snug as a bug. He'd breathed
a huge sigh of relief to discover she adored scrambled
eggs—especially when made with loads of butter and
cream, the way Angel had always made them.

Angel; now there was a topic he'd rather steer clear
of. But then, how could he, when his own daughter
was constantly bringing her up? Sure, he wanted to
view Katie's first word as a fluke, but it'd grown too
consistent to have been anything other than the real
deal.

Kind of like the hole in his heart was feeling more
like the real deal.

Fifty times a day he wondered if he should swallow
his pride, fasten Katie into her car seat, and head for

LA. Fifty times more, he called himself a fool for even considering such a thing. Angel had been Geneva times ten. Geneva had never changed. Odds were, once Angel got a fresh taste of her former rock star lifestyle, she'd never give him and Katie a second thought.

"Mmm-ah!" Katie clanged on the high-chair tray with her teething biscuit.

"I'm coming, I'm coming, squirt." He added a dash of salt to her eggs. "Geez, and I thought old Earl down at the diner was a pain in my—"

A knock sounded at the back door.

Speaking of pains.

Before turning off the stove, Jonah shot a glance at the counter loaded with tinfoil-covered serving dishes. He had enough sugar cookies, banana bread, and chocolate cake to land him in the hospital with diabetes. Why wouldn't the good citizens of Blue Moon leave him alone? He knew they meant well, but when would they get it through their heads that there was no cheering him up? What he felt for Angel couldn't be fixed with a whole houseful of baked goods.

"Mmm-ah! Mmm-ah!"

Another knock sounded. This time sharper.

"Keep your pants on, I'm—" Door open, Jonah had to blink.

Angel, wearing figure-hugging jean cutoffs and a painted-on DON'T MESS WITH TEXAS T-shirt, stood right there on the back porch. Hands behind her back. Long, tan legs going on for miles. White Keds touching at the toes.

His mouth went dry. Was she real or a mirage?

"Hi . . ." the mirage said. Aquamarine eyes shimmering, she reached her hand out for him to shake. "We haven't formally been introduced. I'm Rose Sherman."

He grasped her hand. "Angel, you came back."

"No, Jonah, I'm Rose."

"Mmm-ah! Mmm-ah!" Katie lurched so hard in her high chair that the feet clanked against the floor.

"Katie? Is that you, baby?" The woman so familiar, yet so foreign, rushed past him to unfasten his baby from her chair and clutch her into her arms. "Katie, Katie," she sang, raining the infant's forehead with kisses. "I missed you. You'll never know how much I missed you."

"What about me?" Jonah asked, closing the door.

"Of course, that goes without saying."

"But . . ."

"But, with Liz—Katie, what we share is an unconditional bond."

"And with me, there's baggage?" From somewhere, he managed to find a weak smile.

"I suppose that's one way of putting it." She smiled, too, and the sight of it tilted his carefully balanced world off axis.

What was wrong with him? He was over her. Had convinced himself he'd never truly fallen for her in the first place, so how could his pulse be pounding to such a degree? How come he couldn't breathe and the tips of his fingers itched from wanting to smooth her luminous hair?

She swallowed hard, cupped the back of Katie's head, cuddling her ever closer. "I suppose since I left, I should be the one who starts things off with an apology."

Jonah shook his head. "I should apologize. I should've—"

"What? There wasn't anything anyone could do. Yes, we both made mistakes, but those are behind us now."

She looked to Katie, then eventually back to him. "I'm here with hopes of looking forward."

"Together?"

"If that's what you want."

"That what you want?"

"I think so, but other times . . ." She shrugged. "I just wish there was some way to know for sure."

"Don't we all," he said with a forced chuckle.

Her gaze darted from his face to the kitchen as a whole. "I like what you've done with the place. Looks cozy."

"Thanks." Soiled baby clothes and his jeans and T-shirts overflowed the laundry basket. Dirty dishes languished in the sink. Fast-food wrappers littered the tabletop and spilled onto the floor.

"Need a housekeeper?"

Yes.

No. Hell, no, he didn't need a housekeeper, he needed a wife. Not to clean house for him, but to be his best friend and lover for the rest of his life.

"Make love to me, Jonah."

"What?"

Hand on his sleeve, his baby—her baby—in her arms, she said, "I know this must sound crazy, but please. I've come so far. I have to know if any of what we shared is real."

"What about Katie?"

"Knowing Esther, she'd pay you to watch her."

Fifteen minutes later, Rose had proven herself right. Esther did take Katie, as well as welcome Rose back with a crushing hug.

"Mmm, I missed you," Esther said. "Don't ever leave us like that again."

"I can't make any promises," Rose said, "other than that I promise to try."

"Good enough for me." Esther grabbed Katie. "You gonna be good this time, you little monster?"

The baby grinned.

"Okay," Esther said. "Guess you can stay." To Rose and Jonah, she added, "Go on. I wasn't born yesterday. I know you didn't drop Katie off so you two could attend the Bible breakfast meetin' down at Blue Moon Baptist Church."

Rose gave her friend a wink, then wrapped her in a hug. "Thank you," she whispered in Esther's good ear. "You're an amazing friend."

"Ditto."

Five minutes after that, hand at the small of Rose's back, Jonah ushered her through the front door of his house. "Don't think I've ever come through the front door before," she said, covering her nerves with a giggle. What had she been thinking? Was she out of her mind asking him to make love?

"Then it's about time," Jonah said, closing and locking the door behind him.

The grandfather clock greeted them with disapproving ticks.

Downtown, the morning coal train blew its lonely whistle. It was late. Was she too late to repair the damage her leaving had done?

"How's the diner?" she asked, suddenly eager to discuss anything but the deed they'd supposedly come home to do.

"Good." He perched on the arm of the sofa. "Not quite as good as when you were performing, but the singing waitresses turned out to be one hell of a great gimmick. Much better than Happy Meals or Buy-One,

326

Get-One-Free burger specials." He looked to his feet. "My great-grandfather would be proud."

"I'm glad." Worrying her lower lip, she flashed him a shy smile.

"Guess I should probably call down there, huh? Tell them I'm going to be late." He'd already headed for the phone.

"If you need to work," she called out after him, "I'll understand. I'm good at hanging out around here."

Guess he hadn't heard her, as he was already talking to Leon or Pauline on the other end of the phone line.

Rose's gaze fell to the drooping peace lily, the dust on the piano. This house needed her. Katie needed her. Did Jonah? She'd jokingly asked if he needed a house-keeper, but she hadn't come back here looking for a job. She was looking for a life.

Jonah was back. "That's done."

"All set?"

"All set."

"Good." Again came that annoying giggle. Geesh, it wasn't as if she was a virgin.

Oh, yes, you are. The first time you and Jonah made love, he thought it was a dream—even you weren't so sure if that night was reality or fantasy.

"So," Jonah said, tucking his hands in his pockets. "Want to head upstairs, or . . ."

"What I want is to stop feeling like we're strangers." She searched his dear face. His deep brown eyes that had comforted her through her most terrifying storm. Those firm lips that held the power to kiss her to diz-zying heights, yet reduce her spirit to mush with stony silence. What was he thinking? Did he find her direct approach too forward? Downright brazen?

"We are strangers," he finally said.

327

"So, what do you think we should do to fix that?"

"What we *should* do is buy you the old Griffin place down the road. Fix it up cute. Spend the next two or three years dating, then invite the whole town to our big church wedding, but . . ."

"But what?"

"But that would take two or three years."

Pulse racing, she licked her lips. "And that's a problem?"

He grinned. "Look at my fly. You tell me."

Sure enough, he seemed a bit crowded down there. She'd barely had time to laugh before he crossed the room, cupping her face in his hands to grace her with a powerful, mind-blowing, heart-shattering kiss before scooping her into his arms and carrying her up the stairs.

"You passed our room," she said when he ambled toward the guest room.

"That's not *our* room," he said. "That was the room I shared with my wife. Geneva."

"Sam told me you were married. And that your wife died."

"Yeah, well, there's a whole lot of messy stuff in between. If you're planning on staying, we'll have to get a new bed for that room and change the wallpaper."

"That room has paint—no paper."

"Does it matter?" he asked, laying her on the bed.

"Not a bit."

He straddled her, whipped his navy blue T-shirt over his head. Magnificent didn't do his body justice. His chest and shoulders were unyielding steel rising into a face so handsome, she was almost afraid to gaze upon him for fear he wouldn't be real. But as he tugged at the hem of her T-shirt, pulling it over her head and tossing it to the floor, she felt not the sterile chill of her LA home but a sultry southern breeze blended with the heat of Jonah's appreciative stare.

Oh, he was real, all right, as real as this moment they'd stolen in time. There was nothing fancy about their coupling as they took turns nipping kisses and scooting each other out of their clothes.

Rose thought their reunion would be tender and slow, and it had started out that way, but then desire grabbed hold, with every fevered openmouthed kiss and groan reminding her of the secret places that for weeks she'd dreamt of but been forbidden to touch.

When Jonah's explorations moved between her legs, she was ready for him, wet and hungry and throbbing for more than his inquisitive fingers, but then sighing from the hedonistic pleasure of his deceptively simple touch.

He was power in motion and she joined him for the ride as they tumbled topsy-turvy among cool cotton sheets, reveling in each other and their rekindled love.

He entered her in one swift, gasping thrust and she accepted all of him, closing her eyes and moaning with pleasure, pressing the tips of her fingers into the muscles of his back. This was no time for talking but for feeling, for reassuring each other that they were gloriously, wondrously together and alive and setting course on a journey neither would ever forget.

Such was their urgency that both soon peaked. In Jonah, Rose hadn't found a storybook hero who lasted for days and nights without end. She'd found a real man, with real strengths and weaknesses. And at the moment, she was all too happy to seek shelter in his arms.

Glowing with sweat, her face wreathed in a brilliant

smile all of his making, she rested on her side, tracing the outlines of his brows, nose, and cheeks.

"Woman," he said, smoothing back her hair, "you wore me out."

"Sorry," she said, playing the innocent while batting her lashes.

"The hell you are." He cupped her cheeks, pulling her in for another kiss.

"Okay, so I'm not. Are you?" She searched his face for signs of regret.

"Nope."

"Cool. Now, how about us scrounging up some breakfast?"

CHAPTER NINETEEN

While Jonah fetched Katie from Esther's, Rose happily puttered about the kitchen, whipping up pancakes and sausage, filling the sink with warm, sudsy water, and relishing the simple, homespun task of washing dishes that she knew most women thought a bore. Maybe one day she would, too, but for now any task concerning the care of her family was a task she'd treasure.

After breakfast, Rose put Jonah to work. Playfully scolding him about having let her house fall to ruin in the short time she'd been gone. While she happily scrubbed the kitchen floor, singing to Katie, who cooed in her swing, she had Jonah folding laundry and making sure the washer and dryer kept up their steady hums. After changing bed linens and dusting and weeding and watering the garden and fixing a simple supper of pork chops, frozen green beans, and baked potatoes, Rose helped Jonah bathe Katie in the big, claw-footed tub, remembering the time he'd brought her so much comfort there.

Would there be more of those times to come?

There would if she had any say in the matter—and sooner as opposed to later!

After the dinner dishes were washed and put away, and the baby long since lotioned and powdered and tucked in for the night, Rose said, "How about letting me give you a bath?"

"What?" he said with a grin, kneeling to put the skillet in the cabinet beside the stove. "The warden's giving me a break?"

"Watch it, mister, or I might just get in the tub to pleasure myself and force you to watch."

"Damn," he said with a slight shake of his head. "That doesn't sound too bad, either. And here I thought you were still my Angel."

Rose froze.

"Why do I get the feeling that was the wrong thing to say?" Easing behind her at the sink, he curved his fingers over her shoulders and rubbed.

She spun about to face him. "Why do I suddenly get the feeling nothing has changed?"

"What do you mean?"

She paused a moment before saying, "This angel thing has to stop. I haven't mentioned it before, but that's the third time you've said something along those same lines today. If we're to have any kind of a future—which, by the way, are we?"

"I don't know." He raked his fingers through his hair. "I guess I assumed we'd get married for real, but maybe we still have a few things to work out."

"Okay, starting with the fact that I'm not now, nor

have I ever been since I was ten, an angel. Right up-front, you have to know I used to have a serious drink-ing problem—serious enough that on the night you found me, I was checking myself into a clinic."

"I know. Sam told me."

"Maybe something he didn't tell you was that grow-ing up, in my teenage years and even as an adult, I've done things I'm not proud of. Day by day, I'm forgiving myself, but they're still there. I can't change the past any more than I can predict the future." She shook her head, slapped her hands to her sides. "Who's to say if small town life is for me? I mean, truthfully, right now I can't imagine ever living any other way than right here, in this house, you and Katie by my side, but I worked hard to achieve the level of success I have. Growing up, I dreamed of becoming a star, of escaping my small town. So you can see why now I'm confused to find myself dreaming of not just returning to a small town but you. As much as right now I think I'm ready to give up my career, it's only fair to tell you how much I enjoyed singing at the diner. That could only mean I must at some level miss the limelight. And I know I miss the booze that kept me company on the road. Every day without it is a struggle, but that's just some-thing I'm going to have to battle through."

Jonah looked to his feet, worked the muscle in his jaw.

"Well? Aren't you going to say anything?"

"Don't you want this to work?"

"What do you mean?"

"I mean, why are you standing here doing this re-verse sell job? I was all set to ask you to marry me tonight, yet you've listed a half-dozen reasons why I shouldn't."

"Because just like Sam told you about facets of my former life, he also told me a lot about you. He told me about Geneva and how the two of you mixed like oil and water. He told me what a constant disappointment she was to you—to the whole town. I'd rather die than hurt you the way she did, Jonah. Maybe that's why I'm dredging all this up, because you have to know up-front that I'm trouble with a capital T. I'm also tired of being used, and on the flip side of the coin, I'm scared to death that what we feel for me isn't real, but just a passing infatuation. I'm good for your baby. Good for your diner and house. And after what we shared this morning, I hope you could even say I was good in your bed—but maybe that's all I am, good for temporary fun, but not forever."

"Stop," he said, hands to his forehead. "You've made your point."

"Have I? So now, knowing my good points and bad, do you still think this is ever going to work? Because if you have even a glimmer of a doubt, now's the time to 'fess up."

Jonah searched her gaze for signs that this brave speech was just a bluff, but her aquamarine eyes blazed cold. In all the time he'd known her, she'd burst into tears at the briefest hint of emotion, yet now, at this most crucial point in their relationship, she stood before him dry-eyed and daring.

He thought he knew her so well—better than he knew himself. How could he have been so wrong?

He took a deep breath. "I'll be the first to admit I've had grave misgivings about a relationship between us having any real chance at lasting, but after today, you showing up here out of the blue, professing not just your love, but your forgiveness for my not telling you the truth about your identity back on the very first day we met, I thought, screw my fears. I'm just going to go for it. Fate wouldn't be so cruel as to bring us together, split us apart, then do it all over again just for the hell of it. But you know what? Guess I was wrong."

"Okay, then," she said, swallowing hard.

Was this it? Jonah wondered. Was this the part where she told him her speech had only been a test designed to see how far his love would bend? Or was she exploring boundaries, like Geneva, afraid marriage to him would ultimately end up trapping her in an emotional cage?

Still, she hadn't shed so much as a single tear, and as much as he hated to admit it, that had to mean something. A something he instinctively knew he wouldn't like.

"Want me to leave?" she asked, looking small but proud before him. She raised her chin, daring him to argue a single word of what she'd said.

He wanted to deny her but lacked the energy. And truth was, he loved her too much to trap her.

Maybe she was too cowardly to admit the real reasons she was letting him go, but he'd been down that road before. Being married to a woman who didn't share his hopes and dreams had been hell. Almost as painful as he knew the next decades would be without Rose in his and Katie's lives. "No," he finally said, "I don't want you to leave—at least not tonight, anyway."

"What's that mean?"

"It means I've got paperwork to do down at the diner. You bunk down in your old room and we'll say our good-byes in the morning."

"What about Katie?"

"I'll take her with me."

"Oh, Jonah, why? She's sound asleep. There's no reason to wake her."

"She'll be fine."

"Better awake with you than asleep with me?"

He said nothing.

"Oh, my God," she said, covering her mouth with her hands. "Do you think I'd try to take her?"

He looked away. He couldn't say the thought hadn't crossed his mind. After all, up to twenty minutes earlier he'd have sworn he knew her well enough to want to spend the rest of his life with her. But now she might as well have been the Queen Bitch of Rock and Roll she was evidently dying to once again portray.

"You do. You actually distrust me enough to think I'd stoop to kidnapping." Now she was crying, and his arms ached from the strain of not reaching out to her.

"I'd better get going. Make yourself comfortable. I'll be back after a while."

Rose stood in the kitchen trying to stop shaking but couldn't. Soon enough Jonah left, Katie in his arms, not even looking at her on his way out the back door.

What had she done? she thought, sinking to her knees. *Oh, God, what have I done?*

"What have I done to deserve being saddled with you two?"

Geneva rolled her eyes heavenward only to kick herself for forgetting she was already in Heaven—at least for the next three or so hours.

What was up with those two? Just that morning they'd been going at it like bunnies. Okay, so sure, neither Rose nor Jonah had clean slates, but why couldn't they just work around each other's dirty laundry?

"What're you going to do?" Teach asked, not fazing her when he popped alongside her on her cloud's couch.

"Good question." She pressed her fingers to her forehead—or at least where she thought her forehead used to be. "You know," she said, angling Teach's way, "I could think a lot more clearly with a margarita."

He snapped his fingers and, voilà, in his hand he held a cobalt blue glass festively lined with salt and a lime garnish. "I shouldn't be encouraging you to imbibe, but this close to your unfortunate ultimate demise, I fail to see how a little pick-me-up could hurt."

"Gee, thanks," she said, downing her first gulp. "I think." After a few more sips she said, "So how come I can drink this when I have no body?"

"Long story. One I'm afraid you don't have time to hear."

Geneva's throat tightened. For all her brave talk, she was afraid. She'd had such high hopes for a second chance. She'd worked hard—and she had changed—so how come just because Blondie and Jonah failed to get their acts together, she was still getting a one way ticket to hell?

Rose wasn't sure how long she'd lain on the kitchen floor until she finally found sense enough to drag herself to bed.

She should have hopped in her car the minute Jonah left. If she'd had one bit of sense, she could have been halfway to Little Rock by now, but after driving without stopping all the way to Blue Moon from Sulphur, then climbing onto that emotional roller coaster with Jonah, she knew she'd not only be a danger to herself on the road but to others.

In the upstairs hall she found her toothbrush still in its slot in the hot pink holder. She brushed her teeth, ran a warm cloth over her face, then stepped into the hall, warily eyeing her choices. On the one hand was her old room, but the room she yearned for was Jonah's.

Why had she gone off on him like that? What had she been trying to prove? He hadn't meant anything by the Angel crack. He'd said that morning he loved her; couldn't she have just left it at that?

Yes, but how many other men in her life had told her they loved her, only as a means to use her?

Yes, Geneva wanted to scream at her, but for the last time, Jonah isn't like any other men. He's unique in the whole world. Precious and kind. He only used you to save his baby. Was that really so bad? Can you honestly say that faced with the same situation you wouldn't have done the same—that you haven't done virtually the same over the years in trying to save yourself?

Rose ultimately made the short trip to her old room. Geneva's room. Learning about her, she felt an odd kinship with the woman who'd first claimed the title of Mrs. Jonah McBride.

Crawling into bed, drawing up just the sheet to shelter herself from the balmy night air, she said, "Did you love him, Geneva? Truly love him the way I'm afraid I do?"

"Yes." Only just that moment did Geneva realize how much she had loved her husband. And how very much she missed him and her child now that she was gone.

Sam jolted awake to pick up the ringing phone. "Yeah?"

"Hey, it's Frank. Listen, bud, you better get downtown. We got another fire, and this time it's a doozy."

Sam pulled on jeans and a T-shirt, slipped bare feet into Birkenstocks a nagging voice told him to purchase, then made it downtown in ten minutes only to be faced with an image straight from hell.

From the looks of it, most of downtown was on fire, and next in line to go was the Blue Moon Diner. As if just thinking it had made it so, the building beside it collapsed, raining burning timbers on Jonah's roof.

Damn that mayor. Evidently their talk on the matter of arson carrying stiff prison terms hadn't had much of an effect. Oh—of course, he'd sworn to having been lily white when it came to the subject of all these downtown fires, but Sam had been sniffing out criminals all his life and one thing was for certain: while he couldn't yet prove the mayor was connected to all this, he for damn sure wouldn't rest until he could.

Aching for his best friend but damned glad that he'd heard Rose was back in town. At least Jonah would have Rose back where she belonged to help him through it. Sam flicked open his cell phone and punched in Jonah's home number.

After eight rings, a woman picked up. "Rose?"

"Yes." Her voice was groggy. She must've been sleeping.

"Hey, it's Sam. Look, wish I had time for pleasantries, but I'm afraid I've got bad news. Can you grab Jonah for me?"

"No. Is there something I can do?"

No? "Where is he?"

"At the diner. We had a fight and—"

"Christ." Sam's heart roared like the fire. "Get downtown, Rose. Jonah's in trouble."

Rose shook so badly she could hardly get dressed, let alone insert the key into her car. Sam had been cryptic, but she wasn't dense. She'd heard sirens in the background, along with shouts. There was another fire. Only this time it was closer to home.

Dear God, she prayed, running every stop sign and light. *Please let Jonah and Katie be all right.* Looking back on it, she couldn't even remember what had prompted her to turn all snippy with Jonah earlier in the evening. If she had to take a guess—insecurity. Fear. Some crazy desire to dump him before he dumped her.

But what if, as he'd said, he had been about to propose? If she'd just shut up and let him, he and Katie would be home safe right now, Katie in her crib, Jonah in Rose's arms.

Stepping harder on the gas, she tightened her grip on the wheel.

As long as there was breath in her body, she would die before harm came to those two.

Sam's deputies had both ends of Main Street blocked off, protecting passersby from what appeared at the distance of about a block to be a solid wall of fire. Five—maybe even six—storefronts were burning, the last one in line being the diner.

"Noooo!" Rose screamed, running down the street.

When she'd come close enough to be slapped by the heat, yet still fully intending to charge inside, Sam dragged her back."

"No way," he said. "The backside already caved in. And in front the flames àre too hot. Frank came damned close to losing two men. Face it, Rose. I'm sorry. I loved him, too, but it's time for you to face facts—Jonah's gone. Sacrificing yourself won't bring him back."

"It's not just Jonah," she cried, frantic to get out from his hold, "but Katie, too. I've already lost one baby, Sam, and no one, not you—or the very devil himself—is going to hold me back."

Sam grabbed hold of Rose's sleeve to stop her, but

he only had hold of her light jacket. She wriggled out of it to get free, then ran with total disregard for her safety straight into the living wall of flame.

"Oh, no," Geneva said. "Oh, hell, no." *Jonah, Katie, and Rose—they were a family. What would be the point of Geneva's trying to get into Heaven were she to lose all of them now?*

Teach popped up beside her. "Remember, Geneva, you're strictly forbidden to perform physical manifestations. You must allow fate to take its course."

"I'll give you fate," she said, letting Teach have it right in the kisser before scrunching her eyes shut tight and willing herself into the heart of the flame.

"Jonah?!" Rose screamed, now on her knees, crawling through cloaking darkness, fighting for every breath as she felt her way across the dining room floor. "Jonah, baby, please! Can you hear me?!" Her fingertips met with the heated chrome of what she could only guess was one of the counter stools. Knowing the kitchen and office were directly in line with that, she scrambled all the faster, getting by on little more than a prayer and her unwavering will to succeed.

"I love you and your daughter, Jonah. Don't you dare die on me now."

A flaming timber crashed to the floor beside her and she screamed. Hell itself couldn't be any worse than this, she thought, crawling, crawling, not knowing if she was even getting close. But then she felt the foot of the stove, and the stainless-steel work counter, and she knew from there the office door opened onto her right. "Jonah?!"

In the office the air wasn't quite as thick, and flames from the kitchen helped guide her way.

There they were, Jonah sprawled out on the sofa

with Katie on his chest. They both appeared deathly still.

"Nooo!" she screamed, scrambling to her feet to shake them. "Don't you dare leave me, Jonah and Katie McBride! Not when I've only just now figured out how much I need you."

From over their heads came a terrible shudder and a roar.

Rose looked up.

In slow motion, ceiling tiles tumbled toward her in a shower of sparks and flame. She hugged herself over Jonah and Katie, sheltering them with her own body from the hellish storm. If they were going to die, then at least they'd die together, for there would be no life for her without them.

She'd resigned herself to this fate when a brilliant light descended upon the room. A light far brighter than the flame.

A woman dressed in flowing white emerged. She didn't speak, just extended her hand.

Convinced she must have already died and was now in the tunnel folks talked about on late-night TV, Rose shook her head. "I'm not leaving until you promise Jonah and Katie will survive."

All the more animated, the woman again reached for Rose's hand, this time making contact in shimmering waves of ice.

Before she could even think to fight, the light was lifting not just her, but Jonah and Katie. Lifting, lifting, flying them magic carpet–style across the office, the kitchen, and finally out the front door, landing them in a heap, Katie cradled in Rose's arms.

"I'll be damned!" Sam shouted. "Look, they're all three alive!"

"Thank God," Frank said, gesturing like mad toward the paramedics, who hefted all three to safety, then administered oxygen.

"What the hell happened?" Jonah asked minutes later, sputtering awake with a cough as he slipped the plastic mask off his face. "Katie? Where's Katie?"

"She's right here, Jonah"—held in Rose's protective arms. Rose had slipped off her oxygen but held Katie's firm. "The diner—it's gone, but Katie's okay."

"You okay, too?"

She nodded, eyes shimmering with tears. "I'm so sorry," she said. "I don't know what made me go off on you that way."

Scooting across the pavement to pull her into a hug, he said, "I'm the one who's sorry. I thought I had everything under control. Katie, the diner, you—but that control was an illusion. I'm just a man, Rose, a man who's finally wised up enough to realize all the perceived control in the world means nothing without you. I was planning on going home to you, you know, to force you to hammer all this out, tell you I'd be proud to marry a rock star if you'd deign to hook yourself up with a lowly cook, but I must've drifted off. I can't remember anything past that. Now"—he looked to the ground, reached for a pebble he rolled with his fingers against the pavement—"now, I look back on all the petty things I've been so caught up in and they seem like nothing. This diner being one," he said. "I was actually prepared to lose you just to keep up this same day-in, day-out existence. I mean, where's the fun? The passion? Geneva was right. I am boring."

"You? Boring?" Rose cupped her hand to his soot-shadowed cheek, thinking that never had she seen him look more handsome. "Not a chance. And I do have some money set aside, you know. True, the original diner held a ton of great memories, but we can make new ones, Jonah. The three of us—together."

With Katie asleep in the cradle formed by Rose's cross-legged lap, Jonah took his future wife's hands in his. "Without you, there wouldn't be a three of us. You're the one who saved us, aren't you?"

She shook her head, tears of relief falling freely. "I tried, but the ceiling was falling. I remember trying to shelter you, but I thought it was too late and we were all going to die. But . . ."

"But what?" he asked, tipping up her chin.

"I thought I saw this light lifting us, but . . ." She shrugged. "I had to have been dreaming. We must've all somehow crawled out."

He shook his head, pressing a tender kiss to her cracked lips. "Naw, I know exactly what happened."

"You do?"

He nodded. "Me and Katie were once again saved by our own personal Angel." Tweaking her nose, he added, "And this time, don't you dare try to deny it."

Rose wouldn't have dared—wouldn't have cared, actually. As long as her adopted daughter and husband were safe in her arms, the rest of the world happily faded from view.

"Am I too late?"

Sam turned from Frank to a wide-eyed Leon.

"They're okay, aren't they? I heard on the scanner Jonah was inside—little Katie, too. If I did something to them, I swear, I'll kill myself right along with 'em."

"Whoa," Sam said, clapping his hand over Leon's shoulder. "Hold on a minute. They're fine." He narrowed his eyes. "How'd you hear about the fire?"

"Police scanner. Delilah's cousin always keeps one on."

Sam nodded. "And what did you mean when you said if you did something to them?"

The diner's roof gave way, collapsing in a crackling burst that shot sparks and flames twenty feet high.

Quivering head to toe, Leon burst into tears. "I'm sorry. I didn't know it would be like this. He said it would be easy. If I just did my job no one would get hurt, and the insurance would make us all rich. He promised no one would ever have to work—or worry 'bout money—again. I thought I'd be doin' poor Jonah a favor. I never meant to kill him." He dropped to his knees, covering his sobs with his hands.

Sam touched his shoulder. "Who said this, Leon?"

"The mayor—he hired me. Found out through town gossip how bad in debt I am. Wife's got to have new hats and shoes every Sunday. Got that no count son and his three young'uns to raise. Chevis is too proud to say, but he needed money, too. I was drownin', Sam. I didn't know what to do. Mayor said Jonah wouldn't be out any money, what with the insurance. All he wanted was to get the diner out of downtown."

"Did he say why?"

"Shut up, Leon." The boy mayor stepped up beside them, brandishing a sickly grin. "This is a sad night for our fair city, isn't it, Chief Lawson?"

Sam refused to give the man who was barely one step above a murderer the respect of even looking him in the eye. Turning back to Leon, he repeated, his voice deadly calm, "Stand up, and then tell me why."

Leon, still sniffling, looking from the mayor to Sam, grappled to his feet.

The mayor's icy stare would've froze anyone's lips, so

Sam gave Leon a little encouragement in the form of cuffing the mayor, then asking one of his deputies to read him his rights before locking him into their worst iron-barred suite.

Once the mayor and deputy were out of earshot, Leon asked, "You gonna lock me in the same cell as him?"

"Nope."

"Okay, then; all I know is that the mayor's been gettin' big money—and I mean *big*—from some Texas company wantin' to put in a power plant. Guess with that new highway, the governor's been tellin' folks outside the state that this whole area's fixin' to boom. Mayor says all that power company needed to set up shop, we have right here. A river, railroad—only thing is, best spot for the plant is Riverside Park. Mayor knew he'd never get folks to vote for their downtown to be 'dozed, so he thought he'd do it for 'em. From what he told me, that company's gonna pay a whole lot of money to give us better schools and electric rates, and they'll even put in a new park. Got the land all set aside over by the new highway. Gonna be a fancy rest stop, with toilets and picnic tables and everything."

Sam eyed his other deputy. "Do me a favor."

"Yeah, Chief?"

"Cuff this one, and read him his rights, too."

"Hey, Chief?" Leon called out on his walk to the station.

"Yeah?"

"Tell Jonah I'm sorry."

Mouth set in grim disgust, Sam waved him off. "Tell him yourself. You owe him at least that much."

Watching Leon and the deputy go, Sam rubbed his hands over his face and sighed. Damn, what a night.

How was he going to tell Jonah one of his oldest friends—a guy who'd been working in the diner longer than Jonah—had been responsible for torching it to the ground?

He shot a look Jonah's way. He and Rose were kissing, smoothing each other's faces and hair, almost as if they were testing the fact that they were still there.

Sam figured he oughtta tell Jonah the news about Leon, but he didn't have the heart. Not tonight. This was one time when bad news could wait.

While the two lovebirds leaned against the ambulance's rear tire, hugging and kissing and telling each other how lonely they've been, yadda, yadda, yadda, Geneva eyed the old courthouse's tower clock.

Eleven forty-five. Ah-cha-cha-cha.

Mission accomplished with fifteen minutes to spare!

"Hey, Teach!" she called out from her perch on the front seat of the biggest fire truck—she always had had a thing for firemen—"I did my job, now what about those wings you promised?"

Teach popped onto the seat beside her, turning up his nose at the smell of sweat-stained upholstery and smoke. "Honestly, Geneva, doesn't this town have any classier places in which we might conduct our final round of business?"

She shrugged, glanced at the two brawny studs just outside the window rolling up hose. "Looks all right around here to me."

He sighed. "As usual, I can see I'm getting nowhere, so I might as well commence with what needs to be said."

"Oh, goody," Geneva said with an animated clap of her hands. "Is this where I get winged?"

Teach gritted his teeth. "I'm afraid not."

347

Geneva caught her breath. "What do you mean? Look at those two." She pointed across the square to where Jonah and Blondie and Katie were well on their way to establishing a permanent bond. *"I did everything you and Mr. Big requested."*

"True," he said with a solemn nod. *"It's not so much that you didn't accomplish your mission that's displeased Mr. Big, it's more the way you went about it."*

"Oh, so I get it. What? I'm disqualified for breaking a few rules?"

He squashed his already reedy lips even tighter than usual. *"In a manner of speaking. Good luck, Geneva. . . . Although with any luck on my part, it'll be a long time before we meet again."*

"Wait!" she called out, but it was no use, he was gone.

So, great. What did this mean? Was she headed for Heaven or hell or someplace in between?

Scowling, she tried floating her way out of the truck to spend a little quality time spying on Sam, but when she tried her usual think-it mode of transportation, she got nowhere quick.

And, whew, was it hot in the truck's cab.

Had to have been like a hundred degrees.

She hadn't felt heat like this since that summer before she'd had Katie and Jonah had taken her on that week-long vacation in Pensacola. Man, it'd been hot. She'd tried daintily glowing like good southern women were supposed to, but seeing how Geneva had never placed too high a priority on being good, she'd just gone ahead and sweat like a stuck hog.

Back sticky with sweat, she rubbed against the seat, reached for a tissue from a box on the dash to dab at her forehead. Who'd have thought Blue Moon's downtown barbeque would've beat Florida in a heat war?

She'd just taken a final dab at her forehead when she froze.

Wait just a doggone minute.

Teach might not have thought she'd learned much in Heaven, but one thing she had learned was that angels don't sweat.

She pinched her arm and yelped.

Chomped on the tip of her pinkie finger and felt tears spring to her eyes.

"I'm alive!"

"Lady, what the hell are you doing up there?" The cutest of the firemen waved her out of the truck.

"You can see me?" she asked.

"Uh, yeah. Mind getting out?"

"Sure," she said, flashing him a grin. "Just one more thing." She angled the rearview mirror her way and gasped.

She was alive all right, but not in her body!

Her black and fuchsia hair had been replaced by a profusion of strawberry blond curls framing a prettily freckled face. The Puke & Die concert T-shirt and jeans she'd croaked in had been replaced by the denim shorts and leather halter number she'd sported during her dream night with Sam.

Tearing at not only her second chance but at Teach's awesome taste in clothes, Geneva sent up a silent prayer of thanks. Looking back on it, she might have thought she only imagined it, but as she climbed out of the truck and got her first good glimpse of the sky in nearly five months, she could have sworn she'd caught a star twinkling just for her. Of course, it could've just been a spark from the fire, but hey, she hadn't lost all her selfish tendencies, so she preferred to think of it as all hers.

"Lady?" Frowning, the biggest of the two fire hunks strolled her way. "You ever gonna get down from there? As you can see, we've got a lot going on."

Sam pulled up. Not in his boring old squad car, but in a hot, red '68 Mustang convertible—top down. The car looked familiar. Could it—no. No way this was the same car Kent Holloway traded Moody Roach for doing all that work on his Caddy?

Left hand on the wheel, Sam said, "You guys having trouble?"

"Yeah," the fire hunk called out. "We can't seem to get this chick down from there."

"I'm going, I'm going," Geneva said, casting him a glare before scooting down from the truck and over to Sam. Dizzy from the brief yet exhilarating walk on legs grown accustomed to floating, she said, "Hey. Long time no see."

"Do I know you?" he asked.

"No, but you should." Bold as brass, she sashayed right on over to his passenger-side door and climbed in. "Hi," she said, thrusting out her hand for him to shake. "I'm, ah, Bernadette Sparks."

"New to town, Bernadette?"

"You might say that. Got any coffee around here?"

"Closest place just burned down, but we do have a few all-night places out by the highway."

"Sounds good to me," she said. "If you'd give me a lift, I'd be most appreciative." Hmm, she thought, had it really been she who'd once said small town life was dull?

Grinning, Sam shot her a look before slipping the car into gear and easing down the street. He flipped on the radio, and what should be playing but Geneva's sixth and final Elvis song, "Earth Angel."

CUPID.COM
Karen Lee

Chloe Phillips has found the killer idea that will save her creative investment firm. Cupid.com, a website that reveals your true love, is sure to be a moneymaker. But soon Chloe wonders if it is more of a cosmic joke. First, the men who view the test product all become bewitched with her, turning her life into a three-ring circus. Then the software pairs her up with AJ Lockhart, the business consultant who's been hired to shut down her company. Worse still, when AJ helps to fend off her unwanted suitors, Chloe finds herself ensnared in a web of desire. Leaving Chloe to consider the scariest option of all: What if her attraction to AJ is no random hookup, but a true love connection?

THE SELKIE
MELANIE JACKSON

While the war to end all wars has changed the face of Europe, some things stay the same; the tempestuous Scottish coast remains a place of unquenchable magic and mystery. Sequestered at Fintry Castle by the whim of her mistress, Hexy Garrow spares seven tears for her past—all of which are swallowed by the waves.

By joining the water, those tears complete a ritual, and that ritual summons a prince. He is a man of myth whose eyes hold the dark secrets of the sea, and whose silken touch is the caress of the tide. His very nature goes against all Hexy has ever believed, but his love is everything she's ever desired.

Aphrodite's Secret

JULIE KENNER

Jason Murphy can talk to creatures of the sea. He also has other superpowers like all Protectors, but none of them really help his situation. The love of his life doesn't trust him anymore. Sure, she has her reasons: When she needed him most, he was focusing on his super-career. But that is all over. He vows to reel her back in.

It won't be easy. His outcast father is still plotting world domination, and Jason's other Protector friends fear his commitment to justice. And though Lane still loves him, how to win her hand in marriage seems the best-kept secret ever. Soon Jason will swear that beating up the bad guys is easy. It is this relationship stuff that takes a true superman!

- -

Aphrodite's Passion

JULIE KENNER

Aphrodite's Girdle is missing, and Hale knows the artifact will take all his superpowers to retrieve. The mortal who's found and donned it—one Tracy Tannin, the descendent of a goddess of the silver screen—wasn't exactly popular before the belt. Now everyone wants her. But the golden girdle can only be recovered through honest means, which means there is no chance for Hale to simply become invisible and whisk it away. (Although, watching Tracy, he finds himself imagining other garments he'd like to remove.) Maybe he should convince her she is as desirable as he sees her. Only then will she realize she is worth loving no matter what she is wearing—or what she isn't.

___52474-0 $5.99 US/$7.99 CAN

Aphrodite's Kiss
Julie Kenner

Crazy as it sounds, on her twenty-fifth birthday Zoe has the chance to become a superhero. But x-ray vision and the ability to fly are only two things to consider. There is also her newfound heightened sensitivity. If she can hardly eat a chocolate bar without convulsing in ecstasy, how is she to give herself the birthday gift she's really set her heart on— George Taylor? The handsome P.I.'s dark exterior hides a truly sweet center, and Zoe feels certain that his mere touch will send her spiraling into oblivion. But the man is looking for an average Jane no matter what he claims. He can never love a superhero-to-be—can he? Zoe has to know. With her super powers, she can only see through his clothing; to strip bare the workings of his heart, she'll have to rely on something a little more potent.

___52438-4 $5.99 US/$6.99 CAN

Spellbound
KATHLEEN NANCE

As the Minstrel of Kaf, Zayne keeps the land of the djinn in harmony. Yet lately, he needs a woman to restore balance to his life, a woman with whom he can blend his voice and his body. And according to his destiny, this soul mate can only be found in the strange land of Earth.

Madeline knows to expect a guest while house-sitting, but she didn't expect the man would be so sexy, so potent, so fascinated by the doorbell. With one soul-stirring kiss, she sees colorful sparks dancing on the air. But Madeline wants to make sure her handsome djinni won't pull a disappearing act before she can become utterly spellbound.

Enchantment
KATHLEEN NANCE

The woman in the New Orleans bar is pure sin and sex in a stunning package. And for once, hardworking, practical-minded Jack Montgomery lets himself be charmed. But no sooner has he taken the beautiful stranger in his arms than he discovers his mistake: Lovely, dark-haired Leila is far more than exotic; she is a genie. When he kisses her, heat lightning flashes around them, the air sparkles with color, and a whirlwind transports him out of this world. Literally. Trapped with Leila in the land of the Djinn, Jack will have to choose between the principles of science that have defined his life and something dangerously unpredictable and unsettling.

NINA BANGS
FROM BOARDWALK WITH LOVE

The world's richest man, Owen Sitall, is a flop at a certain game, but now he's built an enormous board so he can win on his own. His island is a playground for the rich. But he doesn't know that L.O.V.E.R.—the League of Violent Economic Revolutionaries—has come to play in his hotels . . . and the plans to bankrupt him have already passed Go.

Camryn, novice agent #36-DD of B.L.I.S.S.—the international organization that fights crime anywhere from St. Croix to St. James Place—finds her assignment clear: Protect the fanatical Sitall from financial ruin. But being a spy doesn't just mean free parking. Before this is over, she'll be rolling the dice with her heart.
